EROTIC LIVES
OF THE SUPERHEROES

EROTIC LIVES OF THE SUPERHEROES

MARCO MANCASSOLA

*Translated from the Italian
by Antony Shugaar*

PRESS LIMITED

First published in the United Kingdom in 2013 by
Salammbo Press
39A Belsize Avenue
London NW3 4BN
www.salammbopress.com

Copyright © 2008 Marco Mancassola

First published in Italy in 2008 by Rizzoli,
an imprint of RCS Libri, S.p.A, Milan

This edition published by agreement with PNLA/Piergiorgio
Nicolazzini Literary Agency

This English translation copyright © Antony Shugaar, 2013

The moral right of Marco Mancassola to be identified as the author of
this work has been asserted in accordance with the
Copyright, Designs and Patents Act 1988

Special thanks to Daniel Morris

A CIP catalogue record for this book is available from the British Library

Cover design by mecompany.com, London

Typeset by Tetragon, London

Printed by Drukarnia Skleniarz, Krakow, Poland

ISBN 978-0-9568082-3-3

This book is a work of fiction. Names, characters, businesses,
organisations, places and events are either the product of the author's
imagination or are used fictitiously. Any resemblance to actual persons,
living or dead, events or locales is entirely coincidental.

Contents

Book One

MISTER FANTASTIC

MAY 2005 — APRIL 2006

There was a time when it was the centre of the world, a bouquet of concrete stalks hammered into granite, a grid of streets dotted with manholes from which there issued, in a never-ending stream, the vapour of dreams. Once this had been his city, a place where he performed great exploits, where he designed wonders, where his wife loved him unconditionally and where every word he uttered rang perfectly true.

Manhattan glistened like a mirage, at his feet, in the late morning light. Reed Richards ran a hand over his forehead. He was looking out at the city through the plate glass window of the panoramic sauna on the twenty-ninth floor of the George Hotel. The temperature was rising and his skin was exuding a sheen of sweat and an elusive, fluid sense of disquiet that even he couldn't put into words. He squinted. This was New York. This was his city, luminous and distant, on the far side of a sheet of glass, outside the panoramic sauna of a luxury hotel.

He tried to relax. After all, this was a place designed for relaxation. Reed used the sauna frequently: he came here to shed toxins and tensions, and to sit, gazing out, in the state of contemplation that view always inspired in him. Around him, other men lay on the wooden benches, silent in the half-shadows, their gazes lost in the view outside. There was nothing here but peace, sweat, and a discreet reciprocal indifference. At least, that's how it usually was. Today, though, things seemed to be different.

There were four men. When he walked into the sauna, Reed had sensed the sudden, unmistakable silence of a conversation interrupted, and once he sat down, he could feel their eyes begin to brush over him, in the half-light, like curious tentacles. Reed felt a slight edge of annoyance. He didn't like being recognised. He hadn't appeared on television for twenty years now, but he knew his picture was sometimes published in pieces about the glories of bygone decades, or in an article about his son Franklin.

Years ago, Reed chose to step out of the spotlight and let Franklin be the famous one. It was with a sense of relief that he had rid himself of other people's eyes. He'd freed himself of the attention of the media, the buzz of gossip, the morbid quivering vibration that clusters around people who are too famous. He'd freed himself of the annoyance of being recognised everywhere he went. So now he felt uneasy, being eyed in the sauna, as the sweat slid down his elastic body.

The wood was scalding hot. A ridiculous awkwardness kept him pinned to the bench. Pretending to be captivated by the view, he let time slide by, minutes and seconds, a succession of instants stretching out in the heat. The men surrounding him were all younger, a piece of data that he found himself registering, unwillingly, more and more these days. What's more, they seemed resistant: no one made a move to leave the sauna. He could hear them breathing in the fiery silence.

He knew it was late and a car was waiting downstairs, in the street, to take him out of town. He knew he had important things to do, that all this was foolish, that the challenge of outlasting the others was senseless. The heat had grown intolerable. He lurched to his feet. The sweat surged down his body as he stood there, his head spinning, trying to picture himself as the others saw him: there's Reed Richards, Mister Fantastic, the Rubber Man, the fading glory of the chronicles of the twentieth century's superheroes. Watch him as he struggles to keep his balance there by the window, naked, dehydrated, with all Manhattan as a glowing backdrop.

Outside the sauna he found the salvation of cool air and of a cooling shower. He clutched the wall, letting the water pour over him. He almost felt as if he would melt. Staying that long in the sauna had been a foolhardy act, the kind of reckless behaviour his doctors had been warning him against for years now. *Your body is special, Reed. It requires special care.*

It took a few minutes before he began to feel better, before his heartbeat began to slow down. His doctors also recommended against using his powers, except for a weekly regimen of exercises performed under the supervision of specialist trainers. In the shower, all the same, he carefully elongated his arms. He stretched them down to the floor and then back up. He felt a slight burning sensation. He did the same with his neck, upwards, and expanded his chest like an accordion. He started stretching out his head, too, trying to give it the rudimentary shape of an umbrella: an old trick he used to do for Franklin when he was a little boy, a trick he sometimes still did under the shower. The effort caused him a sharp stab of pain.

He stopped trying. Anyone watching him would have had the impression that invisible hands were playing with him, manipulating his body, stretching and twisting it only to restore it each time to its original shape. His shape. His body. Over the years, Reed Richards had come to believe that his real talent, his real superpower, was not the ability to deform his body but rather the ability to restore it to its original shape. The rubbery material he was made of had worn out a little as he aged, lost elasticity and become much more sensitive. And yet, in spite of the work of time, in spite of the thousand ways in which it had been elongated and stretched and deformed, his shape had remained roughly unchanged. That was the miracle of Reed Richards. Or perhaps his curse. *I'm still the same. I'm still me*, he said to himself, as his body's temperature slowly dropped.

*

A short while later, he emerged into the changing room, comfortably wrapped in a bathrobe and surrounded by the soft sound of the music that filled the entire floor. A feeling of melancholy satisfaction swept over him. Maybe it was the way the last traces of water vanished, molecule by molecule, from the surface of his skin, or else the feeling of cleanliness that spread through his body, or even just the pure, elementary fact that he had a body: *My arms. My belly. My cock.* He stood motionless next to the wooden locker where he'd left his clothes. He shook his head. He could never resign himself to the sequence of clashing sensations, nameless desires, and obscure instincts that came with ageing. For example, his embarrassment in the sauna just now: so absurd. For him—a mature former superhero, a respected scientist, the chairman of the Richards Foundation—to react in such a paranoid way. Like a fearful little boy. He thought all this over, in the warm air of the changing room, while his skin dried off. Then he opened the locker and saw what someone had left him.

There was a piece of paper inside. It was white, folded in half, perched on top of his trousers. Reed looked at it while his body tensed instinctively, ready to lash out against any potential danger. The world changed consistency around him, turning into a stark list of facts. The light in the room. The sound of a shower. The hum of the ventilation system. Reed had been a warrior, he had survived a thousand ambushes, and he knew that kind of moment. The moment when reality is transformed, and everything becomes important. Everything is a signal. Everything is other than it seems, everything could conceal a threat, or else help to understand the sudden fragment, now, the out-of-place object that had triggered the alarm.

A sheet of paper. In his locker. Reed picked it up, holding it cautiously between his fingertips. He elongated his arm several yards, setting it down at a safe distance. He left it there, in the far corner of the changing room, as if it were a piece of infectious waste. He focused his attention on his clothes. He examined them one by one, carefully, without finding a thing. No suspicious stitching, no evidence of tiny listening devices, no minute drops of epidermic poison, none of the other diabolical contrivances he had encountered in the past, when he was the target of constant attacks. It looked to him that his clothes had not actually been touched. He sighed. The only thing left to do was to stretch out his arm again and pick up the paper. It was a simple white sheet, nothing more, and at last he unfolded it, to read the message written inside:

SO LONG, MY MISTER FANTASTIC

Just that simple phrase, run off by a computer printer in capital letters. Reed couldn't understand. Such a simple phrase; yet at the same time so obscure. Who could have broken into his locker, in the time it took for a sauna, to leave him such a message?

He stood there staring at the words, as though waiting for other phrases, other words to materialise. Was there some reference he was missing? His scientist's brain worked methodically. He tested every conceivable anagram, code, and secret cipher that could be concealed behind that phrase. Over the course of his lifetime, he'd worked with languages of all kinds, real and invented, living or lost, but that message resembled nothing in his experience.

SO LONG, MY MISTER FANTASTIC

Reed gave up. It seemed to be nothing more than a bizarre salutation. Some loony had decided to send him a personal farewell. Maybe it was a longtime fan crossing the line into stalkerdom, someone who believed they'd had a relationship of some kind with him? He refolded the paper and slipped it into his trouser pocket, wondering whether it was worth worrying about this odd prank. Maybe not. He couldn't say. In the solitude of the changing room he began to dress.

*

He heard a noise. It took him a second or two to identify it and associate that sound with a specific thought, a possible source. Tapping. Glass. Reed moved hesitantly, retracing his steps from the changing room back to the sauna. There was no one in sight, complete silence. Only that tapping sound.

He found himself again at the door to the sauna, breathless, incredulous. Someone was knocking on the door from inside. Reed saw the hand against the glass. He had a vague notion that someone might have been locked in and was asking for help. He decided he had to help that person, he had to save a life, exactly the kind of thing he had once done routinely—or at least believed he did. To save someone's life. And yet—that tapping didn't seem like a call for help. It was too unruffled, too *inviting*.

When he opened the door the wave of heat caught him head-on, once again, like a breath from a giant mouth. He was barely able to make out the shape of the person, who had in the meantime moved further into the half-light of the sauna. A woman's shape. Reed waited by the door uneasily, wondering what a woman was doing in a men's sauna, where the men who'd been there earlier had gone, and whether it was safe to go back into the sauna after already spending so much time in there. He hesitated, transfixed by these rational thoughts, until he felt them fade like a dying whisper. He stepped in and shut the door behind him. The silence in the sauna was even more powerful. Only the sound of his own breathing, and the woman's.

They were alone. She withdrew still further, into the hottest alcove at the far end of the sauna, and from that position sat watching him, calmly, as though she'd always been waiting for him. Reed drew closer. He sat down next to her. In the dim light he couldn't distinguish her features. He saw her legs gleaming with sweat, and the blurred sheen of her pubic hair, and the triangle of white flesh left by a swimsuit. He saw her slender arms, the shape of her breasts. They sat there, side by side, sweating and breathing, quivering, each looking at the other's body. Reed felt confusion and heat, a heat that gripped him tighter and tighter, squeezing his chest until he began panting. Against the flesh of his thigh, his penis was a seething rock.

He knew she was smiling. Even though he couldn't really see her, he knew. And he knew he wanted to touch her, and so he reached out a hand, and it struck him as a beautiful thing, deeply moving, that there could be such a simple bond between desire and action. So immediate. His fingers brushed her breast. He followed the curving flesh with astonishment, shyly at first, and then he grasped her. When she reached for his penis he felt firm in her grasp, so real, so definitive, *here I am, here's my body, there's no need for me to stretch or deform myself. Here's my cock in your hands. Here's your crotch under my palm... Here's your soft thatch, the opening fissure. Even our breathing seems solid, scarily heavy, in the extreme heat...*

He awoke with a start. His eyelids fluttered. He was in the back seat of a car. Outside, an impassive landscape was streaming by. Greenery. Trees. They were already deep into New Jersey. Reed took a dazed breath and tried to accommodate this new reality. The car was sailing along a semi-deserted road. He must have fallen asleep the minute the driver picked him up from the front door of the George Hotel, heading out of Manhattan.

He'd been fast asleep the whole way. His eyes met the driver's smiling glance in the rear-view mirror, prompting an unpleasant doubt in Reed's mind. Had Reed sighed once too often as he dreamed about going back into the sauna? Had the driver guessed? He sat up a little straighter, shifting uncomfortably, doing his best to camouflage the partial erection that still jutted between his legs.

"We managed it," said the driver, continuing to smile at him in the mirror. He had a Hispanic accent and the face of a man of about thirty. It wasn't the first time he'd had this driver. Reed knew he was from Ecuador but couldn't retrieve his name.

"What?" he replied, in confusion, still dazed from the force of his dream.

"We managed to make up the time," the driver went on. "When we left you told me we were running late, remember?"

Reed nodded, somewhat reassured, even though everything still struck him as strange and vaguely distorted. The driver's voice. His own voice. The excessive light flooding the roadway. The sunshine pouring in the car windows, imposing a sense of suffocating heat. Reed looked at the other man again, making an effort, as though regaining full possession of reality depended on his ability to remember the man's name. He couldn't do it. He was too stunned. "I shouldn't have fallen asleep," he murmured.

"No, it was good for you," the driver responded. Then he slowed down, following the arc of a curve in the road. Only once they were back on a straight stretch did he add, with a sigh, "Sleep heals the soul. If only I could get some."

Their eyes met again in the rear-view mirror. Reed noticed the young man's face: it was open, but marked by unmistakable signs of torment. "Woman trouble," Reed said instinctively, in an almost fatherly tone, like a doctor diagnosing a patient's illness.

"My wife," the driver agreed. After another sigh, he went to the heart of the matter: "It's not the same as it used to be with us. New York has gone to her head."

Reed nodded. He didn't have much to add. Unhappy love stories all struck him as sad, and all more or less alike. All made up of urgent confessions, all just so much torment marking the face.

Reed touched his own face, at that point, amidst the vibration of the moving car. He'd always been satisfied with his appearance. He'd experienced a thousand triumphant victories but his features had never twisted into arrogance; he'd encountered a thousand disappointments, including a divorce, without taking on any marks of bitterness. Nothing ever sticks to a rubber face. Everything slides off it without leaving marks.

And yet he was worried. He wondered whether he looked sleepy, he wondered if any trace of that absorbing dream had congealed on his features. *I have to get a grip on myself,* he thought. *I have an intense afternoon ahead of me.* He lowered the window to get a little oxygen, letting the rushing wind blow everything away: the last traces of sleep, hangovers from erotic dreams, and the melancholy notes of the driver's voice.

They remained silent for the rest of the trip. Two men immersed in their respective anxieties. Then the car turned into a service road running through the woods and Reed recognised, in the distance, the peculiar structure of the space centre.

*

It looked like an enormous mushroom without a stalk. A nipple jutting up from the line of the land. A sort of swollen blister. Every time he came here, Reed found new comparisons for the space centre's shape: a low, flattened hemisphere that rose out of nowhere, in the midst of the green countryside. A strange place. You spontaneously found yourself wondering what on earth the designers had in mind, and it was just as spontaneous, just as inevitable, to leap to conclusions about the era in which it was built. The Seventies—too much LSD on the street.

Actually, Reed knew precisely what the designers had had in mind. He knew that the flattened curve was meant to evoke a certain organ of the human body, and that if you looked down on the structure from the air you would see, on the roof, an enormous green-glass iris. An eye. The space centre was a gigantic eyeball protruding from the ground, scrutinising the sky in eternal astonishment.

Reed went through security at the front entrance. The guards waved him through respectfully. After all, he was still an important man. A venerable figure, a member of the scientific advisory boards of half a dozen institutions, including this space centre. Reed indulged in these thoughts, smiling to himself, knowing well that if he went back, he would hear the guards exchanging very different remarks. *Hey, was that…? Yeah, that was him. Franklin Richards' father.*

The temperature inside was pleasantly cool. A few young scholars were loitering in the front lobby. The atmosphere was somewhere between that of a government agency and a small college. The structure was used for training young astronauts, for lectures, and other institutional activities: the kind of place where schoolchildren from New York City came once a year on field trips, where diplomats passing through New York City were brought to listen to reports on the state of American space research.

"Richards!" A voice called his name. He didn't turn around at once. There was no need. He knew that right now a woman was heading across the lobby straight for him. He knew that the woman was walking with a brisk, almost mannish stride, and that although she was not a member of the armed forces or any other official corps, every aspect of her appearance smacked of some kind of uniform: the elegant attire with its rigid cut, the hair gathered back in a bun, and even the expression, a blend of the seductive and the ironic, that certain women of her type, attractive singles in their fifties, wore almost as a badge or an epaulette. Reed knew all this. Last of all, as he was turning to face her, he knew he was about to plummet into the embarrassment that engulfed him every time he was in the presence of Mrs. Glasseye.

"I thought you'd never get here," she said. "Reed Richards arrives somewhere a few minutes late. A red-letter event. I've already called your office in Manhattan," she added, smiling a little too warmly, in a tone that implied an unquestioned intimacy.

Reed smiled in turn, vaguely, barely meeting the gaze of the woman standing in front of him.

"You look good," she continued as she linked arms with him and went on walking at the same brisk pace, dragging him along beside her. "Will you ever tell me your secret?"

Reed made a generic comment about the benefits of saunas. He let himself be led unprotesting down the hardwood-floored corridor.

And so it was that, in front of everyone, he let himself be paraded along, arm-in-arm with Mrs. Glasseye: she who for years had directed the centre with an amiably dictatorial flair. She who—despite a headquarters with a psychedelic appearance, despite the fact that they were working on the margins unoccupied by the major space programmes, and despite the ineptitude of the bigwigs in Washington—had managed to keep the space centre operating at a dignified level of prestige. She who could wear blouses with plunging necklines without undermining her perennial air of a colonel. A woman in her fifties with breasts that still stood to attention and practically saluted. A woman who wasn't afraid to stare at the zipper of a man's trousers. A woman who looked everyone in the eye, with a firm gaze, unaware of or indifferent to the awkwardness that she provoked. She who—leaving aside the fact that she was the chief executive officer of a space centre that stood in the middle of New Jersey, with the unlikely shape of an eye gazing into the firmament—owed her nickname to the additional fact that she possessed, thanks to one of those paradoxical tricks that chance seems to favour, one prosthetic eye.

Mrs. Glasseye walked Reed to one of the lecture halls. "It's an excellent group," she stated, gesturing towards the interior, without missing the opportunity to unfurl another of her too-warm smiles.

Reed looked into the lecture hall. He could only see the legs of the waiting students, but kept his eyes fixed in that direction, with a feigned air of distraction, studiously avoiding her glance. He couldn't look her in the eye. He couldn't and he wouldn't. Never so much as when he was in the presence of Mrs. Glasseye did he understand the tremendous fact that looking someone in the eye meant exactly that—looking into just one eye. Staring at a single point. A single iris, a single pupil. The point where one gaze meets another can only be singular, and he was terrified he would pick the wrong one.

"I'm afraid I have to ask you something," said Mrs. Glasseye, crowding in closer and forcing Reed to make an effort not to snap his neck back a yard or two.

"Ask away," Reed muttered, reluctantly shifting his gaze onto her, onto the thousand details of her ambush-face: a soft and apparently innocuous chin. Lips glistening like a wet street. Skin as firm as an ice rink, along which it was so easy to slide up, up, up to the dizzying curve of her cheekbone, where with fatal centripetal force Reed's gaze was sucked in, only to be spat back out, with even more fatal centrifugal force, towards the precipice of the edge of one eye. He stopped just in the nick of time. *If only I could remember,* he keened, *which one is the glass eye.*

Mrs. Glasseye explained the problem. She explained that she'd encountered snags with next week's workshops. Tremendous scheduling snags. Changes in the programme. She explained that, even though she had originally made different arrangements with Reed's secretary, she now needed him to come back next week to finish training that same group. She knew that what she was asking wasn't easy, but after all it was just one more appointment. She explained all this as she drew closer, inch by inch, until she was on the verge of grazing him with a breast. And since he continued to resist, objecting that it was out of the question, that he was already dramatically overbooked… she started laying insidious traps for him. She now began looking elsewhere, towards abstract points in the distance, so that Reed's gaze would cautiously venture closer, like curious prey, and when it did she looked straight at him, without warning, ambushing him. Reed managed to dodge a couple of these attacks and finally stood there, staring at the floor, paralysed, arms folded across his chest. That woman knew how to corner a person.

"I'll call you tomorrow," he conceded. He had no intention of accepting her request, but it sounded like an adequate answer. Sufficiently ambiguous. Mrs. Glasseye nodded with satisfaction. She took a step backwards, lifting the siege. Reed was free. Free to say goodbye, free to put an end to that scene, at once so awkward and yet reassuring, the role-playing that was a routine for them by now: bold-woman-with-handicap-terrorises-courteous-gentleman. He was free to go, to all appearances safe, untroubled by any trauma, without having gazed deep into any indistinguishable iris, into any black-hole pupil. Free to make his entrance into the lecture hall, at last, where a group of young astronauts was waiting for a lesson taught by Reed Richards himself: ex-superhero, respected scientist, and consultant to the American space agency. Free to move on through the hours of the day, that day so filled with elusive promises, that day he would long remember.

*

"You will do great things. You'll discover new planets. You'll touch comets' tails. You'll see the dust of an exploded world glittering all around you. You'll understand loneliness when you discover satellites without planets, or asteroids that wander through empty space like prophets. You'll write your names on the sand of a deserted world, where no one will ever be able to read it or erase it. You'll celebrate Christmas in a distant constellation. You'll feel time stretching out in the vacuum of space. You'll experience the twenty-fifth hour, the eighth day, and the fifth season. You'll do all this," Reed went on in a dreamlike voice. "Or else," he resumed after a pause, scrutinising the slightly baffled faces that looked up at him, "you'll spend your lives accompanying wealthy Russian mafiosi into space—men who will pay millions for an excursion into geostationary orbit, take pictures for their friends, and tip you like they'd tip their chauffeur."

His audience laughed. He'd broken the ice. There were six people in front of him, six young sets of lungs breathing calmly, six pairs of attentive eyes. Five men and a woman. Reed went on talking about the uncertain, intangible boundary between the possibility of performing glorious exploits and the risk of wasting their lives in mediocre occupations. "Glory and mediocrity," he said, "are like two distinct but contiguous frequencies. There are those who spend their lives hearing echoes from the correct frequency, without ever managing to tune it in. That's hard. It depends as much on you as on the world that surrounds you. An astronaut's career is an ambiguous path, where you can only hope that a crushing burden of sacrifice will allow you one day to experience life without gravity…"

The lesson continued. The words flowed. Reed had to talk fast, without pauses, to keep himself from realising how ridiculous the situation was and bursting out laughing. He believed there was something inherently ridiculous about all lessons. Finding himself teaching other people, the focus of a roomful of eyes, breaking up the flow of normal life to take on the role of professor, someone who administers knowledge, someone who sets forth his own understanding with unshakable confidence. All this had always struck him as hopelessly comical. A sort of embarrassing pantomime.

At the same time, he had to admit, he liked teaching. Despite the ridiculous, ceremonious side of it, despite these lessons, and the conferences and the other institutional roles he played, being nothing more than a way to finance his foundation, despite all that: there was something he liked about it. If he let himself go, if he stopped over-thinking, he could hear his own words vibrate in the air, fitting into the surrounding context. He could feel his words fill the room, accepted and recognised, in a way that rarely happened any more. The right lines for the right stage. He could hear his own phrases spill out, one after the other, with that blend of seriousness, humour, cynicism, and sincerity that over the years had become the hallmark not only of his lessons, but of his very existence. After all, he knew that the people sitting before him had a complete technical education. What they were expecting from him, from his reputation and his white hair, was something else. A little experience. A touch of wisdom. Ridiculous, perhaps, the way old professors and supposed wise men always were. And yet needful.

Class was over. Two hours had gone by. Reed said goodbye to the six young astronauts without anyone referring to another lesson next week. He'd joked with a couple of them, one of whom had Russian origins, about the Russian mafiosi that Reed had mentioned. No one had taken offence. They had laughed together. Reed remained in the empty classroom, organising his notes, in the sudden loneliness of a lesson's end.

"Excuse me?" said a voice.

Reed looked up. The only woman in the group had circled back and was now walking towards him with an enigmatic smile. Reed watched her come closer, surprised, almost afraid, as if he were witnessing the appearance of a ghost. The young woman's hair glowed in the light from the windows. Her green eyes had a deep, marine transparency, almost incorporeal. Reed had already noticed those eyes during the lesson, as well as her hands, lithe, pale as ice. Hands that were holding…

"I don't believe it," Reed commented. He stared at the object the young woman held in her hands, shaking his head in amazement. "I thought it had vanished from general circulation years ago."

"It may have vanished from book stores," she said, continuing to smile. "But not from my bookshelf." With that, she handed the book to him.

Reed took it delicately, like someone handling an ancient artefact, and leafed through a few pages. Then he looked again at the cover, with the title:

REED RICHARDS—A 'FANTASTIC' BIOGRAPHY

Under the title was a picture of him in his official costume. The book must have been published at least fifteen years ago, right after his group of superheroes disbanded. An eternity. He couldn't believe he was holding it in his hands. "When it was published," he said, turning to look at the young woman, "you must have been a little girl."

"I was twelve years old," she replied, sitting on the corner of the table, with an incomprehensible mixture of shyness and nonchalance. Her skin was fair and she had a sprinkling of freckles on her nose; it wasn't hard to glimpse in that face the young girl whose imagination had been captured, fifteen years ago, by the biography of a superhero. Then she ran a hand though her thick, reddish hair and Reed noticed details of another kind. Her cat-like eyes. Her unquestionably athletic body.

"I guess I'll have to sign it for you," he said, looking around for a pen. He patted his pockets. No sign of one. "I know I had one," he muttered.

Somebody appeared at the door to the lecture hall. It was another member of the astronauts' group. A tall guy, with a pair of rimless glasses. He adjusted his glasses and stood at the door, discreetly, shooting the young woman an unmistakable glance.

She leapt to her feet. "Here's what we'll do," she suggested. "You keep the book, and you can give it back to me, signed, next week. They told us you'd be teaching another session, right?"

Reed didn't know what to say. He tried to find the words to explain the situation but he hesitated a little too long.

The young woman had already joined her friend at the door. She squeezed his arm apparently to reassure him, or to emphasise his ownership, *I belong to you* or something of the sort. That gesture struck Reed, in some inexplicable way, leaving him even more tongue-tied. That hand. That arm. He could almost feel that physical contact on his own skin. That white hand which in reality, he imagined, must be dry and scalding hot. He stood there watching them, him and her, framed by the light streaming through the door. *A handsome couple*, he thought. There was something logical, natural, and at the same time heartless about the union of two such young and attractive bodies. Or maybe that's what he thought later, when the image started coming back to him, relentlessly. For the moment he stood there staring at them.

"If you want to sign it for me," she said, "my name is Elaine Ryan."
Then they were gone, leaving him alone, with his biography in his hands.

*

It was a sleepless night. He woke up a number of times, in the dark, in his chilly bed, each time in the same position, as if the same instant were being replayed over and over again, a fragment snagged in the stream of time.

Something must be wrong. An obstacle that kept him from sleep. A thought that refused to untangle, a secret waiting to be grasped. He lay there motionless, eyes wide open, wondering what it could be. He finally slid into sleep, two hours of golden blackness in which his body was able to relax and, in the safety of slumber, perform its nightly labours. Slowing his respiration. Rebuilding tissues. Eliminating toxins, consolidating sensations. The work that any body performs, on any given night, in any given bed, anywhere in the world. But this time, when Reed reawakened, dazed, to the pale blue dawn, he discovered something different had been going on. His arm. It had stretched across the bedroom. It lay on the floor, a tentacle at least ten feet long, extending towards the door as if trying to call for help. Reed tried to remember if he'd had a bad dream. He went on staring at his arm in the pale light. He practically couldn't feel it. Too numb. It was almost like an alien limb, a pitiable, dreary strip of flesh.

Then came the pain. As soon as he tried to move his arm, a shock zapped through him, a burning flash that left him breathless. That was when an aching, crystalline clarity surged up inside him, and everything finally made sense: his tormented night, the elusive thought that had kept him awake. Now he understood. *That wasn't a gesture you'd expect from a couple. A woman wouldn't grab her boyfriend's arm in such a comradely manner*, he whispered to himself in the silence of the dawn, thinking back to the young female astronaut and the male friend who had been waiting for her. *Those two aren't a couple. They're just friends.* He felt certain of it, suddenly, an absurd but convincing certainty. He had no idea why it should even matter. He instantly relaxed. He restored his arm to its normal size and closed his eyes, satisfied, sinking back into slumber.

He thought everything had been resolved. He thought to himself that the sun was rising. He thought to himself that downtown a baker was sliding into the oven the bagel that he'd eat for breakfast, that his secretary was getting out of her bed in Brooklyn to come into the office, and that the new day would be a succession of words, phone calls, emails, coffee breaks, glances out of the window, minutes ticking by, and fleeting distractions. The same as it ever was. In spite of everything, he thought that nothing had changed.

*

Light rose over the city, filtering down the streets and into the shop windows of the bakeries, into the kitchens of the diners that were about to open. Millions of bodies emerged from sleep. Men and women emerged clumsily from their beds, starving, blood sugars plunging, comforted by the prospect of an imminent breakfast. At that hour of the morning, there was something ancestral about hunger, something urgent and universal. Hunger lurked everywhere. Hunger in the apartment houses of Williamsburg, the brownstones of Park Slope, the buildings of Tribeca and in the Barrio and up in Washington Heights. In Central Park, women in nylon running pants were finishing their morning jogs, dreaming of a muffin and a bowl of cereal. In the dozens of NYSC franchises, bulky-armed men were finishing their workouts, hoping they still had time for a plate of lean bacon and a protein shake before heading for the office. Other city-dwellers would start the day with a sandwich. Or a plate of pancakes with maple syrup, fried plantains, a noodle soup, or who knows what else. Breakfast in New York came in a thousand colours, belonged to countless religions. Some preferred a doughnut. Doughnuts and coffee for the guards at the Metropolitan Museum, for the professors at Columbia University, for the bus drivers changing their shift. Doughnuts and coffee for the girls in the nail salons, for the sales assistants in the boutiques of Madison Avenue, for the cashiers in the box offices lining Broadway, and for the art dealers in Chelsea.

Annabel came into the office around eight o'clock. Reed heard her in the room next door, turning on the computers and listening to the messages on the answering machine, and then walking over to the door between their two offices. He called to her to come in before she could knock. He'd been at work for an hour and he was starving. She called out an excessively cheery good morning, handing him the newspapers and the paper bag with a couple of cinnamon bagels that, like every morning, she'd stopped to buy for him on her way in. Reed opened the bag and inhaled in delight.

As she moved off to make the coffee, Annabel announced that the morning outside was, to say the least, *completely heavenly*.

Reed watched her go. In too-skinny women, he mused, there was at times something out of place, an overblown vivaciousness, a kind of pained, fake nonchalance. Not that it constituted a problem. Annabel was a capable assistant. And however disturbing the thought might be, he had to admit it: it was strangely satisfying to eat the food that a skeletal woman, almost surely anorexic, brought him every morning. Certain contrasts gave him that kind of feeling. A perverse feeling of being alive. He pulled out a bagel and bit into it. He loved the taste of cinnamon.

After breakfast, the morning flew by. It was just before lunchtime that the aftermath of his unsettled night began to emerge, making him feel momentarily dazed, as if a sudden, tiny breach had opened up between him and the surrounding world. He took a breath. He stared at the telephone on his desk. That whole morning he'd been putting off a certain phone call, but now the time had come. He had to call. He had to confirm or reject that request for an extra lesson at the space centre. Just then, as if obeying a telepathic impulse, the phone rang.

Reed lifted the receiver. When Annabel said that Raymond Minetta was on the line, it took Reed a few seconds to realise who that was. It had been just twenty-four hours since the last time he'd visited the George Hotel, and yet it seemed a distant memory. As little as he felt like it, he told Annabel to put the call through. "Raymond," he spoke into the receiver, with the courteous yet detached tone he always used with his financiers.

"My dear friend," Raymond breathed into the phone, with an unctuous voice that penetrated into Reed's ear. How he hated that kind of voice. How he hated that person. Not so much for his way of talking, or his manners, or even for his political views. It was the fact that he was such a walking talking stereotype, such an obvious personality type, as uninteresting and unappetising as a bad hamburger. Raymond Minetta, the owner of a luxury hotel, an evident case of a repressed homosexual, an ultra-conservative Christian fundamentalist. For reasons that Reed had never quite understood, that man was one of the financiers of the Richards Foundation. "I haven't seen you in a while," Minetta cooed.

Reed avoided telling him that he'd been in the sauna at his hotel just the day before. Probably, Minetta already knew that. He also avoided telling him about the strange message he'd found in the locker, though for an instant the idea had occurred to him.

"The reason I'm disturbing you," Minetta went on, "and you know how sorry I am when I have to disturb other people, well, the reason is that this morning…" The voice faded away briefly, with a vague moan, perhaps a stifled sneeze or a stab of pain. Who knows. Reed thought of the piece of gossip he'd once heard, namely that Minetta, under his thousand-dollar Italian suit, in fact wore a cilice, or something of the sort. Reed kept from laughing. Self-inflicted pain had always struck him as something ridiculous, absurd, and obscene. *Here I am on the phone with a millionaire who wears a cilice under his trousers.*

His impatience mounted. Now that he was holding the receiver in his hand, he felt the urgent need to make that other call, the one to the space centre, the one he'd been thinking about all morning. He had to make that call. Give that answer.

"This morning," Minetta's voice resumed. "The thing is this morning, actually, I read something about Franklin."

"Franklin?" Reed asked, with a fleeting hint of interest.

"In the *Daily News*," came the answer. "That interview where they ask Franklin what health club he attends…"

Reed pulled the *Daily News* out of the pile of newspapers Annabel had brought in. He hadn't even leafed through it yet. He started turning the pages, with the receiver wedged between his ear and his shoulder, the kind of uncomfortable position that he might once have resolved by deforming a part of his body, say, by reshaping his shoulder into a rudimentary third hand, but which he now chose to accept like this, the way anyone else would. He kept the phone clamped between shoulder and ear. He found the article and the photograph that illustrated it. There was Franklin Richards, the Prince Charming of the morning tabloids, America's most beloved son. His son. A stab of love surged through his chest.

Time was running short. He needed to make the other phone call, the real one, the important one, the call that was becoming more urgent second by second. Minetta wasn't about to hang up: "You can imagine," he was saying, "my bafflement when I saw that Franklin told the interviewer, of all things, that he had a membership in a health club at another hotel. I mean to say, as you know very well, for years he's been our guest, as welcome as can be, as are you for that matter, and our hotel's health club…"

Reed's anxiety intensified. What did Minetta want? Had he taken him for Franklin's publicist? He ran his gaze around the office, exasperated, until it came to rest on the object he was searching for: the book. His biography. He had set it on a shelf at the far side of the office, ready to be signed with a brilliant dedication. He thought back to the young female astronaut. The extra lesson. He restrained the impulse to reach out his arm to grab the book, as well as to put a brusque end to the conversation.

"What I'm trying to say," Minetta said, "is that it would be a pleasure for me to have a chance to express to Franklin my undiminished esteem, perhaps by sending him, that is, in a gesture of friendship…" Reed ran his gaze repeatedly from the book at the other end of the office, to the picture of Franklin in the newspaper, as if there were some link between the two things. Some relationship. His son was smiling in the picture, young and perfect, and a strange sense of melancholy swept over Reed.

"You're right," he said, taking advantage of a new ambiguous pause on Minetta's end of the line. Another stifled sneeze? A spasm of pain as the cilice penetrated into his buttery flesh? Whatever the motive that had triggered the pause, Reed took advantage of it. "It can be tough to get in touch with Franklin. He doesn't even have a secretary. He's what people call an indie star, but that's why America loves him, right?" Without giving Minetta the time to break in, he went on: "Which means that now I'm going to transfer you back to my secretary, who will be more than happy, I feel sure, to give you her advice about when and how you can best get in touch with Franklin, so that you can renew your invitations and send him your gestures of friendship. All the gestures you like. It's been a pleasure, Raymond." Without waiting for an answer, he transferred the call to Annabel.

He rested the receiver against his ear, relieved, listening to the perfect silence of the telephone.

That silence. That instant. If only it had gone on forever. If only he hadn't heaved a sigh, just then, and started punching buttons. If only he'd never done it. Afterwards, more than once, he would wonder whether that had been the point of no return, the irreparable turning point. He would ask himself exactly where the line fell, the moment after which his life no longer belonged to him, the portal that led him onto a different plane of existence, the plane of obsession and need, the plane from which it was not possible to escape, not now, any more than from the orbit of a black hole. The turning point. The threshold.

He listened to the series of rings. Reed waited until he heard the receiver being picked up at the other end, and finally the voice, slightly mannish but nonetheless silky, of Mrs. Glasseye.

She didn't seem very surprised to hear his voice. After all, she'd been expecting his call. She'd been expecting his answer.

Reed took a deep breath, and as the sunlight of Manhattan came in through the window, and lunchtime drew near, and an army of impatient bodies poured out once again into the streets, in search of the perfect meal… As his anorexic secretary in the next room was politely answering the questions of a millionaire who wore a cilice, and everything seemed to be suddenly linked together in Reed's brain, in one last fleeting unified vision: eyes, erotic dreams, mysterious notes, cilices cutting into the flesh, smiling blond sons, biographies rediscovered, arms extending outwards, unhappy drivers, hungry bodies… He gave his answer. He'd be glad to go to the space centre for the extra lesson. "It'll be a pleasure," he said. "A real pleasure to be there again."

*

A week later, he was in a car again, heading back from the space centre, after teaching his extra lesson. A different chauffeur was driving this time, steering quietly through the New Jersey sunset.

Reed felt exhausted, afraid, and triumphant. He'd spent a week practically without anxiety, thinking at times of the space centre and the young female astronaut, and then that day he had appeared to teach his lesson, just as punctual as ever, dressed as neatly as ever, feeling a sort of childish satisfaction at the simple fact that he was there, and she was there too. He'd experienced a sort of primordial wonder: two people, both there, at the same time, in the same place on the face of the planet. More than once his glance had met hers and had rested on her eyes for a moment, like someone peering through a door left half-open.

Otherwise, he'd done a fine job. He'd taught the lesson with confidence. He'd made them laugh and made them reflect. He'd held them in the palm of his hand, those six young astronauts. When the lesson was over, he'd lingered, organising his papers, the way he normally did, so that his audience would leave the room with this perfect image in their minds, an older former hero putting his lecture notes in order.

She had come up to him. Reed had smiled, vaguely, pretending not to remember, then he'd pulled the autographed biography out of his stack of files. "Thanks," she had said, lifting the cover ever so slightly to peek at the dedication. *To Elaine Ryan, who'll fly high.*

She had touched her hair, tucking a lock behind one ear, a gesture that might mean anything, and which Reed had taken for shyness. There wasn't a lot left to say, after all, and everything could have come to an end right there, on an afternoon in May, as the sun sank behind the trees of the grounds outside. Reed had nothing to ask, nothing to add, just a pure and mechanical sense of attraction. Not exactly a sexual attraction, rather something like the pull of gravity, one body sucked into the orbit of another body.

And so in the end he made his proposal. It wasn't a proposal he'd thought out in advance, nor was it entirely innocent. He'd done his homework and learned that she lived in Brooklyn. He'd offered her a ride back to the city in his car... The car slowed down as it approached an intersection. "It's nice to travel in comfort for once," Elaine commented, sitting next to him in the back seat. She smiled and looked calmly at the sunset outside the window.

Reed followed her gaze, losing himself in turn in the vision of the fiery horizon. "I imagine," he said, "that you usually go back to the city with that classmate of yours." He was referring to the young man with rimless glasses, who had waited at the door for Elaine, and who Reed had at first assumed was her boyfriend.

Elaine turned to look at him. "That's right, with Bernard. He has an old beat-up Volvo, without air conditioning, and almost without brakes." She smiled: "Every time I ride with him, it's quite an adventure."

Reed nodded. His brain registered every detail. Words, expressions, the slightest moves. It recorded Elaine's well shaped nose, dusted with freckles like the face of a young urchin, her eyelashes, thick and not too long. The triangle of flesh left naked at the top button of her blouse. The way her wrists emerged from her sleeves. He glanced at each of these details with an astonishment that verged on the scientific, regretting that he was unable to study them openly. Oh, he almost wished she would fall asleep in the back seat next to him so that he could observe her at his leisure. He and she, sitting side by side, in the car flooded with scarlet sunlight. Reed realised that the conversation was languishing. "So, I hope your friend didn't mind having to make the drive all alone in his Volvo, for one evening," he said, returning to the topic of conversation.

"Bernard?!" She seemed to find the idea quite amusing. "I doubt it," she said. "Knowing him, the minute I get home I'll find a dozen messages from him on my voicemail, asking me to call and tell him in detail how this ride back went."

Reed frowned.

"He's a curious friend," Elaine explained. "And you…" she seemed to be searching for the words. "Well, you must know. You tickle people's curiosity. You're a living legend."

Reed had a technique he'd developed for reacting to compliments, or at least to phrases that sounded like compliments. A technique that involved a mixture of more-or-less sincere modesty, self-deprecating irony, and a coolness that sometimes verged on annoyance. In this case, he limited himself to batting his eyelids. He felt her words spreading in his stomach, like a mouthful of scalding-hot food, with their electrifying taste. He tried to play it down: "A legend that's a little rough at the edges, I'm afraid. A legend that's become a little dull," he added, waving his hand at the pile of papers and files that he'd set on the seat, between them, attesting to what he'd become over the years: an ageing professor. Something of an intellectual.

"Don't make fun," Elaine said, placing a hand, with sudden recklessness, on the stack of paper. The outline of a vein ran over the back of her hand like an underground river, and the skin of her knuckles was faceted into minuscule triangles. "A personality like yours," Elaine was saying, "can play an important role these days. I mean, after that horrible murder. Who would have guessed that a legend in his own time, like Batman... We're living in strange times, don't you think?"

Reed wasn't thinking. He didn't want to think. He didn't want to talk about the recent murder of Batman or about the times they were living in or any other grim topics. He was determined to avoid the morass of depressing subjects. Dreariness just tended to engender more dreariness. Instinct told him to move on to other subjects, in order to show Elaine that he knew how to kid around, how to keep it light, and that he didn't always have to carry with him the burden of all his past experience. "Watch this," he said, placing one hand next to Elaine's and starting to model it, shaping it with the dedication of a sculptor, so that the two hands were soon identical. Perfectly identical.

She opened her eyes wide. "But what the..." Then it dawned on her and, enchanted by that little trick, she exclaimed: "My hand!"

"Strange tricks for strange times," Reed commented, restoring his hand to its normal shape, dispelling the illusion. Within seconds, a piercing shock ran through him. The shock he felt every time he used his superpowers without proper preparation. He concealed it and smiled, with satisfaction, at Elaine's laughter in response to his witticism.

He went on making jokes. She went on laughing. He realised, of course, what was happening. He was toying with a woman thirty-five years his junior, using every stratagem to make her laugh like a little girl. He was playing the clown for her, in a way he hadn't done for anyone else in years now, not for any other woman, not for anyone at all, and he still didn't know why.

Elaine was laughing. The green flash of her eyes rose up, from time to time, to seek out Reed's eyes. She seemed far too intelligent to keep on laughing at a succession of stupid wisecracks. If she was doing it, Reed

understood, it meant that a ritual was under way between the two of them.
A form of role-playing, a coded exchange. Reed felt a jolt, a discharge of
gratitude and alarm at the idea that it was all spelled out, explicit by now:
*I'm courting her. I'm coming on to a woman who's younger than my son. She
knows it and she's playing along.*

They were in the city. The car was moving through Manhattan. Reed felt
something come straight at him, a sort of wave, the vibration of the city,
and he wanted Elaine to touch him, right away, so that she too could feel
that tension quiver, on his elastic body, like a sensitive cord.

He looked over at her. He wanted to touch her as the night-time lights
of the city filled the interior of the car, so that she seemed to gleam in the
dim half-light. Her ivory skin. Her legs, encased in tight-fitting jeans.
The car headed south, following the stream of traffic, and when the giant
bridge loomed up before them, Reed could almost hear the ocean, finally,
surge towards them with its insistent hum, murmuring into his ears that
time was running out. Time really was running out. He had to seize this
opportunity. And so he cleared his throat, as the car was hurtling towards
Brooklyn, and with the greatest nonchalance he could muster, asked her
whether some evening soon, maybe, he could take her out to dinner.

*

Red wine. White wine. Italian wine, French wine, California wine. Reed
hadn't expected that selecting a wine in a restaurant in the presence of a
woman, or really he should say, *for* a woman, would ever become a pleasure
for him again. Choosing a bottle meant impressing a taste, a colour to the
evening. The hue of the evening was determined by the wine, by the place
where they ate, by the dress Elaine wore, by the unpredictable tone their conversation took on, and by a thousand other factors. Light, glances, the clink
of a glass. Reed also hadn't expected that a sense of astonishment could come
back into his life, certainly not this intense, not this pure. Still, every evening
he spent with her left him amazed, floating in a dense layer of wonder: *Is this
happening because of me? Is it possible that I'm making all this happen?* They were
drawing closer, evening after evening, like planets on the verge of touching.

He wasn't used to it. For the last several years he'd only gone out with prostitutes. Beautiful, enjoyable, predictable prostitutes. When he was with them, he knew from the very outset exactly where things would wind up. An evening with a prostitute was always the same colour. No surprises lurking around the corner. For years, that is, ever since he and his wife had divorced, Reed's only experience of the world of women was through the reassuring, discreet, honest, functional world of high-end prostitution.

Not that he lacked female admirers, or opportunities to have sex free of charge. There were plenty of women interested in seeing what a rubber man had between his legs. When he was younger, he'd found himself fighting off a continuous barrage of offers, intrusive introductions, and more-or-less explicit come-ons. Back then, women sent him letters which practically singed the envelope. They sent him curly hairs of the intimate kind. He was one of the most prominent superheroes in America, a man with a flexible, stretchable body, and all women wanted was to touch him. But he was untouchable. He had a wife. And by the time he no longer had a wife, he was still untouchable, because now he was a man past the prime of his life, a respected scientist, and his idea of maturity involved dignity, discretion, and self-control, rather than a quest for sex.

He couldn't throw himself into the arms of women who were too explicit. Women of that kind, anyway, had stopped writing to him once he retired as a superhero, and these days they were probably sending emails to his son, although Reed didn't know much about that. He'd always promised himself to ask Franklin about his personal life, but the opportunity never seemed to arise.

At the same time, after the failure of his marriage, he was in no state of mind to court women who might play hard-to-get. That took too much energy. By now, he was devoting all his energies to science, to his foundation, to the challenging task of protecting the meaning of his own life after spending decades trying to protect the world. Sex threatened to become a stumbling block. That's when the carefree era of prostitutes began. Beautiful women who never caused trouble. Young too, but *professionally* young, an ageless youth that was not a complication. No matter what, they were all older than Franklin: that was the boundary, the psychological barrier that Reed had never crossed.

A high-end prostitute had style, a neutral style without sharp edges, like a black suit or a dark sedan car. Reed Richards was an ex-hero. He was terrified of looking ridiculous. Style was all-important, even in sex.

What he'd lost, he now realised, was the ability to court a woman. Really court her. Bend the edges of the world towards another person in such a way that everything would appear easy and perfect to her. Courting someone meant making it possible for her to live in a movie, where everything worked as if by magic: the restaurant, the table, the wine, the timing, the after-dinner drink. No awkwardness, no hesitation between one thing and the next. Enchantment isn't something you can create with a snap of the fingers. That was why Reed felt a sort of disbelief at the thought that this enchantment was still in place, and had been for evening after evening, and that a woman who was far too young, beautiful, and unpaid, was at the centre of it alongside him.

The restaurants where he took Elaine were in fact selected by Annabel. His secretary was the mastermind of their evenings together. They had to be charming places, of course, where there was no danger of Reed being recognised, and ideally where he had never gone in the past with his wife, or with some paid girlfriend. They had to be intimate but also fashionable, the right kind of place for a man to take a woman, to court a woman, to make her feel she was at the centre of something. Sometimes it seemed impossible to Reed that the city could have enough restaurants, and he thought miserably of the day when he would no longer know where to take Elaine.

Annabel reassured him. *The restaurants of New York are endless.* She seemed to know them all, and each time she managed to choose the right one, thanks to her extensive reading of the restaurant columns in the press.

Reed smiled uneasily at the thought of his anorexic secretary busy reading restaurant reviews in *Time Out*. Still, he knew he could rely on her. Annabel's selections were always spot-on.

What's more, she had suggested he skip the usual bouquet of flowers after the first dinner, and instead send Elaine an expensive bonsai. *Brooklyn girls love bonsai plants*—she'd uttered the phrase with an aura of mystery, and to judge from Elaine's reaction, when Reed called her later, this piece of advice had been sound as well.

The bonsai. The restaurants. The density of a wine. The colour of a sunset while he was speeding south in a car to pick her up. The way that she'd looked up at the sky on a summer night. The odour of a freshly cleaned street. Elaine's slightly damp hair, perhaps after a hasty shower. Lipstick traces on the edge of a glass. It was a time made up of details. A series of fragments and images that engraved themselves into Reed's memory, like an alphabet on a wax tablet. In that earliest period, the only way he had of getting to know Elaine and what Elaine represented was this chain of fragments, this collection of microscopic, separate, unexpected facts.

Reed wanted to put Elaine in focus in the most complete way possible. He listened as she spoke about her family, the Staten Island area where she had grown up, how she had seen the ocean every day of her childhood, and the time she decided she wanted to travel, maybe by sea. Then one night she had watched as a ferry boat burned offshore, and the glow of that fire had made her raise her head to the sky. The stars. It was as if she had seen them for the first time, barely distinguishable beyond the light of the fire. Her father had been a fireman, her mother was a nurse, and her sister wanted to study medicine, so the whole family was baffled—if not horrified—when at sixteen she announced that she wanted to be an astronaut. It meant she would have to join the air force, and take on the challenge of years of studying space engineering, and even though no one doubted her determination in the slightest, it still seemed like an unheard-of choice for a sixteen-year-old girl. No one had tried to block her way. Everyone assumed she would change her mind on her own.

He listened as Elaine talked about it, how with each year her ambition only strengthened, and how she felt sure that she would be able to *touch the comet's tail*, just as Reed had said during one of his lectures. He listened to her. He listened, peeking at her lips, her mobile mouth, the opening through which phrases and breath issued, the fissure that sometimes seemed as hard as a blade, and at other times deeply and movingly soft.

Reed sought *the form* of that mouth, the form of that woman, because he had spent his life betraying his own form, elongating and altering it until he had almost forgotten it, but he knew that to love someone, on the other hand, meant first and foremost *having a form*, and loving another form. Two mouths, two bodies.

He should have kissed her, so that he could know once and for all the outlines of that mouth. He hadn't done it yet. Maybe he was afraid of the way those lips shone at times, in the candlelight of some restaurant, or in the dim light of an exclusive cocktail bar. Sometimes, out of the corner of his eye, for a fragment of a second, he saw those lips twist in a smile that was too hard, too knowing, too lacking in innocence. But those were shadows. Nothing but shadows, or at least that's what he thought.

Later, he would think of that period as *their chaste phase*, weeks of reciprocal study and indecision, desire, fear, and enthusiasm, weeks that—as he later understood—were the only time they'd been truly happy.

*

Reed pushed open the door. The cool air of the meeting room poured out towards them, pleasant, welcoming. For the past few evenings, he'd asked Annabel to leave the air conditioning on, knowing that the time had almost come: the time to give Elaine a tour of the foundation's offices. Show her where he worked and lived. "This is the conference room," he told Elaine, who followed him with a look of wonderment.

"It's immense," she said. "Much bigger than I would have expected."

They wandered around the room in silence, like children who had sneaked into an amusement park at night. They walked around the large conference table made of highly polished wood. "To be honest," Reed felt duty-bound to point out, "we barely use this room any more, maybe twice a year. The library and the laboratory are hardly ever used either. The foundation is really just Annabel and me, these days."

"Oh, stop joking," Elaine protested with an enchanting smile. She was wearing a dark-green dress, more or less the shade of her eyes, and her shoulders were bare. "Everyone knows," she went on, "that this conference room is frequented by the biggest names in world science."

"A couple of Nobel laureates," Reed admitted. "But we don't see them much… When the board of advisers meets it's usually just to make routine decisions. Whether to reassign funding or publish a new issue of our scientific journal. And of course to enjoy a good lunch."

Elaine laughed. They moved on. Annabel's office was cool, and the air retained a hint of the dry, almost aseptic scent of his secretary. Her desk was in impeccable order, as though Annabel had known that on this very evening two people would be there, looking at her things, the receiver of her phone, the keyboard of her computer, the blank surface of her sleeping screen. Reed felt an unexpected surge of fondness for his faithful secretary. He was confused for a moment, in the cool air of the office, while outside the summer impregnated the streets.

He thought he saw Elaine shiver. Maybe the air conditioning was set too low. "Come this way," he said, and they walked to the last office. "There was a time," he said, just to continue the conversation, and to conceal his embarrassment as Elaine walked into his personal office... "There was a time when we occupied the whole building. Now we just have two floors."

"I know," Elaine answered, lightly touching the surface of his desk. "I read it in your biography." She ran her hand over the desktop, spreading her fingers as if to test its substance. "A whole building," she mused. "It seems incredible to think of it today."

"That's the way things were back then," Reed smiled. "It was the Seventies. We had lots of different projects under way. Laboratories, a hangar full of aircraft of all kinds, even a small special prison for supercriminals. It was all here, including the residences of the other members of the group."

"The most famous group of superheroes on earth," she mused, in a neutral tone, continuing her exploration.

The comment hung in the air. Reed was touched by the doubt that she might have ventured that statement purely out of courtesy. As she walked over to the framed photographs lining one wall, she looked like a child visiting a grown-up's office. With her hair pulled back, tucked behind her ears, and her luminous skin, and the mantle of freckles dusting her shoulders. For an excruciating instant, Reed perceived the depth of her loveliness. Elaine turned towards him, with a start, and with an eager smile she exclaimed: "I don't believe it... I know this picture!"

Reed moved closer. It was the picture that Richard Avedon had taken of him, twenty or so years ago, in the aftermath of a particularly famous exploit.

"He took that picture after the rescue in Florida," Elaine said with a gleam in her eyes. "I remember it perfectly. You stretched your body for miles in the middle of a hurricane, to grab hold of a boat that had been swept out to sea by the storm. There were children on the boat. The whole world was astounded at what you'd done. Nobody thought you could stretch so far."

"Neither did I," Reed said with a smile, pleased that she remembered the case. He looked at her eyes, with a pleasurable sensation of personal contact. "My body was different back then," he added, almost as an apology: that had been his last great exploit.

"The newspapers talked about it for weeks," Elaine went on dreamily. "When you came back to New York, Avedon came to see you and took your picture. That portrait wound up on the cover of *Time*. I remember when our elementary school teacher brought a copy of the magazine into class. She showed it to us, and asked us each to draw our own portrait of you. My drawing turned out to be something awful!" Elaine shook her head. "There were precocious little girls in my class who giggled as they whispered comments about you, things they'd probably heard their mothers say. You were the man of the hour. Women spoke your name. I remember that I was just small, and I thought to myself how wonderful it would have been to be on that boat, in the middle of a hurricane, and to be rescued by you."

Silence filled the room.

Elaine shivered again. She clutched herself without losing her smile.

Reed wished he could warm her up. He wished he could drape himself around her, be a piece of clothing covering her skin. Maybe long ago, with a tremendous effort, he might have managed to stretch his body to the thickness of fabric. Not any more. He would be happy enough just to hand all his own clothes to Elaine, to strip naked and stand there, in front of her, nude, innocent. He wished he could embrace her and tell her that he'd done it, somehow he'd done it: that day he had saved all the children on earth. Including her.

He reached out a hand and brushed her cheek. An immensely long second went by. Then she too lifted an arm, slowly, and they stood there, touching one another.

Reed was often afraid of other people's hands. Other people's hands were too intrusive, too morbidly curious. They tried to touch him at the drop of a hat. Any excuse would do. Other people's hands gripped his hand too tightly, they rested on his shoulder as though by accident, in an attempt to test his consistency, to feel his rubbery texture. *I shook hands with Reed Richards today. It was like shaking hands with a giant piece of chewing gum.*

Other people's hands were a source of embarrassment, mistrust, and weariness, but her hands... Elaine's hands were sliding over his body, over his neck, his arms, sliding under his shirt to follow the outline of his torso, leaving long burning trails behind them. Their passage seemed to leave a hot fissure, like a crevice on the surface of his body. The biggest fissure gaped open vertically, from his chest down to his hip, and from it there seemed to pour forth a torrent of heat, of gratitude, and some pure and invisible energy.

They embraced. They went on talking as if what their bodies were doing had nothing to do with them, as if it were a detail, something their bodies were doing of their own volition, playing together, unencumbered, innocuously, while Reed and Elaine chattered on imperturbably about old memories, about Florida, about things long lost. They could have gone on talking for hours. At last, the distance between their mouths narrowed, inch by inch, until they were too close, and there was no longer room for a single word, and then they kissed, in the rediscovered silence.

*

He took off her shoes. He tasted with the tip of his tongue the soft flesh of her feet. He caressed her ankles. He gazed in rapt adoration at her extremities, almost afraid to venture towards the centre of that body, until she took it upon herself to slip out of her dress, with nothing left on but a pair of skimpy panties. Lying on the bed in the dim light, Elaine's body seemed devoid of obstacles, smooth and warm. Reed gazed down at her before lowering himself closer to her. In Reed's mouth, her breast had the flavour of a dream.

He continued downwards, tracing a solitary path with his lips towards the little oasis of her belly button. Elaine's belly moved ever so slightly, like a sand dune changing shape, as Reed moved past it. He brushed the strings of her panties. He breathed in her scent through the fabric. It smelt of whiteness, like everything else about her. With his hands he slid the strip of fabric down, along the legs that she lifted, docilely, into the air. Reed wished he could repeat that act, doing it over and over again in an endless replay, the strip of fabric sliding down the smooth legs, frictionless, nothing more than a vague rustling sound.

He traced the reddish fuzz with his lips, an almost respectful gesture, until she sighed. Reed felt a sudden sense of reality rise within him, from his limbs, from his whole body, an intense awareness, a sensation that made him perceive everything, with tremendous clarity: himself. His own sweaty body. His bedroom. The lamp shining out a golden light. The clean sheets. She seized his head and forced him to look her in the eye. "Reed," she sighed.

Until then, he'd kept his clothes on. Now he started undressing. He slipped off his shirt and trousers, with help from Elaine, reassured by the fit look of his abdomen. *Not bad for a man my age.* He kept his underwear on. He went back to playing with her body, again, putting off the moment, even though he could feel the tension dropping, dragged down by that missing step. The tacit schedule of sex. Rhythm had to be maintained. *I can't wait.* He made up his mind to slip off his boxer shorts, a quick, offhand gesture, letting his penis swing free, damp, unhindered.

He closed his eyes when he felt Elaine's hand. His penis was pulsating against her palm. For a moment, Reed was afraid he'd lose his erection, while she went on holding it. *Don't scrutinise it. Don't heft it. My penis. The only part of my body that it's impossible for me to control. The part of my body that tends to modify itself beyond my will, unconsciously obeying what seem to be, in each case, the desires of my partner.*

A spark glinted in Elaine's gaze, perhaps a gleam of understanding. She lay back, relaxed, arms behind her head, in a gesture of complete surrender. Once again, for what seemed like the thousandth time, Reed was astonished by the abyss he'd glimpsed in her eyes. There was something in those depths, far down, and Reed lowered himself towards her, to get a better look… Body on body. Gaze in gaze. Elaine's eyes glowed like the entrance to a secret passageway. In the half-light, her face looked different, bonier, timeless, an arcane face that had waited all this time to reveal itself to him. "Elaine," he whispered, guessing in an instant the history of that face and that body. An ancient story of greatness, of horrifying poverty, of men and women who set out from another continent a century and a half earlier. They had loved and dreamed and wished, they'd made love, panted one above another, venerating the memory of their verdant Ireland, and perhaps they'd killed, and generated new life, one generation after another, following one after another, layer upon layer of humanity, building up over time until, at last, they'd produced the body he was now holding, the mouth he was kissing, the gaze into which he was tumbling. Through the eyes of a single person, it was possible to reconnect with the entire human race.

He was sliding into her. Just don't think about it. Give up all control. If he'd thought about it, every slightest nuance of thought could influence the dimensions of his member. Instead, Reed wanted to be real, natural inside of her. No thoughts, no fears. Not even the absurd terror that seized him sometimes, the fear that he might expand too much inside the other's body. *It won't happen. You won't kill her. Don't think about it.* In his rubbery body, the sensations spread out like regular waves.

Reed went on moving, her legs wrapped around his waist, her face contorted as if on the verge of dissolving. They stopped and remained poised. Reed felt a new wave of lucidity rising inside him. It rose from his legs, flowed towards his face, and out of his eyes. He saw everything. He saw into Elaine's wide-open mouth. He saw the foam sliding down her tongue, and her throat vibrate as she screamed Reed's name. He wished he could vanish into that scream. He wished he could melt into her. Instead, they found themselves side by side, panting, trying to laugh and cough, to find something to say, and to flee the sensation that everything, by now, was consummated.

*

Later, around sunrise, he took her home. They caught a cab because at that time of the morning, Reed didn't have access to a car. The taxi hurtled down the almost empty streets, in the hour just before the new day. They were embracing without speaking. Reed didn't like the idea of having to be apart from her, but in just a few hours Elaine had a flight to Houston and she needed to pack her bags and prepare for the trip.

He stroked her hair. He could feel the warmth of her breath on his chest, through his shirt. When the taxi stopped at an intersection, Reed felt someone watching him. He turned his head and met the gazes of two street-sweepers, a woman at the wheel of a street-cleaning truck and her co-worker, a man standing next to the truck, both looking into the taxi with enchanted expressions on their faces. Then both of them waved at him, with a gesture that resembled a benediction. Reed waved back. The taxi shot across the intersection. Reed decided that he and Elaine must be emanating the unmistakable magnetic glow of a couple who had just made love for the first time. "The world knows about us," he whispered into a sleeping Elaine's ear. "We're as dazzling as the dawn of a new day."

Elaine startled awake as they drove deeper into Brooklyn. She looked around as if she'd slept for hours and gave Reed a fleeting kiss. The taxi came to a halt. They were there. Before letting her get out, Reed nuzzled the back of her neck again. "See you in a few days," he said. When Elaine swung the car door open, a bracing gust of cool air poured into the cab.

He watched her go inside.

The light was rising, as hard as a silver shield. It continued its rise as the taxi drove back towards Manhattan, and the East River ran silently towards the ocean, and the skyscrapers drank in the glow of the day. Reed saw Manhattan coming towards him. He saw the buildings getting brighter and brighter. He saw the city gleam all at once as the sun rose, and he felt dazzled and grateful.

For many years, that city had struck him as alien. For many years, he had considered it a memory of itself, a faded copy, as though day by day the buildings and façades had been replaced by stage backdrops, behind which was nothing but empty space. For many years, in his own city, he had felt intolerably alone.

Now, as the taxi left the big bridge behind and surged uptown towards Little Italy, and the city came to life as if just awakened from an enchantment... As weariness enveloped his body, and the seat seemed to swallow him up... As the city buses began cruising up and down the streets again, majestic like small-scale arks, with their cargoes of men and women of every race... He could sense that he loved it still. That city. That living system of buses, taxis, street-sweepers at work, attentive secretaries, cosy restaurants, that crystal-like city that caught the light, a factory-city that produced impressions, an immense mechanism in the service of desire. New York, the definitive distillate of western romanticism. Reed was certain of this, for an instant, before he dropped into slumber. Before dreaming that he was elastic again, like he was long ago, that he could stretch out over the entire city, the city of arks, the city of rainbows, of bridges that cut the light, the hard-working city, the place where everything had no other purpose—and he was sure of it now—than to fall in love in a pure and eternal way.

*

Autumn came to New York. It emerged with signs that at first were imperceptible, a progressive dimming of the sunlight, uneasy gusts of breeze, and then with starkly cool evenings. Astonishment wreathed the city. Wasn't the planet supposed to be warming? Wasn't the climate supposed to be growing more tropical? And yet people were swathed in layers of clothing. Women were no longer walking around bare-armed, the colours of Central Park were fading, and in the late afternoons light dropped away earlier and earlier.

Every day, Reed worked late into the evening, and when Annabel left he remained in the office, writing a last email or doing a final edit on one of his lectures, waiting for it to be time to call Elaine. He tried to pay no attention to sunsets, which stirred an inexplicable feeling of anxiety in him. Those cruel autumn sunsets.

He hadn't managed to take Elaine to Europe that summer. He'd dreamed of taking her with him to London and Brussels, where he had to attend a couple of international conferences. He'd dreamed of taking her out to dinner in the West End, showing her the Thames from Waterloo Bridge, boarding a small aeroplane, arcing out over the English Channel, and together watching as Europe took form, like an ancient promise, before their eyes. But Elaine had other plans. She'd been commuting all summer between New York and Houston to complete a training course. She was trying to make it into an important programme, and it was now or never, she'd told Reed: she couldn't afford to skip a single day. In the end, Reed cancelled his trip to Europe and spent the summer in Manhattan, seeing Elaine at weekends.

But that wasn't what was making him uneasy. It wasn't even the fact, or at least it wasn't only the fact that Elaine was so ambitious, and that she was dedicated entirely to furthering her career. Nor was it that he saw so little of her, even though he longed for her body every second of every day. The problem was Bernard. It was none other than him. Elaine's classmate, the one that Reed had at first taken for her boyfriend, and whom Elaine introduced as an old friend. Bernard who travelled with her to Houston. Bernard who sometimes stayed overnight at her apartment, when they had an especially early flight. Bernard with his tall physique. Bernard with his fit appearance.

He was surfing the web in search of information about Bernard, one afternoon, typing his name into various databases he knew about, when Annabel buzzed him on the internal line. As usual, there was something falsely cheerful in her voice. "Reed!" she exclaimed. "That police officer is here. Remember? He called this morning."

"Of course," Reed replied mechanically. He felt a burst of annoyance: he had a lot of work to get done by that evening, along with searching for information on Bernard. The police still bothered him sometimes about old legal cases. Almost invariably, it was about criminals he had captured years earlier, when he was an active superhero.

The police officer walked into his office. He was in civilian clothes and wore a rather nice suit. "Detective Dennis De Villa," he introduced himself.

As they were shaking hands, Reed sensed his usual discomfort, wondering whether the man was forming the predictable set of thoughts in his mind. *The hand of Mister Fantastic! It really is rubbery!*

Perhaps the man wasn't thinking anything of the sort. The detective looked serious, almost solemn. Athletic, not too tall. Age: thirty-something. Ever since he'd started dating Elaine, Reed looked at other men with a new focus. He imagined seeing them through her eyes. Were they attractive enough? Could they be serious rivals? More or less serious than Bernard?!

De Villa sat down in front of the desk. He waited for a few seconds, staring at Reed in silence. "Perhaps you're wondering why I'm here."

Actually, that wasn't what Reed was thinking at all. Darn it, how could he get some dirt on Bernard's life? He hadn't found a scrap of information in the confidential archives, and he'd wound up turning to the most ordinary of research tools. On the screen, hidden to the eyes of his visitor, was a Google page with the results of his search. Bernard Dunn. A few dozen pages. Lists of courses he'd taken at college, some old clippings from the sports sections about a basketball team he'd played for. Not much more. The glory of the internet, apparently, still lay in the future as far as this young man was concerned.

"In fact," Detective De Villa was just saying, "I only need a couple of minutes of your time."

Reed sighed. He did his best to focus on the conversation. "Let me guess," he began with a blend of irony and irritation, "this must be about some legal matter. Have you unearthed some old case? Do you need my testimony about something that happened twenty or thirty years ago?"

"Not really," came the answer. Dennis De Villa stared at him again. A stony silence spread between them. There was a certain intensity to the detective's gaze. At last he made up his mind: "You must certainly have followed the case of Batman's murder."

The man's voice sounded soft and sort of scratchy. Reed also noticed that his eyes were red, as if he had recently wept, or as if he had been exposed to a harsh light, or who knows what else. Tiny red capillaries, like the mineral veining in marble. "Of course," Reed nodded, this time in an attentive tone of voice. "A horrible way to die. If I'm not mistaken, the trial will get under way soon."

De Villa nodded as well. "That's right," he said, and let another silence ensue.

The silence extended until the sound of an alert cut through the air, suddenly, making them both start. It had come from his computer. Incoming email. Reed glanced at the screen to see if it was a message from Elaine or something else of importance. It wasn't. His eyes slid over to the other side of the screen, where the Google window floated with its unsatisfactory results: Bernard. Bernard. Bernard. That name started pulsing in his head again.

He went back to looking at Dennis De Villa with a polite expression on his face, but by now his interest had faded. No more desire to look into that man's red eyes, no desire to sit there listening to him. He had practically guessed what the other man was driving at and he was merely waiting for the moment when he could get rid of him.

Part of his brain continued the conversation. He listened as De Villa asked whether anything strange had happened, if he'd had the sensation that anyone was following him or spying on him. He heard how the police were afraid that something was going on in the world of the former superheroes, and that new murders might be about to take place. An array of evidence pointed in this direction.

Reed assured the detective: nothing out of the ordinary had happened to him, and he felt quite safe, because he was sure he was not a cause of annoyance to anyone, he was an *innocuous* citizen by now. Who in the world would want to go to the trouble of conspiring against him, and for what bizarre reason? Reed said this and more, trying to remind De Villa that there was a time when it was the police who came to him for protection, asking him and others like him for help, trying to make the detective understand that the time available was running out, really running out, and that he couldn't spend any more of his working day with a police officer, even if he was well dressed and pleasing in appearance, and even though his eyes seemed to be marked by some strong emotion. He couldn't. He needed to think about Bernard. In fact, the other part of his brain was thinking about Bernard.

He glanced again at the computer screen, restless, eager to plunge back into the world of promise of the search engine. He needed to look for evidence on his enemy. His nefarious adversary. Elaine claimed that Bernard was a homosexual, and there was no reason for him to be jealous. Reed wondered why, then, in his Google searches, Bernard's name failed to appear with any connections to gay topics. An association, a men's gym, the directory of gay ex-basketball players or gay astronauts or any other gay concern imaginable. Didn't gay people band together into association after association? Didn't they spend half their time signing petitions for gay rights, or filling the world with traces of their existence so that everyone, even the most careless observers, would be sure to know about their proud existence? And yet there was no sign of him. Not a single entry, in the entire sphere of the internet, provided a shred of confirmation that Elaine wasn't lying, that Bernard was sexually inoffensive, and that he—Reed—was just being paranoid. A jealous lover. There was not a single trace, in that immense electronic realm, in that virtual world teeming with answers, of the information Reed craved.

De Villa was staring at him, from a distance that seemed to be light years away. There was a final pause. Then the detective got to his feet, saying he'd already taken too much of Reed's time, and asking for the umpteenth time to make sure and call if anything suspicious were to happen. He handed Reed his business card. Reed held it between his fingers, stupefied, like someone unable to remember what a business card was used for, that piece of cardboard with sharp edges. Then he walked him to the door. Now that the detective was leaving, he almost felt a sense of regret. He didn't feel like being alone. Outside the window, the sun was setting. This time, as they were shaking hands, and as he once again tumbled into the red eyes of the other man, Reed felt the need, for an instant, to know more about that man. He wanted to tell him to take care of himself, to protect his eyes, to look out for the air and the allergies and the many dangers that autumn, inevitably, brought with it.

*

Whenever Reed tried to get information about Bernard, she always managed to make him feel like an idiot. *Reed, you amaze me. Bernard is what he is, he doesn't need to prove anything to you. You should be satisfied with what I tell you. Let's not talk about it again, understood?*

Reed understood. At least for a few days. Then the machinery of obsession began grinding away in his brain again, more relentless than before. He fantasised about asking for help from certain old acquaintances of his. Discreet, professional people, who would bring him a complete report on Bernard Dunn's life in just a few days: routines, habits, friends, men or women or whatever might happen to fall within his proclivities. It would be so simple. Those old acquaintances of his would tell him the truth. But he immediately felt like a worm, a tremendous feeling of guilt overcame him for being unable to take Elaine at her word. To rely on Elaine's answers. What an odd sensation. How could he love a person so much and yet be so unsatisfied with her answers?

In fact, he suspected that Bernard was only a part of the problem. Nothing but a single part. The rest of the problem, with Elaine, was how elusive she was capable of being. The indifference with which she had avoided his suggestion of a vacation together, or with which she turned off her phone when she was busy, without worrying that he might try to call her. There was something about her that smacked of a self-contained, unshakable independence. She was certainly not the kind of girl you could control, much less *possess*. For that matter, why on earth would he ever try to *possess* her?

But that was exactly what he was trying to do.

The nights she agreed to sleep at his apartment were minor triumphs for Reed. *She's here. In my arms.* They would fall asleep, naked, under the sheets, and it was so satisfying to hold her close against his body. *In my arms!* At the end of those nights, dawn came early and slipped in the window, stretching out between them like a third lover. That was the time to hug each other closer, to begin touching one another, half-asleep. Sex in the morning, what a wonderful luxury. Reed could slide into her with his eyes still shut, without entirely waking up, and open his eyes just as he came, seeing her, underneath him, like a silvery creature in the light of dawn.

Then came the time to get up. Elaine had to leave in a hurry, to run by her apartment before some appointment that morning, or else straight out to the space centre in New Jersey, or worse still, to the airport. Reed had too much self-control and sense of efficiency to try to detain her. He didn't want to make himself pathetic. He settled for trying to impress a *flavour* upon the rest of her day, attempting to leave an imprint, a sensation in her, something she could carry with her throughout the day.

For instance, breakfast. He would make sumptuous breakfasts for her. He had abandoned his beloved bagels to focus on delicacies, Scottish smoked salmon, French cheeses, organic cereals, exotic fruit, and other choice morsels, the kind of things that you can buy at Dean & DeLuca or other stores with exorbitant prices. After learning that Elaine loved tea, he had spent a fortune to have an exquisite Japanese tea shipped to him. Breakfasts had to be perfect. Every detail had to sparkle. The world needed to look perfect as long as she was with him, so that the hours that followed, the hours without Reed, would seem less rich and less significant to her.

Or else music. The music had to be left in the background, as if by chance, while they were getting dressed or eating breakfast. Jeff Buckley for instance, or any other of those dramatically intense, youthful, romantic singers who were capable of echoing in a person's head, in a subtle, tormenting manner, for hours and hours. That's what he wanted. He wanted to be sure he wouldn't vanish from Elaine's consciousness! He wanted to echo inside her throughout the day, every instant, to haunt her like a ghost! Before that, he'd never experienced worries of that kind, nor had he ever been frightened at the idea that someone could go through their day without thinking of him. *What's happening to me? What the hell kind of things are these to worry about?!*

He'd had to live into his sixties, with white hair and a less omnipotent body, before falling in love like this. He'd had to stop being a superhero, lose part of his superpowers, accept that he had limits, before experiencing unlimited desire for another person. All his life, he'd been able to reach out his arm and take whatever he wanted. And now there was so little he could do, he had such poor resources to make this woman his own.

Elaine was near, Elaine was far. It was a state of peace and eternal conflict. Elaine would take a shower, emerge with a cascade of wet hair, grab a quick bite with him, seize her bag, and then she'd be gone. She'd run far away. Reed would walk her to the elevator. Usually there was a kiss, or perhaps an embrace, and sometimes the fleshy rose that Reed would form, as a joke, out of his hand, pretending to extend it shyly to her. She would smile, pretending to sniff it, unaware of the intermittent stabs of pain that simple rose would cost Reed, in his hand and his whole arm, for the rest of the morning.

Once she was gone, Reed had nothing left to do but go back to his usual pursuits. Sit at his desk and prepare for another productive day. No one would be able to detect the obsession that was seething inside him. Not the people who were calling to invite him to attend a conference at some university, not a member of the board of advisers of the Richards Foundation who had come in to discuss some administrative matter, not even Annabel who was handing him the paper bag of cinnamon bagels, the way she did every morning, with her skeletal hands. No one. Reed appeared the same as always: affable, productive, courteously ironic.

What a tremendous strain! The inhuman effort of mastering an obsession, and keeping in equilibrium his external normality and his internal disquiet. As soon as the day was over, and he found himself alone, a destructive weariness settled down on him.

In the silent evening, he might chance to catch a glimpse of himself in a mirror, and recognise that there was something odd about his appearance. Feverish eyes, ringed with exhaustion. He looked like one of those old lunatics who used to show up occasionally for his lectures, submitting evidence about their alleged discoveries concerning extraterrestrial life forms or molecular energy. Someone possessed by an implacable anxiety. Someone who would never find whatever it was they were looking for. Reed didn't want to have that glint in his eyes. *You've got to have style even when you're feeling lonely. I don't want to look like an unhappy old man.*

He couldn't believe he'd come to this point, much less that he'd got there so quickly, in the space of just a few weeks. He, Reed Richards, the man whose exploits had saved thousands of lives, the man who once issued orders to police chiefs and army colonels, a member of the international scientific community. *I've been a rubber man for my whole life, now I want to be inflexible. I don't want to wriggle into the fissures of her life. I want something more. I want everything. I want to enter into her and stay there for hours. I want to get to know her the way you know the air around you. I want to force her to take a weekend off, I want us to go somewhere together. I want to be the king of her days, I want her to be the queen of mine, and the rest of the world to be nothing more than a detail.*

*

It was a wet day. A pounding rain was beating down on the city, outside, falling for hours now. Rain on the apartment buildings, rain on the streets. Rain on the roofs of cabs and on the backs of city buses. Rain on the umbrellas of hurrying pedestrians, of tourists struggling to consult their guidebooks. Rain on the picture windows of Starbucks where people who had momentarily given up the effort to explore the city, or even just cross it, were nursing cups of expensive coffee, contemplating the world outside or their own reflection in the glass. Rain. At the height of the afternoon, water streamed along the gutters, bathing sidewalks, the traffic was hope-lessly snarled, and people hurried along, overcoats sodden, nerves shot. In the rain, New York went into a state of suspended animation. An enormous short circuit seemed about to jolt through it. The smell of wet asphalt mixed with the aroma of food outside restaurants in Chinatown, outside Mexican restaurants and pizzerias, outside kosher and Russian restaurants, an odour reminiscent of saliva that seemed to make the city resemble a moist, enormous mouth. Raindrops drummed on office windows, laying siege to those working inside.

Reed worked until dark. He had spent the morning at a seminar for university professors, spending two-thirds of the session setting forth some of the current issues of astrophysics, and devoting the last third to stories about his past career as a superhero, at the request of the attendees. It often happened, at the end of a lecture, that the questions he was asked slipped into the realm of the personal. His life. His memories. Normally, Reed was capable of fighting against that drift, and could steer the topic back to the theme of the lecture, but sometimes he wound up giving in. When he was tired, for instance, or when he lacked concentration. Reed didn't think of himself as nostalgic in the least, and he was well aware that there was only one right attitude to adopt in the case of time—not to regret it, but to avoid wasting it. Still, sometimes it was easier to pretend he longed for the past. The past was always an excellent topic, and it satisfied any audience.

He went back to the office in the driving rain, and there he bided his time, ignoring his impatience, by working on an academic article, and with a long telephone conversation with a Washington bigwig who wanted him to be a member of the scientific advisory committee for a new, important government project. Apparently, they needed him. That ought to have pleased him. But all he felt was a pang of anxiety. The idea of making com-mitments of any kind tormented him, and what he wanted most, all of a sudden, was a little room, a little freedom. A little emptiness.

He wound up treating Annabel badly, because she had scheduled two of his meetings the next day too close together.

"You always like to save time in that kind of meeting," she said, in an attempt to justify what she had done, which made Reed even more furious.

"Do you think you have the right to decide what I like and what I don't like? Do you think that you can make decisions for me to cut short my meetings? And come to think of it, why are you still in the office? Do you really have no personal life at all?"

Annabel left the office in tears. *Rain outside, tears inside*, Reed thought with detachment. *A perfect equilibrium of liquids.*

It was six o'clock, and he could stop working. He shut his eyes and tried to stop thinking. To empty his mind. A Tibetan lama had taught him a few basic meditation techniques. He could not now recall any of them. His mind kept wandering in a thousand different directions, restlessly; each idea was an incandescent surface, upon which it was impossible to stay still. Washington. Annabel. Appointments. A yearning for sex. A yearning for a vacation…

Elaine hadn't called him once in the past week. Nor had he called her. Dignity, the important thing was to preserve his dignity. At last, she had got in touch that morning, with a message suggesting they get together that evening.

Reed took a sharp breath. Elaine was the most incandescent thought of all, the surface his mind kept bumping up against, without ever being able to touch it. Impossible to touch it. She was a glowing ember in his head.

He went back to his private suite, where he took a shower and picked out a dark shirt. There was still time. He turned on the TV, something he hadn't done in months, and that show appeared on the screen. The female mutant who assumed the bodies of celebrities. One of the most famous superwomen in America. *I could have recycled myself that way, I guess. I could have had a television comedy, or I could have been the regular host of some talk show or something like that.*

Still, he enjoyed the show. It helped him to clear his head for a while and kill time until Elaine was due to be there. He heard the doorbell. Reed stood up with a poker face. He was never just happy when she came to see him. It was more like a sense of restlessness, almost a sense of disturbance, like when one radio frequency comes into contact with another frequency.

He had sent a car to pick her up. Elaine walked in, complaining about the traffic. "It took forever!" she said. They exchanged a glancing kiss. Under her coat she was wearing a tight black dress. Short, with a low neckline. The most feminine astronaut Reed had ever seen. There they both were, elegantly garbed, standing in Reed's living room. Annabel, as far as he could remember, must have reserved a table for them in a Cambodian restaurant. Or was it Laotian?

In fact, he didn't feel like going out. He didn't feel like worrying about whether someone had recognised him, or if someone was wondering how old the woman he was with might happen to be. "I was thinking," he said, "maybe tonight we could just eat in. What do you say to some takeout?"

"That would be great," Elaine replied, without a flicker of surprise. "This evening I'm completely beat."

Forty minutes later, they were sitting on the carpet, eating from takeout boxes. Thai food. Classical music in the background, mixed with the sound of the rain drumming down outside. The most informal dinner they'd ever had together.

They could have been comfortable and happy, in the warmth, in the dim light. They'd both taken off their shoes, and Reed's eyes kept sliding down, to their extremities, the feet of a man and the feet of a woman, and everything seemed pleasantly intimate, suffused with a warm erotic promise.

But the conversation was languishing. Reed could feel an unease between them. Later, he couldn't have said exactly what started the argument. There are certain conversations, as he well knew, that can lead only in one direction. No matter where they start, the end point is inevitable. The point of friction. The open wound. "In fact," Reed found himself saying, "I'll admit that there's a problem." He took a sip of white wine from his glass, to show just how unruffled he was. "The problem," he resumed, "is that I can't seem to understand your, how to put this… your *nonchalance*. Showing up so nonchalantly when it's been days since you last called me."

Elaine also took a sip from her glass. She watched the wine forming tiny golden ripples as she swirled it ever so slightly. "Reed, you know perfectly well where I was. And in any case, you could have called me yourself."

Reed maintained an even tone, so that everything would continue to seem innocuous. "Certainly," he said. "I knew where you were. Your training and all that. I can imagine it was tough to find a few minutes, maybe late in the evening. Yes, I can imagine how busy you were, what with your training, and what with your colleagues, and what with Bernard…"

Elaine put down her glass. "My God," she groaned.

Reed pretended he hadn't heard her, aware that he was irritating her, and that the intimacy of the scene was beginning to wither. The enchantment of the low lighting and the music by Schubert, their bare feet, and everything else.

"I can't believe it," Elaine said. "Again with Bernard?! Can I ask you why you're so obsessed with him?"

Reed decided to get up, and started collecting the empty takeout boxes. "I'm not obsessed in the slightest," he replied, continuing to put on an impassive tone of voice. "You told me that he's gay, right? Why should I worry about him?"

"He's not gay," Elaine sighed. "He's a homosexual. Those are two somewhat different things."

Reed froze for a second, trying to grasp the difference. Then he went back to collecting the boxes. "Great," he said, with angry sarcasm. "Now that I know it, I'll stop worrying."

"I can't believe it," Elaine said again, in a harsh voice, shaking her head. She got up too, and started gathering the remains from their dinner.

"You have such an evasive way of dismissing things," he accused her.

"Reed, I'm not being evasive. You're the one who wants too much. You want to occupy every part of my life. You behave as if we were married."

Reed was suffocating. The air had turned hard. He could feel something unpleasant about to happen, increasingly ineluctable, but he couldn't help asking: "What are you saying?"

Now they were in the kitchen, where they set down their empty trays and boxes and glasses on the table, and then stood there, facing each other. Without the protection of the carpet, the chilly floor was painful against Reed's bare feet.

"Meeting you was a wonderful surprise," Elaine said in a gentler tone of voice. "You were a childhood legend to me, and that day at the space centre you materialised, in the flesh, and there was a spark between us.

Between your eyes and mine." She looked around uneasily: "Isn't there any light around here?"

Reed remained motionless. There was plenty of light available. There were halogen lamps in all sizes, ready to light up the room at the touch of a button. A world-renowned lighting designer had worked on the apartment a few decades ago, along with carpenters and electricians, many of them long since retired. There were yards and yards of fibre optics and electric wiring, and dozens of light bulbs that had been replaced over the course of time, and all of this had been done expressly to create the powerful lighting resources that waited, latent, around them. But Reed chose not to use them. He allowed the kitchen to remain illuminated by nothing other than the glow from the adjoining room, so that Elaine's face would be left as it was, before his eyes, carved out of the uncertain light. "Go on," was all he said.

Elaine forgot about the light and went on delivering a speech that, it dawned on Reed, she must have rehearsed long before: "You're an important man," she said. "You're respected, attractive, and you haven't become ridiculous the way other superheroes have. It was incredible to find that you liked me. It was incredible to start dating you, and be able to get to know you, and those other things I wasn't used to, I mean, being courted the old-fashioned way, with a car coming to pick me up, a different restaurant every time, and waiting such a long time before going to bed together..."

"Wait a minute," Reed broke in. He had expected her to slip in a mortal blow at some point, but not that little revelation. "Do you mean to say," he asked, "that's not how it usually went? That you didn't wait so long with other men?"

The question seemed to surprise her. She ventured a smile in the half-light. "Reed," she whispered. She spread her arms: "I'm a big-city woman, I'm twenty-seven years old, I'm in training sixty hours a week, I live for my work. I take sex when it comes around."

Reed nodded, without quite knowing why. Words were beginning to elude him. "And with me?" he asked.

Elaine seemed to think it over. "With you... I couldn't say. I just thought that was the style of a man your age."

Reed felt scalded. His face, in particular, but also down on a line with his hip, where lately all his emotions had been concentrated, and where there seemed to be a very sensitive fissure. "A man my age," he echoed. He stood there, gazing at Elaine's face, or maybe just imagining it, in the scant light. That face. It seemed as hard as a diamond. That face, so intense, so determined. The kind of face that would remain unchanged as it aged, with perhaps a few lines here and there. Just like Sue's face. *Like my wife's face*, he thought, almost grateful to be able to make that comparison, to be able to draw a line between his own past life and this uncertain, prickly instant.

"Reed?" Elaine called to him.

He came to with a start. There was complete silence. The music had ended some time ago, and even the sound of falling rain had stopped. Now there was a sense of nudity in the air. "Go on," he said.

"There's not much more," Elaine sighed. "I was intrigued by the situation. They've been wonderful months for me. But you seem to expect too much from this, Reed. I don't think…" She seemed to experience a last instant of embarrassment. "I don't think the two of us have the same perception of the importance of this relationship."

Reed nodded again.

"I think we'd better stop seeing each other, Reed."

"You're right," he answered, in the most neutral voice he could muster.

*

His life belonged to him again. No more obsession, no more stupid waits, no more dreary insomnia before dawn. Or at least that's what he promised himself. Reed wanted to become himself again. The eternal, original, incorruptible Reed. There were moments when this objective seemed to loom close, be attainable, when everything that had happened over the past few months turned into a mirage, nothing more than a momentary blur. He went out clothes shopping. Simple, elegant suits, designed by a well-known Italian designer, the kind of suits he'd always worn but which only now, in the last few years, seemed to fit him to a T. *Look at me now*, he said to himself in front of the mirror, in the shop, as a chubby sales assistant looked on approvingly. *Here I am. I am what I want to be. Elegant and solitary.* He also bought some flowers as an apology to Annabel. At first he'd thought of a box of chocolates, but then chose to spare her sensibilities.

And there were other moments… As he was collecting his clothes to send them to the laundry, or when he was reading the Sunday sections of the *New York Times*, or while carefully fishing the anti-theft strip out of a book he'd purchased at Barnes & Noble… When he was touching his body, his immutable body, under the spray of a warm shower, or while performing his stretching exercises, in a special gymnasium, under the watchful eyes of his trainers… As he was doing the things he'd always done, the usual everyday actions, and the air had that unmistakable colour of *absence*… At any given instant, he might be struck by the perception that Elaine was out there, in the city, in the vastness of the world at large. Elaine was the wind that buffeted the windows. She was the spirit that pervaded the entire outside world. And he could lay no claim to her.

It was during one of those moments, as he sat at his desk trying to regain possession of his thoughts, that an email arrived from Franklin. Reed looked at the name of the sender, almost stunned to remember that someone out there in the world carried the same last name as him. Franklin Richards. His son. Reed hadn't communicated with him for the past few weeks, and he didn't even know whether he was in New York. *I keep forgetting to tell you about that guy from the George Hotel, what's his name?, the one that everyone says wears a ball-crushing cilice, you know the one I mean… Anyway, he sent me a Cartier watch, the package reached me while I was still in Baghdad, you can imagine for yourself what it was like to find myself holding a Cartier over there. Of course, the first thing I did was to put it up for auction on eBay. More than anything else, I was curious to know how he found out my address, but I guess he must have spoken with you.*

Reed thought back to the day, thousands of years ago, when Raymond Minetta had called him. It happened in the period after he'd seen Elaine for the first time, in passing, and he had little idea of what was waiting for him. How long had it been? Not many months, after all, but it seemed like a day from another lifetime, a fragment scattered in a distant fog.

It seems to me, Franklin went on, *that he wants me back at the health club at his hotel. I honestly can't understand this obsession with health clubs, every time I go back to NY somebody's asking me where I go to work out or take a sauna. What do I know? Wherever, I tell them. I mean, I spend so little time in NY… But the real reason for this email is to remind you that tonight they're showing the documentary about me. Even though I know you never watch TV, I thought I'd remind you all the same.*

Reed drafted a reply but he wound up deleting it. He felt like writing something true, something intensely sincere, because if there was one thing he had been missing over the last few months it was sincerity, that sensation of something capable of flowing between two people, without hindrance, naked and straightforward. *I have a crush on a girl who's younger than you. I'm getting over it now.*

He'd better not. It wasn't like him to write anything so explicit. So sentimental. The idea of opening up to his son both repelled and attracted him, because like any jilted lover he wanted to be understood, by everyone, but he didn't want to risk being pitied. Commiseration was a mediocre sentiment.

There were things that mattered more, after all, than the end of an affair. There was his work, his diplomatic meetings. There were dozens of reasons not to think about her. Dozens of reasons to stop waking up at sunrise, with a start, in the livid light of day, incredulous to discover he was alone. *Sleeping alone is a crime. There ought to be a law against it. Still, I'll have to get used to it. I just have to get used to it.*

*

That night, after work, he went to dinner in a pretentious restaurant with a functionary from the UN, who talked to him at length about a new scientific training programme in the universities of Eastern Europe. It was pretty boring. He went home early, and since he had no other obligations that day, he turned on the TV.

Lately, he'd been watching it a little more than usual. Generally, he didn't like it. He believed that television was what had destroyed the old world of the superheroes. As everyone knew, once the superheroes started appearing on television, people stopped thinking of them as heroes and began thinking of them as entertainers. What's more, he found it embarrassing. It didn't suit him. He was embarrassed by the idea of a grown man going on television, under the spotlights, with make-up and everything that went with it, and he found equally embarrassing the idea of a grown man watching television, on his sofa, slippers on his feet, and his gaze dead.

But Franklin was on. The documentary seemed to have started a few minutes before. Reed went on watching the reconstruction of his son's life; the story of the boy with two superheroes for parents, both fodder for the press throughout the Seventies and Eighties, who in his turn developed superpowers as a child but lost them with the onset of puberty. The story of his troubled adolescence, the arrest at sixteen for possession of marijuana, how he left college at eighteen to take passage on a Greenpeace schooner, and finally the sensational kidnapping. Franklin taken hostage by a pirate crew in international waters, off the coast of Indonesia, and the American mass media reporting on the case day and night, the entire nation watching with bated breath. An army special operations force sent to rescue him, another Swedish hostage killed in the rescue attempt, the political earthquake over who exactly had authorised the operation. Franklin returning home, America's prodigal son, and talk shows receiving incredible ratings whenever he appeared as a guest. Scenes of female admirers laying siege to a restaurant where he was having lunch. An interview with a Hollywood agent who claimed to have offered him a contract. Franklin smiling at everyone he met, inaugurating centres for Alzheimer's victims, popular with mothers seeking husbands for their daughters, and never missing an opportunity to denounce the government's environmental policies. An adorable rebel. Franklin the pacifist, marching against the war. Franklin the ecologist, founding his association, in partnership with a famous rock star, and raising millions of dollars to protect the Amazon. When his friend the rock star was arrested for rape, the case did nothing to undermine Franklin's popularity. America always forgave its favourite sons. Franklin agreed to work for an NGO, began going on missions into combat zones, reporting on the environmental damage caused by warfare. He launched a campaign against the use of depleted uranium. Franklin shown with a helmet on his head. In an elegant shirt during a diplomatic meeting. Bare-chested in the Iraqi desert. Franklin as a special model during a Gucci fashion show in Miami, donating his fee to the environmentalist cause. Franklin living as a globetrotter, making sporadic appearances in New York, just long enough to have his picture taken with some new love interest. He loved young up-and-coming actresses. No one ever seemed to know exactly where he was. Not easy to track him down for an interview. Franklin was a genuine indie star and was on more magazine covers than Johnny Depp.

Reed laughed a lot. The commentator's voice was reeling off one exaggeration after another: like when he said that Franklin was the last role model left to America's youth, or when he said that *Franklin Richards is a sex idol for an uneasy America*. Reed imagined his son laughing, in front of his TV, with his blond shock of hair and his ironic grin, pleased at having pulled it off, having charmed them all, once again. He was thirty years old, but he was still America's most beloved son, the nation's golden boy. No doubt about it, America would forgive him his next exploit, whatever it turned out to be.

Reed had no idea what kind of a father he'd been. *If your worth as a parent can be measured by your appreciation of what your son has become, then I must have been a good father.* He was happy with the way Franklin had grown up. But it had been a challenging task. Reed, who was so *rubbery*, so elastic, who for many years had a personality that matched his body perfectly, smooth and elusive, had found it difficult to raise another person. To know how to treat him. A person who depended on you without actually being you, a person who had a body of their own, demands of their own, and an unmistakable need to have solid figures around them. Solid figures around them! Franklin had had the Rubber Man as a father and the Invisible Woman as a mother. A fine couple of parents…

In the old days, when there was still a feeling of fellowship among the superheroes, someone had proposed founding an association of superhero fathers, to share their experiences and discuss their problems. But it never came to be. The superheroes had been incapable of presenting a united front. Reed had learned how to deal with it on his own, to reconcile the conflicting needs of being a paragon of normality, like all fathers, and a paragon of exceptionality, as a superhero.

He remembered when Franklin was small, and father and son showered together: every time, Franklin waited for him to perform one of his marvels under the spray of water. *Daddy's head is shaped like an umbrella. Daddy's arm is shaped like a drainpipe.*

Reed had loved his son's laughter more than anything else in the world. The laughter of his child. He'd loved Franklin's body as it grew day by day, the way you love a miracle or a fabulous mystery: with adoration, with pride, with an astonishment so vast that it verged on terror. Franklin. As long as the two of them had lived together, Reed had never felt he was alone, because feeling you're alone means feeling that you have no meaning, and Franklin filled his life with meaning. Even when the heroic exploits began to thin out. Even when the world started to change.

Once Franklin had become independent, Reed dreamed for years of seeing him come home, and maybe taking the second floor as his headquarters. Reed didn't need that second floor, he used it—if at all—as a storage area for old equipment. He would have been happy to give it to Franklin. But his son wasn't interested. Reed had been forced to strip his dreams, little by little, away from his son's dreams, as in a delicate operation of ungluing.

Franklin had his own plans. All things considered, Franklin was like Elaine. They were both out in the world, masters of their fate, happy and free.

*

Elaine's message came in a couple of days later. Reed felt the vibration of his cell phone, tucked away in some jacket pocket, transmitted to his chest with a shiver. He pulled it out and stared in disbelief at the words on the small luminous screen. *I watched the documentary about your son. It made me think of you.*

At first he decided to ignore it. After all, it wasn't the kind of message that required an answer. And by now he felt he was leaving their story behind him. Elaine's smile, Elaine's flesh, Elaine's liquid voice, her unattainable youth, the white scent of her sex: it was all fading away, Reed felt certain, like the symptoms of a disease. Soon he too would be free again. He would begin waking up without those scathing depressions, and go out once a month with some paid-for girlfriend. That's what would happen. That's what was about to happen.

But there was the message on his phone. He had no idea what it signified, and the smartest thing would be to delete it. *When something seems to be too ambiguous, don't force yourself to interpret it. Forget it.*

By that evening he'd read it dozens of times, each time feeling even more confused. Outside, darkness had fallen long ago. The tip of the Chrysler Building was illuminated on the horizon, and one by one the buildings around it had lit up, silent, impassive like giant guardsmen.

By the light of his desk lamp, Reed studied the message. More than once he'd been on the verge of deleting it. More than once on the verge of responding. He kept rereading it with all the focus of a scholar perusing an ancient scroll, until he realised how late it had become, and that a long report he needed to finish by morning was waiting on his computer screen. To hell with it. Incredible that he was devoting so much energy to such a trivial decision. In exasperation, he pecked out a response: *I've thought about you sometimes, too.*

Elaine replied. He wrote to her again. They wound up exchanging messages all evening like a couple of teenagers. Reed had to stay in the office until two in the morning to finish his report.

When he woke up a few hours later, his mind was fuzzy and his memory of the text messages hovered like a dream, like a nocturnal illusion. In fact, they hadn't said anything compromising. They'd exchanged news on their lives, they'd confessed that they missed each other. Normal things. Very natural things, in the end, for two people who had been lovers. In the silence of the early morning, Reed checked his cell phone, reflexively, with a predictable mixture of anxiety and desire, but there were no other messages. *That's that. It was just a passing moment, an interlude of weakness.* The day stretched out ahead of him. A productive day in late autumn, a day made up of emails to be sent, new phone calls from Washington, his participation in a videoconference with, among others, Tim Berners-Lee. Reed generally didn't let himself be impressed by other people's celebrity, but he still had a certain admiration for the gurus of the tech world. He focused deeply on the videoconference, then he cleared a thousand other tasks and a thousand other messages off his desk. No more text messages on his cell phone. The day went by, as busy as any other, as nondescript as any other but for two unexpected things.

Towards the end of the afternoon, Reed walked over to Annabel's desk. "Could you scan this for me?" he asked as he handed her a sketch of a micro-device he planned to patent. In his spare time, he sometimes came up with ideas of this kind. Nothing revolutionary, just small devices that the micro-technology industry was always happy to take under consideration.

"Certainly," Annabel said. She took the sketch and laid it on top of a pile of letters, documents, and other papers she needed to deal with.

"Hold on," Reed said. Something had caught his attention. He grabbed a sheet of paper that lay on top of another pile, in the same corner of her desk.

"Oh, right," said Annabel, without understanding the sudden change in Reed's voice. "That came in the mail a couple of days ago. Don't worry: it's just nonsense. A meaningless prank. I meant to throw it in the trash, but I forgot."

Reed froze to the spot. He stood there, reading and rereading that phrase, the sole phrase written on that sheet of paper, printed in capitals. Something stirred in his memory, blurry at first, and then swimming into focus, until he remembered where he'd read it before. That phrase. Those bizarre words:

SO LONG, MY MISTER FANTASTIC

Annabel was baffled. "Something wrong?" she asked, fearful she'd made a mistake. "It hardly seemed worth bothering you about such an absurd note."

"How did it get here?" Reed asked.

Annabel rummaged through the pile of mail where Reed had found the note, and extracted a stamped envelope. "In this," she said.

Naturally, there was no evidence. The envelope was white, the stamp standard postage, no return address. The printer used for Reed's address was the same as the one used for the phrase. Reed shook his head. What an incomprehensible prank. He decided that this time he couldn't ignore it. Could that anonymous sheet of paper be considered a suspicious development? Was that phrase a threat of some kind? "No problem, don't think twice about it," he reassured Annabel, walking back to his office with envelope and note in his hand.

Now it was his turn to rummage through various piles of paper. He started with the desk drawer where he kept his business cards, but didn't find the card he was looking for. He went on with various piles of documents on his desk, but didn't find anything there either. *What was the name of that detective? He had an Italian surname. Where could I have put his card?* Usually, his desk was in impeccable order. It rarely happened that he had to look for anything for more than a few seconds.

Just then, Annabel put through an incoming phone call. As soon as he finished that call, another one came in. Reed wound up spending the rest of the afternoon on the phone, without a break and, when he was finally free, the issue of the anonymous note seemed less urgent. Absurd, yes, but less serious. Once again, he tried to find the card of the detective who had come to see him some time ago. That he wasn't able to find it could mean he'd just thrown it away. He started to wonder what he might say to him. *Oh, detective! This is the second time that someone sent a note to me with an enigmatic phrase of farewell! I'm so frightened, Mr. Detective Man, please help me!*

Ridiculous, he thought. The note was ridiculous, the situation was ridiculous, and the idea of asking for help from the police was ridiculous. He'd always taken care of his own protection. Or, if there was any protecting to be done, it was him protecting others. Basically, more than a threat, that phrase continued to strike him as a sort of hail and farewell on the part of some nutcase. He tossed the note into the bin. He heaved a sigh, his body relaxed, and almost as a comment on the situation his belly produced an unmistakable sound. *It even happens to Mister Fantastic every once in a while.*

Annabel had left. Another workday was drawing to a close. He knew that it was time to turn off his computer, his desk lamp, time to take a shower and think about his own concerns. *They called me Mister Fantastic because I did fantastic things. I can't even remember what I expected in those years, what I imagined would happen when I finally stopped feeling superhuman. Now, that moment is here. In this sequence of days, in this flow of data to transmit, broadband connections, videoconferences with Tim Berners-Lee, inventions to patent, seminars on astrophysics, intercontinental conversations, time zones to take into account, and sentimental depressions.*

There's nothing so bad about getting old. I just wish I could be sure I'm doing it the right way.

He turned off the light. In the protective darkness he left the office and went into his private rooms, where he started undressing in the dim light.

It was then, as the sad touch of evening wrapped around him like a cape, and the muffled buzz of the city filtered in through the window, that the second unexpected event of the day happened.

He heard the elevator stop at his floor. He heard the door slide open. Reed threw his clothes back on, with a sense of alarm, wondering who the hell that could be. Someone that the doorman had let in. Someone who had the code to stop the elevator at his floor. He strode through the rooms of the apartment, in silence and still in the dark, ready to spring into action and defend himself, if that proved necessary, with all the strength of his rubbery old body. He reached the last room, took a deep breath, flipped on the light switch, and in the sudden glare he saw a person. He saw her standing there, in front of him, one hand thrown up to shield her eyes. "Reed!" Elaine exclaimed. "Turn off that light, you're blinding me."

*

"You've come back," Reed whispered as they embraced on the bed, undressing each other, and their breathing grew heavier. "You're here, in my arms."

Reed kept brushing against her body, shoulders, arms, breasts, the flat line of her belly, exerting only the slightest pressure, like a doctor examining a patient. He couldn't bring himself to believe that her body was real. He tried to look into her eyes. She kept them closed, breathing harder and harder, and his voice eventually turned dubious, his repeated words almost becoming a question: "You've come back?"

Elaine started ever so slightly, rubbing her pelvis against his. "Reed, stop talking… Let's make love."

Reed lay on top of her. He absorbed her warmth, he recognised her scent. He couldn't seem to concentrate. A layer of moisture was forming between them, a patina that kept their bodies from adhering one to the other. He wanted there to be nothing between them, no perspiration, almost no layers of skin. He wanted her to open her eyes and tell him that she had come back to stay with him for good.

Elaine only moaned. Instinctively he hugged her tighter, then something happened. He did what he'd never done before. He elongated his arms like a pair of cables, wrapping them around her, to imprison her, to squeeze her tighter, to hold her motionless as though in an interrogation. Reed's arms entwined around her body, arms around her torso, arms around her arms, and Elaine struggled for an instant, perhaps trying to break free, and then surrendered. She started moaning again.

Reed moved slightly away, overwhelmed, but didn't release her. He didn't really know what he was doing any more. He wanted to fully understand her, he wanted to take her prisoner. He turned her around, with a sigh. As she wriggled and twisted, he rubbed his penis between the cheeks of her bottom, staring at the constellation of freckles and moles on her back. Her hair had fallen to either side of her face, laying bare the nape of her neck and her shoulders, and Reed gazed lost in reverie at that starry sky. Elaine's voice seemed to come from a great distance. "Reed, harder… Squeeze me harder."

He held her locked in a vice-like embrace. She was his. He could do what he wished with that body. Then why didn't he feel more satisfied? He felt his arms begin to burn, and he didn't know how far he'd extended them, wrapping them around Elaine's body over and over again. He felt a wave of alienation sweep through him, furious, as he entered her, and everything seemed to become automatic: his penis plunging deep, time after time, the moans from both their mouths. *This isn't me. This isn't how I make love, this isn't my kind of sex.*

And yet there in the scene was a Reed, panting, gripping Elaine's body, almost suffocating her, fucking her, expanding his penis inside her. His penis, his unknowable penis, the least spontaneous part of his entire body, the part he had no control over, whose original size he couldn't even remember. The only part of him whose true length he couldn't distinguish: impossible to tell its natural state from the lengthening due to his superpowers. His penis swollen inside her. He couldn't stop it, not now, not any more, he could feel it grow, with terror, panting more intensely. Elaine screamed, twisting, panting like him, while Reed lost himself in the starry sky, the sky on her back, a constellation, a horoscope on her white flesh, in which he once again tried to divine the answer: *why did you come back?*

They froze. Reed felt the pain surge upwards, without warning, from his arms, his penis, and his whole body burning as though a new, devastating fever were rushing through it. He shouted. He was coming, spurting dense drops into Elaine's body, as his vision blurred and he lost himself, once again, in the milky sky of her back.

*

Everything started again. Nothing had changed. Elaine frequented the space centre in New Jersey, flew to Houston with Bernard every other week, often had her phone off, and showed up, spectacularly beautiful, to spend the night with Reed a couple of times a week. Theirs was a low-frequency relationship. They saw each other often enough to maintain a relationship, without letting it cut into the rest of their lives. Often, they said goodbye without any clear idea of when they'd next see each other. Exactly opposite to the way Reed would have liked it. He hadn't tamed Elaine; she had finally forced him to accept the kind of relationship she wanted.

At first Reed adapted. He was dazed that she had come back and he was convinced that, all things considered, a little independence was probably good for him, too. He wanted to stay trained in detachment. He wanted to have her and at the same time be ready not to have her at a moment's notice. He could do that. He thought that if he'd let her go once, he could let her go again.

Most of all, he wanted to know why she had come back, and why she had appeared that evening, unexpected, mysterious as a comet, allowing him to embrace her and adore her and fuck her. But maybe there was no reason to waste time thinking about it. There's not always an explanation when someone comes back. Sometimes a person returns like the tide. Like seasons change and animals migrate.

Was it conceivable that she had come back for the sex? Elaine let herself go so completely, every time they had sex. She screamed. She pleaded. Reed was almost afraid of her. And yet he was the one who fucked her, who expanded inside her, who wrapped her in the arms that he stretched out for yards and yards. It had become their usual way. Elaine liked it when he tied her up with his arms. She liked to pretend that she was surrendering to him, even though she was always ready to dart away.

65

Every time, Reed felt his body burn, and came in a rush of pain: as he collapsed onto Elaine's body, he cursed himself for having done it. He couldn't survive that pain. He couldn't ever do it again. He couldn't afford to have sex like that. For every dose of wonder, his body set aside at least twice as much pain, punctual and unappealable.

Then he would open his eyes again, and she was next to him, naked, white, and an uncontrollable surge of love gushed out of him. It was practically a chemical reaction. The particles of pain were transformed into love. He knew that he would do it again. He knew that he would push his body to its extreme limits, that he'd wrap her in his arms again, that he'd spurt out his sperm shouting with pain. He knew that the desire would come back. It always came back. It all came back, whether or not there was a reason.

Other things came back too, more and more often. The sensation in his hip, for instance. Not exactly pain, but something closer to a trace, like a memory his body preserved, a sediment of the first time that Elaine had put her hand there, her intensely hot hand, leaving a scalding trail forever. That's when the sensation had begun. It seemed like a fissure. A sort of internal tear that Reed could feel whenever he moved, in the uniform elastic tissue of his body. In a body made of rubber, there could be no lacerations. *I should mention this to my trainers at the gym. Or even better, to Doctor Szepanski. I should tell somebody about the sensations I've felt for months now, about the constant feeling of being poised between a delightful pleasure and an infinite pain. I should talk about it. There was a time when I talked constantly about my body. I subjected it to thousands of examinations and tests and talked about it objectively with other scientists, as if it belonged equally to them and to me. My body was a subject of study. It was something to conduct experiments upon. But now that my body is only mine, I don't know what to do with it. I'm like an inexperienced parent with a newborn baby. What can I do with this body to make it happy?*

*

Work had always been an article of faith with him, and not because he was in search of something to fill his life, or to distract him from the loneliness of his apartment, but rather because he loved logic. His work was a field where logic had some chance of reigning supreme, where there seemed to be a relationship between cause and effect, and where he could count on the fact that, the more demanding the work, the more significant the results. Work seemed like a safe investment. It was the best place to put his time, the least risky shelter against the waste of oneself. Of course, it wasn't the same as catching dangerous supercriminals, or thwarting conspiracies by corrupt industrialists, or hurtling headlong into an alley to rescue a girl from imminent rape. Not any more. Still, even now, as he was asking for new funds for research, or focusing on the first draft of a scientific paper, or delivering a lecture in a conference centre, or just asking Annabel to deal with some piece of business… Even now, Reed could still enjoy the logical order underlying his actions, the way each step determined the following step, and he could surrender to this flow of events, finding himself tired but satisfied at the end of the day. That's the way things had been progressing for years. Or at least up until now.

Outside, the winter advanced. On many days, you could barely make out the sun, no more than the glow of a distant explosion. Reed would sometimes sit there, dazed, in the middle of a pale morning or a chilly afternoon, and suddenly snap to, realising that he'd been at his desk and staring into the void, for a minute or two.

He realised that he wasn't himself any more. He noticed the number of unread emails clogging his inbox, how slowly the writing of his articles proceeded, how often his attention veered away, like a spur line from the main track, from whatever someone was saying to him on the phone. He realised that his efficiency had declined. Some part of his capacity for concentration seemed to be dwindling away. There was a leak in his energy system. Maybe it was right there, in his hip, where he still felt a sort of laceration, or in some other hidden part of his body. Maybe it was wherever Elaine had pressed her lips. Or maybe wherever she hadn't.

He had stopped googling Bernard's name, resigned to the idea that he'd never know the truth about that man, but he still frequently googled her name, sometimes every day, as if the search engine could supply him with an updated daily index of how much Elaine did or didn't love him. Actually, though, he found nothing. A few dozen pages, just like for Bernard. Reed wound up googling his own name, occasionally, imagining that it was Elaine doing the search, so that he could see what would scroll past her eyes. Perhaps he was no longer a star of the first magnitude, but there were still hundreds of thousands of pages containing his name.

Reed had a hard time recognising himself in what he read online. It all smacked of idle gossip, vague, remote, something that resembled the narrative of a narrative. *Is that me? Who are all these people talking about, on their websites, in their blogs, in the entries in their digital encyclopedias?*

It was during one of these moments that Annabel came into his office, wobbling on her high heels, to have him sign a couple of papers. A Google page was open on Reed's computer, and he noticed that she shot a worried glance at the screen as she walked past his desk.

They exchanged a long look heavy with meaning, and that was when Reed understood. Annabel knew. She knew he was wasting time on the web, and that he wasn't focusing on his work, his precious work, the work that was an article of faith with him. She knew he wasn't answering all his emails, that he was turning his articles in late, that he was forgetting to make certain phone calls. She knew that something was draining his energy and she knew what that was. She knew all these things because she was his assistant, she worked with him day after day, with unflagging devotion, and Reed both loved and hated her for that.

In the following days he did his best to appear the same as ever. Reliable, productive. He felt like an alien who had taken possession of someone's body and needed to allay the suspicions of those around him. He was Reed Richards. The man who'd had white hair ever since he was young, almost as a sign of some inborn wisdom. The man with an elastic body and brain, capable of containing anything and everything without contradictions. The authoritative man who could still call the editor of the *New York Times* and have an editorial published on any topic he wanted. That's who Reed Richards was.

All the same, sooner or later Reed Richards was forced to go to his secretary and ask her, with feigned nonchalance, to reserve a table for him in a restaurant, or to take care of buying a present. For Elaine. For the woman who had punched the leak into his life. For the woman who had insinuated herself into his days, until she had saturated them.

Annabel implemented his instructions without a word. There was no mistaking what she thought. It was by her glances that Reed began to realise something had happened, something grave and irreversible. *Annabel doesn't recognise me any more. I don't recognise myself either. I'm losing all sense of order. I'm abandoning the realm of logic.*

When Elaine came back, he'd fooled himself into believing that everything was the same as before, but now he understood that it was all much worse. The obsession was far more intense. The insecurity much more destructive. *When a fever returns, it's a thousand times more lethal.* The winter had scarcely begun, but the season of suffering was at its peak.

*

By now it was almost Christmas, and once again Reed had been lulled by the illusion that he could take Elaine away somewhere, to Europe, for a short vacation. Elaine had smiled, the way you smile at a child with an overactive imagination, and told him that leaving was unthinkable for her. "Why don't you go on your own?" she'd said with sadistic aplomb.

Reed didn't go anywhere. All he did was attend a few Christmas parties, shaking hands, raising glasses of champagne in toasts, applauding chamber music concertos. If there was an alien inside him, if Reed Richards really had been replaced by some restless, irrational creature, it was certainly a creature that knew how to camouflage itself. Reed chatted with elderly ladies of the wealthier classes, indulged the insipid gossip of the wives of the foundation's financiers and sipped brandy with potential new financiers. Only occasionally did he feel obliged to retreat to a corner, or lock himself into a bathroom to see whether Elaine had tried to call him, or if she'd left him a message, or else to try to call her himself.

On December 20th a car came to pick him up and drive him to New Jersey; for the first time since Elaine entered his life, the car conveyed him to the eye-shaped space centre, along a road lined with marshlands. The snow in the woods had already vanished, melted by a wave of warmer weather, a bubble of heat in the midst of winter. It would be a suffocating Christmas.

The sight of the space centre stirred a mixture of sarcasm and discomfort in him. A shaft of reddish light illuminated the building from inside, making him think of a gigantic, terrible case of conjunctivitis, spreading through the plate glass windows of the lobby out onto the puddles dotting the lawn, like a slow-welling haemorrhage. A number of parked cars lined the access road, suggesting that the party was already in full swing, and Reed felt a stab—practically a flash of premonitory embarrassment—as he thought of all the heads that would swivel in his direction when he entered the room, the too many eyes that would size him up.

He got out of the car and headed for the side entrance, cutting across the lawn, which had been reduced almost to a swamp by the radical shifts in climate. He wound up getting his shoes all muddied. His footsteps produced a squishy sound. The evening wind blew around him, warm and lonely, as a muffled sound came from within: music, voices. *I don't want to attract attention. I want to appear from out of nowhere, as though I'd been there all along.* But once he reached the side entrance he found a pair of guards, who looked at him curiously and told him, in the tone of someone speaking to a cantankerous old eccentric, that the guest entrance was on the other side of the building.

"I know that," said Reed. "It's just that I parked close to this entrance and you understand, I don't want to have to walk back through the mud…" He gazed down at his feet, hoping the two guards would take pity on his poor muddy shoes.

"You should take the path, sir. That way you won't get your shoes dirty. You can take the path and go in through the guest entrance."

Young Americans, thought Reed, looking the two young security men up and down. *So polite and such assholes.* "Of course," he replied. "But guys, let me explain… I'm Reed Richards. I'm a member of the scientific board of advisers here. What do you say you just let me in through this entrance?"

The two men at the door exchanged a glance, then looked back at Reed. "Did you say Richards?" the younger of the pair asked. They finally waved him through, although still with a dubious expression on their faces.

Inside, he rubbed his shoes clean on a mat. He reached the lobby, where he was pleased to discover that a musical performance was under way, attracting the interest of the crowd. Behind the solid wall of partygoers, someone with an androgynous voice was at the piano, accompanying themselves in a ballad. Reed had time to leave his overcoat in the cloakroom, grab a glass from a passing tray, and look around to get a sense of the situation. The room was full of men in tuxedos and women in evening gowns. The average age was pretty old. As far as he could see, the astronauts attending sessions at the space centre either hadn't been invited or were celebrating elsewhere. As for Elaine, he knew she was still in Houston. Obviously, with Bernard.

Not a sign of Mrs. Glasseye. In the middle of the room was a large Christmas tree, its decorations glittering in the reddish light. The resinous odour of the fir tree filled the room, and Reed walked closer to it, glass in hand, to get a better whiff of the scent. That was when he took a look at the ornaments. Little glass balls dangling from the branches. To be accurate, *little glass eyes*. Reed emitted a groan, horrified, and then took a look around him, incredulous that the rest of the crowd was placidly watching the show and sipping from their glasses. *The Christmas ornaments on the tree are glass eyes. Good God, am I the only one here that finds that embarrassing?!*

"A bit much, isn't it?" said a deep voice behind him.

Reed turned around and found himself looking at a half-naked man, dressed in nothing but a pair of emerald-green briefs. "Namor," he said, without much joy in his voice. When he met other former superheroes he rarely reacted with real enthusiasm. Especially when they were Namor. "What are you doing here?"

Namor shrugged with his usual scornful air. "Getting drunk," he said, raising the glass he held in his hand, "and just like you, taking a look at these lovely ornaments. Our hostess enjoys the occasional self-referential bit of irony, have you noticed?" He shot Reed a penetrating look, as if he could read his thoughts. "But more than anything else," he added, "she enjoys putting gentlemen like you in awkward situations." He burst into arrogant laughter, underscoring how superior he felt to all this, and gulped down a hefty swig of wine.

Reed just barely smiled, already annoyed. He never could stand being around that man for more than thirty seconds at a time. *If there's someone who ought to feel awkward, it's you, who still walks around in that outfit. Pathetic. A guy in his sixties with pointy ears and sagging pectorals, a guy*

who has a TV show where he talks to the audience from inside an enormous
aquarium, swimming around with schools of coloured fish.

"I can't stand this caterwauling," Namor said, referring to the musical performance, probably irritated that he had no one around him, no audience to regale with his typical stories. The kingdom of the undersea depths and the rest of his repertoire. No one had ever been able to ascertain Namor's true origins, but he'd been spouting those stories for decades. Namor took another swig, and then with an allusive glance he shot out a question: "And how is your lovely ex-wife?"

"She's fine," Reed replied, without grasping the reason for that glance and that conspiratorial tone.

They ran through a few more conversational gambits. They talked about people they both knew, what had ever become of Captain America and other old colleagues, what they'd heard about Superman, who was now an elderly and sick man, and other things, but they never exchanged more than a couple of sentences about any given topic.

At last, as the performance was coming to an end and a round of applause was swelling from the crowd, Reed broke away from the other man with relief. He circulated through the room, greeting a number of acquaintances. He didn't feel uncomfortable, exactly, but even if he'd successfully avoided entering the room while everyone was looking, he continued to sense something. A feeling. Something around him. It was there, something rough, under the ceremonious smiles, under the conversation as soft and smooth as velvet. Then someone grabbed his arm, and even before turning around he realised that he'd been taken prisoner—as he knew had to happen—by Mrs. Glasseye. "There you are," she said, kissing him on both cheeks as ostentatiously as she could. She was wearing a dress with a plunging neckline, and she must have done something to her hair: blond, or no, maybe darker. Anyway, different. Mrs. Glasseye went on gripping his arm in a confidential manner: "It's been a lifetime since I've had news from you," she said. "But don't worry, I have my sources."

"Such as?" asked Reed with a hint of anxiety, carefully avoiding her glance.

"Such as," said Mrs. Glasseye as she moved a little closer, "I know that you were asked to sit on that committee. In Washington."

Reed heaved a brief sigh. "Oh, that. I haven't really had time yet to look into it."

Mrs. Glasseye wasn't about to let go of his arm. She sent a greeting to someone across the room, waving with a bright smile. Then, moving her lips slowly, in a way that somehow struck Reed as almost obscene, she said: "I assume you'll say you can't do it."

Reed turned his eyes away from those lips, still uncertain where to look instead, letting his gaze roam the room until it settled on the Christmas tree. A thousand little eyes looked back at him. "Say I can't join the committee?" he asked in confusion. "Um… Is that what you think I should do?"

Mrs. Glasseye let go of his arm. The mask of a perky impertinent fifty-year-old woman seemed to slip for an instant, and she said in a heartfelt tone: "Reed, of course that's what you should do."

He gave her the barest hint of a smile. He had no idea what this was all about, but he didn't feel like admitting that. He didn't want to confess that he hadn't been paying much attention to his work recently, didn't want to tell her that he had a somewhat—how to put this?—*nebulous* idea of his coming commitments. Washington? What the devil was going to happen in Washington?! He continued to let his gaze wander, hoping that someone would come over and interrupt their conversation, or that he could change the subject. "How about *him?*" he asked, gesturing in the direction of Namor, who was preening himself at the far end of the room with a couple of women who looked more or less like retired porn stars.

Mrs. Glasseye followed his gaze. "Old Namor? He keeps himself busy," she said.

"He's just pathetic," Reed replied, glad for an opportunity to take it out on someone else.

Mrs. Glasseye went on looking at Namor, raptly, in the manner of a zoologist studying the behaviour of a very rare species of monkey. "You just say that because you're afraid of the competition," she said without smiling, without resuming her usual languid tone.

"Competition? What would I have to fear from that man? Unlike him, I've chosen to maintain my dignity. I stopped wearing my skintight costume twenty years ago, and I don't spend my time seducing forty-year-old bombshells like those two. What are those people even doing here?!" He drained his glass, satisfied with his own indignant outburst.

Mrs. Glasseye shook her head, though she kept looking off into the distance. She seemed worried about something. Or maybe, Reed realised with a little shock, *she's trying not to look at me. Maybe I make her uncomfortable.* Perhaps, for the first time in their acquaintance, the roles were reversed. Now, it was she who was avoiding his glance. Reed took a deep breath, upset, suddenly guessing what was about to happen.

"Oh Reed," she said, with something bordering on sadness. "Don't worry, we all know you have no interest in women in their forties." She looked at him, and for a brief instant their eyes met, his eyes locked on her eyes, on the real eye and the fake eye, producing a sort of dazzling spark. "We all know," she concluded, "that you've found something better."

Reed was petrified. He felt like asking her to repeat what she'd said, even though there was no mistaking her words. *We all know that you've found something better.*

The music started up again.

Reed didn't dare to move and stood there, overcome, furious, conscious of the thousand eyes all around him. Now he understood. Now he knew. He knew they were all focused on him, eyes of flesh and eyes of glass, the eyes of Mrs. Glasseye, the eyes dangling from the branches of the Christmas tree, and the eyes of Namor the goddamned lord of the depths, Prince of Atlantis my ass: that's what that allusive tone had been all about, that idiot smile of his! The eyes of the two women standing with Namor, with their tits pumped up in some clinic in Mexico, and the eyes of that roomful of people. Their sidelong glances, the glances he had felt on his back that whole evening, without knowing how to read them, the glances he'd caught in the past few days, at every damned Christmas party he'd attended. Those looks. Those half-smiles. Everyone knew, the news had travelled.

The singer's androgynous voice rose again, romantic and stirring, and the scene seemed to freeze in place, as if by magic. The guests all stood listening. Reed slipped away quietly, taking advantage of the interlude, even though he was well aware that, no matter what he did, there was no hope of going unnoticed. *Even if they don't look at me, they know about me. They know I'm running away.* He couldn't fool them any more. Everyone knew that he was involved in an inappropriate affair. Everyone knew, Reed felt certain, that he'd become another person, unrecognisable, neglecting his work, and everyone thought—of this he also felt certain—that it wasn't *moral* to fall in love the way he had. At his age, in his position. *The world's falling apart, there are wars and environmental catastrophes, pandemic menaces, terror attacks, oil is running out, civilisation is on the verge of collapse, and he wastes his time mooning over a young girl. A man as stylish as him. As dignified.*

He made it to the door, this time the main entrance, and rushed outside onto the muddy lawn, without even stopping to get his coat. Air, he needed to get some air. He heard the singer from inside, still intoning his song of love, a melancholy song Reed had never heard before. Reed stumbled in the mud, in the chilly night, shaken by a succession of shivers. *Fine*, he thought. *I don't care if they know. I don't care if they look at me, or if they're appalled. I don't care*, he went on saying, astonished to discover that he meant it, and that he wasn't ashamed, that he felt no embarrassment at being unmasked. He was too tired to worry about them. *Fuck style, fuck dignity.* You can't fall in love and keep your dignity intact. To love, Reed realised, you have to be willing to accept some humiliation.

*

A couple of weeks later, he caught a plane to Washington. The sky had a silver sheen as he climbed the steps to the plane. He had in his bag a memorandum that they'd faxed him about the work the committee was about to undertake, and he'd promised himself he'd take a look at it during the flight. After taking his seat, he smiled at the hostess who brought him some coffee. The plane was half-empty. The few faces present seemed sleepy. There was that touch of desolation in the air that seems typical of early January, after the holidays are finished and all that remains is a long, barren winter. *There's something bleak about the passage of time*, thought Reed as he fastened his seat belt and the plane taxied out onto the runway. *There's even something vulgar about it.*

The plane accelerated and lifted off. Reed looked out of the window at the city down below. His city. He caught a fleeting glimpse of the East River, grey and powerful, and the FDR Drive with its already heavy traffic.

Then everything vanished into a whitish mist. The plane had climbed into low-hanging cloud cover. It went on climbing and then stopped, suspended for an instant in an air pocket. Reed closed his eyes. He wished he could just push a button and stay there, hanging, forever, at seven thirty on a Monday morning.

All things considered, he'd had a couple of enjoyable weeks. Sad, yet enjoyable. On Christmas Day he'd talked on the phone to Franklin, who had called him from some obscure African country and had promised he'd be back in New York soon. Reed had also talked to his ex-wife, who as always was polite and remote, as well as with his old friend Ben. For lunch, he'd gone to a charity banquet, despite the risk of sly looks, despite his dislike of handshakes, despite his desire just to stay at home and read a book in peace, something he hadn't been able to do for years. He'd gone so that he wouldn't look like a freak in Elaine's eyes; she was spending the day with her family. In fact, he didn't want to look like a freak to anyone. Dining alone on Christmas Day was not accepted. *It's not a good thing to look too solitary. People are afraid of lonely people.*

In the end, the banquet wasn't all that bad, and Reed had even managed to have a couple of interesting conversations. That didn't happen often. At his age, he considered it to be a treat. Having a conversational exchange worth engaging in at a social event now constituted a precious occasion.

The following days had been half vacation, because Annabel had taken a week off, with the official excuse of going to Florida for New Year, but more likely to check into a clinic for anorexics.

So now it was the last day of the year. Around sunset an unnatural silence had already settled over the city, almost in expectation of some inconceivable detonation. Reed waited for Elaine, who had agreed to spend the night with him, and together they'd strolled down Broadway, hand in hand, as all around them fireworks crackled and people shouted. Passing strangers had hugged them, and they'd received and returned a thousand Happy New Years, and laughed when they slipped on the wet sidewalk. They managed to find a taxi and headed south, all the way to Battery Park, and had looked out over the parapet at the water of the harbour as it reflected the blurry sparkles of distant fireworks.

They stood, arms wrapped around each other. They stood there, on that point at the far end of the island, where the city narrowed with a rounded curve, spraying its breath out towards the ocean, towards Ellis Island, down towards the statue with the torch and the enigmatic face, towards the ferry boats cruising the harbour, towards Staten Island with its secrets, with its giant dump that housed the debris of fallen towers and the city's grief and pain. "I come here every year," Reed told her, and Elaine had nodded, wordlessly, her hair tossing in the wind.

Later, they'd undressed, in Reed's bedroom, as the chaotic din outside began to subside. Elaine's flesh had the white gleam of the inside of a seashell. Reed had turned her over and lain down on her, admiring her back, feeling her breathe. Feeling her vibrate. Reed understood that he would desire that woman forever, and not because she was good or bad, not because she was skilful at keeping him on tenterhooks, nor because she was beautiful and had a lovely starry back. He would desire her because something vibrated within her, something that Reed found familiar, as if the two of them were ancient radio sources meeting again, after an era, to exchange an arcane message. He would go on wanting her because her skin glowed, and in the low light of his bedroom her body seemed to lose its outlines, becoming something close to a shimmer, a wave, a vibration of restless energy. "I love you," he whispered, resting his swollen penis on her white skin.

"Oh Reed," she sighed. "You know the way I feel about…"

"Hush," he said as he slipped between her legs.

But she went on: "You're not in love with me, Reed. You're obsessed with me, and that's something else."

"Hush," he said again. He extended his arms to take her prisoner. "Hush," he whispered again, stretching out a section of flesh until it reached her mouth, so that she could suck on it. "Hush," he went on as he began fucking her, and could feel her heart beating beneath him, a pulse so powerful that it frightened him.

Even now, Elaine was able to speak. She told him to get ready.

"Get ready for what?" Reed moaned, on the verge of coming.

"Oh Reed," she replied, moaning in turn. Her heart was pounding harder. That was when Reed felt her heartbeat stop, suddenly, and emit a sinister *click*. He barely had time to guess. Then there was a flash of light. Reed felt an explosive burst of heat, and a shattering shockwave blew everything to pieces. He felt his own body dissolve in that surge of light and heat, and his own flesh spatter into shreds. The roar was immense and liberating. The bomb had wiped the room out of existence. Reed had felt it all with surprise, as well as an odd sense of satisfaction, as if part of him had foreseen all this, as if he'd somehow been expecting it.

He must be dead by now, or so he assumed, and yet he continued to see the scene. He saw it from above, now, from higher in the air, until it came to resemble an aerial camera shot. He saw the building smoking after the explosion, down there, a solitary smokestack in the middle of the city. He saw the column of smoke rise, bend, assuming the shape of a giant question mark. He saw the crews of firemen come tearing down the street, and the crowd of rubberneckers cautiously edging closer. He hovered there, watching the fire, floating in mid-air, until he noticed that someone was touching his shoulder, and then at last he opened his eyes.

The stewardess smiled. "We're landing, sir."

Reed looked around in confusion. He was in a passenger plane. The New York-Washington shuttle. "Of course," he replied automatically, checking to make sure his seat belt was fastened.

He glanced out of the window. Beneath them the Washington suburbs were streaming past. Reed watched the landscape, blinking his eyes, struggling to separate reality from the sensations of his dream. He had no idea when he'd fallen asleep, when his memories of the last night of the year had mutated into that strange incomprehensible dream.

The captain announced that they were landing. Reed tried to relax. In his mouth, he could taste the flavour of Elaine, of her kisses. His heart went on beating as the plane set down: his body seemed unable to resign itself to the idea that none of it was true, that Elaine wasn't there, she'd never been there.

*

NASA headquarters was a long, rigidly squared-off steel-and-glass parallelepiped. The car that had picked Reed up at the airport deposited him at the front door of the massive building, where he was greeted by a flock of assistants. "Mr. Richards, happy to see you again," the head of security said. He escorted Reed through the main lobby to the elevator bank. Reed had no time to look around. Upstairs, other assistants accompanied him down a hallway, until they reached a hardwood door where the assistants scattered, all at once, like so many nocturnal apparitions at the dawn of day. Reed found himself inside, in the luminous meeting room, his respiration slightly heavier.

A profound calm reigned over the room, a muffled, protected atmosphere. *Everything's slower. Everything's denser. The control room, where decisions are made.*

A man he knew well came towards him, smiling, striding across the gleaming floor.

Reed gripped his hand. "It's a pleasure to see you, Michael."

The head of NASA had a candid gaze and a surprisingly boyish smile. He shook Reed's hand and held it for a moment in a friendly way, looking him in the eye: "The pleasure's all mine, Reed. Glad to have you with us. We're on a very tight schedule, the place is a madhouse. We need a clear mind like yours."

"That's fine," Reed replied, not sure what else to say.

Four men were sitting at the table. Three space agency executives and an outside consultant. Reed knew them all. One last person, a renowned professor of psychology who consulted for a number of government agencies, showed up a minute later. Reed knew her too. Now the group was complete. A silent assistant served coffee before moving quietly out of the conference room, while the last two arrivals took their seats at the table.

The master of the house began his address. "Thank you all for being here today, and I especially want to thank our guests who travelled to Washington to attend this meeting. I hope at least that our coffee is better than they served you on the plane." A few polite smiles flashed in response to the humorous barb. "I imagine you've noticed that this committee was put together in something of a hurry. In this project, the usual protocols have been to some extent shunted aside. That's not something I'm especially happy about, but let me just assure you that we had no other choice." He paused, to allow a moment for anyone wishing to comment, then nodded towards one of the NASA executives: "Jonathan will be chairing your session today, as a voting member."

Jonathan nodded slightly, to greet again the members of the committee.

"I have complete faith in your judgement," the director went on. "The one thing I would ask you, as you examine the profiles of the candidates, is to do your best to put together a diverse group. This project needs to be staffed by a crew that represents—how shall I put this?—a variety of points of view."

Helen Kippenberg, the psychologist, broke in with her deep voice: "Michael, can't you give us a few details about this mission? How can I evaluate the profiles of the candidates if I have no idea what the devil they're going to be doing up there?"

The director smiled at no one in particular, as though he hadn't heard the question. His face looked like the face of a tired child. He said nothing more, except to wish them the best in their endeavours. He got to his feet and walked softly out of the room.

The six people who remained were disconcerted for a moment. They glanced at one another with a mixture of fellowship and suspicion, each one wondering what the others knew. At last, since there were many candidates to be considered, and part of the morning was already gone, they set to work. They started examining and debating the profiles of the candidates, on each of whom Jonathan extracted from a leather briefcase, one after another, a slender bound file. Nearly all the candidates were familiar names to the committee members. It wasn't especially hard to evaluate their profiles. The discussion seemed to be moving forward, around the table, in a general climate of agreement.

Reed commented. He offered concise opinions. He played his role. This wasn't the first time that the space agency had summoned him to headquarters with a similar protocol, and he wasn't so alarmed at the project's apparent secrecy. He wasn't overwhelmed by the air of importance that surrounded the meeting, nor by the cryptic attitude of the NASA officers. He'd attended much stranger meetings in his life. He'd been in far more tense situations. What was worrying him was something else.

Something was surging up inside him. It had begun bubbling immediately, the minute Michael began his opening speech, or perhaps even earlier. Perhaps when Mrs. Glasseye spoke to him during the Christmas party, or even earlier, when he had first been summoned, and he had been sent that memorandum by fax, and he'd avoided reading it and focusing his mind on exactly what that summons meant. On what he would be asked to do in Washington, on the task that would be awaiting him there. *To select the candidates for the crew of a space probe.*

Each time that Jonathan pulled a new file out of the leather briefcase, Reed felt his stomach cramp up. His body, his elastic body, seemed to contract like a piece of fabric drying out in the sun. Then he would relax. Oh, it just couldn't be. That sort of coincidence couldn't happen. It couldn't. Or could it? A tremendous, embarrassing suspicion had surged up inside him. The suspicion kept coming in waves, and went on that way until lunchtime, when the others decided to take a forty-minute break. They had already selected half a dozen profiles.

During lunch, in a comfortable private dining room adjoining the cafeteria, they chatted about the Batman case, the complexities of the trial, with mentions of the obscene manner in which the corpse had been defiled. They talked about the president's latest foot-in-mouth gaffes, and the recent study on oral gonorrhoea among American teenage girls, and all the other topics that millions of people were talking about that day, at lunch, in a more-or-less distracted, more-or-less worried, more-or-less frivolous tone of voice. It was all normal. A group of famous experts eating lunch in a dining room, drinking iced water, diverting themselves with the news of the day. Reed took part in the conversation, happy that no one was talking in depth about anything, happy just to be skimming the surface: their conversation, even their acquaintance with one another. Things that remained on the surface seemed more normal. Decidedly more innocuous.

He had almost regained his composure when they returned to the conference room, each of them carrying a cup of coffee. He took his seat at the table, slumping into his chair with a sigh, and that was when the situation collapsed around him. The inevitable finally happened.

"Bernard Dunn." The name was read out by Jonathan, in a neutral tone, from the cover page of the new file he'd extracted from the leather briefcase.

Reed kept his eyes down, focused on the small notepad in front of him. The air had dried up and seemed to scratch him with every breath he took.

"Here comes the new blood," someone commented. It was the outside consultant. "I suppose that when Michael talked about diversity," he added, "this is some of what he had in mind, right? Considering candidate astronauts who will be flying their first mission?"

"I was in charge of him during a training session in Houston," one of the NASA executives said. "Remarkable subject, highly ambitious."

Reed took a covert glance at the file Jonathan was holding. He recognised a small photograph of Bernard, and the sight triggered a familiar stab in his hip, a microscopic crater gaping open, for the umpteenth time, spitting forth its seething flow of lava. Jealousy. Resentment. Hostility. *Damned cocksucker. You're even tormenting me here.*

"I remember meeting him at a seminar in New Jersey," Helen Kippenberg was saying. "I didn't have the chance to get an accurate impression. Reed, what do you say about him?"

Reed didn't react right away. "Bernard Dunn?..." He pretended to struggle to remember the name. "I think I saw him at a lecture or two."

There was a pause. "Well?" Jonathan asked.

"Well, what?" Reed echoed him.

"What I mean to say," Jonathan said, "is we'd like your opinion. Do we put him in the candidate pile or the reject pile?"

Reed closed his eyes, in an apparent attempt to concentrate. He couldn't look his fellow committee members in the eye. He felt unpleasantly transparent. He plunged into an abyss of indecision, then felt the answer rising from his guts, as fast as a ricocheting pinball, scurrying up through his stomach and hurtling out through his lips: "Reject pile."

The discussion of Bernard's CV lasted a few more minutes. Reed paid no attention to it; he was too busy trying to comprehend what he had done. *I didn't give it a second's thought. It was a purely instinctive response.* His negative opinion seemed to influence the others, and in the end the panel voted to reject Bernard's candidacy. Reed felt like asking them to think it over. *Give him a little more consideration. Don't let my answer sway you. I don't want to cast the deciding vote…* There was no time. They were moving on to the next profile. Reed closed his eyes, again, breathing in as much air as he could, praying that it wouldn't happen.

But it happened.

"Elaine Ryan," Jonathan read out this time.

A surge of panic shot through Reed, mixed with a kind of intense astonishment. That name. He couldn't believe that it could be uttered like that, aloud, by a stranger, by someone who knew nothing about her skin, her scent, the warmth of the person to whom that name corresponded. *You can't say that name. That name is for me, and me alone.*

And yet it was there. That name was filling the space around the table, in the conference room with its muffled atmosphere, in the headquarters of a government agency. "Elaine Ryan," Jonathan said again, looking up from the file. "One of the few female candidates," he pointed out.

"And in absolute terms, the youngest candidate," said Helen Kippenberg, who seemed to have studied Elaine's profile. Reed was afraid that she too was about to utter her name, the forbidden name, the heart-stopping name, with that perfectly poised voice of hers, the voice of a fashionable psychologist. "In my opinion," the woman said, "she has a very interesting profile."

For several long minutes, the tableful of people spoke about Elaine. Reed didn't dare to breathe a word. It all seemed so surreal, so impossible, and he sat there staring into the middle distance as if trying to blend in with the air in the room. He thought about pretending to feel unwell, a coughing fit or something of the kind, any excuse to get out. But that would have just attracted more attention. He sat there, petrified, while Helen took the floor. "Elaine Ryan's educational transcript is virtually perfect," said the psychologist. She had an affected accent, like someone doing elocution exercises or rehearsing for an interview on the radio. Reed hated that voice. He hated the way she pronounced *the name* and absolutely hated the moment when she said: "Reed, you must have run into her more than once at the space centre in New Jersey. What do you think of her?"

Every eye in the room turned towards him. For one horrible instant he thought he was about to blush. "I guess you're right," he said, laconically.

"It's a good profile," he added, without emotion, without meeting the gaze of the psychologist who was looking at him, in expectation, dissatisfied with his answer. He wondered whether Helen Kippenberg was trying to put him in a corner. Maybe she knows. *Maybe she's been in New York recently, or at the space centre in New Jersey, and she's heard some talk.*

"All right," Jonathan broke in, "what do you say? Candidate pile or reject pile?"

Reed gulped. "Oh," he did his best to smile. "You're not going to ask me to be the first to express an opinion again, are you?!"

"Why not?" Jonathan replied. "As far as the New York candidates go, you're probably the one who knows them best."

Everyone went on looking at him. Reed started sweating under the crossfire of those stares, at the edge of that table. He felt he had no way out. He couldn't stand up to all those stares at once. Perhaps he'd have to give in, confess that he couldn't answer, that he had no right, that he was personally involved. *Unless they already know that.* As soon as that thought surfaced in his mind, he felt he was lost. There really was no way out. No avoiding the weight of those eyes, no escape from the torment of doubt: was the rumour of his relationship with Elaine common knowledge in Washington, too? Was that meeting really what it appeared? Or had they summoned him just to put him in a false position, to test his professional ethics?

"Reed?" he heard someone call. Maybe it was Jonathan. The scene had taken on a strange texture. *Focus. You have to get yourself out of this situation.* "Reed, are you all right?"

"The fact is," Helen Kippenberg said, filling the gap in the conversation, throwing him a moment's temporary salvation, "that Elaine Ryan has passed every kind of test with flying colours." Reed went so far as to wonder whether the psychologist was a lesbian. Whether she'd fallen for Elaine. The thought rocketed through him, without a purpose, without a source, a meteor flashing across the sky of his mind, before the woman could lob the question back in his direction: "So, Reed. Given the apparently brilliant foundations of this candidate, it's crucial for us to have your opinion. Should we consider this candidate, yes or no?"

Reed felt like screaming. He felt like ordering those people to stop it, to stop talking about Elaine, he felt an urge to protect his love and to envelop it, now, in a blanket of blessed silence. He wanted to call her and beg her forgiveness for having talked about her from a distance, in a detached manner, or maybe he felt like berating her violently—my God—and forcing her to confess the way things truly stood. *Did you know what would happen? Did you know that I would be a member of the committee?!* The enormity of this suspicion made him black out for a second, but then he came to in the room, once again, without knowing what Elaine knew, without knowing what the other committee members knew, without knowing, without knowing. He was the man who didn't know, and all he knew for certain was one thing. *If Elaine is accepted, I might not be able to see her for months.*

This thought too made him feel worn out, almost on the point of vanishing. He thought about Mrs. Glasseye, who had recommended that he decline the invitation. For some reason, he was sorry that she wasn't there, next to him, with her magnificent cleavage, with her provocative ways. Mrs. Glasseye wasn't a bad person. She'd had her share of trouble in life, and at the Christmas party she'd done her best to warn him. But she wasn't there. Reed was alone, and he had to give them a reply.

He had such a powerful urge to scream. But it was with a calm and measured voice, on the verge of the robotic, that he finally gave his reply.

*

That evening he returned to New York in a daze, exhausted as if from a weeks-long trip. As soon as he got home, he took off his shirt and shoes and wandered through the rooms of his apartment, half-naked, with a glass of wine in his hand. Outside, the rain was pounding down. Practically a tropical downpour. Reed stared out of the window, hypnotised, sipping wine, doing his best to rinse away the taste of anxiety, of suspicion, that had swept over him that afternoon in Washington. He set down his glass and finished undressing. In the shower, he turned the water on as hot as it would go, well aware it wasn't good for him, that the elastic structure of his body tended to deteriorate with heat. *Dissolve, doubt. Slide away, torment.*

When he got out of the shower his skin was reddened and his hair smelt of shampoo, but his mood hadn't improved. It was nearly midnight, he hadn't eaten dinner, and yet had no desire to eat or sleep. All he could manage was to turn on his laptop, search for the folder where he stored his pictures of Elaine, and study them one by one like an investigator looking for a clue. That face. That reddish hair. It seemed intolerable, almost obscene, to imagine that lovely mouth uttering lies. Oh, even if Elaine did know about the committee, she hadn't technically lied. It was if anything a crime of omission: she had just failed to tell him something.

Reed decided that he needed to know. There was no point in standing there, naked, brushing the computer screen with his fingertips. He hastily dressed and called a taxi.

Later on, as the taxi was wending its way through the streets of South Brooklyn, and the rain drummed on the vehicle's roof, Reed wondered whether he'd made the right decision. He wanted to turn back, seek the protective shelter of the bright lights of Manhattan, or better still, his own apartment. But now he was here, and he hated the idea of changing course. He had always considered himself a decisive person, someone who was able to face up, with courage, without uncertainty, to the solitary pain of making decisions. All kinds of decisions. That was why he hated it so much, lately, when he discovered that he was incapable of making a firm decision. It must be an effect of his relationship with Elaine. *She's proved that she's more determined than I am. She's showing a stronger will than mine. Every relationship is a meeting place of two wills: when the weaker will comes into contact with the stronger one, it collapses.*

There was her window. The light was on. He asked the cab driver to stop and wait while he made a phone call. He imagined the ringtone of Elaine's cell phone, its vibration on the table or on her pillow, he imagined Elaine picking it up and reading Reed's name on the display. "Hello?" said her voice.

"Hello. Were you sleeping?" he asked pointlessly, and without waiting for an answer: "I'm downstairs. Can I come up?"

There was a moment's silence. "Come on up," Elaine replied.

Reed paid the cabbie, embarrassed that the man had listened to the phone call. He stepped out into the rain. He hurried across the sidewalk and was swallowed up by the dark-coloured street door.

Upstairs, he found the apartment door ajar. There was a small living room, flooded with the orange light of a lamp, and a door leading into another room. Elaine emerged from there. "Reed...what a surprise." She was wearing a pair of jeans and a T-shirt with a rock group emblazoned on it. Bare feet. A stab of unease, verging on panic, pulsed in Reed when he saw her looking like this. She looked like a young girl. A teenager. They stood there staring at each other, both dazzled, until she shook herself and ran into his arms. She hugged him tight. "Oh Reed!" she sighed, her face radiant. "I've been summoned for the space mission. I have to go to Washington tomorrow!"

"I know," he said, stiffly, keeping himself from returning her embrace. "I was on the committee. We examined dozens of profiles and selected ten or so candidates. Tomorrow you'll all be in Washington. A different committee will select the final four members of the space probe crew. You've got a good shot at it. I know everything. I was in Washington today. I gave a positive vote on you and the rest of the committee went along with my opinion. I know everything, you see? And you knew everything too. You knew that I was going to be on that committee."

Elaine broke away from him. She looked at him as if he had spoken to her in some exotic foreign language. With a smile still on her face, she moved into the other room. "Come on in," she said.

The bedroom was furnished soberly, in an almost minimalist style, with a small cream-coloured armoire, and a futon on the wooden floor. The bonsai that Reed had sent her months ago sat on the window sill, looking slightly sickly. A bookshelf contained, arranged in order, dozens of volumes on astronomy, meteorology, physics, and space engineering. Reed looked at the books, one by one, relieved to find something familiar in that setting. This was his first time here. His first time in Elaine's home. Every detail of that bedroom struck him as wonderful, in some sense disconcerting, but most of all there was the suitcase. Reed felt a painful pulsing in his hip. There was an oversized suitcase lying open on the floor, and Elaine was filling it with clothes. "If they pick me tomorrow, I'll have to fly straight to Houston," she explained. "At least three months of continuous training at the Johnson Space Center. This mission is proceeding according to a record time frame. Everything will be very intense."

"I know," Reed said again. He sat down on the only chair in the room, a small white chair, and watched Elaine folding and packing her clothes.

"I can't believe it, I still can't believe it," she said, as she slipped a pile of underwear into her suitcase. "I've been called in for the interview. I feel like I'm dreaming."

Reed stared at the underwear lying in the suitcase, feeling a surge of yearning and angry physical desire. "Elaine," he implored. "We need to talk."

"So let's talk," she replied, without interrupting her packing.

Reed waited, to restore his tone of voice to a semblance of calm. He didn't want to seem upset. He noticed the music, at very low volume, just above a whisper, coming from a stereo set on the bookshelf. He noticed that sound, and heard the rain falling outside the window, and the sound of his own breathing. He heaved a sigh: "Did you know I'd be on the committee?"

Elaine tucked a stray lock of hair behind one ear. "Well... I imagined you might," she said, continuing to focus on the suitcase. "Two days ago, when you told me that you would be going to Washington."

"You imagined I might," Reed echoed her words. "You didn't tell me that you would be one of the candidates. Do you realise what an awkward position that put me in?"

Elaine decided to look him in the eye. "Oh, come on. Nothing's really happened yet. I still have to go through another level of the selection process, don't I? And after all, no one knows about us."

"You're wrong." Reed stood up, intending to walk over to the window, but he gave up the idea and dropped back onto the chair. The room was too small to move around. Too small to hold them both. Too small to hold everything in it: the two of them, the suitcase, the fresh memories of that afternoon in Washington. "There are people who know about us, here in New York. And the people in New York can talk to the people in Washington."

"Someone knows about us?" Elaine said. "That seems impossible. With your obsessive attention to detail, the way you keep from being recognised in restaurants, the way you avoid being photographed by the paparazzi."

"They know."

Elaine seemed to give the matter a moment's consideration before getting back to the job of packing her suitcase. "It's funny to think of anyone wasting their time talking about us," she said. "People are weird," she added, as if this settled any issue.

"Elaine," Reed sighed, beginning to lose his patience. "Don't pretend you don't understand. I was put into a critical position today. I was forced to act unethically, and I committed a grave violation of my responsibilities. I had to pretend I had no relationship with you. I was forced to play-act, and it's not something I enjoyed one little bit, it's not the way I work." He crossed his arms and gave her a serious look. "It's not my style," he added.

"Oh," she said. "It's not your style," she echoed him, in a vague tone, tucking her hair behind her ear again.

Reed felt like telling her to stop doing it. That gesture. That typical gesture of hers, tucking a lock of hair behind her ear, almost shyly. One of the gestures he'd fallen in love with, at the beginning, gestures that were like movements of an imperceptible dance. Now he understood that there was more to them, and that everything he had at first taken for shyness, mysterious and enchanting, was most likely indifference. Profound indifference. *Here you are before me. You're tired, excited, you want to finish packing. Tomorrow you're leaving for Washington. You got what you wanted.*

Reed stood up, at that point, determined to ask the question. The real question, the terrifying question. "Is that why you came back to me?" he asked. "After we broke up? Did you come back because you knew I'd be sitting on that committee?"

Elaine shut her suitcase. She snapped the lock. She unlocked it and relocked it a couple of times. "Sometimes I just don't know what to say to you," she said. "I really just don't know what to say to you at all. Do you think I'm that much of a grifter? To come back to you in the hope of gaining some personal advantage for myself?" She pulled the suitcase upright, as if she were about to leave that very moment, and gave Reed a weary look. "If I'd really wanted to take advantage of you, I would have told you that I loved you, I would have led you on. But I didn't. I never said that I loved you, just that I missed you. I came back to you because I missed you. Is that so hard to understand?" She stood waiting for a few seconds. "I guess it is," she went on. "It's complicated for you. You need to complicate things. You need to imagine my coldness, my harshness, in a thousand different ways. I know that's what you do. I could practically not exist for you, Reed. You aren't in love with me, you're in love with the image you've constructed of me. Fine, do whatever you like. You can keep the ghost of me. But the real me, the real Elaine, has a flight to Washington in a few hours." She took a step forward, almost touching him. "The point is," she hissed, "that, no matter how things went, I deserve this candidacy. I know it, and you know it too."

Reed embraced her. There was nothing else he could do. He gripped her so tight, for a moment, that he could sense the fragility of her bones. He hugged her so tight he could kill her. Elaine issued no cry of pain. He might possess superhuman strength, but she had strength of a different kind, a nameless strength, obstinate, unpredictable.

He kept embracing her. He could feel her heart pounding against him. He wished he could leave her, leave and never come back. He wished he could fall at her feet and wriggle, naked, extending around her legs, become a worm imploring her for pity. He wished he could do all these things.

Then they kissed. Everything happened in a flash. They fell onto the bed, grappling together, desperate and on fire like a pair of falling stars, starting to undress, continuing to kiss, exchanging saliva, the fluids of one in the mouth of the other. Reed was appalled. He felt excited and yet impotent, hopeless. Their bodies. Their panting. Elaine was stimulating his penis with delicacy, with fury, pulling it towards her, persuading it to elongate, and Reed let himself go, let the flesh flow forth, without restriction of any kind. His penis had become a tentacle. Elaine wrapped it around her, panting, bringing the tip of it to her mouth. Reed shaped one of his fingers into the form of a penis, a second penis to slide into her, feeling his own body undulating in an unstable fashion, ready to stretch out into a thousand tentacles, to wrap himself around her with the suppleness of a demon. It occurred to him that there was no desire in all this. Only a need for union, the necessity of fusion, the need to possess the other, in order to make her forget what it felt like not to be possessed.

"Elaine," he breathed as he came on her, and for an instant he saw the scene as though from a distance, from far away, from an infinitely remote point of view, he saw the monster-man spurt his sperm, and the snow-coloured girl take it all over her face, he saw them together on the bed, in that room, on the surface of the city, in the middle of the nation, on that planet surrounded by empty void, by dying stars, by galaxies striving to wrap themselves around each other.

He spat out the last few drops. With a dissatisfied sigh he recomposed his body.

*

A few hours later he woke up in Elaine's bed, cold, naked. The minute he tried to move, he felt all hell break loose in his body; he lay there contorting, breathless, under the sheets. That pain. He thought back to the sex they'd had that night. His own body, deformed, on top of hers. Was that real? Did that actually happen? No question, the pain he was feeling right now was real. And so was the sense of emptiness. Elaine had vanished. In the half-light of the bedroom, Reed could see enough to know that the suitcase was gone. He lay motionless, trying to master the pain and anxiety by listening to the traffic noise outside as it slowly grew louder.

It was still dark. Reed reckoned it must be about six. He ought to get moving. There he lay, in that bed that wasn't his, in that unfamiliar apartment. *I suppose this is a romantic scene. Or maybe just a depressing one.* Oh, the scene in which he finally got up, groaning with pain, and donned his clothes. He looked for a note, a message from Elaine. He found nothing. He called a cab. Back home, he took a shower, and even before Annabel got in, he was already at his place, seated at his desk, the way he was every morning. It was all so romantic, it really was depressing. The gleaming surface of his desk reflected his silhouette. The telephone was chilly after its night of sleep. The computer screen came back to life with a whisper, and he stared at it hesitantly, as if in a dream. Here was his life, here were his everyday things.

Even the thoughts that surfaced intermittently in his mind, over the course of the morning, had an unreal flavour to them. But they kept coming back. *Why did I do it? Why did I give a positive vote on her application? My God, what have I done?*

At least Bernard isn't with her.

The morning went by. The afternoon went by too. Reed tried to focus on his work, without much success, and to brace himself against the chaos of his own thoughts. The telephone emitted a low-battery signal, a solitary electronic lament that made Reed jump in his seat. He rummaged through a drawer in search of his charger, and that was when his fingers chanced to close around the business card he had been looking for some time ago. Dennis De Villa. The police officer who was convinced that the superheroes of the old guard were in some kind of danger. Reed smiled a weary, disenchanted smile, and thought to himself that no one could help him now, and the only real danger he faced, at this point, was to go even further out of his mind, sink still deeper into the morass of ridicule and torment.

He'd heard nothing from Elaine. He began fooling himself that everything was just fading into oblivion, into a glimpse of unreality. *Nothing's going to happen. She won't be selected for that mission. No one will be selected, no one is going.* But in the end his phone vibrated, and reality surged back, iron-hard and relentless. A few words on the screen of his phone. That ruthless message. *I made it,* Elaine wrote in the message. *I was selected, I'm going up in the space probe.*

*

A month later, in a morning washed with whitish light, while outside the erratic winter held the city in its fist, Reed found himself in Doctor Szepanski's consulting room. He was naked, lying on an examination table. The room was immersed in silence: only the breathing of the two men and the noise of the ultrasound machine that emitted distant signals, intermittently, like those of an underwater sonar device.

"Everything's fine here too," the doctor said, staring into the monitor next to the exam table, while his right hand manoeuvred the ultrasound probe over Reed's lower belly. Without raising his eyes from the monitor he flashed a self-satisfied smile. "It's funny," he said. "After all these years I still get a charge out of seeing what's in there. Inside the body of a superhero. It somehow takes me back to when I worked for the government—I mean, you remember what it was like back then, too, don't you?"

Reed took a deep breath. He could feel the probe sliding over his belly, skating along on a layer of chilly gel. "I never took part in your research programme," he said. "I wasn't willing to put myself into the hands of you government doctors."

Szepanski gave no sign that he had heard him. He sat there, gazing raptly into the monitor, repeating several times: "All good. All good here, too." Without warning he grabbed the tube of gel with his free hand and absent-mindedly squeezed out a freezing cold spurt onto Reed's groin. "Let's take a look down here," he said.

Reed kept himself from complaining. It was he who had requested a complete ultrasound check-up. He tried to catch a glimpse of the monitor. From where he lay, he couldn't see a thing. At most, he could see Doctor Szepanski's profile, his weirdly tiny nose, his exaggeratedly taut cheekbone. Szepanski must be seventy-five by now, but his face looked almost ageless, in a disquieting way.

"In those days," the doctor resumed, "every time a new superhero agreed to be examined, it was like a party. We were as excited as little children. We expected to discover who knows what, inside the bodies of you super-people." Then, trying to justify himself: "You could have been a strategic resource for the nation, that's why we had to study you."

"Sure." Reed didn't have much more to add. Back in the days when Szepanski was the head of the government centre for medical research on superheroes, he too had assembled a small team of scientists to subject his own body to experiments, along with the bodies of the other members of his group. That's the way things were back then. People thought it was possible to learn the secrets of any given body. They were convinced that they could plumb the depths of who knows what truth. It was the end of the Sixties, the Seventies, with a tail stretching on into the Eighties. The golden years of his life. The authentic era of the superheroes.

"Everything I know I learned back then," Szepanski summed up with a triumphant smile, grooming his dyed hair as if the monitor were a mirror on a vanity table.

Reed noticed the doctor's taut cheek, the lack of wrinkles or any creases of expression. *Here we go again. He must have had more surgery done.* The doctor had had his first facelift twenty years ago, and he hadn't stopped since, it seemed... "Oh!" Reed cried out. A shiver had run through him after Szepanski squeezed more gel onto an especially sensitive part of his body.

"Since we're at it, let's check things out down here too," said the doctor distractedly, manoeuvring the probe onto Reed's testicles.

Reed heaved a sigh. The only thing that worked with doctors was patience. He turned his head and looked away, tired of trying to divine the theoretical findings of the ultrasound, by reflection, on the cosmetically enhanced face of Doctor Szepanski. He lay there, looking out of the window. Dust motes floated in the shafts of light that filtered through the glass, like so many microscopic worlds. He could feel the probe sliding, almost caressing now, on the small mass of his testicles, and he was just beginning to feel more relaxed when Szepanski started up again: "And your sex life? What can you tell me about your sex life?"

Reed looked over at him again. "Why do you ask? Something wrong down there?" he asked, nodding towards his lower body. Then, since the doctor was not saying anything, he replied wearily: "Non-existent, I would say. No sex life to speak of in the past month."

"Not even masturbation?" Szepanski inquired.

"Do we have to be so specific?" Reed objected.

"You superheroes always have troubles with sex," the doctor said, pushing the probe against one of Reed's testicles, making him start in response. "Believe me, by now, I know enough about it. None of you seem to understand other people's bodies, because they're so different from your own. That's why you feel so lonely all the time." He turned to look at Reed, just long enough to bestow one more tight little smile upon him. In the harsh light of day, his too-tanned skin shone with a sinister gleam.

Reed started to feel a little exasperated. "Joseph," he sighed. "If there's something wrong with me, I wish you'd just say so... But I can't imagine that my sex life has anything to do with it..."

"You superheroes have gone beyond desire, that's it," the doctor went on without listening. "Your bodies have ventured too far, so you can no longer feel ordinary human desires. You're stuck in some remote limbo. You don't have sex for the sake of pleasure, you do it out of a terror of no longer possessing anyone. You can't manage to come and if you do, you don't feel a thing." He put down the probe, and handed Reed a handful of paper towels.

Reed tried to wipe the gooey substance off his body. He had gel on his torso, abdomen, and groin. He felt like the newborn spawn of some monstrous creature, freshly emerged from the gelatinous womb of its mother. "Interesting… theories," he commented. "But I already told you what my symptoms are: fatigue. I can't seem to concentrate…"

"These days, that's something three-quarters of humanity is struggling with," was the doctor's response.

"…and this pain in my hip that keeps tormenting me. It's like there's an internal tear, a laceration in the elastic tissue of my body," Reed complained, taking care not to mention that the tear seemed to have a *flavour*, it was a sensation, it was something so definite that it had a name. *Elaine. This tear is her imprint. Her indelible bite.*

"We looked at the hip, too. I didn't see a thing." Szepanski pulled a face, something he may have intended as a furrowing of his brow. Whatever it was meant to be, all it actually resulted in was a single, strange, worrisome movement of his hairline. He decreed: "There's nothing wrong with your hip. There's nothing wrong with your belly. There's nothing wrong with your testicles. In fact, there's nothing wrong with you at all."

Even though he'd been unable to clean himself entirely, Reed started putting on his clothes. He was dissatisfied with Szepanski's diagnosis. "Okay," he said. "Taken individually, every part of my body seems to work fine. But what about if you take them all together? Couldn't you take a look at the body as a whole?" He pulled on his trousers and, feeling a little stronger, stated: "I know something's wrong with me. I can feel it."

The telephone on Szepanski's desk rang. The doctor picked up the receiver. From his tone of voice it was clear that he was talking to the nurse in the adjoining office. "Just a few minutes," he said, then hung up and turned to Reed. "Symptoms, Reed. My job is to judge from symptoms. *Feeling like something's wrong* is not a symptom. We've looked, and there's nothing in your body." As he spoke, the flesh around his mouth remained immobile—it had the consistency of setting cement. There was something feminine about his rebuilt cheekbones, and it clashed with the hairy hands, dotted with liver spots, that he rested on his desk. He added: "Perhaps…"

"Perhaps?" Reed asked as he finished getting dressed.

"If you were to talk to me about your sexual problems, we could find out more. Certain symptoms are often concealed in that area." He underscored the last phrase by spreading his hands in an affable manner.

"I have no sexual problems," Reed dismissed the subject. He was accustomed to Szepanski's quirks, but he couldn't figure out why the doctor was so insistent on talking about sex. His instinct told him to beware. He wanted the doctor to help him without forcing him to talk about his intimate life. Was that so hard? My God, wasn't that the job doctors were paid to do?

The telephone rang again, emitting a couple of beeps. "I'm afraid I'm going to have to let you go now," Szepanski said. "You understand, a patient's been waiting and I'm going to have to see her."

"Of course. Good to see you, Joseph." Reed put on his jacket and left. He glanced into the waiting room. He saw a woman with a cascade of tawny hair, about forty or so, dressed expensively, and blessed with a shamelessly healthy appearance. Reed doubted she was a patient and wondered whether she was one of the doctor's lovers. He'd heard rumours that Szepanski cheated on his wife with his female patients, both superwomen and other women. The thought of the elderly doctor's rebuilt face sweating in the throes of intercourse made Reed queasy. He preferred to think she was just a patient. One of the numerous millionaires that Szepanski had acquired as clients over the years, thanks to his reputation as physician to the superheroes. Rich people liked having that kind of a doctor. Being touched by hands that a few minutes earlier might have palpated the belly of some former superhero. *Or maybe even Mister Fantastic's balls.*

He still felt the viscous chill of the ultrasound gel on his skin. He shivered as he hurried towards the elevator. Once at the ground floor, he walked out onto the street and was taken aback by the violent glare of daylight. He took a few steps across the sidewalk, amazed to find himself there, in the flow of foot traffic, fully dressed and standing erect, officially pronounced healthy. A car was waiting for him. But he felt like going back. He felt like running back into the doctor's consulting room and confronting Joseph Szepanski, the celebrity and luminary, doctor to the superheroes, the man whose skin was pulled tighter than a drum, and shouting the truth into his face. The razor-sharp truth. Telling him that what he felt had a name and this name was burning in his hip, in his body.

*

He got into the car. His brain was too rational to accept all this. To admit that unhappiness in love could clamp his body the way a hand clenches a glass, and that what had reduced him to his present state were the months of emotional highs and lows, torment, and jealousy, since the day he first heard Elaine's name. Elaine. Elaine. Reed had believed that the day of the committee meeting in Washington was the darkest abyss, the most miserable emotional bedrock he was likely to hit, but ever since she left for Houston matters had only got worse.

It was a state of constant agony. He felt sleepless, exhausted, and it hurt him to move, it hurt him to think. It hurt him to smile, talk, look out of the window. Part of him realised, with lucid clarity, that he had crossed a border of some kind, and what at first had been a limited, surmountable malaise had begun to grow into a limitless, open-ended sickness. Nearly infinite. Reed suspected he was suffering from depression. He refused to admit it to himself—as he refused to admit that he had fallen down there, into the black hole, into the quicksand where fate led all those who had pursued stupidly, obtusely, the fatal path of obsession with another person.

*

He opened his eyes. A burning sensation. The light was stabbing them with a thousand tiny blades. He found himself immersed in a white light, between white sheets, on a hard bed that smelt of whiteness. There was a needle stuck into his arm. The room he was lying in looked unfamiliar, but as soon as he was capable of looking around, it wasn't hard to figure out where he was. The neon light on the wall, the nondescript furniture. He was in a hospital room.

The silence was soothing. He closed his eyes for a moment. The moment must have been a long one, because when he opened them he was no longer alone. "There you are," Doctor Szepanski said to him. He was standing next to the bed. "You had us worried there, Reed."

Reed did his best to understand. He tried to establish some order to his thoughts, fit together what data he had. The effort was pointless. He had no data. Everything was immersed in a white glow. A terrible hollowness in his head. "What's that?" was all he could get out, in a whisper, gesturing to the IV bottle and the tube taped to his arm.

"Just a little glucose and mineral salts," Szepanski said. "You were unconscious for a while," he explained. He moved a little closer to the bed and looked at Reed as though he'd never seen him before: "For God's sake, when you were in my office you should have told me, Reed. You should have told me that you were abusing your body that way."

Reed felt like telling him to go away. He felt like closing his eyes again. He wanted to burrow comfortably into that emptiness, that distance, because he knew it wouldn't last long, that soon everything would resurface into his mind: what had happened, and the reason why it had happened. He tried to hoist himself up on his pillows. He was very weak. His body had taken on a curious consistency, like something that had melted and then congealed again. "Annabel," he uttered. "Where's Annabel? I need my diary."

"Don't worry about your diary," Szepanski said. "You won't be able to work for at least a couple of days. Don't even think about it." He went on staring at Reed, giving him an odd, almost aghast look. "It was Annabel who found you this morning. You'd been lying on the floor of your room for who knows how many hours. Your body was an unholy mess. I don't want to know what you were trying to do, but I do want to tell you this: your body was a mess."

Reed nodded, uncertain about any other reaction. The memories were starting to condense in his head, like a sort of slow haematoma. Everything still seemed unreal, and sufficiently distant for him to confess: "Joseph, did you know that I don't even know how long my own cock is?"

Szepanski's inexpressive face seemed to crumble. No matter how tight his skin might be pulled, you could sense a grimace of discomfort. "You need rest," he said. "I'm going to leave you alone."

"Weren't you the one who was so interested in my secrets?" Reed insisted. He couldn't even say why, but it seemed a matter of fundamental importance to tell him about it: "One day I downloaded a porn movie from the internet. I know everyone says the same thing, but it really was an accident. I don't like pornography."

"Reed, this hardly seems like the time," said Szepanski, though he still remained at the bedside, his eyes increasingly glassy.

"When I opened it," Reed went on, appalled at his own flow of sincerity, "it took me a few seconds to realise what it was. Long enough to get a good look at the actor's cock. It was big, hefty." Reed closed his eyes in exhaustion and went on talking: "You won't believe this. The next time I had sex, my cock took on the same shape, without my having any say in the matter." He knew that there was no point to confessing these things, not now, not to this man, and yet he felt the need to say something true, something secret, as some kind of offering to thank destiny for the fact that he was still here, still alive, still conscious. A tribute to the god of intimacy, to the lord of sincerity. "I have no control over that part of my body. It extends and contracts in response to every slightest nuance of my thoughts, even my subconscious thoughts. Especially my subconscious ones. My cock follows the secret flows of my thoughts and of my paranoia. My cock is made of paranoia. It happens even if I'm alone. I can't tell its original size any more."

There was a moment of profound silence.

"Now you rest," Szepanski said. It was impossible to tell from his tone whether he was satisfied or appalled. Probably both. Reed heard him move away and then say again, from the doorway: "Rest."

It wasn't difficult to follow his advice.

*

In the hours that followed he fell asleep and reawakened several times, leaving and returning to the world around him, in waves, like the movement of a rip tide. With each reawakening the memory grew sharper. The memory of the reason he'd wound up in that hospital. The memory came back to him with all its weight, with all its embarrassing details.

It had happened the day before. Reed had spent a frantic afternoon, working furiously, in an attempt to make up for how distracted he'd been recently and to show that he was the usual Reed. He had told off Annabel for the way she answered the telephone, with an emphasis that he considered inappropriate, asking her maliciously whether she had by any chance *a little excess blood sugar to metabolise.* He'd upbraided a consultant who was guilty of turning a report in late, reading him, at a sadistically slow speed, a list of the dozens of consultants over the course of the foundation's existence who had all turned their reports in with admirable punctuality. He'd called the cell phone of the president of the company that provided the office with computer tech assistance, reaching him of all places in the middle of a Basque pelota game. Reed had been quite sarcastic about the recent lapses and shortcomings in the service that the company provided, forcing a promise of a full quarter's free service, while in the background he could hear the audience roar as a player scored a point. *¡Viva la pelota!*

He'd done that, and it had made him feel better. *I can do it. I can still take charge of situations. My will hasn't lost its grip on the world. I can push, I can persuade. I can act, achieve, and feel. Give me a day and I'll make full use of it.*

But later, in the silence of his apartment, all that force of will slid off him. The evening lay before him, empty and tedious. Lately, things had been going that way: the energy of the day tumbled into the apathy of the night, daytime confidence turned into nocturnal malaise. The more he instilled his will into his work, the greater grew the yearning to strip himself of that will, annul himself, become putty in someone else's hands. Elaine's hands.

She wasn't there. She was in some absolute, distant elsewhere. Houston seemed like another dimension. She was down there, as if she had fallen through the looking glass, to a place where other rules applied, other thoughts prevailed. Reed knew she wasn't thinking about him. Every night he waited for her to call. He avoided going out or making plans. He knew she wouldn't call, and that in the end he would be the one who called, and yet that night too he had waited, without being able to sit down, or even eat dinner, his appetite killed by the flavour of his own obsession. He just wandered from room to room in his apartment, raving, dizzy with excitement, his body on high alert, while his head went on fantasising.

He'd fantasised about her hands, her mouth, the soft folds between her toes, the hollow behind her knees, the map of freckles on her back. He could almost draw that map from memory. He was happy to remember every bit of that body, and yet aghast at the way he was scattering himself into the recollection of a thousand details. A thousand images. There was one Elaine; there were millions of images inside him. He could see her through the thousands of reflections of his imagination as if he were looking through the multifaceted eyes of an insect.

Elaine didn't love him, that much was clear, unmistakable on the face of it. It was all over, and yet no final, definitive words had been uttered. Even though he knew well that it was pointless to hope—not again, not any longer—something inside him kept hoping. To start over again, to be reborn. To die and be reborn, isn't that what he was hoping for? He kept thinking about her, incessantly, invoking the thought of her body the way a sorcerer invokes a spell.

Years earlier, he remembered, when the group of superheroes that he and his wife had led for decades broke up, and the two of them realised there wasn't much else keeping them both together, Reed had spent a period when, every night before going to sleep, he deformed his face for hours, stretching it every which way. He could extend his cheekbones for yards, stretch his forehead like a chest expander, and he could press his hand on his face until he was able to feel the back of his head. It was horrifying. It hurt. What no one understood, what no one thought, was that a rubber face did have feelings. An elastic flesh was a flesh filled with tense nerves, flaring like wooden matches. Reed kept doing it, all the same, because it was the only way to get some rest, in the end: with his face reborn, identical to the way it was before. He needed to work on his face, annihilate it and reassemble it dozens of times, until he felt that there was nothing left on it. Not a trace, no expression of sorrow. His face, remodelled, virgin again. Deforming his face had been his form of self-destructive behaviour, his self-inflicted damage and his therapy at the same time, his method of dealing with his marriage breakup. *I must destroy my face. I must destroy it and reassemble it.*

At the time, he had told himself that that would be the last crisis in his life. Reed clearly remembered his resolution, *I will never feel pain again, not like this, the next time I'll just prevent the pain.* Thinking back on it now, it almost seemed funny. Prevent the pain? Pain springs up out of nowhere, it comes at you like a car hurtling out of the fog. It's a hard thing to dodge. Actually, he had to admit, the emotional state of that long-ago time seemed to vanish in comparison with the way he felt now. The fresh pain made the old pain fade into insignificance. It turned it into a blurry, amusing memory. All things considered, Sue leaving him after years of reciprocal indifference couldn't have hurt him that badly. Giving up Elaine now, in the midst of the raging flame, was quite another matter.

I could try it again. I could try breaking down and reassembling my face, it had occurred to him that evening, while he was still hoping for a phone call from Elaine. But he didn't want to focus on his own body. It was Elaine's body that he wanted to think about, that body that was now absent, that body that had once lain in his bed, and yet left no trace. It seemed impossible that he had once touched that body. Impossible that he had held it in his arms. He'd twisted on the bed, alone, incredulous, as a ravaging tension seized him. He'd wound up staring at his hand in the lamplight, and then he'd started shaping it, transforming it from memory to make it identical to her hand. Fingers, knuckles. Elaine's hand. He'd started to touch himself, with that hand, on the clean white sheets, breathing harder and harder.

He'd kissed his hand. He'd sucked on its fingers. It wasn't enough. Where was Elaine, where was her body? He'd gone on twisting and turning, possessed, so frenzied that he couldn't feel the burning sensation come over him. He'd started shaping his chest. He'd thrust it out, manipulating it, until he made it look like a pair of female breasts. He'd touched them. They were too hard. A flash of self-awareness swept over him, at that point, and he'd glimpsed himself on the bed, a naked man with the breasts of his lost lover, and he'd burst into laughter, in horror and bafflement. *Ladies and gentlemen, Reed Richards with tits.*

The laughter had turned into contractions in his belly, something close to labour pains, as he continued to twist himself, lying on his side, lifting his legs to twist his body into a U-shape. He'd joined his legs together. He'd fused their rubbery mass, and he'd started modelling that mass, laboriously, cursing at the first stabbing pains. A second body attached to his own. Two bodies looking at one another, legless, lying on the bed, joined by a single curve of flesh. He realised he was doing something demented, improbable, something he had never done before, something that would cost him dearly… But he went on. He wanted to recreate Elaine. He'd continued modelling that rudimentary body, doing his best to impress upon it the desired shape, face, breasts, extruding the arms, but it wasn't easy, and once again he started laughing, looking at that shapeless body, that sort of monster, that ridiculous foetus.

Something was awakening in him. A mass of icy, sinister pain, a pain so intense that it could only be guessed at, for now, only hinted at. He hadn't stopped. He had continued, trembling, laughing, hiccoughing, drooling from the effort, panting in excitement, his penis hard, his muscles straining, his hands shaping that twin body. Elaine's neck. Elaine's abdomen. Reed remained in that position, touching Elaine, and for an instant he had felt her, under his hands, it was her, Elaine's body, her soft, tenacious body, her warmth, and Reed tried to hold her, to keep her form from escaping, even if Elaine was already crumbling, vanishing like a mirage.

Something new was about to happen. Something immense, beyond pain, beyond any sensation. Reed had felt it from afar. It was the echo of an impending event, the heralding of some approaching thing, in his nerves, in his flesh on the verge of snapping. His vision was blurred, his body had lost all sensation. He understood that he had ventured too far, beyond limit, that there was no going back, and before he passed out, a phrase had resurfaced inside him: in a shock of lucidity, an unexpected phrase popped into his head. *So long, my Mister Fantastic*, he had whispered with his last voice. Then the reality around him had blanked out, and a flowing darkness had carried him away.

*

He had requested that no one be informed of his condition. Not Franklin, not Sue, and especially not Elaine. He didn't want to worry anyone. He didn't want anyone to feel sorry for him. He couldn't bear the idea of being so weak, so needy, in Elaine's eyes. He made a point of not calling during his time in the hospital, painfully aware that she was unlikely to notice the absence of his calls. She was in the midst of the training for her mission, and as far as she was concerned nothing else existed in the world.

Only Annabel knew. For a couple of days she shuttled back and forth between the office and the hospital, bringing documents and conveying messages, so that Reed could deal with the most urgent matters and no one, from outside, would be able to tell that he wasn't in the office.

On the third day he was able to get dressed, gather his things, and leave the hospital. He left the building alone, with an apparently nonchalant step, like a friend come to visit a patient. Only his little overnight bag gave away that he himself had been a patient. Someone who had been or was still sick. The hustle and bustle of pedestrians in the street at first prompted his resentment, as though he couldn't accept that the world was the same—exactly the same—as before. But by the time he'd walked a short distance and felt the blood circulate in his legs, he began to have different feelings. He was strangely and deeply moved. He had no idea why. He looked at the bodies around him. Those bodies, so complex, so vulnerable, that would one day malfunction and break. The bodies of the pedestrians around him. The men's bodies covered by their coats, the women's bodies with their legs lengthened by high heels, the bodies of the policemen on the street corners, those mortal bodies, without superpowers, so defenceless that they were pitiable. Moving.

Reed felt a quiver inside. He thought back to the sensation that had come over him just before he passed out, the sensation of something impending. The sensation of an unimaginable, unequalled event, something that would sweep away the world as he knew it. He hurried towards the waiting car and climbed in quickly, like someone with a pack of invisible hunters at his heels.

The driver pulled away. He slipped into the stream of traffic with a velvety move and, looking into the rear-view mirror, he enquired: "Everything all right, sir?"

"Fine," Reed reassured him as the hospital building vanished into the distance behind them.

"I hope it was nothing serious," the driver ventured.

"No, nothing serious," Reed replied without adding any information. He had no interest in discussing his hospital stay with a chauffeur. He looked out of the window and watched the city stream past. Then he turned back to the driver, sensing a stirring in his memory. That Hispanic accent. That open, slightly tormented face… Reed realised he'd had this driver other times before, and it dawned on him when the last time had been. *That day. That fatal day.*

"Your name is Santiago," he said, plucking the name, to his own surprise, from some hidden recess of his memory.

"That's right, sir," the man said, with a smile.

Reed thought back to that day months ago. The day when the Ecuadorian driver had transported him to the space centre in New Jersey, where he was scheduled to teach a class, after a sauna at the George Hotel. The day when everything seemed to be the same as it ever was, and the farthest thing from his mind was the possibility of falling in love or becoming a slave to an obsession. He wasn't thinking about those things. In fact, that day he wasn't thinking about anything at all. If asked, he would have said that being with someone else wasn't right for him, not now, not any more. He would have answered that in any case, to the best of his knowledge, being with someone was a good idea if it made you feel good, if each member of the couple reduced the loneliness of the other. He would have said that he couldn't understand people who remained in unhappy, unsatisfying relationships. That's what he would have said. He would have provided a logical, unruffled answer, on that bright spring afternoon.

Yet now, at the immeasurable distance that separated him from that day, Reed could look back on it and see that everything was there from the very outset. The obsession, the frenzy. Everything that would happen later was implicit, from the beginning, all bound up with the strange melancholy of that day. It was all there, like an entire body contained in a gene. Reed had walked into the space centre, laid eyes on Elaine, and from that point forward everything was decided once and for all. In the first glance. In the first shiver.

If only I were capable, he thought, *of seeing in the present what's waiting for me in the future. The way reality will develop. And yet it's here, around me, already engraved in the things that surround me on all sides.*

He went on staring at the nape of Santiago's neck. He continued to try to catch the driver's eye in the rear-view mirror, as if that man could tell him the secret, reveal the formula for avoiding events that were yet to come. "Your wife," he finally asked. "I remember that you told me about your wife. Are you still having problems?"

Santiago's smile turned off. He shot a suspicious glance at the mirror. "My wife? I talked to you about my wife?"

"That's right," Reed replied. "She was causing you a great deal of suffering. You tried to tell me your story. I'm afraid I wasn't a very good listener that day."

Santiago still seemed baffled. "That's amazing, sir. Do you really still remember that conversation?" The way he said it sounded almost indignant, as if there were something scandalous about the fact that he, Reed Richards, should remember the marital problems of a chauffeur he'd met many months ago.

Reed leaned back wearily in the seat. "Yes, I remember," he said. "But forget about it, I didn't mean to pry." He lay there watching the panorama outside, the traffic and the pedestrians, and the prospects of cross streets that opened out, at regular intervals, at every intersection. Down there. In the ambiguous blur that marked the end of each of those streets, it was just possible to make out the edge of the island. The beginning of the watery realm that surrounded it. Reed mused that it had been weeks since he'd taken a stroll along the waterfront or looked out on the ocean. Maybe not since New Year's Eve. He thought longingly of that night. He longed for the ocean. He longed for an afternoon on the beach, a trip to somewhere far away. He missed Europe, Spain, the coasts of Italy, and every other place he hadn't visited in years. He found himself missing the whole world, as the car crept slowly through the streets of New York.

He decided to try talking to the driver again. It seemed important to let the driver know that now he understood more about the grief of love. "Maybe that time I should have told you…" He groped for the right words. "Let's say… the fact is that often people can be enigmatic," he declared wisely, in a paternal voice, appearing to offer advice rather than look for understanding, which is what in fact he was doing. "I mean, people give ambiguous signals about what they want from us."

"Maybe they don't want anything at all," the driver replied, without shedding his suspicious glare. For some reason, the topic seemed to make him anxious.

"But maybe," Reed gave it another try, eager to establish a link with the young man, "I mean… Maybe loving someone means loving her in spite of her mystery. Maybe we are too rational, too presumptuous in our idea that we can control everything. Maybe that's just the way things are meant to be. If you want to love, you have to accept a certain amount of humiliation."

"I don't understand, sir," Santiago replied, swinging around past a bus that was blocking the road. "I think I've already been humiliated enough," he added, giving him a glance in the mirror that seemed to say that Reed, too, looked like he'd been humiliated enough.

Reed decided to drop the matter. It wasn't like him to insist. He sat there, staring out of the window, watching mankind flow past along the Midtown sidewalks, wondering how it was possible to feel so vulnerable, so helpless after a life like the one he'd led. *In other people's eyes, I'm still Reed Richards. A man who has defeated thousands of enemies and withstood thousands of ambushes. A man who is sufficient unto himself. A man who never speaks about feelings. When I try to talk about certain things, I wind up making other people feel awkward.*

At the next intersection, Santiago slowed down, and perhaps with regret, he spoke again. "I appreciate your advice, Mr. Richards. Let's say… Let's just say that I don't need it any more. Not now," he said, in a mysterious tone.

Reed nodded, puzzled, wondering what the reason for such secrecy might be.

"I believe… The time is past for thinking about that kind of thing," said Santiago, as he pressed down on the accelerator. His Hispanic accent sounded odd and at the same time vibrant. "I mean to say, that time is over, the time of… How should I put this? *Romanticism.* When we talk so much about romantic matters, we end up talking only about ourselves. About our own personal lives. We talk and talk about our lives as if they were all so important. As if we were all Hollywood movie stars. That time is over, it's gone now," he said again, shaking his head, as his face darkened. "Oh, I know that you're sort of famous. I wasn't in this country yet, but I know that people like you were important. Sure, superheroes, people capable of shaping the course of destiny with greater strength than anyone else. But you understand…" he focused on a taxi that was trying to pass the car. Then, his voice quivering with some obscure emotion: "These days, people don't think much of the idea of controlling their own destiny. Ask around. Talk to people. Everyone's a fatalist now. No one would be surprised to be swept away by a hurricane tomorrow morning, or to see an alien invasion, or who knows what else. It's just nonsense of course. But it's destiny. Whatever destiny might mean, nobody even thinks of mastering it any more. Destiny, you see, is pretty heavy-handed when it comes to dealing with our plans, our unique affairs, with our…what should I call them? With our *romantic egos*. In the eyes of destiny, we're all just tiny."

Santiago fell silent, breathing heavily. Reed scrutinised the driver's face in the rear-view mirror, wondering whether he felt well. *Maybe I've been a little weird recently, but there are people who are doing worse than me.* He slumped back, eager for a little silence, regretting the decision to strike up the conversation. *I asked for it. I shouldn't have prodded him. I wanted to talk about the troubles of love, and I've been served up a tidy little lecture by my philosopher-chauffeur.* He wondered who could have imparted those ideas to the driver and taught him those peculiar expressions. And where did that sinister gleam in his eyes come from? Twelve hours a day driving in city traffic, and that's what the effect seemed to be. "Wise words," he said, cutting it short.

He couldn't foresee that one day he would think back on this, and realise just how right the driver had been.

*

Ben got in touch late one afternoon, when a warm breeze was blowing outside and the first signs of another spring were starting to pop out all over. Reed was sitting at his desk. When the phone rang, he picked up the receiver, expecting as usual to hear Annabel's voice. To his surprise, what he heard instead was a gruff unmistakable voice saying, point-blank: "How the hell are you doing, you old slab of chewing gum?"

"Benjamin!" Reed exclaimed. He hadn't heard from him in weeks. His old friend belonged to the category of people who appear and disappear all the time, unpredictably.

"That angel of a secretary of yours just adores you," Ben said. "I have no idea why. Poor little thing. I'm pretty sure that if she didn't waste her time working for you, she wouldn't be such a scraggy little darling. I had to pester her for ages before she agreed to put the call through direct, without announcing me. She was afraid you'd be mad at her."

Reed shook his head, suppressing a smile. "Can I ask why you didn't want to let her announce the call?"

"To surprise you, man. To hear the sound of your faggoty little voice, before you had a chance to put on your *I am so cool* one." Reed smiled again, imagining his corpulent friend in his usual get-up, T-shirt and fishing trousers, talking on the phone, sitting on his reinforced couch. "Ben, have I ever told you to go to hell?"

"Plenty of times."

The two men chuckled. Reed was happy to get this call. He'd known Benjamin Grimm since college, and he'd been sorry, years ago, when his old friend moved out of the city. "Anyway, if it matters to you," Ben went on, "yours truly is doing pretty well these days. This old rock isn't crumbling away, that's for sure. Every morning I go out on the water, every night I sleep like a baby. What about you?"

"Don't ask," Reed sighed. He stopped to think for a second, and then tried to explain: "I feel like I'm surrounded by lunatics. Everyone I meet talks about the weirdest things. New York is an insane asylum, you can't trust anyone."

"I know what you mean. Why do you think I holed up out here?" Ben paused, and Reed distinctly heard him take a sip of a drink. Suddenly Reed wished he could be with him, in the small fishing village where he lived, looking out at the beach through the picture window in his living room, drinking the first beer of the evening. "It's that shit," Ben continued. "They all have brains clogged with cocaine. They're all up to their necks in debt and paranoia. People aren't teetering on the brink of insanity any more, they've plunged in headfirst and they're pretending that it's normal. Listen to this. There's some guy who keeps writing to me, as a matter of fact I think it's from New York City, anyway he's convinced that I can procure some strange superhero drug…"

"Good God. Are people still deluding themselves with those fantasies?"

"Sure. There's still plenty of people who believe all that bullshit about superheroes. So I told him that the formula is simple. I told him that the secret drug of the superheroes is made by grinding up salicylic acid crystals. Then he just needs to find someone who's willing to take a straw and blow the stuff up his ass."

Reed burst out laughing. The elastic walls of his stomach contracted and relaxed rhythmically, almost to his surprise, for the first time in weeks. It was a strange sensation: the enjoyment of real laughter. The pleasure of letting himself go. "I can't believe you said that," he chuckled as he caught his breath.

"Believe it," Ben replied. His voice had a gruff warmth. His tone was untroubled, and it was in that same tone that, after another pause, he fired off his unexpected question. "So I heard about your little vacation," he said. "How was that lovely clinic?"

The laughter died in Reed's mouth. The taste on his tongue turned sharp, the acid flavour of sudden discomfort. Damn. He thought no one knew about it. He thought it was a dead letter, a forgotten matter, and that he'd never have to talk about it again. "Nice," he tossed out, pretending indifference. "But how…"

"Old Ben doesn't miss a thing. Let's just say that I have my sources."

Reed sat silently, waiting, like an animal paralysed by imminent danger. He could hear Ben breathing into the receiver. He sensed that his friend was not going to add anything more and it was up to him to provide explanations. "Your sources must also have told you that I was only there for a couple of days," he said. "It's not like I meant to keep it a secret. It's just that nothing really serious happened."

"I'm glad to hear that," Ben exclaimed, without losing the ironic inflection in his voice. "I heard that when they found you, you were twisted in knots, with your head where your dick ought to be. I knew that was a pretty good description of your true personality normally, but I was starting to get a little worried in spite of myself."

Reed smiled again. A smile of gratitude and grief. He began to understand the purpose of that call, and imagined that before long Ben would ask even more uncomfortable questions. He could feel something shifting in his chest, a surge of annoyance and deep-rooted affection, that choked his breath and left him speechless. "Jesus, Ben."

"Anyhow," the other man went on. "When someone's body is made of the same material as a condom, I can imagine that he'd be sensitive about the subject. He should be careful. Careful about where his dick winds up."

"Let's get on with it," Reed huffed. "Get to the point."

But the man on the phone wasn't ready for that part yet. He seemed determined to encircle Reed slowly, waiting for the right time to get him with his back against the wall. "For instance, I was wondering. Whatever happened to your girlfriends, those girls you used to date? Little darlings with adorable names like Paris, Jenna, Gisele..."

"They must have moved on to other clients," Reed replied, trying to think of some wisecrack to toss out. "If you're interested, I can give you the phone number," was all he could come up with.

"Better not. Big as I am, you think I could go out on a date with a little darling? No, what I need is a lady sumo wrestler." Ben heaved a deep, theatrical sigh, like a comic giving his audience time to take in a joke, and then resumed: "Really, I'm just worried about you. I know how it is at our age. A man needs to let off steam, a man needs the occasional satisfaction."

"In fact I consider myself satisfied," Reed stated, well aware that he was skating close to a defensive whine. "Satisfied with my work."

Ben stopped for one of his beer sips. "It's funny that you say that. Funny," he repeated, with a hint of sarcasm. "I hear that funny things have been happening to you. They say that you've changed, that you're grumpy. They say you mistreat the people who work with you, that you've lost your sense of humour. That you're not as reliable as you used to be. Not to mention that you wind up in the hospital for mysterious reasons. In short, funny things for a man who says he's satisfied."

Reed started to feel tired. The phone was warm against his ear, and the thought of the work he still had to get through was starting to press against his brain. An email he'd been in the middle of writing beckoned from his computer screen. In fact, a pretty important email. "Good God almighty," he counter-attacked. "How on earth do you hear all these things from where you live, holed up there on your beach?"

Ben said nothing, and waited a while before resuming, this time without much irony. Stripped of all jocularity, his voice sounded rockier than ever. "I've seen a picture of her, Reed. No question, she's an attractive young woman. Red hair, hell, and those exquisite freckles on her nose. I can understand that a guy could lose control with someone like that."

Reed slumped in his chair. The afternoon light was dying, leaving the office in a growing penumbra. "A picture of her," he echoed.

"Don't put on that voice. You know that word gets around. You know it's easy to get hold of someone's picture." Ben sighed, like someone faced with an unpleasant task, and then said: "I know you, and I know that right now you're thinking of the best way to put an end to this call, you're thinking that you have a lot of work to do and so forth. So I'll get to the point. Reed, if I didn't know you better, I'd tell you that I'm worried about you."

"There's no reason to be worried," Reed lied instinctively. "Everything's fine, everything's under control."

Ben swallowed a large gulp of beer. "Go fuck yourself, Reed. Don't play-act with me. We've been friends for more than forty years, we worked together for twenty-five years, I don't deserve to have you trying to pull the wool over my eyes." His voice was so deep now that it made the receiver vibrate in Reed's hand. "Why don't you answer this question instead: is she worth it? Sure, she's cute, but she's not all that remarkable. You could do better. What do you see in that girl? Don't you think that whatever it is you see is actually in your mind?"

"I don't want to talk about her any more," Reed rebelled. He felt his face burning, the corners of his mouth drying out. "I'm not ready, not yet."

"You're not ready?!" Ben seemed to be on the verge of breaking into laughter again. "I can't say if all this is funny or tragic. If I compare the Reed I know with the Reed who's spouting these idiotic replies…"

"Ben, please."

"Man, just don't tell me that you're not ready," Ben growled, making the phone vibrate again. "I'm pretty sure the two of you have been dating for a while."

Reed made an effort at self-control. He didn't want to fight with his old friend. "As far as that goes, we haven't been seeing much of each other lately," he let slip, as if it were the most uninteresting of facts. As though that break in his relationship with Elaine weren't pushing him towards madness, as though he didn't feel relegated to a terrible, obscene limbo, and as though he weren't secretly scrambling to do anything he could to get out of his exile. To be redeemed from limbo. To see Elaine again. To have Elaine's body, the real one, back in his arms.

"Listen, you old slab of gum, stop telling me things that I know already. The girl is in Houston. Everyone knows that. And everyone is wondering, by the way, just how you dared to show up for that committee in Washington."

Reed closed his eyes. "Jesus," he whispered. "Everyone who?"

"The thing is," Ben kept going, without giving a sign that he'd heard what Reed said, "she'll come back to New York sooner or later. And what will you do then?" He stopped, and a flash of suspicion entered his voice: "That is, of course, unless you show up in Houston in the meantime..."

Reed said nothing. Now he felt totally exposed. He shot a guilty glance at his computer screen, where the email waited, silently, for him to finish it. That email. Those words, so carefully chosen, those formal phrases. Reed stared at the letters on the screen, hypnotised, trying to find his next line in them like in the words of a script.

"Reed? You wouldn't be thinking of..." Ben was talking softly, like to a child. "Don't do it, Reed. Don't make yourself ridiculous, that wouldn't be like you. Listen to an old friend. You've fallen hard, that's something that happens. But this is enough. Don't scrape the bottom. There's nothing romantic about hitting the bottom, however romantic it might look from a distance." He took a deep breath, and continued: "When it's all said and done, what is it you want to do with this girl? You want to have children? Do you want to marry her and introduce her as the new Mrs. Richards? You know that's not possible, Reed. You know that perfectly well. You've got too much personal style to try pulling a prank like that. Even you have no idea what to do with this woman. You want to have her, but you don't know why. I know you, believe me, I really know you. If you truly thought you could build something with her, you would have introduced her to the world. You would have brought her down here, to meet your friend, the old rock man, so I could give you my blessing. And you know I would have given it. I would have done it, Reed, if I'd seen that you believed in her. But you don't. You're just luxuriating in the role of the hopeless lover. You've decided to cause yourself some pain, to play the role of a martyr to love. It's a dangerous game, Reed. New York is full of lunatics, you don't want to be the king of the lunatics."

Reed felt a twinge. He felt as soft as a piece of butter, while the words of his friend stabbed into him like a hot knife. He thought of his friend's body, that body of massive rock. From that throat of rock, only words like those could have emerged. Gruff. Heavy. Reed recognised that it was true, it was the pure truth, he'd avoided introducing Elaine to anyone, he'd kept her a secret, *she's the one person who has caused the greatest turmoil in my life in the past several years, and no one I know has seen her but the doorman of my building.* Not even Annabel had met her. Ben had seen a picture of her, and as for Franklin, the very thought pushed him to the brink of panic. He could never introduce Elaine to Franklin. He could never imagine them side by side. Maybe because if they were in the same place, it would become impossible to ignore that Elaine was a perfect girl for his son, certainly not for him. Or maybe it was because Elaine herself had never seemed very eager to be introduced to Franklin or to anyone else, and that fact had always stirred up a mixture of relief and bitterness in him. *She doesn't want to be acknowledged. She has no interest in having the world know about us.*

"Reed?"

He had to say something. He had to reassure his friend, start talking again. He heaved a sigh, and did his best to soft-pedal: "Thanks, old rock. I'll keep your words in mind."

Ben didn't seem reassured. "The time is past for falling in love like that, Reed. This is not the time to be distracted by things like that."

"Now you too?!" Reed said. "I've already heard this lecture."

"Then maybe it's a good lecture."

Outside it was evening, the room was dark.

The computer screen illuminated his desk, spreading a vague glow around his body, like luminescent plankton in the ocean depths. Reed continued to stare at the screen. He continued to stare at the half-written message. The message that he would soon send, that would travel through miles of wires, connections, and radio relays, broken down into elementary electric impulses, after which it would reach its destination, on another screen, and reassemble itself before the eyes of a stranger. The message that he had long imagined writing. The message in which he invented imaginary research requirements. The message in which he requested, with the deployment of some adroit diplomacy, the use of certain laboratories at the Johnson Space Centre, in Houston. The message with which, in practical terms, he was inviting himself to come to Houston.

*

New York was suffocating, and it wasn't even April yet. A mantle of stunning heat descended upon the city. Reed would spend long minutes scrutinising the street, from his office window, as though he were waiting for a signal of some kind. Lost in a reverie, watching the numbered roofs of the buses going by below, the incessant movement of the swarms of taxis. For the first time, the idea of the work awaiting him failed to trigger a flow of energy in him; instead, it prompted a surge of nausea.

The last few days had been a sort of blurry patch. He'd taught a class at Columbia University, where he'd lost his temper with some of the students because, in his view, they were asking stupid questions. He'd eaten solitary meals in a restaurant where he'd once had dinner with Elaine. He'd missed a number of appointments without much remorse, he'd avoided answering a fair number of phone calls, and hadn't even bothered to upbraid that foundation consultant when he was late turning in a report once again. He'd found a message from Franklin, saying that he would be coming to New York, and a couple of messages from Dennis De Villa, the police officer, who was apparently trying to get in touch with him. He'd sent a short reply to his son but had avoided answering the detective's messages. He didn't feel like dealing with the paranoid ideas of the police.

Even enjoyable things seemed to have become impossible. He had skipped several of his sessions at the gym and missed a sauna he'd reserved at the George Hotel. He could feel the days slip through his hands. He could feel time dripping through his fingers. All his life, he'd been able to impose order on the weeks, the days, he'd known how to govern the elusive material of the everyday. He'd been able to keep from squandering his energy. He'd focused, he'd imposed a form upon himself, and the last thing he'd have expected, now, was to lose that form. He'd tricked himself into believing that once he was past a certain age, order would become implicit, inseparable from his life itself.

The only thing he managed was to check the mail on his computer. He was waiting for an answer from Houston. In the meantime, he continued calling Elaine every other night or so, ignoring the weary, possibly bored tone of her voice when she answered. He avoided making any reference to his possible visit to Houston. He wanted it to be a surprise. Whether a welcome or unwelcome one, a surprise nonetheless. He wanted to be the kind of man who was still capable of astonishing her. A man who was capable of showing up, without warning, and claiming his share of attention.

Elaine told him about her days. She told him about classes in meteorology, parachute training, zero-gravity simulations, lift-off and landing tests, complicated software for handling the spacecraft. She told him all these things as if she were talking about an enchanted world to which he would never have access. Reed felt like laughing at her stories. He felt like telling her that he knew every detail of that world backwards and forwards, and that a 300-million-dollar mission, organised on the fly for obscure reasons, didn't impress him. He'd seen better than that in his career. But he couldn't laugh. He could only grip the telephone, hang on to her accounts, and focus on her voice with a blend of wonderment, resentment, and adoration.

He pretended that everything was still the same. He pretended not to know that Elaine, by now, had got everything she could have wanted from him. *She's satisfied her curiosity. She's had the experience of taking her old childhood hero as a lover and she even got a boost in getting selected for this mission. What else can I offer her now?*

Night after night, her voice grew increasingly distant. "You're already in outer space in your mind," he said one evening, putting on a playful tone of voice.

"It's the chance of a lifetime," was her pragmatic reply.

Reed dreamed often. He dreamed about the colour of her flesh, like a magnolia petal, the curve of her smile when she came. He dreamed of scenes with embraces, rediscovered intimacy, that crystalline happiness that only revealed itself in dreams. Elaine welcoming him into her apartment in Brooklyn on an afternoon of bright sunlight. Elaine in the sauna with him, massaging him without haste. Reed woke up at dawn, sweaty, his penis pulsating, a stabbing pain in his hip and limbs. Since the evening of his collapse that pain had come back constantly. Dreams of idyllic scenes filled his nights, but it was pain that permeated every reawakening. The pain came in waves, not unlike Morse code, and seemed to herald an enigmatic announcement.

Maybe Ben was right. Maybe the Ecuadorian driver was too. That time had passed. You couldn't live in that kind of exalted melancholy any more, not here, not now, it was an excessive luxury, something that belonged to bygone times. The heartbreaking yearning, the outsized passion: straight out of a nineteenth-century French novel. Strictly for mid-twentieth-century Hollywood studio movies. Reed had always been happy to live in his own time, and he didn't care much for people who fantasised about living in other periods of history. Yet here he was, just like them, dreaming about living in other times. Oh, to fall in love the way people fell in love in the Twenties, in silent movies. To fall in love the way they did in Europe, during the war, with the sensation that the world was about to end, but that it would eventually rise from the ashes. To fall in love the way they did in the Fifties, the way an existentialist loved a woman in Paris, or the way a vagabond beat loved a girl in San Francisco. To fall in love like in the Sixties, when he met Sue for the first time, at college, and the air felt a thousand times less hard than it was now. To fall in love like in the Seventies, when in New York you could go out every night, to dance, to love, to fight, when the superheroes patrolled the neighbourhoods, drinking in the city's bottomless energy. To fall in love like in the Eighties, when everyone wore a mask of cynicism as if they were going to a masquerade, without realising that they'd never be able to take off that mask again. Or like in the Nineties, when the internet promised to make everyone happy, or at least wealthy.

Or maybe to fall in love, who knows, the way people will fall in love in the future, in some as yet unknown manner. To fall in love like in the years to come, when people will look back on that horrible time, the early years of the millennium, a time when everyone lived in a state of panic, hurtling to and fro in the dark like inside an anthill, and every project appeared impossible, including the idea of an encounter, two people meeting, and actually recognising each other.

*

Ben popped up again a few days later, this time in person. He presented himself in Reed's office dressed in an elegant custom-tailored suit which barely disguised his massive body. On his head he wore a panama hat that gave him a whimsical holiday look, and his leather shoes came in a size that, at a glance, must be half again as big as Reed's shoes.

"Richards, what reason would you have to give me that look of amazement? I live just a three-hour drive from New York, not in some other universe." Without a lot of ceremony, Ben added that he was hungry, that outside the sky was blue, and that he wanted to see the beaches of New York again. "So move your skinny rubber ass," he said to Reed, sticking a large cigar into his mouth.

Reed shook his head in disbelief. "I can't leave the office."

"Who's keeping you?" Ben asked, sitting in a chair that creaked ominously under his weight.

Reed didn't know what to say. That day he had no appointments. The only work he would do, most likely, would be checking his emails a thousand times or so. He was speechless, still amazed at this visit from his friend, and overwhelmed by the sudden revelation: he could do it. In fact, no one would keep him from doing it. He could leave the office at 11:30 on a weekday morning.

Even Annabel was somewhat astonished. She sat there watching as the two of them left the office, possibly appalled at Ben's orange rocky body and his five hundred pounds of sheer mass. Or perhaps just at the fact that

Reed was leaving the office. "See you around, little darling," Ben said, and her jaw dropped a little further.

Outside, the weather was balmy. Reed inhaled deeply, feeling a blend of remorse and a sense of freedom. Ben pointed him towards his pickup truck parked at an angle, wheels on the sidewalk. A young female traffic cop was writing out a ticket, but her face drained when she saw Ben coming. "My God, I know you... You were in that commercial... You're...you..."

"Sweetheart, if you're about to ask me whether I'm the Incredible Hulk, you'd do better to keep your mouth shut." He smacked a kiss into the air with his rock lips, and climbed into the vehicle. The truck sank a good five inches. "Reed, are you going to get in, or do you want to roll up in a circle and act as my spare tyre?"

They headed south. Manhattan looked like an anthill that had been ripped open. Ben immediately started cursing the midday traffic that threatened to delay his lunchtime. "I know a fabulous Japanese place along the road to Jamaica Bay," he announced.

"It'll take at least an hour to get down there!" Reed objected. "Jesus, I ought to be in the office," he added, even though he knew it was too late to change his mind. He settled back in his seat, suddenly relaxed, glancing over at his friend's profile. His rough facial features, the familiar physiognomy. The passage of time had partly smoothed out Ben's expression. But it was still Benjamin Grimm, the legendary rock man, a daunting colossus with a rocky body, his one-time adventure companion. Reed felt like reaching out and touching the rough, warm material that made up that body.

The sun went on shining along the road. They drove with the windows down. "I can't believe you left your idyllic village on a day like this," Reed resumed. "You must have had to give up a morning of great fishing."

"You're wrong about that," Ben sneered. "I can see you don't have a clue about fishing. Bright sunny days are no good for fishing." Ben jammed his foot down on the gas pedal as they crossed the bridge over the East River, with the enthusiasm of a Renaissance paladin riding to conquer new realms. He was enjoying the excursion. Although he had chosen to live holed up like a bear, he still liked to get out and about now and then. Ten years ago, he'd received an offer to appear in a television commercial for an insurance company: *your policy will be as solid as a rock*. He hadn't thought twice. He pocketed the money and fled north to New England, where he bought himself a house in a small coastal town and a pickup truck with the most spacious cab and the sturdiest seats available. For a while, after that commercial, he'd received other offers for television work. *Are you kidding?! Only losers appear on TV. People who are no good to the world any more. I have plenty of things to do here, in my little house, paid for with your very nice money.* He didn't want to hear about it. He'd got everything he needed, enough to live untroubled, and from then on he had decided to leave well enough alone.

They stopped for lunch not far from the Brooklyn Museum, in a Japanese restaurant where Ben said he had eaten before, and where they served awesome nattō beans. "Oh, no," Reed moaned. "Don't tell me you still eat that stuff."

"Of course I do. How do you think I stay in such fine shape?" Ben asked, launching into a rudimentary pirouette on the sidewalk, under the astonished eyes of the passersby.

At the restaurant, Ben ordered a double helping of soba noodles as well as various dishes of fried vegetables, along with his beloved nattō.

"Disgusting," Reed sniffed, as he watched his friend scoop the slimy beans into his mouth. "Who would ever have thought that Ben Grimm, the stone colossus, would eat that stuff?"

"Hey. I know that Brooklyn makes you irritable. But leave off my food and keep your nose in your own plate of tasteless white rice."

Half an hour later, they reached the ocean. Suddenly, the city fell away, and the glittering water advertised its presence as the truck hurtled across the steel bridge extending towards the strip of land of the Rockaways. They drove a couple of miles along the peninsula, until they decided to park the truck and walk, finally, on the sandy beach. "I can't believe it," said Reed, almost stunned to discover that here, an hour's drive from his office, such a sense of peace could be found. A warm breeze was blowing off the ocean. The sky was bright as a pearl, streaked slightly to the north by planes taking off from JFK. A few surfers were bobbing erect in the waves, and strollers went by up and down the beach.

Reed scrutinised the face of everyone he passed on the strand. Men and women, couples, solitary runners, white-haired men out walking their dogs. He eyed them curiously, unsettled, seized by an unexpected hunger for faces. He watched those people walking on the beach, on an early April day, sensing they were like him and close to him, and yet at the same time light years away. It was like looking at them from some remote standpoint. A motionless observation point, imperturbable, a place from which everything appeared clear and even ordinary: the history of each and every individual was stamped on their faces. He could recognise on the face of a mature person the kind of youngster they had been, he could intuit in the proud young men and women the feeble geriatrics they would someday become. He could see them like so many backlit figures. The life of each of them was there, in its entirety, on that beach, in that light.

Just then, someone came towards them. Reed shook himself out of his reverie. It was a little boy, a child of no more than five, and he was tiptoeing in their direction until coming to a stop in front of them, like an emissary bearing a message. He stood there, staring wide-eyed at Ben. The moment stretched out. Ben restrained himself for a few seconds, and then puffed out his cheeks: "Listen, kid. I know that your parents have told you different, but you're not the centre of the universe. Was there something you wanted to tell us? Did you want to describe the delight of two-ply Huggies diapers? Because if not, you see, my friend and I were taking a walk."

"Ben..." Reed admonished him. He leaned down towards the child, worried that Ben had frightened him, though the boy gave no sign of intimidation. "Hi," said Reed.

The boy finally seemed to notice that he was there, and in a bold voice asked: "Is your friend real?"

Ben puffed out his cheeks again, rolling his eyes.

"I think he wants to know if you're wearing a costume, Ben."

"I understand that, you old slab of gum." Then, to the child: "Of course I'm real, kid. I'm Benjamin Grimm, the Rock Man. Hey, we're superheroes. You know what a superhero is? Did your mom ever tell you about us?"

Like an actress answering her cue, a young woman broke away from a group not far away and came over to them at a trot. She reached down and took the little boy by the arm. "I'm sorry about this," she said with a smile.

"No problem at all," Ben replied, eyeing the young mother's tight-fitting T-shirt. "In fact, your son was entertaining us in the most *delightful* way."

Once they were alone again, the two men exchanged a glance. There was a moment of silence, then they burst into the inevitable laughter. "You realise," Reed asked, "that this is the kind of thing we'll remember one day, years from now, when we're decrepit codgers in a care home somewhere, passing our time reminiscing about old stories?"

"Speak for yourself," Ben replied. "I'm made of rock, the one thing I'll never be is a decrepit codger." He walked whistling through the sand, barefoot, shoes in hand. Apart from the episode with the little boy, most people seemed to pay no particular attention to him. In general, Ben did not pass unobserved. Maybe that day people just failed to recognise him, or like the little boy they assumed he was wearing a costume, or else that his rocky body belonged to just another nameless mutant of the many that filled the airwaves these days. Or maybe everyone recognised him. Maybe everyone recognised Ben, and recognised Reed, but decided to leave them in peace, lost in their thoughts, lost in the embrace of the ocean breeze, in the gentle sensation of being friends. They kept walking, with the sun in their faces, two old heroes in their sixties.

The sand was warm beneath their feet. The sound of the waves crashing on the shore hovered in the air, like a word on the point of blossoming into existence, a sweet and indefinable word, made up of scudding foam and a gleaming nostalgia. Reed took a deep breath, sensing the perfection of the moment. A heartbreaking curtain of calm. He wished he could shout to Ben, shout to all the people on the beach, shout to the open ocean and the row of apartment houses lining the beach. Shout Elaine's name. Shout the name of she who was absent. *If only she were here*, he thought, and wondered what she was doing now, and who she was with.

"After our phone call, I kept thinking," Ben said at that point, as if he'd guessed Reed's thoughts. His voice seemed to merge with the hypnotic sound of the tide. "I felt like I no longer recognised you, my friend, I told myself that you had never loved little darlings that were just too damned young, and that you'd always mocked guys who wound up with girls thirty years younger than them. That's what I told myself. Not because I wanted to accuse you of anything, but because I wanted to figure out where all this was coming from. I mean, with all the years we spent together... Whatever you do, it seems like it reflects on me, somehow. You know what I'm saying, Reed?"

Reed nodded in silence.

"I thought about the old days," Ben resumed, as his rocky feet sank into the sand. "I wondered whether this part of you had always been there... Even when you had everyone by the balls, and you were giving orders to the highest officials in the police department, and you went to the White House for dinner every other month. Even when you were Mister Fantastic, the leader of our group, the global superstar on the superhero scene. Even then, maybe there was this part of you, soft, almost feminine..." He stopped. "Don't get me wrong!" he said, slapping Reed's shoulder. "I'm not saying you're a girly man. I'm just wondering whether even then there was a part of you that was just waiting to...ahem...*die for love.*"

Reed was rubbing the shoulder where his friend had brought down his hand. "Ben, you don't exactly have a light touch." He shook his head and commented: "Thanks for thinking so much about me, but I don't really know what to say to you. With Sue, I don't think I ever showed this aspect you're talking about..."

Ben seemed to think that over, and burst out laughing: "Of course not! Sue would have punched you if you'd acted all romantic. She would have flipped a force field right in your face." With an amused smile, he walked on. "You and Sue were busy doing other things," he added. "You worked together. I imagine that what kept you together wasn't your obsession with one another as much as with your mission. You were convinced..."

"...that we were freeing the world," Reed finished the sentence. "Just like you, and like all the other superheroes." Reed sniffed the smell of the ocean. The noise of the waves crashing onto the shore kept getting louder. He went on walking next to his friend, at a steady pace, in the slowly declining afternoon light. "It was a long time ago, Ben. To think back on it now, it seems to me that we were all just playing a role. Each had their part to play. We believed in our ideal, and our lives were bent to fit it. The reporters told our stories and often exaggerated, the screenwriters made movies inspired by our lives. Half the kids on the planet adored us. There were student groups and politicians who sang our praises and there were others who opposed us, police chiefs who loved us and police chiefs who detested us. We stirred up a lot of passion. Maybe you're right, there was already a certain weakness in me, and yet the way I remember things, it was a whole different sensation. I felt like I was at the centre of something."

"Hey! I sure didn't mean to suggest that you're a weakling somehow. You're an example to me and you're like a brother, Reed. You always will be." Ben adjusted his hat, and pulled one of his cigars out of a pocket. "Hell. I'm not used to all this soppy talk. And all these people parading up and down the beach with smiles on their faces. Is that what our faces look like, too? They all look like they're on Xanax." He shook his head, put on his usual sarcastic smile, but immediately went back to a heartfelt tone: "Let me tell you something. You and me, our group and very few others, we managed to get out with our dignity intact. Without recycling ourselves as paid clowns on TV or idiots on some reality show, the way plenty of the old guard wound up doing." Reed nodded again. He wished he could just walk along in silence, now, and listen to the sound of the wind, but he let his friend go on: "If only there was someone who could take our place, we could stop worrying. We could put our hearts at rest."

"Times have changed," Reed pointed out. "Young people nowadays are different. I imagine that it is we who are often incapable of recognising what they can do."

Ben chomped his cigar. The topic of young people invariably started his heart fibrillating. "You know what I think? They don't know how to do a thing," he decreed.

Reed stood looking along the beach. "I hear that old Superman has opened a centre or a school of some sort around Park Slope," he ventured. "A place for young people with superpowers and with serious intentions."

"*Serious intentions?*" Ben's voice was more sceptical than ever. "Don't make me laugh. For years, people have been whispering about this idea of old Superman's." He stopped again, as the sun lit up his rocky face. "The truth is that the quality of kids has been declining over time, cut in half with each new generation, like some kind of radioactive isotope. Each new generation is worth half of the previous one. Which I'm sorry to say, seeing as you have a son."

"Franklin has no superpowers. He's not a real superhero, strictly speaking."

"I know that. I mean to say… You know how I feel about that boy. I'd sell my soul for him. Still, I can't stand the things he does, I don't like his image as a harmless alternative star, good for nothing but providing copy for the gossip columns. In his position, there's so much more he could do. He really could shatter the system."

"I'm not so sure about that," Reed sighed. He furrowed his brow and added, in a firm voice: "At times, I've found myself thinking exactly like you. But given the times we live in, I think that Franklin is even too active. The environmental movement is very grateful to him. And anyway, we can't expect everybody to be a revolutionary. Not now, not here."

At that point, Ben stared at him with a satisfied expression.

"What?" asked Reed.

"Nothing," Ben replied. "I don't agree with what you're saying, but let's just say that this is what I wanted. I wanted to talk with the old Reed. To hear him making sense, the way he used to."

Reed looked away. He didn't know whether he should feel complimented or offended. "Oh, Ben. I just went off the rails over a girl. It's not like I had a massive stroke or anything."

Ben's smile broadened. "Excellent," he said, like a doctor pronouncing a diagnosis. "You seem about to get back on your feet."

They turned around and headed back, taking their time, as the sun sank behind them. Their shadows stretched out before them. Reed stared at the sand, looking for the footprints of their previous walk in the opposite direction, trying to capture the sensations: the wind, the heat on his back, his closeness with Ben, that sense of timelessness. It seemed impossible that an afternoon like that could ever come to an end. Impossible that everyone was about to leave, the walkers on the beach, the little boy from before, the youngsters with their surfboards.

Reed sighed. Sunsets always saddened him. He knew that everyone was leaving. He knew that all he could expect at home was an empty apartment. Still, he could do it, even Ben had told him so. Get back on his feet.

He kept listening to the sound of the ocean. He tried to impress it on his memory, to capture it like a seashell, and to keep from shivering, now, as the sun sank into the horizon.

*

It was April 11th, and although that day was destined to go down in history, it started like any other day. The dawn came up suddenly, setting fire to the few smoke-grey clouds that had been caught napping in the sky. Aeroplanes glided slowly out of the east, fresh from their crossings over the watery wastes of the Atlantic, bringing with them the melancholy of old Europe. Ferry boats heavy with freight docked at the wharfs of the harbour, their bows glowing in the fiery dawn, as the East River and the Hudson flowed past impassively, absorbing the heat of the new day.

Up and down the riverbanks the first runners appeared, chests puffed out, already panting, lungs working to burn oxygen. Oxygen was burning in the apartments, too, in the gas flames of the hobs cooking breakfast, in the ovens of the thousand bakeries of downtown Manhattan. The bus engines coughed into life in chorus. The taxis slid along the artery of Broadway, agile as so many fish swimming upstream, leaving a trail of small puffs of smog in the morning air, transporting their human cargo of travellers, early-rising managers, journalists with laptops already on their knees, lovers returning home after the night's adventure. Police officers at the end of their shift were driving home, eager to strip off and climb into bed next to the warm body of their woman, or their man, while others who were just starting their shift roamed the streets, observing the world with a vague disgust.

The hum of the city grew louder. The animals in the Central Park Zoo listened with amazement, unable to grasp the mystery of that man-made world, so alien to them, whose noises came from beyond the trees of the park. The animals in the Bronx Zoo cried out in chorus, in the morning, and so did the animals in the Queens Zoo and the Prospect Park Zoo, perhaps torn by the yearning for their lost freedom, and possibly sensing the tragedy around them. The unmistakable vibration of the human tragedy. Unhappy lovers stirred uneasily side by side, in their sweat, lost in the last dreams of the night, while lonely men woke up between cold sheets, or at the table where they'd fallen asleep in front of their computers, with a message still blinking on the screen from some anonymous chat-room user. Those who had stayed up all night now jerked to attention, and studied the light filtering into the room, with weary eyes and feverish foreheads. Day had dawned. Thousands of cell phones were being turned on, thousands of computers awakened from their sleep, and thousands of television screens were being illuminated, as if by enchantment, to spit out their stream of news.

Reed opened his eyes around six, drifting in the tail end of some tangled dream. He'd been dreaming about Elaine, of that he was certain, because his penis was pulsating, lolling on his belly, dreary, useless, and he sensed that his body was slightly deformed, his arms extended by an inch or two, or perhaps his chest larger than normal. He breathed deeply and whipped the sheet aside. Every morning, in the fragile instant of the first awakening, the thought of Elaine struck him like a slap in the face.

He took refuge in the shower, trying to rinse away all traces of nocturnal melancholy, though a sense of anxiety persisted. He barely managed to gulp down a little food. Small stabs of panic pricked at his stomach, inexplicably, and he decided that as usual it must be about her. The thought of her absence. The thought that Elaine wasn't near him, eating breakfast, eating the food that he had prepared. Without her, Reed's kitchen resembled an empty stage set. *Cut it out,* he told himself. *Even if she were here, she wouldn't be eating your food. She's certainly on some special pre-mission diet.*

He forced his thoughts to change direction, and yet that anxiety persisted. He could feel his heart beating unnaturally, his throat tied in a knot, and tiny shivers running up from his hip. Reed didn't understand. It was as if his body knew something that he didn't know yet. Afterwards, he would think back to those last hours, that last morning of blissful unawareness, that blind disquiet that ran through him. He'd think back to those moments, wondering how he could have failed to see what was coming. That event that was drawing closer, heading straight at him, fatal as a house fire, silent as an eclipse.

He spent the following hours in a sort of limbo, incapable of concentrating, losing the thread of his thoughts, leaving even the simplest sentences half-finished. He finally told Annabel just to hold all calls. Late that morning he took a car, travelling across the city, whose streets were immersed in a dreamlike glow. A white sun scattered an elusive liquid light, and in that light reality seemed to flicker, like a mirage, in every gust of wind. Deep-reaching shivers shook Reed when he got out of the car. The wind was sneaking under his clothes. Out of the corner of his eye, he spotted a paparazzo loitering around a few yards away.

For the past few days, Reed had regained the interest of the gossip columns. Reports of his relationship with a younger woman must have reached a newsroom somewhere. How odd that it should have happened just as that relationship was at its bitter end, and when Elaine had in fact left New York. The paparazzo wouldn't be getting many compromising photos today. Reed let out a sigh. Throughout his career, he'd been very skilful at eluding those columns. He'd taken care not to toss his name into the cauldron of their vapid chatter, their overimaginative ravings, not to offer his likeness to their greedy pages. Even at the height of his exploits as a superhero, he had never been fond of that kind of attention. He'd never liked having a lot of eyes on him, never even particularly enjoyed being the object of applause. That was why more than one person had called him paranoid, but Reed felt sure that he was anything but. People didn't understand the difference between paranoia and discretion. People didn't understand the meaning of dignity.

The paparazzo loitered for another few minutes, like a hesitant shark, lurking outside the plate glass windows of the restaurant that Reed had entered. Then he vanished. Inside, Reed had joined the members of the scientific advisory board of a research institute where he sat as an honorary member. A dozen elderly luminaries who wouldn't look that sexy, all things considered, to the readers of a gossip column. Reed took a seat between two ancient professors. The presence of the paparazzo had distracted him for a moment from his restlessness, but now his mind began wandering again. It was impossible to concentrate on the conversations of his fellow diners. Impossible to focus on their faces. Impossible to focus on their manicured hands, dotted with liver spots, as they waved in the air in elegant emphasis, underscoring some concept. Impossible to listen to the amusing anecdotes recounted by one of them, impossible even to fix his eyes on the menu. Reed wound up ordering ginger chicken and a salad, the first two items he noticed on the day's specials, without knowing that the flavour of those two dishes would remain in his throat, for the rest of his days, like the taste of a last meal.

Then it was time to leave the restaurant and get back in the car, as the wind swept the city with increasingly powerful gusts. People walked down the street clutching their clothes to their bodies, as if they were afraid they'd be stripped naked in the clear afternoon light. The rustle of the wind and the hum of the traffic amplified each other, creating a sound reminiscent of a distant scream. An indefinable black hole had opened up inside Reed, absorbing all thought, all attention, all sense of reality... He walked back with relief into the familiar shell of his office. He went into the bathroom to splash some water on his face. He looked in the mirror, waiting, observing his own restless eyes, the glittering silver of his hair. *What's going on, Mister Fantastic?*

He went back to his desk. He brushed the keyboard of his computer, checked what emails he'd received while he was out. The message was there, apparently innocuous, blending in with the other messages in the queue, with no special features to call out its nature, its crucial importance. Oh, damn! The answer from Houston. For an instant Reed thought he'd understood, and the idea that the nervous anxiety he'd felt all day might just be the product of a presentiment of that message gave him a short-lived sense of calm. *Oh, that's why. That's the explanation.* But after he read the message nothing changed, and the same anxiety kept slithering through his stomach.

There was no explanation offered for the delay. Reed imagined that the Johnson Space Center was in full pre-launch chaos. However, his request had finally been accepted. He'd got what he wanted. He could drop in there, a few days before launch, to remind Elaine of his existence. He could do it. He'd been invited. Reed should have been satisfied, yet he felt no enthusiasm. No triumph. Only a sudden weariness which made him close his eyes and lean his head back against the chair, with a sigh. *It must be on account of that lunch. That ginger chicken still sitting in my stomach.* He felt his thoughts grow heavy, plummeting into a distant elsewhere...

He found himself in a dimly lit room, where sound spread in a muffled fashion. When he tried to move, he sensed a liquid resistance around him, as if he were at the bottom of a swimming pool. In fact, it looked like the bottom of a swimming pool. Around him there were other people, silent, motionless, and Reed started parading through them, feeling their gazes. There was Annabel and the paparazzo he'd seen a short while before. There was Elaine, and Ben, and the little boy on the beach, and Bernard Dunn, the NASA officials, the psychologist Helen Kippenberg, the astronauts he'd known, and Mrs. Glasseye. There were all the members of the scientific board of advisers with whom he'd eaten lunch, the consultants to the Richards Foundation, its financiers, Raymond Minetta, the doorman from his building, Detective Dennis De Villa, the Ecuadorian driver, and the other drivers he'd had recently. There really were a lot of people. All of them, dressed elegantly, watching him wordlessly, and he was amazed at how many of them there were, how many people he knew. "You're all here," he said. Last of all, he found Sue, his wife, who was waiting for him at the far end of the room, as pale as an ice statue.

Sue shook her head, and her lips barely parted. "Oh Reed," she said, in a heartbroken voice. "You still don't understand." Reed started trembling. "Look around, Reed. We're not all here. Don't you see who's missing?" Reed's eyes ran over the room, instinctively seeking out Elaine, and he saw her, there, in the midst of the crowd. Elaine was there. Reed turned to look at his wife without understanding. "Reed, don't you see who's missing?" Reed concentrated then, feeling something begin to emerge, from a deep place, the seed of something he had always known. It was rising to the surface. It was taking shape. A trace of truth that he could feel inside himself, uncertain at first, then clearer and clearer, hard as a diamond, painful as a blade, oh my God, my God, something unutterable, something so terrifying that it was starting to make him weep, even before he knew what on earth it was. He was about to know what it was. He sensed that he was about to find out. Then there was a sound, small at first, then increasingly insistent…

Reed shook himself awake. He found himself back in his office, dazed, agitated. The late-afternoon sunlight was slanting in through the window and the phone on his desk was ringing. Reed stared at it, his thoughts still befuddled by his brief sleep. A blade of anguish sliced into his throat. He hoped that the phone would just stop ringing, stop bothering him. After all, he had asked Annabel to hold his calls. After all, he'd just emerged from a weird nightmare. He had the right not to pick up, the right to do nothing. But the phone went on ringing, and he decided to pick up the icy receiver, with a trembling hand. "Hello?" he finally said.

There was a long silence. Through the receiver he could hear Annabel's broken breathing. His skin crawled in a single, violent wave of goosebumps. "Annabel? Annabel, what's happening?"

"Reed…" He'd never heard Annabel's voice so overwrought. "Reed… It's Mister Grimm on the phone for you…" She seemed to be about to add something, then she gulped back a sudden sob, and brusquely transferred Ben's call. The phone plunged into abysmal silence. "Ben… Ben, is that you?"

The first thing he heard was the sobbing. Ben's rocky voice seemed to have shattered into a thousand pieces, a thousand chaotic sobs that, for some reason, made Reed think of the chirping of some nocturnal songbird. "Ben, what is this, some sort of joke? Ben, do you mind telling me what's going on?"

Then Ben took a deep, enormous breath, and in a voice Reed had never heard before, he shouted: "My God, Reed! My God! Reed!…"

The phone dropped out of Reed's hand. He leapt to his feet, panting, gripped by a dizziness so powerful that it forced him to lean against the wall. He grabbed his head, telling himself he was still stuck in that dream, in that mysterious dream, in that part of reality where nothing was definitive, where nothing had consequences. But here, in this part of reality, the receiver was still spitting out Ben's howling voice. Reed staggered across the office, like a drunk, until he reached the door and violently yanked it open, causing a rush of air. Sheets of paper flew off Annabel's desk. He and she stared at each other, horrified, appalled, each terrorised by the other, and Annabel's face was streaked with tears.

The television was on. Reed looked at it, hypnotised, as if he were seeing it for the first time, studying the images of a special edition from ABC News. Footage shot from a helicopter showed a column of smoke rising from a tall building, dark, dense, practically motionless, curving like a giant question mark. Reed looked at the smoke. He looked at the gutted building. He found the scene familiar, he recognised Manhattan. That building. He let out a moan. The saliva dried up in his mouth, and the blood slowed down in his veins, nearly congealing. Everything became infinitely slow. He turned to look out of the window: he saw the same column of smoke down there, beyond the line of buildings across the street. He saw the half-dozen police helicopters, apparently immobile, hanging in mid-air. He saw the direction from which the smoke was streaming, and all of the elements started to slide together, lock into place. All his suspicions. All his fears. He let out another moan, incredulous, while his thoughts began to collapse, hopelessly, into a state of panic.

He left the office at a dead run, pursued by Annabel's screams, and hurled himself into the elevator. Downstairs in the lobby, he set off at a run again, shoving past the doorman, who was yelling too and trying to stop him, for some reason, like he wanted to protect him, to spare him the horror of the outside world. In the street the silence was surreal. The only sound was that of the helicopters and the hollow echoes of the sirens. Traffic had stopped, and people were out of their cars, out of the buses, their faces tilted upwards, staring in dismay at the column of smoke. Reed ran. There was nothing else he could do. He ran for blocks and blocks, as in dreamlike slow-motion. He ran breathlessly, with the impulse to scream, cry, vomit, his chest shaking with the slow, deep thumps of his heartbeat. *Don't let it be true. Let it just be a mistake. Don't let this be reality, and tomorrow let this all be a weird memory, funny, almost, just make it not be real, don't let it happen...* A crowd of people was coming towards him, moving away from the area of the explosion. Men and women of all ages, of all races, with expressions of shock, eyes wet with tears, faces, legs, arms, haircuts, expensive suits, cut-price clothes, plans for dinner, cell phones in their pockets, loved ones in their minds, people to call, *it happened, it really happened, in our neighbourhood, at the George Hotel, apparently it was a bomb, there have been victims, one of them is...* Men and women, bodies, one after another like a dense stream, and Reed pushing against them, labouring, working his way upstream, he alone pushing against the crowd, still shouting, panting, until he got there, exhausted, standing at the foot of the wounded building.

He froze. He stood there looking up at the George Hotel, at the gaping hole on the twenty-ninth floor, the flames that shot out intermittently. Teams of firemen surrounded the building, while swarms of newsmen rushed about, appalled, excited, shouting snatches of news into microphones. Women in tears wandered around in dressing gowns, probably guests of the hotel who had been evacuated, and a half-naked man walked around in a state of shock, like a prophet in the middle of the desert. Reed saw everything. He saw the blood-red paint of the fire trucks, the darting tongues of flame from the hotel. He took it all in at a glance, a broad and detailed glance, a glance that seemed to spread out, for an instant, practically to infinity.

He took a few hesitant, wavering steps forward, just as it dawned on the first few reporters who he was, and they began clustering around him, as a policeman came towards him, both arms spread out, perhaps to stop him or else to embrace him. Reed collapsed on the policeman. He tried to stretch his arms upwards, towards the gaping hole in the building, towards the murderous flames, but his arms fell among the crowd, two arms a few yards long, two helpless tentacles. The policeman gripped him tight. He was shouting at him to calm down. Reed felt quite calm, actually, calm enough to observe the faces of the journalists packed around him, in an instant of disconcerting silence. Calm enough to hear the voice of one of them, not far away, announcing the news into a microphone: *a sad day for New York, a sad day for the world. At about six o'clock this evening, April 11th, an explosive device planted by nameless attackers destroyed the health club of the George Hotel, in the heart of Manhattan, causing numerous injuries and two deaths, one of which appears to have been the young star of our time, Franklin Richards, America's most beloved son.*

*

For days, it was the only news covered in the media. The nation was in shock. The day after the attack various national newspapers published the same headline, FRANKLIN IS DEAD, as if they were incapable of using any other words or devising any other phrases. The picture of America's most beloved son filled every cover and was splashed across every front page. Regular television programming was scrapped. Screens obsessively broadcast the images of the building in flames, rerunning the horrified faces of the eyewitnesses, the heartbreaking arrival of Franklin's father, the ex-superhero, and his futile attempt to extend his arms towards the burning twenty-ninth floor of the hotel. They broadcast, over and over, the bunches of flowers piled up at the foot of the George Hotel. They broadcast the thousands of young people who took to the streets, on the evening after the attack, singing Franklin's name in chorus. They broadcast the documentary on Franklin Richards, which had already been shown on the air, promoting it as a world premiere and chalking up record viewing figures. They broadcast interviews with famous ex-superheroes who had known him as a boy, members of Greenpeace with whom he had worked, young starlets with whom he was said to have had relationships. They broadcast the interview with Raymond Minetta, owner of the George Hotel, replaying again and again the part where Minetta burst into tears, with a grimace of pain, repeating in a nasal voice: *that boy, that poor boy.* They broadcast the statement of the Secretary of State, who appeared on TV immediately after the attack to reassure the nation and declare that the cowardly act of terrorism would not strike fear into the heart of the United States of America. They broadcast interviews with officials of the special investigative teams who were working day and night, it was reported, to find out who was behind this crime. They broadcast the face of Detective Dennis De Villa, his red eyes, emotional and strangely cold at the same time, his regular features, his solemn expression as he answered the journalist's frenzied questions. The world had a thousand questions. *Did they know who had planted the bomb?* They still weren't sure who had masterminded the bombing, though the theory of a clandestine organisation was gaining strength. A deadly group whose aim, it was believed, was the murder of a number of individuals with ties to the old world of the superheroes. *Franklin wasn't a superhero, strictly speaking. Might he have been a chance victim of this attack?* For now the police weren't sure whether the bomb set off on the twenty-ninth floor of the building, while the younger Richards was in the famous panoramic sauna of the George Hotel, was meant to kill him or his father, Reed Richards, who was known to frequent the same health club. *Why weren't the Richardses under security protection? Had there not been indications of an impending attack?* The police had explored the idea of giving Reed Richards a security detail, and had contacted him on more than one occasion, but there had never been any confirmation of the need for that measure. As for the younger Richards, implementing a plan for his protection would have been impossible, as he had been overseas until the day before the attack. *Was this attack linked in any way with the murder of Batman?* There were surely ties with Batman's murder. *Were there likely to be any other murder attempts?* Unfortunately the police had no way of ruling out that possibility.

At first the television programmes chose to overlook Reed, disconcerted as they were by the reactions of that dry-eyed father, restrained even in that circumstance, faithful to his reputation as a controlled individual. Except for his dramatic arrival at the scene of the bombing, Reed had avoided the television cameras. He gave no interviews. He wept no tears in public. He had immediately made himself available to the police, offering his help in the investigation, and he had issued a laconic statement in which he declared his determination to do everything within his power, by any and all means possible, to catch his son's murderers. Strong words. Efficient words. Two days later, Reed assaulted an overly intrusive cameraman, damaging his equipment, and finally everyone understood. Reed Richards' mask was about to crack. His self-control was on the verge of giving way like a faulty dam. Just wait a little, and his tears would flow, along with the tears of all the others, along with the tears of the entire nation.

*

In the first few days, something similar to rage had acted as an anaesthetic, leaving Reed empty of feeling. He was unable to cry. He was unable to respond to the embraces of the people crowding into his home, he couldn't eat or sleep. Everyone told him to get some rest. How was he supposed to rest? He was too busy thinking about Franklin's murderers, whoever they turned out to be, that band of fanatics who had toiled away in the shadows, emerged from the shadows, and vanished back into the shadows, while Reed now sat nailed in place beneath a scalding shaft of light, the light of horror, the blinding spotlight of grief.

He sat there brooding, determined to track them down, one by one, at least find them, at least get a glimpse. He sat there fantasising about wrapping his arms around those murderers. He dreamt of holding them with homicidal strength, like a boa constrictor, squeezing them with his elastic body. He sat there, swearing revenge. He sat there breathing, keeping his eyes wide open, minute by minute, in the strange hallucination that the world around him had become: so absurd, so luminous. He sat there cursing Raymond Minetta, ridiculous man that he was, who had sent Franklin a watch, a goddamned watch, with an invitation to frequent his health club, where he had been vulnerable to the attack… He sat there cursing the police, that flock of nobodies, and that Detective De Villa with his red-streaked eyes, and his fellow detectives who were unable to come up with a shred of evidence. Unable to say where this clandestine band of fanatics had come from, who was their mastermind, whether any suspicious individuals had been observed passing through the hotel building. How could he rest, until someone could tell him something, anything at all?

He sat there nodding at each formulaic expression of condolence. He sat there handling the details of the funeral. He sat there hating everyone around him, all those people dressed in black, capable of doing nothing but looking at him with faces oozing concern. Hating Ben with every fibre, the way he was constantly underfoot consoling him, or being consoled, hating Szepanski and his cosmetically enhanced face, always offering him a calming injection, and more than anyone else, hating Annabel, that anorexic idiot, locked in the bathroom to throw up every few minutes. My God, was it really too much to ask for a competent assistant at a time like this?

Rage had surged into him like an electric discharge. He responded with hostility to other people's glances. People treated him in a strange way. They spoke slowly, they blew words at him as if they were trying to make them penetrate into him. *Reed, you're in a state of shock. Reed, Franklin is dead.* Of course he was dead. He knew that for himself, he wasn't a child. He knew the meaning of the word *dead*. He could feel that word bobbing on the surface of his consciousness, he recognised the sound of it. It was one of the simplest words in the language and he understood what it meant. The last thing he needed was other people's help. He felt no need to hold their hands. He didn't like other people's hands. And he didn't need their grieving looks. He was allergic to being looked at, by people or by television cameras. That was why he'd assaulted that cameraman, when he loomed up before him two days after the bombing. He'd felt hatred for the cameraman, so he hit him: wasn't that logical, the most normal thing he could have done? So the first few days went by filled with fury, filled with logic, with actions tied to other actions, as if a back-up engine had started in his brain, and was steadily preserving cause-and-effect relationships.

Reed, you need to go to see him. They've finished the autopsy. You and Sue can go and take the body away. He found himself standing in a chilly room, immersed in the light of a neon tube. It was a room at the coroner's laboratory, and that body lying on the table, covered with a sheet, must be their son. He and Sue drew closer to the table. Sue was wearing dark clothes, and didn't say a word. Reed avoided her gaze. They had seen each other since the day of the attack, of course, but they'd never really spoken, as if there was no need, as if *talking* had become something impossible by now. Nor did they talk there, in that room filled with the smell of formaldehyde. They did nothing more than to stop beside the table. Without making any conscious decision, Reed reached out and seized the hem of the sheet.

It was a blackened corpse. The face was gone, charred, and not a trace remained of the hair. The chest was a road map of patches ranging from black to red, depending on how much the skin had resisted the heat, with the large Y shape of the autopsy incision, stitched back up hastily, like some incomprehensible signature. Reed looked at the body. He wasn't overwhelmed by the sight: he'd seen dead bodies in his time. He'd seen burnt, skinned, exploded corpses. In the old days, that was just part of the fighting. What he did feel was uncertainty. There was nothing in that blackened body on a lab table that resembled his son. He stood there, for a long string of seconds, trying to recognise a detail, a fragment that would allow him to draw a line between his son, the person he had helped to bring into the world, and that corpse. He couldn't see it. There was no evidence that the body belonged to Franklin, and he was just about to say so to Sue, in the grip of a demented sense of relief, when his gaze happened to rest on the corpse's right hand.

It was intact. It was clenched into a fist, in a defenceless way that reminded

Reed, somehow, of the clenched fist of a newborn baby. Reed studied the hand. He stared at the knuckles, the creases of the fingers, until something stirred inside him, and the image that he still had of Franklin, the blond youth, the athletic young man, the pride of liberal America, suddenly aligned with the corpse before his eyes.

He felt a sort of dolorous spark. Reed closed his eyes, opened them again, and understood that in that instant the universe had changed. *It's me. I'm right here. All this is real, Franklin is dead.*

The cloak of stunned bafflement of the past few days slipped off him. The truth came down upon him like a sword. His mouth fell open, his eyes lifted. He saw his wife standing in a halo of light, an older woman, her hair a mix of blond and grey, her face still pretty, but too pale, twisted in a grimace of intolerable pain. He saw her mouth, and recognised in it the mouth of his son. He saw her eyes wide open, and in them he recognised the eyes of his son. He mirrored himself in her eyes, and she saw her own reflection in his, and the torment passed back and forth, from one to the other, over and over again, strengthening as it did, leaving them paralysed, speechless, unable to touch, each on the opposite side of the table. Each of them chained to the eyes of the other, as if suspended in some equilibrium, aware that the minute they untangled themselves they would both fall, hurtling in opposite directions, plummeting down into horrifying chasms, towards their own lonely hells.

*

The hardest day of Reed Richards' life dawned cloudless, from early morning, dominated by a cruel and magnificent sun. Light filtered down onto the city like a ghost, whitening the streets and polishing the air.

In mid-morning Ben showed up, wearing a large pair of sunglasses which made him look like an old-fashioned gangster. "Here," he said to Reed, holding out another pair of sunglasses.

"I don't need them," Reed said. "Never worn sunglasses in my life." He was sitting on the edge of the bed, in his bedroom, already dressed for the ceremony. From the adjoining room came the muffled voices of Annabel and Doctor Szepanski.

"Take them," Ben insisted, slipping the sunglasses into the breast pocket of Reed's suit jacket. His rocky hands seemed incredibly delicate. He stood there in front of Reed for a few seconds before asking: "Did you get any sleep last night?"

"I don't know," Reed answered, turning his head away. Ben's physical proximity wounded his eyes. He had always assumed that in this kind of situation reality would simply blur, dimming like in a dream, but since he'd laid eyes on Franklin's corpse the day before, everything appeared crystal-clear and very close. Faces and objects seemed to press against him. Now that the blinding rage had vanished, things appeared so distinct. So sharp-edged. "I don't know," he said again, turning away even further. "I might have closed my eyes, I'm not really sure. I don't think it makes a lot of difference."

"It'll make a difference soon. You're going to need some strength, Reed. There's going to be a big crowd, and you'll need to be strong."

Maybe Ben was right. When they left later in a car with dark-tinted windows and drove across the city, the streets were half-deserted. There was almost no traffic. Many shops had their shutters rolled down. The waiters in the few restaurants that were open stood, behind the plate glass windows, like guards standing watch over a long-lost monument. The mayor had proclaimed a city-wide day of mourning. New York was weeping over its latest wound, the death of its latest idol. In the pitiless sun, groups of people walked in silence towards the cathedral. Half of the city seemed to have converged on the site of the ceremony.

Looking out of the car window, Ben began to cry. At first Reed didn't notice because his friend was wearing dark glasses, and his tears flowed silently. "This city still has a soul," Ben said. "Everyone loved him, they really did love him."

Reed looked at that rock face and felt an urge to move away from him and from his tears, but the car was too small. He couldn't get any further away. So he lifted his arms and took the rough wet face of his friend in his hands. He held it close.

"Forgive me for what I said," Ben sobbed. "That day on the beach. When I said that Franklin wasn't doing enough. When I said…" By now the car was within sight of the cathedral. Hard to say how big the crowd outside the church must have been. At a glance, tens of thousands of people. Special military squads were patrolling the neighbourhood, dozens of television crews dotted the scene. Ben glanced out of the window. He gave himself a shake, rummaging through his pockets in search of a cigar, to regain his self-control.

Reed let go of his face. His friend's tears were scalding his fingers.

Ben took a chomp of his cigar and spat it out in disgust. He started crying again. "They killed him because they were trying to harm us," he said, as the car pulled up to the kerb. His massive body vibrated like a meteorite. He grabbed Reed by the arm, and added with a burst of rage: "They killed him because they've got it in for us, for what we were, for what we represented. But I still can't understand it. Whatever we old superheroes might ever have done, how could they bring themselves to do this to us?"

"I don't know, Ben." Reed wriggled free. He put on the sunglasses that his friend had given him and opened the car door.

The crowd fell silent. A sudden vacuum seemed to settle onto the street as Reed got out of the car. Tall, stiff, alone. Thousands of throats tightened, while he entered the cathedral, his shoulders bent under the weight of thousands of eyes.

Inside, in the dim shadows of one of the largest cathedrals on earth, another crowd was waiting. The country's most important men and women filled the front pews. Reed was escorted to the central pew. Sue was there, motionless, her face as white as ice. Reed sat down next to her. In the absolute silence, he could hear the rustle of their clothes coming into contact, and Sue's jagged breathing. He could imagine the effort and the pain it cost her to sit there, under all those eyes, without giving in to the temptation to turn invisible. The same effort that it cost him to stay still, without deforming, without plunging his hands into his own chest, into his hip, to try to tear the pain out of there. A million shards of glass seemed to be plunged into his rubber flesh.

It was Sue who had insisted on a public funeral. *For Franklin. Because that's how he would have wanted it.* So they sat there, side by side, motionless, the Rubber Man and the Invisible Woman, while the pipes of the majestic organ swelled, spreading their music throughout the nave. At that sound, the crowd shivered. A thousand necks bent forward. A thousand hands gripped the wooden benches. The mystery of death was among them, once again, with all its vast, indifferent power.

This is the day of our heartache, uttered the amplified voice of the bishop of New York. *Today anyone who still has a heart can feel it breaking. This is the day of the heartbreak of our America...* Reed listened, his attention fluctuating. He heard the speech in waves, alternating moments of unbearable intensity with moments when he listened from a distance, from some remote and unknown place. *That scene down there: the funeral of my son.* From time to time he felt the urge to turn around, look behind him, and search for a certain pair of green eyes. The gleam of a reddish head of hair. He knew that she had come, that Elaine was there, somewhere in the crowd, and the thought wrapped itself around his head like a bandage, without alleviating the pain.

At the end of the ceremony he was finally able to turn around, but what he saw, with a start, was an army of people marching towards him and Sue. It was time for the condolences. The parents of the dead man were surrounded. The first mourner to shake Reed's hand was the President of the United States, with an indecipherable grimace on his face. Reed shook the president's hand under a barrage of photographers' flashes, despite the contempt he felt for that man. He accepted his conventional words of loss. A disagreeable sensation remained in his hand, and yet at the same time a hint of ridiculous gratitude. The president was followed by the mayor, the chief of police, the editors of the New York dailies, the head of NASA, diplomatic representatives of major foreign countries, and officials from the world's leading scientific institutions. Not all those people commanded Reed's esteem. He shook each of their hands with nausea, yet with gratitude, wishing in spite of himself that those hands would never come to an end, that they'd go on touching him, as if those hands, with their damp palms, could suffocate the fire inside him.

Then came the family of the other victim of the attack, a businessman from Boston who just happened to have been in the George Hotel at the wrong time, from all the police had been able to gather. The widow came up to him, dignified, vaguely hostile, holding her son, perhaps six years old, by the hand. Reed embraced her with a lump in his throat. "My husband was a big fan of yours when he was a boy," the woman said. "Who'd have ever thought…"

"I'm sorry," Reed whispered.

"We need to be strong. God will help us," she sobbed.

Reed was on the verge of collapse. Out of the corner of his eye he could see the television cameras ready to ambush him, drawing closer and closer, waiting implacably for the collapse, the tears of Mister Fantastic. The man who could once stretch out his arms for miles and miles and save a boat that was being swept away by the ocean waves. The man who could join together, like an enormous elastic band, the two ends of a collapsing bridge. Mister Fantastic himself was about to collapse. They could sense it, they could predict it, and they leaned closer now, as another great hero, the greatest of all time, made his way laboriously up the aisle of the church.

It was old Superman. The crowd parted before him. The living legend made his way forward slowly, trembling, helping himself along with a cane. He wore his old costume with the red cape. Reed walked towards him, and the two aged heroes, distraught, embraced before the cameras of the whole planet.

Superman wasn't alone. Reed received embraces from Captain America, Daredevil, Mystique, Thor, and all the others. The entire old guard of superheroes had come. Some of them wore their old battle costumes. The following day, the newspapers would publish photographs of the ceremony, with a list of those who had attended, as well as those who weren't there: Batman, whose brutal murder was the subject of an ongoing criminal trial. And poor Robin, now practically forgotten, who had also been killed in mysterious circumstances several years ago.

Namor was there too. The so-called Prince of Atlantis was dressed in an unprecedented black suit. As Reed embraced him he caught a whiff of his brackish scent, the scent of ocean, seaweed, and tears, and it dawned on him that he'd never seen that man wear clothes before. Reed remembered that Franklin had always enjoyed making fun of Namor, *that elderly exhibitionist. The man without a shirt. The prince of pectorals.* He imagined seeing Namor through the gleaming, endlessly amused eyes of Franklin. He looked at Namor with his pointy ears, moving awkwardly in his black cotton suit, and he saw him through the eyes of his son, the cheerful young man always ready to laugh. He saw the other superheroes, their sagging faces, he saw the television stars waiting nearby, ready for their moment on camera. He saw Dr. Szepanski with his too-shiny face, probably the result of a quick facelift done especially for his appearance at the funeral. He saw all of this and, for an instant, he sensed how grotesque it was, and sensed something unexpected, almost unrecognisable. A spasm of dark, dolorous sarcasm.

At that point a panting lament broke out in the church. Raymond Minetta was sobbing, leaning against a column and shouting incomprehensible words. Embarrassment spread through the crowd. Many looked away, perhaps feeling pity, or maybe remembering that old rumour. The cilice. The ball-crushing torture. There was a strange undulating surge in the church, as grief washed up against a wave of guilty amusement. Reed wondered if this is what Sue had had in mind when she'd said that Franklin would have wanted a public funeral. He sought her out with his gaze, but just then she was squeezed, practically suffocated in the emotional embrace of Namor. *There's something grotesque about funerals. Franklin would be laughing at us*, he thought, but it did nothing to calm his torment.

Last of all, Mrs. Glasseye came forward. Reed trembled, afraid he would break into tears. He didn't try to avoid her glance this time, and she refrained from the usual provocations. This was no time for those sorts of games. It was time to look at each other, to embrace in the awareness of what they'd lost. Reed knew that she could understand him. He knew the real tragedy that woman had experienced. "Reed," she whispered. "Listen to me. Listen to me, Reed. The coming days will be hard. The coming months will be hard. The coming years will be hard. The pain won't go away, but you'll become stronger. If you're strong enough, you'll find something to believe in, something to have faith in, and that will help you."

Reed held her. He could smell her sweet-scented breath, her hard breasts pressing against him.

"Your work," she went on. "You and I were born to hold tight to our work, weren't we?" she said with a wise smile.

Mrs. Glasseye moved on to Sue. The two women looked at each other, intuiting the other's emotions. Sue knew as well. She knew that in the car crash that cost her her eye, years ago, the other woman had also lost her young son. That was her tragedy. That was her grief.

And so they embraced. The two mothers who had lost their sons stood with their arms wrapped around one another, each breathing through the other's hair. That day Mrs. Glasseye was revealing a secret. If anyone still wondered which was her real eye, the mystery was solved once and for all. Her real eye was weeping.

*

The most spectacular funeral of the decade was over, and the body of America's most beloved son had been reduced to ashes, and the television crews had gone back to their studios. Hundreds of people had embraced the parents of the dead man—intending to transmit their warmth to them, but in reality leaving them sucked dry like statues eroded by the caress of too many hands. The crowd had begun to scatter, but the day wasn't entirely over. Reed noticed that Sue was leaving. He saw her go, surrounded by a small entourage of friends and assistants. Breaking away from Ben and the other superheroes who had stayed behind, he hurried to catch up with her.

"Sue…"

They were outside, at the kerbside, and the light had softened by this time of day. A car was pulling up silently to pick up Sue. "Are you leaving?" asked Reed.

Sue turned to look at him. She was wearing dark glasses too.

"We'll have to decide what to do with his things. We'll have to go to his apartment," Reed said. The words in his mouth were as heavy as pieces of lead.

"We'll talk about that," she said in a distant voice. She adjusted the sunglasses on her face. Her expression was harsh and pinched. "I have to go," she whispered.

"My God," he said, fighting back. "This thing happened to both of us, Sue. He was *our* son. Don't treat me like an enemy." Reed gulped, exhausted by the weight of his own words: "Are you punishing me because you think that Franklin was killed by mistake?"

"We can't know if that's true right now."

"If it turns out that I was the real target of that bomb…"

"We can't know what happened," she said again.

"Sue, I think…" Reed gasped. "We should talk… Sue, I think we should at least hug each other."

She wavered. For a moment she seemed to lose control. Her body began to turn transparent. She cleared her throat and her face became fully visible again. "Reed," she finally replied. "There's someone else who can hug you. I know everything. There's someone who's even younger than Franklin."

Reed shook his head. He stood there, staring at her, afraid that she would vanish once again before his eyes, but what he saw was his own face reflected in Sue's sunglasses. A tired, vaguely puffy face, the face of a man who hadn't slept for days out of fear that grief might suffocate him in his sleep. He resisted the impulse to yank off her sunglasses. "That has nothing to do with it," he moaned.

She hesitated. She touched her hair, cautiously, as if it were so many delicate filaments, bundles of nerves. "Good luck, Reed," she said as she got into the car.

"That has nothing to do with it," he repeated.

"Good luck."

The car pulled away. Reed considered extending his arms towards the departing car. Grabbing it by the bumpers, preventing it from leaving. The kind of thing he used to be able to do. *Maybe I still could. I wonder. I can certainly still stretch my body. I can extend legs and arms, I can still stretch, but I'm not sure what towards.*

When he turned around he encountered the eyes of the people who had remained behind. Pitying, embarrassed glances. Reed met their gaze and stared back, feeling himself wrapped in layers of chilly solitude, until he recognised a face in that crowd. Green eyes. Reddish hair. Reed looked at her, stunned, blinking in the afternoon glare.

Elaine was coming towards him, walking lightly as if trying not to frighten him. She stopped a few feet from him. They stood without touching. The silence lengthened, increasingly painful, until she decided to speak: "Hell,

Reed. I don't know what to say. Whatever I might say would only sound stupid."

"There's nothing to say," he found the strength to respond.

"As soon as you let me know that the ceremony was scheduled for today, I asked for leave and caught a plane from Houston."

"Houston," he echoed, astonished to be reminded of the existence of that place. He looked at Elaine through half-shut eyes, finding it hard to put her face in focus just after seeing Sue.

She was prettier than he had remembered. Her skin was pure and glowing. Reed felt so deeply moved, he could scarcely bring himself to look at her. *I once held you in my arms. We were together, you and I, at a time when it seemed the world was still intact.* He opened his mouth and entreated her: "Come with me…"

Elaine looked at him with a shocked expression. "You're…" she began, and then, struggling to finish the phrase, "…crying."

"I can't stay here any longer," Reed implored. "I can't. Come take a drive with me. Take me home."

"My God, Reed," she said, shaking her head. "I have a plane to catch, I've got to get back to Houston." She went on looking at him, uneasily. "I can't stand seeing you like this."

Reed moved off. Perhaps she'd changed her mind, because at that point she followed him. They walked along together, a few yards apart, until they reached the car. The sun hanging low in the sky caressed their shoulders. They got in the car, in silence. The engine started up smoothly, and the car edged away from the remaining funeral crowd. Reed had left without saying goodbye to Ben and the others. He felt no remorse. All he wanted was to go.

They rode side by side, looking out of the windows. New York was there, as always, and had resumed its busy life. Taxis cruised up and down, and people entered and exited the doors of the shops, the Greek diners, the fast-food places, the Starbucks, the Barnes & Nobles, the organic food shops, the private members clubs. There was something mechanical about all that movement. People appeared and vanished from Reed's sight, swallowed up by the mouth of an office building, disappearing into the mystery of a door, like figures in an enormous animated puppet theatre. A grotesque, ancient, illusory puppet theatre, the most glittering one on earth. *My city is a cruel theatre. It always has been and I pretended not to know that...* When the car came to a halt, they sat motionless, frightened, until Reed asked the driver to leave them alone.

The driver got out. They remained in the car with its smoked-glass windows, parked by a sidewalk in Manhattan, both of them exhausted, speechless, aware of the distance between them. The man at the bottom of the abyss. The girl about to reach for the stars.

Reed was terrified by the thought of going upstairs, to his empty apartment, but he knew Elaine would never agree to go up with him. He limited himself to touching her hand. He was thinking of nothing. The sensation was not that of seeing an old lover again, nor was it even the feeling of achieving a long-held wish, even though he had in fact dreamed of a moment like this, for a long time, in what now seemed like another life. Rather, it was the sensation of following a script that had already been written. The heartbreaking screenplay of the animated puppet theatre. Reed half-closed his eyes, dazzled by Elaine's fair white skin, while the picture of Franklin's charred corpse surfaced in his head. Sue's pinched face. Ben's sunglasses.

"Reed," Elaine whispered in a voice cringing with embarrassment. "You're exhausted. You need to get some rest."

He came to with a start. He wanted to ask her to touch him. He wanted to ask her to lay her hands on him, like a healer, even though he understood that no one could heal him. "Do you remember the first time I asked you out to dinner?" he asked. "We were in a car just like this one. It's been less than a year. Do you remember when I took you home at dawn, after we made love? Again, we were in a car like this one. It seems impossible that it's been such a short time."

Elaine appeared increasingly uncomfortable. She nodded distantly. "You're exhausted," she repeated.

"Time has strange effects when you have a body made of rubber. Time rolls up, stretches out, and contracts. Everyone's time resembles their body."

"My God, Reed."

"I suppose there's no point," he sighed then, "in asking you not to leave me. I suppose there's no point in asking you to come away with me, to Europe, for a few weeks."

Elaine averted her eyes. "Don't ask me that," she said, staring out of the window. "It's not fair of you to ask me that."

"You're right," Reed acknowledged, as he observed Elaine's pale profile. There wasn't much he could add to that. He didn't feel surprised, just worn out. After all, it really was such a simple matter: the silence, Elaine's face turned towards the window, the smell of the leather upholstery. The need Reed felt not to be left alone, and the fact that in just a few moments he would be.

"I remember when you invited me to dinner, I remember when you took me home at dawn, through the damp city streets. I remember everything, Reed, I was there at your side." She turned to look at him, abruptly, forcing him to shut both eyes tight, with a moan, as if completely dazzled. "Look at me, Reed. I have a plan, and you've always known that. In just five days I'm leaving on a mission. It was insane for me to come here today, during the final operative phase. In a short while I have my flight back to Houston. In a short while, I have to leave, Reed. Don't ask me for impossible things. I'm not a superhero, I can't perform the impossible."

Reed let out another moan.

And you have things to do, too," Elaine said in a patient tone, "something much more important than running away to Europe with me. You need to stay in New York, keep tabs on the investigation into what happened to Franklin. Isn't that your job now?"

Reed kept his eyes shut tight. Against his eyelids, the afternoon light was a sharp blade. Reed could sense the dazzling glow of the world, increasing like a raging fire, like the glare from a great desert. "The investigation," he sighed. "It would be reassuring to clutch at that hope. To go on living in order to make sure justice is done." His voice broke. "I wonder just what the investigation will tell us. I wonder if the same thing that happened with Batman will happen here. Whether the police will go mad on the case but never identify a mastermind. I wonder what can ever be said, what can ever be discovered that will pay me back for all this, that will shield me from this pain."

Elaine didn't reply. Reed could sense her presence on the seat beside him. There she was, the girl he could no longer see, lost in the glow beyond his eyelids, the girl with skin as luminous as a ghost, the girl he had once thought he held in his arms, but whom he had only brushed with his fingertips. The mirage-girl, the illusion-girl. The girl whom he had placed at the centre of the world, pointlessly, fatally, just as the world around him was spiralling off-kilter, faster and faster, without him noticing.

Outside, Manhattan was sliding towards sunset. The rush of the city was softening, and the passersby walked past the car without realising who was in it. In a nearby Starbucks people were reading the news on their laptop computers: FAREWELL TO FRANKLIN RICHARDS. NEW YORK COMES TO A STANDSTILL FOR FRANKLIN. The driver was loitering nearby, vaguely worried, peeking at the car's impenetrable smoked-glass windows. Then he saw the car door swing open, and Reed Richards crawled out, both eyes closed, as if someone had just sprayed him with salt water. Reed stumbled into him, and the driver held him up. "Are you all right, sir?"

Reed opened his eyes, slowly, looking at the man who was holding him up, at first failing to recognise the man. Then it dawned on him. A driver. A stocky man in his early fifties, one of the hundreds of chauffeurs who had driven him in his lifetime, one of the men who had transported him, for years, back and forth against the backdrop of this ambiguous city. He managed to muster a smile. "Yes, I'm fine. Please take the lady to the airport."

*

After the funeral, Reed found his place empty. He walked through the conference room, past Annabel's office, and reached his own private suite of rooms. Everything was immersed in a profound motionlessness. The sofa where Ben had sat sobbing for hours still bore the imprint of his heavy body. In the kitchen, the scent of the thousand or so teas brewed in the past several days by Annabel still hung in the air. Empty mugs. Dirty glasses.

Everyone had assured him that when he got home that night he would be wrecked, and he'd just collapse into sleep. *Luckily, that's how grief works. The minute your head hits the pillow, sleep will save you.* In fact, he was weary, inconceivably weary, and his body felt like a distant abstract entity, as if drained of blood. But his consciousness wouldn't give up. The long day refused to come to an end. And so they dragged themselves—he and his body—through the silent rooms. The rooms where Franklin grew up. The rooms where his son had lived, breathed, and sensed the world. The rooms Elaine had passed through, where the two had never met, where now they never would.

He undressed furiously, hurled himself into the shower so that the splash of water would overwhelm the silence. The water enveloped his body, tepid at first, then hotter. Reed turned up the temperature. Hotter still. When the water had become scalding, he opened his mouth wide, soundlessly, and stumbled out of the shower, dripping wet, trembling, his skin burning, his muscles sagging… He fell to the ground. His rubbery body was deforming, stretching out like a streamer of drool, and he went on crawling, naked, through the emptiness of those rooms.

Szepanski walked in the next morning on him, still awake, sitting naked on the edge of the bed. "My God, Reed," the doctor said, as he prepared an injection. "You haven't pulled another one of your foolish pranks, have you?" He inspected him visually, looking for suspicious deformations. "I told you to call me any time of the day or night."

Reed barely moved. "What could you have done?" he asked in a harsh tone.

Szepanski stepped back in surprise, but immediately regained his confident air. "I suppose I know what you mean. A superhero helps others, but no one can help him, is that what you're saying? Now I'll tell you what Doctor Szepanski can do." The morning light glided down his polished skin. "I can give you a nice injection of diazepam. I can make you sleep like an angel. If you don't get some sleep, you know what'll happen. The brain needs regular doses of dream activity. If you deny your brain that dream activity, it'll start dreaming when you're awake, and pretty soon you won't know the difference between dreaming and waking."

Reed saw the doctor coming towards him with a syringe. He wondered what a man who spends most of his time having his face redone would know about reality. "I'm not sure if I want to sleep," he said.

"Come on, Reed," and a crease of disappointment appeared on Szepanski's face. "You know that I want to help you, but I can't stay here all morning. I have a lunch meeting with my publisher."

Reed didn't know what he was talking about. Maybe Szepanski had written a book, perhaps a book about cosmetic surgery. *Oh well*, he thought. *People go to lunch with their publisher. People have their faces redone in time for summer. People go online to find out if there have been other attacks, other murders in the world of the superheroes. People waste themselves on thousands of wishes and desires, people fall in love with a thousand will o' the wisps, people have children and then watch them die. People are trapped on this planet. People really do lots of different things.*

He felt the needle pierce his skin. He had time to lie down and realise that Szepanski was observing his naked body, with an indiscreet gaze, before spreading a blanket over him.

*

He was in the panoramic sauna of the George Hotel. He knew right away that it was a dream, *this sauna no longer exists. This sauna was destroyed by a bomb.* And yet everything seemed so alive: the bodies of the other men in the half-light, the intense heat, the scent of the wooden benches. He felt sweat slide down his back, as slowly as a tear. He thought back on what Szepanski had told him, and decided that the doctor had lied to him. *It's not reality that starts to resemble a dream. It's dreams that become more solid than reality.*

When the other men left the sauna, only one remained behind. He was young, and he was sitting next to him. With a sudden start of awareness, Reed knew who it was. Franklin looked at him with a smile. His sweat-drenched face gleamed in the shadows. They sat there, father and son, looking out at the panorama beyond the plate glass. New York was motionless before their eyes. Reed didn't know whether he was sweating or crying, on that bench, sitting next to the naked body of his son. When he could no longer resist, he hugged him, tight, feeling his son's youthful muscles, his hot skin. "You're here, you're here with me," he sighed.

Franklin smiled awkwardly, and all he said in reply was: "We're not alone, Dad."

Reed perceived another figure in the far corner of the sauna. The mysterious person slithered slowly in the shadows. Reed guessed that it was a woman, and then something stirred in his memories. Everything became clear. Instinctively he took Franklin by the hand and led him towards the woman. The air was a hot gust of breath around them. The sauna was as dark and hot as a mouth. They sat down side by side, close together: Reed, Franklin, and Elaine. Nude, deeply moving, entirely pure. Feeling that he was on the verge of tears, Reed brushed his son's and Elaine's lips, and then gently pushed their heads together. Franklin and Elaine looked at each other and laughed. They turned to Reed as if asking final permission, then they kissed. Reed felt something dissolve in his chest, and the tears finally began to flow.

He knew that it was all about to end. He knew that an explosion was about to blow them away. And yet time lengthened. Reed looked at their bodies, and the faint swimsuit marks on their skin, and the hands of each in the hair of the other. It was all very physical. It was all so real, and an absurd hope rose inside Reed, *this isn't a dream. He's still alive. This isn't a dream, the dream was everything else.*

He woke up with a start.

Even though the clock said that he had been asleep for fourteen hours straight, he felt instantly clear-headed. Exhausted, the same as before. In his memory, the dream lacked the flavour of a dream, rather it seemed like another reality, as detailed as the one he was experiencing right now. He started wandering around the apartment in the night. He wondered if this was what his life would be like from now on. *A long day without breaks. Asleep or awake, always immersed in the same torment.*

It wasn't yet dawn when he went into his office, carefully dressed, even though he knew he wouldn't be working that day. Annabel would only drop in for a few minutes to deal with the mail. The Richards Foundation had suspended all activity for a few days. The following week it would start back up with a meeting of the board which, Reed knew, would propose renaming the foundation after Franklin.

He sat in the darkness, waiting for his computer to boot up. He began googling his son's name. He typed it in over and over—maybe the search engine was hiding something from him, maybe it was refusing to tell him the whole truth. It said that half a million people had attended the funeral of Franklin Richards. It said that there had already been two cases of teen suicides, youngsters who had killed themselves with a picture of Franklin in their hands. It said that the offices of the diplomatic corps were concerned, because *that young man not only travelled the world to clear up polluted war zones, but he also worked to bolster what remained of the country's good name. Now that he is dead, who will clean up America's conscience?* It said that, in the comments of widely read blogs, blame was being assigned to him, Reed Richards, *that ageing "hero" who proved incapable of protecting his son, and who was probably himself the target of the attack.*

It said a thousand other things, and Reed continued reading until his eyes started to burn. Later, he heard sounds from the adjoining office. Annabel. Reed withdrew into his private suite, determined to avoid any contact with his secretary. He locked himself in the bathroom, letting the water run in the shower, just in case she ventured back there in search of him. He lost himself in the noise of rushing water, like in the roar of distant waves, allowing his thoughts to swirl around the things he'd read online, around the dream he'd had, around the last conversation he'd had with Elaine. When he emerged, all was quiet. Walking cautiously, he went back to the office. On his desk was a stack of letters, and a paper bag with his favourite bagels.

He sniffed at them. In his previous life, those bagels had been a happy ritual. Now he stood there, contemplating them, as if he were musing about their probable use. He moved on to the mail on his desk. It was almost all letters of condolence, and the first few letters from women who had seen him on TV. *My heart ached for you. I know that this may sound stupid, but when I saw you in the midst of that funeral, all I wanted to do was wrap you in my arms. Here's my phone number if you feel like calling me.* The aura of tragedy must have given him some new form of sex appeal. He knew he'd have to expect more letters like that in the coming days. He knew that he'd have to keep his guard up, now more than ever, and protect his own grief, to make sure no one took advantage of it for their own stupid fantasies.

He was braced to not answer letters, not reply to emails, and even to ignore calls. He was braced to tell everyone that he just wanted to be left alone. But what happened that day was that no calls came in, and there were none in the days that followed either. Silence enveloped his life. His friends respected his grief, or more likely they were embarrassed by it. *People are embarrassed by other people's pain. They are relieved by thinking that there is nothing more they can do for you.*

He wondered whether Sue's friends were different. He wondered what she was doing during these days of aftermath, whether she had managed to cry, or if she was just sitting, invisible, in the corner of a room. Thinking about Sue filled him with anguish. *She was his mother. Sue was his mother, and I was his father.*

*

In the following days, the dreams with Franklin came back often, as did the dreams with Elaine. Each time, he woke up smoothly, as though it were a minor transition, and as though dream state and waking state had the same substance. There was no break in continuity. There was no difference. Both when dreaming and when awake, he felt his body burn, both dreaming and awake he felt the same impulse. The impulse to stretch without knowing towards what.

Sometimes the telephone startled him awake in the early morning. It was almost always the police calling, about logistical issues with the security detail assigned to guard his apartment. On a couple of occasions, the investigators had come to talk to him about progress on the case. When Reed told them about the anonymous notes he'd received over the previous months, saying SO LONG, MY MISTER FANTASTIC, Detective De Villa had nodded with a look of surprise. He stood there, thinking, cautiously stroking his chin. "I really would like to know who's sending these notes. Apparently Batman received a similar farewell note. You should have told us about them, Mr. Richards."

"My God." Reed could barely speak. Words continued to have an unsustainable weight on his lips. "Do you think that these notes were a warning of some kind?"

"Let's just say…" De Villa had seemed about to utter something. Then he decided against it and limited himself to observing: "We don't know whether they were sent by the same people who organised the attack. In any case, you should have told us about them."

Then one afternoon it was Ben's turn. Reed had just woken up from one of his restless naps to hear the phone ringing, and he got up to answer it. His old friend's gruff voice filled the receiver. "Listen, Reed. Don't let your sense of helplessness weigh you down; don't let your sense of guilt crush you. We still don't know for sure if the bomb was meant for you, and even if it was, there was nothing you could do to prevent what happened."

Reed listened to the breathing of his faraway friend. He let a long pause go by, hypnotised by the sound of that respiration that echoed in his ear, like the hum of a waiting ocean. "I could have taken those notes seriously. I could have taken Detective De Villa's visits and calls seriously while we were still in time. Maybe there was something we could have done. Now it's too late. It's too late even to understand."

"What are you talking about?" Ben asked. "It's not your fault that Franklin's dead. But it's your duty to figure out who was responsible."

"We know who it was. A group of anti-superhero fanatics. The same group that plotted Batman's murder."

"Okay. But who's the mastermind behind that group? Reed, we need to learn every detail. Unless we manage to find out everything, how are we supposed to survive?"

"I don't know." He gulped uneasily and tried to explain the way he felt: "Look at the Batman case. The trial has been going on for weeks and by now it's obvious that there will never be a complete resolution. Something horrible is happening, Ben. If you want, you can call it terrorism. You can call it a plot, you can call it what you want. We're bound to lose our minds no matter what we do, whether we try to find out more or we give up. And if we really do find out that the bomb was meant for me…" He closed his eyes and shivered. "I don't even want to think about it."

Ben let out a groan. "I can't believe you're talking this way. For the first few days you were furious, vowing revenge and pledging to do all you could to help the police." His voice was quivering with indignation. "If it's the way you say now, what's left for us to do? If we can't find out everything about the perpetrators, then what's left for us to do? What's left for *you*? Reed, what'll you do?" Ben took a deep breath and then, with unexpected cruelty, suggested: "Will you just run away with your little darling?"

Reed coughed. A thorn of sadness had just sunk into his throat. He sat there gaping until he answered in a woeful tone: "No, Ben. I won't run away. There is no little darling."

Finally, two days later Detective De Villa came back. He was alone this time, without his fellow investigators. He said that there were some new developments and he seemed to hesitate, awkwardly, unsure whether Reed was ready to hear about them. According to the detective, several details seemed to point to the conclusion that Franklin might have been mistaken for his father. For example, the fact that the sauna reservation had been entered in the computer of the George Hotel under the simple heading: *Richards*. The fact that the hotel computer system had been hacked into, evidence that someone might have been able to access the reservation list. These circumstances, along with further details, suggested that Reed was the real target. The detective seemed pretty confident on this point.

"Do you consider this evidence to be definitive?" Reed tried toughing it out.

De Villa took his time before answering, his eyes inflamed like small embers, letting his gaze wander—indecipherable, serious—over Reed's face. "These people didn't want to kill *the son* of a superhero. This was just a horrendous mistake."

Reed lowered his head. "Do you have a family, Detective?" was the only thing he could think of asking.

The detective gave a start. "No." He took a step backwards, then corrected himself: "Actually, a brother. We don't see much of each other." Although he must have been at least thirty, in the light of day his face now seemed very young. That man with a cold, vulnerable face cleared his throat, and in a hoarse voice that sounded somehow emotional, he said: "Mr. Richards, I understand what you're trying to say. You want to know whether I'm capable of imagining your loss. Believe me, I am. I can also imagine that what I came here today to tell you must have come as a further shock."

Reed dismissed the detective without another word. His throat was dry, all the moisture had been sucked out of it. There really was nothing more to be said. *They killed the wrong Richards. My son died instead of me. The real target of the attack was Mister Fantastic. The real target was the old hero.*

*

There was a time when that was the promised city, the place where everyone would be able to become themselves, a maze of crystal palaces capable of reflecting the sky in all its light. There was a time when that was the holy city, the chosen city, the city whose own salvation represented the salvation of all other cities, the city whose splendour was the very splendour of the world. Once that had been his city. Once he would have uttered the names—his name and the name of the city—as if they were the names of a pair of age-old lovers, who had existed for millennia one for the other.

Reed went out in mid-morning. He took his guards by surprise, but they hastily followed him downstairs into the lobby and out into the street. There, instead of climbing into a car as he usually did, he turned and hurried away, merging into the stream of pedestrians.

"Mr. Richards... Sir!" he heard one of the bodyguards call.

Reed quickened his pace. New York pulsed like a quasar around him. Reed could feel the city's vibration, made up of a thousand overlapping echoes, car engines, underground trains, multitudes of hearts beating as one on the surrounding sidewalks. He started to run, pursued by the increasingly concerned bodyguards, fishtailing among the crowds, zigzagging through the streets. He felt the pulsation of the city in his rubber legs. More and more powerful, similar to a countdown.

He wondered whether New York City, in spite of the distance, was vibrating expectantly for what would happen that day more than a thousand miles south of there. At the Kennedy Space Center, in Florida. The space probe would launch from there. A mission was about to leave the earth's surface. This was Elaine's big day, the day she'd leave for outer space.

Reed raised his eyes to the sky, suffocating, as it dawned on him that Elaine was about to punch through that very same sky, escape into distant space, while he'd be left here, a prisoner, trapped under that white blanket, in that stifling greenhouse. The sun stung his skin. A layer of dampness had formed beneath Reed's clothes, and his elastic body was growing wearier. He ducked into a subway entrance, giving his bodyguards the slip once and for all, and found himself on the station platform, looking down onto the tracks.

He had to calm down. Catch his breath. Instead, he kept walking anxiously back and forth, along the platform, exchanging glances with other passengers who might, perhaps, have started to recognise him. An ageing superhero wearing a sweat-stained shirt. An old man, his face puffy, his hair a drab silvery colour.

At last the tracks began to hiss. In the far distance, the lights of an oncoming train appeared, fast, bright, preceded by a gust of hot wind. Reed boarded and remained standing, balancing, without any idea of the train's direction. He let himself be transported through the dark tunnel, piercing the bowels of the city. The train gathered speed. Away from the torment, away from everything. Away from the office, away from home, away from the bedroom where he dreamed of Franklin, where he dreamed of Elaine. Away from the streets where he'd been a hero, where everything had been within reach of his arms, and where now everything only stirred regret.

Up there, the city continued to vibrate. Up there, people cut along the sidewalks, drank coffee, ate sandwiches, or reserved tables for lunch. Up there, people read the *Village Voice*, carried on conversations on their cell phones, piled up debt on their credit cards, looked for opportunities for the perfect vacation, dreamt of getting clean from their addictions, or simply of being able to fall in love once again. Up there, people lived their illusions, their disenchantments, repeating their time-worn actions, playing the same eternal roles.

The train had stopped and pulled out of a series of stations. When Reed recognised the name of a stop in Brooklyn, something began to light up in his head. He got out at the next stop. He'd decided on his destination. He took a different train, this time heading east.

Time passed. Reed let himself be carried along, increasingly certain about his destination, until he reached the last stop. Rockaway Beach. As he left the station he noticed that the temperature had risen. He walked towards the beach. The strip of sand lay before him, hot, brilliant, bordered further out by the line of the crashing waves. The murmur of the ocean came towards him, and the breeze pushed, through his shirt, against his rubbery chest.

Reed took a breath. He took off his shoes. The sand was scorching hot, fragments of seashells pricked the soles of his feet. The sun forced him to lower his gaze. The footprints of a thousand strollers jumbled across the sand: *maybe Ben's and my footprints are still here. Or the footprints of that little boy who came up to us, asking Ben if his body was real. Just two weeks. Two weeks ago I was here, on this same beach, knowing nothing and foreseeing nothing.*

He wasn't alone on the beach. People walked along the water's edge, in silence, or lay on the sand basking in the sunlight, flattened by the touch of that powerful shaft of heat. People just as unsettled as he was. As estranged as he was. Shadow-people who slipped along, elusive, practically weightless, on the sun-whitened sand. Reed walked for a long time, pushed forward by the wind. The roar of the ocean seemed to be inciting him and whispering something into his ear. Reed thought he understood. He mustn't stop here, he needed to continue his journey. He pushed on with his last remaining funds of energy, solemn, desperate, feeling his limbs straining, becoming tense. He stumbled and crashed to the ground. "Are you all right, sir? Do you need some help?"

Whoever it was that spoke to him, they got no answer. Reed stood up, cut across the beach, heading towards the line of apartment buildings, and made his way back into the train station. This is what he needed: a ride north until he reached the Long Island Railroad, where he could catch a train heading east. Now he knew his final destination. Heading east, in the direction of Montauk.

On the train, he felt other passengers watching him. His clothes were covered with sand, and only now did he realise that he was missing something. *My shoes. I must have lost them somewhere on the beach.* He sat there staring at his feet, unembarrassed, somehow deeply moved by the sight of those extremities, so naked, so helpless. He thought of Elaine's feet, the feet of women he'd loved. He thought of Ben's rock feet, of Franklin's soft baby feet. He thought of people's feet, their hands, the places where people came to an end, meeting the external world. The train was speeding along

Long Island, lengthwise, towards the Hamptons and then leaving them behind. Village after village. Outside the window, the island sailed past like a dense, prolonged dream, and the ocean glittered in snatches, in the distance, parallel to the tracks.

It was a fairly long ride. It took a couple of hours. At last, Reed got off the train at the end of the line, in the small town with an Indian name. Montauk, the last outpost. The tip of the island, the farthest extremity. The point where this rich island came to an end, yawning out into the void, into the vastness of the ocean, out towards the dark belly of the Atlantic. Waiting outside the station was a single taxi. Reed got in without a word, meeting the driver's startled glance.

"Where do you want to go?" the driver asked his passenger, staring at him in the rear-view mirror.

"To the lighthouse," Reed replied.

"Beautiful place," the taxi driver said. "It's a romantic place, in fact. Young lovers go crazy for that lighthouse." He let a moment pass: "Are you coming from New York, sir? Are you sure you feel all right?" he asked immediately after that, as though the two questions were linked.

"Don't worry," Reed said. "I have money for the fare. Just take me to the lighthouse, please. I've been travelling all day to get here."

The car pulled out almost without a sound. The streets of the town were steeped in calm. Silent tourists wandered around like phantoms. The taxi left the residential section and pushed out into the greenery of the promontory, gliding along with the utmost apparent tranquillity in the silvery light. The sky seemed made of crystal. The lighthouse loomed up before them, coming closer and closer, like the stalk of a giant, solitary flower. The ocean foamed past the rocky shoreline. The car came to a halt in the parking area, where an American flag fluttered in the breeze and Reed got out of the cab, greeted by the roar of the ocean.

He bought a ticket to the top of the lighthouse. He started climbing the iron steps. He must be the only visitor. His breathing echoed throughout the stairwell, until he emerged into the open at the top of the tower. He gripped the handrail, trembling. *At last I'm here. It took me so long. When was I last here? Maybe when Franklin was still a little boy.*

He really was the only visitor, and suddenly he relaxed, grateful for the solitude, grateful for the sound of the sea and the waves. For the first time in days, maybe in months, he felt something resembling peace. There was a sense to his being here. There was a sense to the lighthouse itself. Oh, that beacon had guided generations of sailors. From the top of that tower, generations of lighthouse-keepers had sent out beams of light, over the centuries, and had scanned the horizon with eyes full of hope, terror, or yearning. Off to the left, you could just make out the coast of New England; straight ahead, the deep blue vastness. Ocean, and nothing but ocean. Scudding foam, flowing current, a liquid mirror covering seismic faults, seabeds, underwater mountain chains, shipwrecks, a mass of salty water that smacked of tears: the tears of America, the tears of Europe.

Reed went on scrutinising the horizon. "Europe," he whispered. "Europe," he said again, savouring the sound of that word, like the sound of a forgotten promise. Then he uttered other names, one by one, letting the wind carry them off: "Franklin." "Elaine." "Sue." He cleared his throat. "Reed," he said the name last, as an evocation, as if on the far side of the ocean, on the distant coast of the other continent, a new Reed might stand listening.

He began taking off his clothes. His body shivered in spite of the heat. Once stripped bare, he felt a shock, something ambiguous and almost erotic, a quiver not entirely disagreeable. He wished he could touch someone. He felt the lack of everyone, he missed everything. *The world is here in front of me.* He needed something to grab onto. After extending his legs until they had stretched out into two thin ropes, he knotted them tightly to the railing. There, that's it. He felt no pain. It was as if he were anaesthetised, possessed, as if his body had ceased to be his own. As if his body were making decisions for itself, finally free. Reed felt confused and yet clear-minded. *It's absurd. I have to do this. My God,* he thought, tempted to laugh at himself, high atop that lighthouse, naked, knotted to the railing. He extended his torso out into the void. He took a breath and launched himself.

He stretched out, hurtling past the rocky coast. He extended beyond the shoreline. He reached further, out over the strip of transparent water, out to where the vast depths began. He sailed on for miles, effortlessly, driven forward by his own momentum, by the tension of his muscles, thrusting back against his legs knotted to the lighthouse. He pushed forward, extending out over the ocean surface, travelling out to sea, towards the faraway opposite shore, towards the rest of the world. He stretched, straining, weeping with effort, his face disfigured, certain that he could make it, *I'm going to embrace the world, I'm going to wrap myself around the entire planet.* But when he felt the ripping tear, it came as no surprise. *I knew it. I knew there was something in my hip. A seed of pain that was destined to blossom.*

Back there, miles behind him, he felt the wound opening, and even though he knew that minutes of agony awaited him, he remained calm. *I'm Reed Richards. I'm Mister Fantastic. My son died in the flames, I'm going to die in the ocean.* He fell into the waves, twisting like a serpent, his mouth full of salt water. His screams were lost somewhere, in the watery depths, resembling echoes of distant whales, and all the pain he'd felt in his life seemed to come back, all at once, one last time, before tumbling forth into a neutral, perfectly new sensation. *This time it's true. I'll never go back to my original shape. I'll never go back again, I'll never go back.*

There, where his body had torn open, the blood issued in a steady stream, a slow pour made up of cells that kept enlarging, once they'd left his body, stretching out in the water like jellyfish. The red stain spread out for miles, and for a moment it seemed to take on the form of a face, before that was lost in the ocean currents. The ocean lay immensely mute, a silence as piercing as a scream. Everything was concluded. All pain seemed to have ceased. In the distance it was just possible to make out the hum of an aeroplane or two, and perhaps a passing melancholy freighter.

A thousand imperceptible sounds crossed paths in the air. Echoing radio and magnetic waves vibrated in all directions, igniting the air with their elusive chant, enveloping the earth with their rivers of information. Soon the news would ricochet around the globe that another hero was dead. Reed Richards, father of Franklin, the old glory of the superhero scene, had left this world.

But for now, other news filled the airwaves. News that was as shocking as ever, as routine as ever. The world's stock exchanges had taken a jolt. American soldiers had been killed in the Middle East. NASA had successfully launched a space mission from its base in Florida. The launch had gone well, the spacecraft had left the earth's atmosphere. Aboard the spacecraft, it was reported, three men and a woman were in perfect condition…

*

On board the space probe, the crew members were in fact doing fine. Especially Elaine Ryan. To tell the truth, she'd never felt better in her life. She'd witnessed the take-off with a sense of panic and peace, a clarity of mind unlike anything she'd ever experienced before. She'd heard the fuel roar in the combustion chamber, the friction of the atmosphere against the side of the probe. She'd felt the pounding in her chest, the flow of blood in her veins. She'd done it. She'd lived for years holding her breath, focusing on this single objective, facing down other people's scepticism, and uncountable times she'd felt utterly alone. She'd nurtured her desire over time, she'd dragged its weight for years. But she felt as light as a snowflake now, as the spacecraft left the earth's gravitational field, as the commander issued orders to the crew.

Elaine stirred. There was a new amazement in her body, a profound sense of both yearning and breaking away. She turned her gaze towards the spacecraft's porthole. Her eyes opened wide, her pupils dilated like the blossoming of a flower. The earth was down there. A luminous, solitary sphere, fragile in appearance. It seemed moulded from pure light. Oh, there was her planet. The layer of water and air where reality took shape, and broke down, where everything was designed to be sensed, where memory accumulated everywhere. In that fluorescent atmosphere she had been born. In that atmosphere she had grown up. In that exquisite blue light she'd gone to school, she'd read biographies of superheroes, and she'd become acquainted with the taste of tears, with the disconcerting flavours of truth and falsehood. *It's actually happened. I'm on my way to outer space.* In spite of all the obstacles, in spite of the enormity of the effort. In spite of Reed…

Elaine thought of that man, down there, and the strange love affair she'd had with him. She thought of her embarrassment when Reed asked her not to go. He'd tried to make her feel sorry for him, he'd tried to exploit the death of his son. That was an ugly thing to do. Elaine had felt disappointed. For a while, at first, her affair with Reed had been an intense one, because older men know how to court a girl; plus going to bed with a childhood hero certainly had its appeal… Sometimes, with him, she'd even let herself go. Too bad Reed had stirred up all those fantasies in his mind. There was something deeply egotistical about men of that generation, they'd grown up in a greedy time, they came from a century when people thought you could conquer everything, whatever you wanted: freedom, fame, public glory and private delights. The way she saw it, times had changed, long ago. Most important of all, people couldn't possess one another any more. *I couldn't stay with you. When I was with you, I wasn't even real, I was just an obsession you had.*

The spacecraft was vibrating slightly. Elaine took a last look through the porthole, trying to pinpoint the place where her city stood. New York. She looked down on the coastline as if it were a distant mirage. It was too far away to make out Staten Island, but she could recognise the slender fragment of Long Island. Off the coast of Long Island, she noticed something odd. She blinked and went on looking.

"Do you see that too?" she heard the commander ask, as he looked out in the same direction from the porthole next to hers.

"Yes," Elaine responded, unsettled by that sight.

"You think it's an oil slick?"

"No, I don't think so," said the commander. "Not with that colour."

Elaine studied the tiny patch of colour far beneath her, the red striation in the blue of the ocean. She decided that the commander had a point. Maybe it was a natural phenomenon of some sort. Maybe a giant colony of algae, or a huge school of scarlet fish, or who knows what else. What an incredible spectacle. That red, so vivid. A series of shivers ran through her body, and a surge of absolute, desperate love filled her veins. "Whatever it is, it's incredibly beautiful," she declared, her voice quivering. Unexpectedly, she felt about to cry. "Don't you think it looks sort of like a face?"

"That's true," acknowledged the commander with the same emotion. There was a moment of awed silence. "This planet," the commander mused, "just never seems to run out of surprises, does it?"

Book Two

BATMAN

APRIL 2005
&
1980S – 1990S

He was in the bathroom, wearing nothing but a pair of two-hundred-dollar boxer shorts. His skin was bronzed and his abs were taut. Bruce Wayne looked into the mirror, smiled at himself, and started to dance, feeling a pleasurable surge of energy inside him, as an old disco song pounded out from the stereo in the living room. Still dancing, he spread a moisturising lotion over his body. He massaged his chest and shoulder muscles. When the song reached its chorus, he swivelled his pelvis with rhythmic thrusts and began singing, in a velvety voice: *You are the best in town. You take me up and down.*

He slipped on a pair of black socks and, dressed that way, in boxer shorts and socks, he started moving through the house, singing to himself as he went. He did a spot check: everything seemed to be ready. Shafts of discreet light illuminated the place, silhouetting the large cactus plants with their thorny arms, in the corners of the rooms, as if they were trees lit up by a distant fire. The light was perfect, fleshy, the kind of light that would set off his tan—he felt sure—to its best effect. The same light bounced off the crystal glass tabletops, the books on the shelves, the movie posters framed on the walls, the collection of old vinyl LPs piled in stacks. The stereo still blared out the disco song. Bruce started dancing again, in delight, contracting his abs, raising both arms, smiling at an imaginary audience. Bruce Wayne, lithe dancer. Bruce Wayne, the most seductive ex-superhero on earth, the sexiest man of his generation, in underwear and socks, in all his splendour.

That afternoon, the cleaning woman had done the rooms, leaving them in a state of almost excessive tidiness. Bruce began moving the occasional object, a cushion, a book, the hem of a curtain, to bring back a lived-in look and avoid having the place appear too contrived. He sprayed an air freshener around. Minuscule drops settled on his skin. Next to the sofa, a pile of carefully arranged magazines testified to the broad range of his interests: *The Economist, The New Yorker, Variety,* and *Sports Illustrated.* Among the magazines, apparently by chance, were a couple of older issues that contained articles about him: BRUCE WAYNE: STILL RIDING THE WAVE. BATMAN: 'SEX APPEAL ISN'T KIDS' STUFF'.

And now, the final touch. Bruce set an elegant steel ice bucket on the table, full of ice cubes, with a bottle of white wine inside. Outstanding. The stage was set. A new evening of delightful entertainment was about to unfold. He took an ice cube from the bucket and went back to the bathroom, where he stood before the mirror and tapped his face with the ice. He worked on his cheekbones. On his cheeks. He carefully tapped along the contour of his jawline. He moved down his neck and that's when he saw it: there was something on his chest. He picked up a pair of tweezers and yanked out a white chest hair. *You little bastard,* he whispered, dropping it into the sink with a sigh.

It was time to start getting dressed. He slipped on a white shirt. He had bought the shirt, made of a fine mother-of-pearly fabric, earlier that day. As he did every Friday, Bruce had spent half the afternoon in a boutique on Madison Avenue, trying on clothes, looking for items that showed off his athletic figure. It was never easy to make a choice. The clothes had to be understated, suitable for someone his age, and at the same time a little cheeky, capable of showcasing his body. A mature style, a sexy style. That afternoon, he'd tried on dozens of shirts, sensing the friction of the fabric over his muscles, as well as dozens of pairs of trousers, scrutinising in the mirrors of the fitting room how they made his bottom appear. It took patience. It was nerve-racking work, but someone had to do it. He had always had a precise understanding of the importance of clothes. He'd always believed that it was crucial to dress as if there were a chance you might die that day, and choose each outfit as if it were the last: the outfit in which you wouldn't mind being found, dead, sprawled out in the street.

He remembered the days when he was active as Batman. The time when he'd put on his skintight suit every night, after sprinkling his body with talc to make sure the suit slipped on. The period when he wore his dark cape, well aware that in that outfit, indeed, he might have died. One thing was certain, he wasn't going out for fun or to take the poodle for a walk. He was going out to wage combat, to take on the city's criminals. Every night, for many long years, he'd left home unsure whether he'd ever return, and yet he'd been comfortable in his clothes: that suit did honour to his body and that cape wrapped him in gloomy splendour. To die in that outfit wouldn't have been unseemly. And even though his clothing was different now, clothing that would never be worn to fight crime or wage ferocious battles… still, the principle remained the same. An outfit that you could imagine as your last was an outfit that was worth putting on in the first place.

That day, in the leisurely atmosphere of the boutique, he'd spent quite some time in the fitting room, while two ceremonious sales assistants handed him garment after garment, commenting every time with sighs of approval. "That's a very nice drop, Mr. Wayne." "The shoulders on this jacket, Mr. Wayne…" As the proceedings went on, he ventured out of the fitting room and noticed another customer. A well-built young guy was standing in front of the large mirror that screened the fitting area, bare-chested, lazily waiting for the sales assistants to bring him another item. Bruce couldn't help but give the guy a glance. Almost without fail, the physical beauty of other men both enchanted and annoyed him. The guy had smiled that particular kind of smile that people seem to put on when they recognise someone famous. It was a smile that seemed to say *hey-I-know-who-you-are* but it could just as easily have been a smile that said *how-about-we-get-to-know-each-other-a-little-better*, and Bruce had turned his eyes away and withdrawn, with a grimace, into his own fitting room. Damn it. Come-ons from other men always made him cringe. He had decided it was time to leave the store and it was then that he noticed on the floor of the fitting room…

Bruce's thoughts were suddenly interrupted. The sound of the doorbell had rung through the house. The sound echoed through the rooms, causing the air to reverberate, startling him ever so slightly, but pleasurably. Nine o'clock on the dot. Right on time. Punctual people put him in a good mood. He had just finished dressing and all he needed to do now was put on his jacket. The stereo was pumping out the tail end of the disco song, and Bruce hurried to replace it with an album of atmospheric music by a refined French band, although in his head the refrain continued: *You are the best in town. You take me up and down.*

He slipped the jacket on over his shirt of mother-of-pearly fabric. He touched up his hair, donned the most seductive expression he could muster, and went to open the door.

*

The girl was tall, androgynous, unquestionably his type. She wore stiletto heels and skintight jeans. She had narrow, almost masculine hips, and under her T-shirt you could make out a pair of small breasts, like a young girl's. Her face seemed carved from some precious glowing metal. Short dirty-blond hair, twenty at the oldest. She walked through the door and stood there, allowing him to admire her, blinking in the warm light of the living room. Then Bruce offered her some wine.

Bruce studied the hand with which she had taken the glass. It was a small, delicate, determined hand. He raised his own glass with satisfaction: "Here's to us," he toasted.

"To us," she said, looking at him with half-closed eyes.

Bruce took a sip, even more pleased for having chosen the right wine. Light and aromatic. He sensed the flavour wash over his tongue and spread in his mouth, slowly, delightfully, a domino effect of sensations that seemed to reach, without effort, the most sensitive regions of his throat. He wondered whether the girl knew anything about wine. He noticed that she seemed to be sunk in who knows what obscure thought. "What is it?" he smiled at her.

She shook her head and laughed briefly. "Sorry," she said. She shook her head again and explained: "I was just thinking… I just thought, for some reason, that you'd come to the door in your costume."

Bruce continued to smile affably. "I hope you weren't disappointed."

"Oh no," she hastened to reply, wavering in a moment of apparent uncertainty. Her eyes were a chilly, vague colour, somewhere in the shifting chromatic scale between grey and green. She looked around, perhaps in search of a distraction, and made up her mind to ask a question: "Do you mind showing me around?"

"Of course not," Bruce said. He stood there, peeking at the girl's face as she wandered around the room.

She let her eyes slide over the walls, halting for a few moments on the framed movie posters. There was a mixture of shyness and indifference about her that Bruce seemed to find, almost always, in people her age. An indecipherable expression flashed over the girl's face, then she said: "This is an interesting place you live in."

Bruce nodded as he took another sip from his glass. He found enigmatic people sexy. "Come with me," he invited. "I'll show you the rest."

They walked down the carpeted, arched hallway, proceeding silently like two explorers in an enchanted grotto. The girl followed him with a tranquil air. "Are we alone?" was her only question. "I mean, what about your butler?"

"My butler?" Bruce asked, baffled. He wondered if she was talking about the butler that often appeared in movies inspired by his life. In fact, there had been someone more or less like that, many years ago, but the movies had definitely embroidered reality. "Little one, I think he died before you were born."

"Oh," she sighed, with a hint of disappointment, or perhaps it was relief.

"Come with me," Bruce urged her. He led her into a small room, where a vast wooden armoire covered three of the four walls. Pointing to one of the doors, he challenged her: "Guess what's in here."

She looked at the door of the armoire. "I couldn't say," she said, cautiously. "Guess."

"I'm afraid I don't know."

"Come on," Bruce said, touching her hair nonchalantly, as if he'd done it a thousand other times, or as if that gesture might help her to think of the answer. "Something we just talked about," he suggested.

She seemed to concentrate and ventured to laugh. "Your butler's corpse?" she joked.

Bruce laughed too, and decided that the girl had a sense of humour. Not all the girls did. In fact, almost none of them. He made a mental note to call the friend who had sent this one, to thank him for his stimulating selection. "Come on," he said again. "Don't tell me you can't guess?"

She shook her head with a sigh. Bruce stood looking at her for another moment, letting the suspense grow, before making up his mind. He opened the armoire. Inside, stored in a nylon slipcase, draped over a transparent plastic hanger, there was a shiny black costume. "Batman's costume," he announced.

"Oh," she said.

"You can touch it," said Bruce.

The girl hesitated. She stared at the costume, perplexed, as if she'd been confronted with a strange animal specimen.

"Touch it," Bruce urged her.

She reached out a hand. She slipped her fingers under the nylon slipcase and touched the fabric of a sleeve. "Oh," she repeated. "I like it," as she began caressing the costume, sliding her hand towards the shoulders and chest.

Bruce watched her hand slide over the black cloth. "It's a special fabric," he breathed. "As a matter of fact, it's not really a fabric. It's a kind of latex. Can you feel how moist it is, almost tepid? It absorbs your body heat. It reacts to the touch of your fingertips," he said, taking a deeper breath, drawing a little closer, pulling together the threads of that improvised threesome: him, the girl, and the old superhero costume.

She nodded with a conspiratorial air. She didn't seem too surprised. "I can feel it," she said, looking deep into his eyes.

Bruce avoided telling her that she actually couldn't feel a thing, because the properties that he had just described belonged to the original costume, while this was a far less sophisticated reproduction. The original costume had been stolen years ago. He spared her the details of the troublesome aftermath of that theft. He spared her the story of how he'd tried to get the stolen costume back by going to a club for fetishists near Chelsea Park, where he'd heard that stolen costumes often wound up, and how he'd wandered through a crowd of people dressed up as superheroes, reeking with the scents of leather and rubber, sweat, and amyl nitrate, including a number of men dressed as Batman. He spared her the information that none of those people were wearing the original costume, and that at that point he had given up all hope of getting the costume back, but to make up for it he'd spent a very agreeable evening, in a small dimly lit room with a number of nice young people whose acquaintance he had made in the club.

He spared her all that knowledge. All he did instead was to draw a little closer. Breathing hard, he whispered: "Try slipping your other hand in."

The girl put her other hand into the nylon slipcase. She resumed caressing the costume with sweeping circular gestures, breathing hard too. She seemed to get the game. She ran her fingertips over the ribbed shell, over the curves designed to adhere to the chest, the folds of the abdominal muscles. She let her hands drift downwards, caressing the rubbery fabric.

"That's enough," Bruce said all of a sudden. He could feel the blood flowing in dense, vigorous surges inside him, a warm erection pressing against his trousers. He didn't want to push the game too far. Too early, there was still plenty of time. "The night is long," he declared. "I still have to show you the rest of the place."

*

In the Madison Avenue boutique, that afternoon, after retreating into his fitting room, his mind made up to put on his clothes and leave, he'd glimpsed something on the floor. It was a sheet of paper. He couldn't have said how long that sheet of paper had been there. Maybe someone had slipped it under the door just a few seconds ago, who knows, or maybe it had already been there when he stepped out of the booth for a moment, or maybe it had been there for a while. He was too involved in trying on his shirts with their mother-of-pearly fabric and with the comings and goings of the sales assistants to pay any attention to the floor of the fitting room.

A white sheet of paper. Folded in half. Bruce bent to pick it up and sensed with his fingertips the texture of the paper, smooth, fine, as though that very same paper had been a fabric, a scrap of clothing, the hem of a garment that he could try on and wear. Of course. The whole world was a garment that he wanted to wear. A part of his brain thought back to the guy he'd just seen in front of the fitting area mirror, the one who might have shot him an allusive glance. Bruce was seized by a mixture of irritation and flattered enjoyment at the thought that the guy had been so bold as to slip a note under the door of his fitting room, maybe a note with a phone number or an admiring phrase, or perhaps a crude proposition, a proposition that would have left Bruce cold since the guy wasn't young enough for him, and he was a male, and he wasn't his type. He'd smiled a vain, slightly contemptuous smile, then he'd unfolded the note and felt only disappointment when he read:

SO LONG, MY BATMAN

That wasn't what he'd expected. It really wasn't. He'd turned the note over in his hands. What the hell did that message mean and who the hell… All right. He guessed that the right thing to do now was to try to find out what was going on here. He'd swung open the fitting room door and slowly poked his head out. The guy from before was still there, involved in consultation with one of the sales assistants about the cut of a jacket, and when the two men noticed Bruce they both stopped talking and stared at him.

Bruce had pulled his head back in, with the movement of a very proud turtle. He had heard them resume their discussion on the strategic importance of a jacket's rear vent. Once again, Bruce stuck his head out to spy on them, and once again they had stopped talking, staring at him in bewilderment.

There'd been a moment of thorny awkwardness. The guy no longer had a smile of pleased recognition on his face. If anything, he seemed to be baffled by Bruce's behaviour. "Is something wrong, sir?" the sales assistant was asking. "Should I have some other shirts brought for you to try? Let me call my colleague."

"It doesn't matter." Bruce had grimaced in disappointment. At first glance, the guy had nothing to do with the message and neither did the sales assistant. Then who could it be? The other sales assistant? Some other customer? He had asked whether anyone had passed by the fitting booths in the past few minutes and the sales assistant had replied with a glassy look: "I don't think so, sir. What do you mean by *anyone*? Are you sure you're all right?"

Bruce had slammed the fitting room door and stayed there, mulling over his doubts. He had no idea what this whole thing meant, but he was determined not to worry about it. It was Friday, he was planning to see a girl that night, and he didn't need some absurd prank putting him off track. *Every night with a girl demands my utmost concentration. Every encounter demands exclusive attention.* No need to be distracted by a sheet of paper that had somehow materialised beneath his feet, or by the phrase written on it, a phrase that—come to think of it—he'd seen before. This wasn't the first time. Not at all. A couple of identical notes had been delivered in the mail in the past few weeks.

SO LONG, MY BATMAN

Given the tone of the message, he half-suspected that some disappointed lover from his past might be behind the notes. Why not? It was plausible. Maybe one of the many girls he'd seen just once and immediately dropped. Wasn't it the most obvious solution to a mystery of that kind? Bruce's past was punctuated with broken hearts, the way a city street was littered with broken glass the morning after a riot. He sniggered with pride and a vague sadness. Of course, the idea that some nameless broken heart might be so audacious as to follow him into a boutique to slip him yet another farewell note struck him as odd and slightly disconcerting. In any case, he decided to overlook it for the moment.

The night, the night awaited him! A night in the company of a new girl. The night, with its rituals, its sublime promises. The night demanded his undivided attention.

*

After the little game with the latex costume, he and the girl walked into the next room, still breathing hard, each of them deeply aware of the other. They advanced with silent footsteps. It was quite a large room, with a wooden floor. A couple of thousand-dollar lamps cast a creamy light, almost painted, creating a succession of patches of brightness and shadow. The girl swayed over to the middle of the room, looking around her quizzically.

"This is my study," Bruce explained.

She smiled and seemed to relax. "Actually, I was wondering what your place would look like," she admitted as she looked around again. "Whether it would be full of electronic equipment, or strange devices you invented when you were still a superhero."

"A lot of that stuff is still in storage in the old mansion," Bruce breathed, coming to a halt at a spot in the room where he knew, with great precision, that the lighting would strike him in an evocative manner. He rolled out one of his best smiles. "The rest of it I donated to museums. By now, it's just ludicrous junk. Technology ages so quickly. I don't like things that get old," he said with a wave of his hand, taking in the timeless, exquisitely classical style in which his study had been furnished: red leather armchairs, a black wooden desk, a crystal-fronted bookcase. A paperweight glittered on the desktop. It was also made of crystal, shaped like a turtle, the shell faceted like an enormous diamond. Bruce's smile was increasingly confident. "I was told that you grew up on the Upper East Side. I imagine your home was similar to this."

The girl nodded. "Similar," she limited herself to saying, resuming her cautious attitude. "So, no strange gadgets. No complicated closed-circuit video surveillance systems, no environmental sensor apparatus, no central computer running the place…"

Bruce burst out laughing. "None of those things. I used to have fun with gadgets. But even back then, believe me, they weren't such special things." He hesitated, afraid of looking too modest, before adding: "I have something better to show you. Something more interesting than an old electronic device."

The girl did nothing more than gaze at him, expectant, pale, and magnificent. She was standing in a dimly lit corner and her face seemed to fade, now, as in a strange video effect. Bruce looked at her, hypnotised. Then he came to, and drew closer to her. He touched one of her hands, carefully, as if he were afraid of receiving an electric shock.

The girl seemed to be tangled in confusion. At last, her face softened. Bruce kept looking in the half-light at that face; it struck him as blurred, elusive, and arcane. *That's odd*, he mused. *Certain faces seem to transform themselves in dim light, suddenly reminiscent of a thousand other faces, or perhaps they're just revealing their unique, eternal appearance, capable of emerging from beneath the semblance of any and all faces.* The faces he liked best, in the final analysis, were all the same. That's how it had always been, even back when he preferred boys. Bruce had always liked young people with regular features, light-coloured eyes, blond hair with that exact honeyed shade, a faint dusting of freckles, that same shape to the mouth, that particular expression, at once angelic and remote. Male or female, they were all incarnations of a single type, like different faces of a single person.

"Your face…" Bruce breathed. Again, he came to and recovered his affable tone. "You have a nice face. And nice hands," he added, looking down at the hand that she was now holding out to him like a delicate offering. Bruce seized that hand. He considered its texture, its dewy warmth. "Come with me," he said, pulling her towards a door on the far side of his study.

The girl followed him obediently. They walked into a small gymnasium. There was a scent in the air of cast iron weights. "Is this what you wanted to show me?" she asked, looking at the equipment in the room: a weight bench upholstered in leather, sparkling weights arranged in order of size, a couple of multifunctional machines.

Bruce dropped the girl's hand. "We're in one of my favourite rooms," he preened, standing for a moment in a pose, muscles contracted, so that she'd notice them bulging under his shirt. "But this isn't where I wanted to bring you." He walked across the gym and approached another door. After pushing it open with the merest touch, he gestured for the girl to follow him.

It was a small display room.

In the middle of the room, illuminated by a couple of white spotlights, another Bruce Wayne stood before them, legs spread slightly, a shameless expression on its face. The sculpture was life-size, and made of black resin. It portrayed Batman in his costume, with the top part of the suit partially open. A sort of tear separated the costume at the chest as if there were an invisible zipper. Bruce was pulling the left side open with one hand, offering to the sight of the audience his shapely pectoral muscle, like a woman producing her breast to nurse an infant. There was a challenging look on his face. His eyes stared straight ahead, and his mouth was twisted in a vaguely obscene grimace.

They both looked at the statue without speaking. Bruce waited for the girl to ask a question so that he could explain the history behind this work of art, the creation of Nathan Quirst, the famous hyperrealist, who had attained stardom years ago with a life-size sculpture, disturbingly realistic, of a nude woman down on all fours, giving a blow job to Hitler while being sodomised from behind by Stalin. Bruce had seen that sculpture at the opening of a controversial art show. He'd looked at it with mixed emotions, something midway between annoyance and admiration. A few weeks later, he'd attended a magazine party, where he happened to be introduced to the artist. Nathan Quirst was drinking cherry-flavoured vodka and was surrounded by an entourage of art students, all eagerly awaiting another of his outrageous comments. Rumours were circulating that he was at work on a new statue of the pope. It took only minutes for the two men to establish a certain rapport, and for the artist to start getting a cunning appreciation of the ex-superhero's physique. The encounter had flattered Bruce's ego. The next day, Quirst gave him a call, with the voice of someone who'd just woken up with a bad hangover, and asked Bruce to pose for him.

"It's by Nathan Quirst," Bruce said, after waiting in vain for the girl to react in some way. He said it in a quiet voice, as though providing an obvious piece of information.

"I see," she replied. The name didn't seem to mean a thing to her.

Bruce found it remarkable. Remarkable that she would know nothing about the artist who scandalised half the world, who had been banished from the museums of at least four conservative states, who sold his artworks at prices that would easily purchase a penthouse overlooking Central Park, who had left a statue of the pope unfinished to start work on a portrait of him—the statue of Batman showing off his pecs. "Nathan Quirst!" he reiterated.

"I see," she said again, in a tone that, to Bruce's ear, smacked vaguely of irony.

That really was something. Damn. Not to know who one of the highest-priced artists on earth was, the artist who had become famous by depicting Hitler and Stalin banging the same woman. Come to think of it, though, he had to wonder if the girl even knew who Hitler and Stalin were. These days, kids knew nothing. They seemed to have just landed from a different planet. "He's a rather well-known artist," he explained.

Disappointed at how little impression the statue had made, Bruce kept staring at that reproduction of himself. For the most part, his visitors were dazzled at the sight of the thing. Even Bruce still was. The artwork was charged with an ambiguous, almost violent power, and radiated the subtle aura that the most expensive artworks, often, tend to possess. He'd spent a fortune to acquire it. After Quirst finished working on it, Bruce had been the first to see it. At the beginning, he was thrilled with the way it portrayed his body, with how the costume highlighted his musculature, at how the cape seemed to flow fluidly behind him, like some membranous element of his body. What a magnificent reproduction. Quirst had grasped the force of his body. But there was more than that in the sculpture. There was something stripped bare. It wasn't just the way Bruce bared his chest. There was something in the pose, in the face, something that triggered excitement and unease. There was something excessive about it, some deep absence of innocence. Looking at that sculpture, it seemed to Bruce he was looking in the mirror, and recognised what he'd become: an ageing satyr. A lascivious demon busy trying to seduce the world, offering up a glimpse of his still-youthful body. He remembered that Quirst was smiling triumphantly, while he was unsure whether he should be furious, upset, or overjoyed. He'd offered at once to buy the piece of art. He doubted that other viewers would see in it the same things that he recognised, at least not in such explicit terms, and yet the idea that it might wind up in an art exhibition somewhere frightened him.

The girl had walked a short distance away. She was devoting her attention to the other artworks hanging on the wall, a half-dozen canvases and assorted portraits by big-name photographers. She stopped to study a photographic portrait. "Robin?" she asked, with distinct interest.

Bruce caught up with her reluctantly, annoyed that she should turn up her nose at the sculpture, his contradictory sculpture, his extraordinary sculpture, the sculpture that had immortalised his strength, his sensuality, his disconcerting shadow. Annoyed that she should have chosen to focus instead on that portrait. It was an original photograph by Richard Avedon, dating back to the period when the photographer devoted himself to portraits of superheroes. It showed a young man in his superhero costume, or rather, in his sidekick costume. The young man was looking into the lens with a trusting gaze. Light enveloped him, giving him an angelic appearance. "Robin," Bruce confirmed.

"How long has he been dead?" the girl enquired.

"Years. I can't remember," was the response.

"He had nice eyes."

"Maybe he did," Bruce replied, without much enthusiasm.

"He was very important to you, wasn't he?" she asked, continuing to study the portrait.

Bruce snorted. "Maybe. I don't remember. Why are you young people always so interested in dead heroes?"

The girl seemed to snap out of a trance and smiled apologetically. "Don't be angry." She reached out one hand towards Bruce's chest and put the other hand on her own. She remained in that pose for several seconds, as though waiting to synchronise their hearts. When she was sure she had won him back, her eyes shone. Her gaze was a frighteningly deep grey.

"All right," Bruce conceded. He took a long breath and, following a sudden impulse, he decreed: "It's time for you to do something for me. A nice little something."

*

A long time ago. It was the early Eighties. Robin was almost eighteen when he came into his life, and even though by then Bruce had already had several young men, he'd never had one that was quite so young. Until that day, he'd never even identified his type. Robin appeared one night with his dirty-blond hair, the freckles on his nose, so completely in line with Bruce's subconscious tastes that he seemed to have been designed, like a prototype, by the benevolent god of perfect love affairs.

He was a shy but determined young man. He knew how to get a grip on an idea and hold on to it, with the tenacity of a reptile clamping its jaws down on something. He blushed constantly. He had a hard time looking anyone in the eye. He was athletic, he trained regularly with a Graeco-Roman wrestling team, and out there on the mat he unleashed an unexpected, almost desperate grit. Bruce first ran into him one night in an alley, in the middle of a brawl, one against two, fighting a pair of men who, as Bruce later learned, had called him a faggot. Bruce put the two attackers to flight. Then he'd turned to leave, without a word, ready to move on to other tasks. The young man had asked him to wait. He'd walked over to him, blood streaming from his nose, with his shy, burning gaze. "So you do exist after all," he'd said. "I've always thought so, always hoped you did." Bruce had looked into those green eyes for just a moment too long, and that moment had changed both their lives.

Back then, as far as the world was concerned, Batman's very existence was still an open question. The only ones willing to swear that Batman was real were the criminals who had faced him in combat, a number of eyewitnesses, and a handful of journalists who did investigative work on the mysterious hero. Although most people were convinced of Batman's existence, no one could be fully certain. It was this haze of doubt that made him such an alluring personality. Batman was sort of an ambiguous legend. Until that night, he'd been a legend for Robin, too, he'd been an idea in the boy's mind, a clue, a body made up of dreams for the most part. Until that night, this was all he had been, but in the course of just a few days he'd become real, so real that he was now his lover.

Robin came into Bruce's life with the attitude of someone who meant to stay, and at first Bruce had been impressed, almost amused at the young man's determination, and at the idea that he was being courted by someone twenty years his junior. Robin would show up with presents he'd bought for a few dollars. He'd make awkward declarations. He recited short, clumsy poems into his answering machine. That boy was pathetic, yet somehow exciting. Bruce found it enjoyable to have him around. Enjoyable to be able to rely on his instant loyalty, on his feelings of adoration. Enjoyable to take him out to dinner, enjoyable to take him home afterwards, to fall asleep cuddling him. To wake up and find him there. Enjoyable to think that he was protecting someone, to take him under his wing and start to shape him, forge him; Robin wanted nothing more than to be forged.

The young man had moved into the mansion with him. He'd learned all Batman's secrets. He was strong, he was brave, and before long he'd become Batman's assistant. In fact, he was soon at Bruce's side every minute of the day and night: in the nights they spent patrolling the city, in the nights they spent in the bedroom. He was his assistant in his mission as a superhero, his assistant in the discovery of new sexual impulses. Robin satisfied every request. Robin complied with a smile whenever he was asked, giving in to Bruce's desires, silently offering his white and hairless body, like a sacrifice, like a soft laboratory animal.

With Robin, Bruce had discovered everything. He had discovered the physical type he liked. He had discovered the extremities of another body. Discovered the sensual moistness of toes, the overwhelming attractiveness of a pair of hands. Snow-white, promising hands. He had discovered the secrets of Robin's hands. He'd discovered their power, their flexible softness, discovered the pleasure of giving himself up to the well-trained hands of the other. Feeling Robin's heartbeat, in each of his hands, two small heartbeats in perfect unison. Two hands. Two systems of muscles, flesh, and nerves, two energy terminals, sensitive extremities, two perfect organs, two tiny miracles of evolution. The touch of those hands could fill him up. For years, Robin had filled his life, satisfied his body and his narcissism, his desire to have a disciple, an efficient partner, a pupil ready to believe whatever he said, a lover willing to lend his hands, his hand, from one night to the next with imperishable love.

*

He led the way to a small bathroom. He turned on the vanity lights over the mirror. A spotless granite sink awaited her. "Here's what I want you to do," he told the girl. "Something very simple. Just wash your hands," he explained, satisfied with the sound of his persuasive voice, and with the way in which his words seemed in part to penetrate into the girl, causing her to quiver slightly, and in part to bounce off her, like solar radiation bouncing off a planet's atmosphere. Bruce liked to dominate the person, but not entirely. Bruce liked it when the game had a shade of ambiguity to it. The slippery boundary between domination and being dominated. "Wash your hands," he ordered, in a velvety voice.

The girl obeyed. She betrayed no sign of amazement. She had certainly been instructed in what Bruce preferred. She soaped her hands and scrubbed them, calmly, under the stream of lukewarm water.

"That's right," Bruce panted. He watched her hands, those two white fragments, as they glowed in the silvery rush of water. The foam slid around her wrists like a bracelet, like the slobber of a mysterious animal. In those hands, too, just as in her face, there seemed to be something timeless and impersonal, the incarnation of a perfect principle. Bruce experienced some sort of painful dizziness. He wanted to grab those hands and press them to his face; he wanted to kiss them and gulp them down.

He enjoyed the show for a few minutes. He watched the two hands scrubbing, polished and smooth, one against the other. He watched the slender fingers. He could have gone on admiring them for hours. At last he decided it was enough, at least for the moment, and gave her a towel. "You did a good job," he said.

She dried her hands without haste, lazily. "I thought you'd want to watch me longer than that," was all she said. Her face was the picture of absolute calm.

Bruce decided that this girl would never be amazed at anything, any demand, any surprise, and that she would always preserve that same unruffled demeanour. That's what she was. Innocent and impassive. The girl looked up at him, without warning, a green-grey bolt that left him breathless. The friend who had sent her had guessed right. This girl definitely was his type.

They went back into the living room. The music welled up around them, welcoming them back, and the light from the lamps had the warmth of a sunset. The girl got comfortable on the sofa. "Oh," she said, as if relaxing after a strenuous effort.

Bruce filled two more glasses. He dropped a couple of ice cubes into each glass and stirred them with his finger. "Now, then," he said, as he handed the girl her drink. "What do you feel like talking about?"

The girl gave him one of her vague looks. "Talking about?" She seemed to think that over. "I couldn't say."

Bruce drew closer, touched her glass with the rim of his own. The two glass edges produced an almost imperceptible sound. "Tell me," he said, sitting down beside her. "Tell me what you did today."

"What I did today?" The girl dipped a finger into her own glass, to stir it the way Bruce had just done, then ran her wet finger over her lips. "Is that important?"

"No," Bruce admitted, staring at her finger, her inviting lips. "But still.

Just for something to talk about, just to get to know you a little better."
With a well-rehearsed smile, he prompted her: "I imagine you already
know all about me."

"Of course," she said, breaking eye contact. "You're Batman. Batman," she
said, uttering the name in an even voice, almost like a kind of watchword.
"Can I call you that? That is, can I call you Batman?"

"Sure. Call me whatever you want," he replied, sipping from his glass.
He imagined someone watching them right now, the two of them, the man
with the well-cared-for physique, bronzed, relaxed, sitting next to the sexy
girl. They must make quite a pretty picture. He felt pleasantly confident. He
reached out a hand and brushed the girl's lips, finding a fresh, damp trace.

She didn't seem to register his touch. She seemed capable of letting herself
be touched a thousand times, by a thousand hands, with the indifference
of a cat. "I'd say that today I got ready. I got ready for tonight."

Bruce laughed briefly. Not that there was anything funny, it just seemed
like the right moment for him to laugh. He let his hand slide towards the
nape of her smooth neck. "You got ready all day long?"

She seemed to stop and think it over again. "No, I went... Central Park.
I went to Central Park."

"You went to the park. And in fact, it was a beautiful day," Bruce conceded, feeling a sudden, indistinct pang of jealousy at the idea that she
had moved around the city that day without him. That happened to him
sometimes. The thought left him aghast. The thought that out there in
the world were girls and boys who were his type, girls and boys with that
gaze, that light in their eyes, those freckles on their noses. The thought that
they were out there, and he hadn't had them yet. It was stupid, he knew
that, but there wasn't much he could do about it. He went on caressing the
nape of her neck. He waited for the thought to go away. The nape of the
girl's neck was smooth and slender, and Bruce clutched it with a powerful,
almost violent grip.

She remained unfazed. "A beautiful day. Yes, it was. I lay on the grass
and read a book."

"That's nice," he said, taking his hand off her neck and letting it slide down
her back, exploring as it went. "All those trees, all those lovely squirrels." Her

back, too, was slender, and at the same time fairly powerful. He wondered what sports this girl played. He let his hand slide further down, discovering the knobs of her spinal column, counting them one by one, like the grains of a precious rosary. "Are you nervous?" he smiled, sensing tension at the base of her spine.

She ignored the question. "To tell the truth, the squirrels are the thing I like least. They make me think of rats." She took a sip from her glass, then asked with sudden emphasis: "Don't you think there's a relationship? I mean, a link between the squirrels in Central Park and the rats on the subway tracks."

Bruce smiled again, amused at her reasoning. "I don't know," he replied. "I never take the subway." He leaned in towards her, closer, until he could smell the scent of the wine on her breath. He could sense the moisture of her respiration. He could observe her heartbeat pulsating in her temple, and could feel the echo of that heartbeat down there, under his hand, where it lay confidently at the base of her back.

"You know what?" she went on. "I read that none of us are ever more than five metres away from the nearest rodent," she said, in the tone of someone revealing an important piece of information.

"You read a lot," he said, taking her hand.

The girl must have sensed a hint of irony in Bruce's voice, because she abruptly changed the subject: "And you?" she asked. "How did you spend your day?"

Bruce looked at her in surprise. People her age, and with her looks, rarely reciprocated a question with another. They usually just answered. They usually seemed incurious. "I bought some clothes. I worked out. I waited for you to arrive," he whispered, lifting her hand. He brushed the tips of her fingers with his lips. Then he extended his tongue and, with a shiver, sampled the flavour of her fingernails.

"I was convinced…" the girl stopped, trying to find the words to express her thought. "I was convinced you went to some exclusive health club to work out. I was convinced there was a gym where superheroes go. Where do you meet each other, you superheroes?"

"We don't," Bruce answered. He explored another one of her fingernails with his tongue. It tasted of iron, of seashell, of salt. He took the fingertip into his mouth and remained, for a few seconds, in complete peace.

"Oh," she said. "I thought superheroes saw each other socially."

Bruce could have explained it to her. He could have said that, in effect, the superheroes used to get together every now and then: they did the same work, they shared the same mission. Once most of them retired, though, they'd stopped seeing each other as often. Bruce remembered seeing Reed Richards, that old piece of gum, at the George Hotel's health club a couple of times. He remembered noticing that Reed was still in decent physical shape, though nowhere near his level. What had they talked about on those occasions? They must have chatted about the old days. They must have sat together in the panoramic sauna and watched the sunset. Later, Bruce had a home gym installed. He'd stopped going to the George Hotel, stopped meeting Reed or anyone else from the old scene. There was just no occasion. There was no reason. There really was nothing left for them to say to each other.

Bruce didn't explain all that to the girl. It wasn't a very sexy topic for discussion. It wasn't a topic suitable to the moment.

He let go of the delicious finger, having sucked it from top to bottom, realising that both their glasses were empty. He got to his feet but then changed his mind. He'd better not overdo it with the wine. Instead, he realised that the girl hadn't paid enough attention to the posters from the various movies inspired by his life, nor to the magazines with articles about him, nor to a certain object that was on the table. The precious object. The famous object. "Come here," he said. "Let's see if this time I can amaze you."

*

A few years had passed. Bruce and Robin still lived together. Their relationship was still intact, to all appearances anyway, even though many things had changed. Their life together would have seemed unchanged to outside eyes, like the shell of a shiny insect whose body was being devoured, in actuality, by a ravenous larva.

Bruce had started seeing other boys. At first it wasn't because he'd grown tired of Robin. It happened because those boys were young and available—each of them like the last one, and yet at the same time new—and he couldn't seem to remember, quite simply, a single good reason why he should remain faithful to just one person. The mystery of their faces and their elusive gazes. When a young man of the right type crossed his path, Bruce couldn't help but welcome him, with wonder, with gratitude, as if every young man were an emissary from the same distant land, the bearer of a secret that he was called upon to comprehend.

As for Robin, he watched in silence. His jealousy consisted of dismayed glances, sudden blushes, profound sadness. As he grew older, he had preserved his clear boyish face, a face that appeared to be immune to the complications of the outside world and the increasingly perverse, ever more fragmented rules of human desire. "I love you, Bruce. Why can't it be the way it used to be?"

"I love you too," Bruce tended to answer the first few times. "You'll stay with me, you'll go on living with me. But it can't be the same as it was, we're different people now. We've grown older."

Of the two of them, obviously, it was Robin who had committed the unforgivable sin of growing older. He was now a grown man. He had broad shoulders and a bit of a paunch, and two wreaths of golden hair that had sprouted around the buds of his light-coloured nipples. He was a man with a complete, virile body, a man who stood and watched, uncomprehending, as the person he loved got infatuated with boys who could claim only one merit: they were younger than him.

Their relationship had begun to deteriorate. Bruce couldn't have said when he started to find Robin, with his burdensome body, the wounded look on his face, irritating. More and more irritating. He wished Robin would look at the world with a more ironic gaze. Life was grim enough; what need was there for all this tragedy? He would have preferred for Robin to start sleeping around, would have preferred it if Robin had flown into a rage or wrecked the mansion. He would have preferred any reaction instead of that look, a look of love and absurd loyalty, clear as a dawning day, as impossible to look at as the glint of a knife.

After a couple more years, they had left the old mansion and moved into the city. They'd moved into a brownstone in the West Village. It was the end of the Eighties, the superhero scene was changing, word had spread that Reed Richards' old group had disbanded, and by now Bruce had unmasked himself to the public. For years, Batman's actual existence had ceased to be a secret. All that Bruce had done now was to make the matter official, becoming real to the eyes of the world, revealing his everyday identity. He'd started appearing on the occasional TV show and officiating at police ceremonies.

Robin had opposed this change. He thought the world needed its heroes to be legendary, to remain shrouded in the mists of the impossible. "Becoming real," he would say, in his awkward voice. "That's the worst conceivable thing for a hero."

Bruce didn't know what Robin was talking about. He'd lived in the shadows for so many years that he was happy to enjoy a little recognition for a change. In fact, he'd stopped patrolling the streets, but he continued to wear his costume for official occasions.

Without meaning to, they soon became one of New York City's most prominent couples. They were good-looking, famous, and miraculously healthy, a combination that wasn't all that common among the male couples of that period. The gossip columns were full of them. Their mailbox overflowed with invitations to glamorous events. The cult of their relationship spread like wildfire, inflaming the public's imagination. Apparently, people got excited about a love story only once it was on the way out.

At first, Bruce just laughed it off. He asked his acquaintances to tell him about all the absurd, hilarious rumours in circulation. Batman and Robin were about to get married in Hawaii. Batman and Robin had each had the other's name tattooed on his penis. Batman and Robin were about to adopt a Cambodian child, two female Siamese twins, an albino chimpanzee, or perhaps it was really an albino Cambodian child. It was so funny that you could just die laughing. Or else slap your head in amazement. As time passed, Bruce stopped laughing. He'd always liked the idea of people talking about him, but not in such ridiculous terms. Nor was he particularly happy about his name being so bound up with Robin's.

By now, he felt far away from him. Far away from that overgrown, submissive boy, from that heavy man in his thirties who had too long ago given up gyms and wrestling mats. Far away from that man with the overly sensitive skin and the face of an ageing child, with his freckles and his receding hairline, far from his tiresome loyalty, his irritating consistency, and his same old enthusiasm for the same old things. Robin still got excited about every stupid new electronic gadget. He spent hours in the basement of their house in the West Village, like a teenager, modifying electronic circuits and fine-tuning the weapons with which his costume was equipped. He'd never got tired of being a superhero. He was convinced he could go on forever. Compared to him, Bruce felt like he was on another planet. He had long ago grown weary of being the caped defender, of fighting in the streets, of technological gadgets. And above all, he had grown weary of Robin.

The next step had been to start humiliating him in public. It started one summer afternoon, one of those hot afternoons that seem designed to make people edgier, crueller, or more fragile. He'd made a comment about Robin's physical condition in front of strangers, prompting a few embarrassed giggles, and those giggles had rung the starting bell, ushering in a new season of cruelty. On another occasion, he'd taken Robin out to dinner for his birthday, pretending he was being nice, letting Robin order whatever he wanted, then he'd summoned the waiter back to the table and informed him that the gentleman had changed his mind, and that he'd only be eating a salad tonight, because of his *evident weight problems*. Ha ha! The look on Robin's face!

Humiliating his old lover was an amusing pastime. Laughing at him behind his back was even better. At parties, the minute Robin went to get a drink, Bruce would make some wisecrack about him, about the way he dressed or his bad breath, after making sure he had someone around him stupid enough to laugh, and sufficiently insensitive to go on looking at Robin, for the rest of the evening, with a treacherous smile.

When he was certain that Robin was watching from a distance, he'd flirt shamelessly with anyone—male or female—who was young enough, well aware that Robin would be obsessed for days by the faces of those people, even by the faces of those who didn't matter in the slightest, people that Bruce would have forgotten just minutes later. He knew that he'd won when he saw Robin hurry away, crushed, red-faced. "Wasn't that your boyfriend?" someone might chance to ask.

"Him? More like my secretary."

When he chose to take someone home, he'd make sure that Robin knew it. He'd leave the bedroom door open so that Robin would hear every last sound. Bruce's sadism swelled in waves, for days and weeks, only to fall quiet all at once like a wind that had been placated. Then came very different nights. Nights when Bruce would tiptoe into his ex-lover's bedroom. He'd creep silently up to Robin's bedside, careful not to wake him, and he'd watch him sleep, studying him calmly, trying to fathom the mystery of that man's faithfulness. *Why on earth do you still love me?* he'd whisper in the silence of the night. *I'm old, vain, and insufferable. Why on earth are you still with me?*

In the semi-darkness of the bedroom, he stood watching Robin's pale, trusting face, with the inevitable trace of pimples triggered by some psychosomatic disturbance. At times like that, a surge of tenderness bubbled up in Bruce, from some distant forgotten place, and his hand would reach out to stroke that face, tracing small curves, as if filling it with question marks. Was this the fate of every love story? What had happened, and how could it be that things were ending like this? *Was I ever really in love with you, and what did it mean to be in love?*

You're not enough for me, he'd whisper in the end. *You're not enough for me, no one's enough,* he'd add, in the tone of someone asking forgiveness, knowing full well that tomorrow everything would go back to its usual way. The next morning, Robin would still have the same shortcomings, his same introverted, tiresome, annoying ways, his skin problems, his bad digestion, his lack of humour, and Bruce's cruelty would return, the same as ever, atrocious, implacable, the baffling cruelty of unrequited love. On one of those nights, Robin had shivered. His respiration had quickened, and Bruce had understood that he wasn't asleep. Without opening his eyes, Robin had seized his hand, running it over his face and then his chest, sighing, almost sobbing. It must have been close to dawn. Robin's skin had the whiteness of a spectre. "Don't leave me, Bruce. I feel so lonely, Bruce." He'd gone on squeezing his hand, rubbing it over his body, harder and harder, over his white body, ever lower, towards his straining groin.

Bruce stood there, inert, for a few seconds, in a daze, then shook himself, with a stab of pity and disgust. He'd pulled back his hand.

Robin had twisted on the bed like a snake struck by a mortal blow. "On the nights I go out on patrol, everything out there seems so senseless. We were heroes, Bruce, and we were together. I feel lonely. More and more alone."

Bruce had walked away, his head spinning, and after that night he'd never entered Robin's bedroom again. At times he fantasised about Robin leaving, breaking the chains of their reciprocal dependency. But he knew Robin would never leave. He lacked the strength, or perhaps he just didn't know where to go. Robin limited himself to going out three or four nights a week, in his superhero costume, solitary, silent, a hero without his captain, a follower without his leader. He'd come home exhausted at sunrise, after dozens of patrols around the city.

Bruce never knew how many criminals Robin fought on those nights. He didn't even know whether there were still criminals out there to fight, criminals like there were in the old days, on the street, criminals you could identify and challenge to fight. Times had changed. This was New York and these were the Nineties, coordinates in the space-time continuum that one day would be looked back on and regarded as an ambiguous time, full of light and perverse promises. The streets were being cleaned up. The police were using summary methods. According to official figures, major crime was being swept off the streets. Who knows. Did that mean, perhaps, that the crime was moving elsewhere? Bruce had the impression that the world's crime was actually slithering all around, sidling off, blending in everywhere, concealed in every home like the hand of a ventriloquist inside a dummy. Evil still existed, more than ever, it had just got harder to recognise, more difficult to pin down. It reverberated around people like a strange magnetic wave, and you couldn't say where it came from.

He had told Robin to stop it more than once. No one from the old scene went out to patrol the city any more. It made more sense to leave that work to the iron-fisted mayors and the police chiefs, to the Rudolph Giulianis and the William Brattons and all the nice officers of the law who were paid for it. "You're out of shape and you're alone now. When you're the only one still doing something, doing it becomes dangerous. Isn't it time to stop?"

*

Music whispered softly from the stereo. Bruce waited for the girl to join him at the table. She came over with a look of polite interest, glancing at the paper object that he was holding up. "What's that?"

"A calendar," Bruce explained. He smiled indulgently, as if she were begging him to let her see it. Then he handed it over.

The girl laid the calendar down on the table and started turning the pages.

Bruce stayed watching her, waiting, peering at her face as she reacted to each picture.

"They're superheroes," she noted, as she went on turning the pages.

"Of course they are," said Bruce. After all, wasn't she the one who had asked him if superheroes still got together?

In truth, none of those superheroes had met the others for those pictures. Each of them had been photographed on a different set, and practically none of them belonged to the old guard of heroes. For the most part, they belonged to the scarcely known new crew. A certain Iguana Man posed on a desert dune, wearing nothing but a scaly loincloth, his muscles smeared with lubricant. Another named Black Crystal had his picture taken at the mouth of a volcano, with one hand placed to cover his private parts, the other hand lifted to create a small sphere of light. An unlikely Ice Champion had earned the February page, posing in a snow-covered forest, naked and unashamed, leaning back against the trunk of a tree in a lewd pose. Bruce had no idea who any of those people were. He guessed they must be mutants, and that they worked on TV or something like that. You couldn't say that the calendar had actually caused them to meet; however, there they were, one after the other, picture after picture, month by month.

The girl got to July. She paused, staring with a vague expression at the picture of Bruce. In the picture, Bruce was standing by the side of a swimming pool, naked, wet, his body gleaming in the sunlight. His leg muscles were taut, like right after a gym session, and his cock stood out, white, lustrous as a seashell, while the rest of his body was perfectly tanned. His relaxed smile gleamed white too, and tiny drops of water illuminated his hair, making it look as if it were made of light. "You have a nice physique," the girl commented in her polite tone of voice.

Bruce went on looking at the picture. That portrait inspired in him a profound, pure, almost painful pride. It was a different piece of work from Quirst's sculpture. In artistic terms, it was a lesser work, of course, nothing more than an ordinary calendar shot, but still, in that photograph he was beautiful with a tender, almost vulnerable beauty.

Of course, he knew about all the criticism that the photograph had prompted. A superhero like him! A public figure with a past like his, with his prestige, reduced to showing off his dick in a pin-up calendar. He was the only superhero his age featured in the calendar. There he was, with his trim body, surrounded by other men thirty years his junior. There he was, with his muscular legs, with his firm abs. Still riding his wave. Still alive. Bruce could have looked at that photograph for hours, comparing his body with the other bodies on the calendar, every last muscle, every detail, without entirely grasping the truth of that image, without ever being able to reach a final verdict: *it's me, I look great. Do I look a little ridiculous? And if I do, does that matter? Isn't mankind as a whole ridiculous?*

The girl looked at the picture for a few more seconds, before turning to the next page. Disappointed, Bruce found himself studying the portrait for the month of August.

Bruce suppressed his urge to object. He felt sure that none of the portraits after his were of any interest. "Now, you just take him—the Spinning Top," he let slip, noticing she was lingering on that page. "What kind of superhero is he? Nobody knows what he's supposed to be able to do. It isn't clear what superpowers he has." The girl nodded without conviction, and went on studying the picture of the young man with a taut physique, a serious expression on his Hispanic features. Bruce felt increasingly indignant. "It's certainly not clear who that guy's fighting against. Correct me if I'm wrong, but I think he wasn't even born in the U.S., so you tell me what he's doing here. These new superheroes are incomprehensible to me. They have powers that nobody understands but them," he continued, until he sensed that the girl's smile was strained with embarrassment. It dawned on him that he was coming across as an aged scold, with perhaps even a hint of anti-immigrant racism.

The girl decided to shut the calendar. "Don't get mad. The best picture in here is the one of you."

Bruce stepped away, annoyed at his own impatience and at the slightly hypocritical tone in the girl's voice. He didn't want to hear those kinds of remarks. He didn't want pro forma compliments. He expected other people to believe in him, in an absolute manner, without reservations.

He snorted in annoyance, wondering whether he ought to change the music on the stereo. Even that wouldn't be enough though. The intimate atmosphere in the room was dissolving rapidly, like the oxygen in an aeroplane losing air pressure. Now he felt the urge to move around. He left the girl in the living room and shut himself in the bathroom.

He splashed cold water on his face. With his damp hands, he brushed back the hair he'd kept thick over the years by diligent consumption of finasteride tablets. The hair he maintained a natural-looking brown with the assistance of a Bleecker Street hairdresser. He turned on more lights. His face looked radiant in the mirror, almost electric, except for the hint of a shadow under the eyes and around the mouth, as if those areas were beginning to sag. He pondered the option of smoking a little crystal meth. It might be a good idea—who knows—it might make his face luminous and convex again, free of sagging, and get things running fluidly, without a hitch, like in a perfect script. He thought how carefree he'd felt a couple of hours ago, at the start of the evening, when the girl was still a dream, nothing but an expectation, when he was still dancing in front of the mirror. He found himself missing that moment. Missing being alone.

Perhaps he should ask Doctor Szepanski about it. He needed an operation on those marks around his mouth. Doctor Szepanski would have plenty of advice about cosmetic surgery. Bruce had already had a couple of understated facelifts, and in both cases Szepanski, that old reconstructed monster, had recommended the right surgeon. Recently, Bruce had also asked him for advice on the idea of having a little operation done on himself down under, to see if he could become as tight as he used to be.

Plastic surgery on the mouth and plastic surgery on the ass. What could be more complementary? he asked himself, and at that point he burst out laughing, shaking his head, tapping his face with more cold water. *I'm fine, my face is fine,* he decided at last, with a blend of triumph and despair.

He walked back into the living room with a new resolution. Time to get the night moving forward. He headed straight for the couch, from which the girl rose to her feet with an apprehensive look. It must have occurred to her that she'd ticked him off. "I was waiting for you," she said. It looked like she too had touched up her hair. "I wondered what had happened to you. What should we do now? Do you want me to wash my hands again?"

"No," said Bruce in a dry voice, determined to get a firmer rein on the game. He pretended to think it over for a moment, then he relaxed into an amiable smile. "I think it's time to change a little. I think it's time for you to take your clothes off."

*

Robin died one winter night, in the darkest corner of Central Park, where the forensic squad said that he'd been dragged forcibly, and where someone had cut his throat.

He must have taken some time to die. He'd left a long trail of blood down an unpaved path in the park, and a fair amount of dirt under his fingernails suggested that he'd crawled on all fours, dying, perhaps in search of help that never came. More blood pooled around his body. The blood had frozen during the night, forming a dark, gleaming puddle, as if every drop of that blood had been transformed into a tiny bright crystal. His eyes, too, had frozen wide open, and when Bruce arrived the next morning he'd glimpsed his own reflection in them: he'd been able to recognise his face, the face of a mature man, all alone now.

It's happened, he told himself. It had happened, happened for real, happened with no way back. The man who had been his sidekick for years, the man who had always been loyal to him, the man who had offered him his most fervent love, lay there, lifeless, on the grass at his feet.

The policemen on the scene had felt obliged to express condolences appropriate for a widower. "We're so sorry, Mr. Wayne." "Try to be strong, Mr. Wayne."

Bruce was wearing his Batman costume, and wrapped his cape around himself, shivering with a chill in the leaden morning light. They asked him if he knew anything about Robin's nights in recent times, what Robin was up to, if he had any enemies or for that matter, any friends. Bruce shook his head. No idea. There had been such silence between Robin and him in the last period. Silence, distance, and coldness. Before he died, Robin had scratched some marks into the damp soil with his fingers: tangled, meaningless grooves, along which the blood had gathered in a system of minuscule canals, leading nowhere.

A slashing sleet was falling now. He had accepted a cup of coffee from a young policeman named Dennis De Villa, a guy who in a few years would be promoted to detective and whom Bruce would keep running into, from time to time, at police ceremonies and other official events. "Try to be strong," he too had told Bruce. "Try to be strong."

Bruce went home in a cab, soaking the seat with his wet costume. When he got there, he waited to take off the costume, frightened at the thought of being left naked, scared at the idea that maybe, once he took it off, he'd never be able to put it on again. For so many years, that costume had been his life. For years, he had been Batman, the Dark Knight, the caped defender with his trusted sidekick. For years, he and Robin had eluded death, night after night, avoiding death's ambushes, almost laughing in its face.

In the end he took off his costume. He held it in both hands, wet, light-weight, not knowing what to do with it, as though expecting it to take on a life of its own. He had felt naked and empty. Now what should he do? Call someone, go to sleep? Wait for the reporters to start calling him?

The only thing he'd managed to do was to watch a movie. The movie that he'd never stopped watching over the years, ever since he was a child, the movie that had always inspired, frightened, and moved him. The movie he'd watched dozens of times, with Robin as well. That old movie, made decades earlier. He sat there, watching the adventures of Zorro, motionless, lifeless, in the living room of his house in the West Village, while outside the taxis drove past, the pedestrians walked by, and the city seemed absurdly unchanged.

It wasn't until the end, when Zorro took off his mask, that Bruce realised he was crying. The tears poured down freely, almost flavourless, and Bruce imagined someone else looking at him now, seeing a middle-aged man with a worked-out body, lying on a sofa, weeping silently in front of a movie made decades ago. He'd pitied himself. He cursed himself and felt guilty, lost, exhausted, as if some protective coating had vanished from the surface of his body and the weariness of so many years had plummeted down into him, all at once. He'd sat on the sofa long after the movie was over. He sat motionless as the afternoon stretched out, until there was nothing left inside him, not a sniff or a whimper, no emotion, just a sense of reality, a pure shard of awareness, transparent as a sliver of broken glass: it was over now. Robin was dead, truly dead.

*

They had moved into the kitchen. On the crystal shelves were pieces from a porcelain collection, deluxe electric appliances, an Italian-designed espresso maker, and a vase of orchids. Shafts of light filtered down from the ceiling, as all-enveloping as liquid spotlights. The girl was sitting under one of those lights. She was wearing no clothes. She seemed pretty comfortable, perched on a stool, under that light and under Bruce's gaze. She was broad-shouldered, slender though she was. Tapered arms, small erect breasts that remained motionless, like a buoy in the waves, as her breathing raised and lowered her chest. "The thing I like best about your place," she said, in a tone that seemed to seek forgiveness for having annoyed Bruce a short while earlier, "is definitely the light."

"The light?" Bruce said, feigning surprise.

"It's a light that has a certain…" The girl shifted slightly on the stool: "…warmth," she concluded. She had a taut abdomen. A hint of light-coloured hair on her pudendum. Her legs were tapered too, and smooth as a piece of flint.

Bruce moved closer. "They say seduction starts with the lighting," he said, pleased with the timbre of his voice. "A body glistens in the right light. Bodies are like planets, they know how to glisten in the depth of darkness."

"Oh," she said politely.

Bruce walked around the stool and stopped behind the girl. Raising both arms, he formed a shape with his hands so that they cast a shadow onto the floor. It was the silhouette of a bat, or perhaps a vampire, fluttering as it dropped down towards the girl's head. The girl laughed. He smiled. He separated his hands and the bat vanished, leaving only their two shadows, drawing closer and closer. Bruce grazed the nape of her neck. He distinctly saw a shiver run down from her neck and spread across her back. So he stopped grazing her with his fingertips and asked: "Are you hungry?"

"What?" she asked, in a baffled voice.

"Hungry?" Bruce asked again, stepping away from her, satisfied that he'd undermined her confidence. "My housekeeper left us a first-rate dinner," he went on, pulling from the fridge a bowl of salad of bitter lettuce and fruit, and a plate of cold meats garnished with fresh coriander. He set the delicacies on the worktop.

"They look wonderful," she said, somewhat listlessly. "Even though I have to confess… I'm afraid I'm not very hungry."

"I want to watch you eat," Bruce replied in a courteous and inflexible manner. "And get to know you a little better," he added, as he started making up a plate for her.

"You're not going to have anything?"

"Oh no. I'll keep myself free," he smiled, handing her the plate.

The girl seemed about to object, then she accepted the plate. A shadow of resignation passed over her face for an instant, making her even more attractive.

"Get to know me better…" she echoed, crossing her naked legs on the stool.

"Of course." Bruce took a seat on the stool across from her. "Do you think that getting you naked is enough for me?" He smiled indulgently, either at her or at himself, before going on: "For instance, let me see… That thing we were talking about."

"What thing?"

"What you said about what you did today. You went to the park to read a book."

"Oh," she said, poking at the salad on the plate with her fork. "At the park, that's right."

Bruce poured himself a glassful from a pitcher of iced water. He took a sip with a studied gesture. "Tell me more," he prodded. "Tell me about the book you read."

"The book…" The girl stalled for time by taking a few bites of salad, then smiled: "It's almost like you're testing me."

Bruce smiled in turn, aroused by the minor skirmish. Aroused by the way she perched nude on the stool, in that light, by the way she ate and how her hand gripped the fork, calmly spearing one piece of fruit after another. Once again, he felt seduced by the girl's poise and mystery. "I'm just curious," he said. "Tell me about the book you were reading."

"Foucault," she sighed. "I was reading Michel Foucault."

"Foucault?!" Bruce exclaimed. "That's surprising," he admitted. "I didn't think you young people read that stuff."

"I don't know what young people read," she said dryly. "It's what *I'm* reading."

"I understand," he observed, increasingly delighted. Now the girl's skin seemed tense, as delicate as rice paper. "I'm afraid I've never been able to make it through that kind of stuff," he declared. "French philosophy. Verbose French theorising. Verbose pompous French meditations."

"Foucault isn't verbose," she objected.

"Isn't he the one that they say was into S&M?" A provocative spark glinted in his eyes. "I'm not sure that I could take a philosopher seriously if I knew he was into S&M," he said, dismissing the topic with calculated arrogance.

The girl couldn't stop a doubtful expression from crossing her face. She looked at her own naked body and then looked at Bruce, sitting in the middle of this luxurious kitchen. The circumstances hardly seemed appropriate, after all, for criticising someone else's sexual conduct.

He burst out laughing. "You have a point," he said, and dropped the subject. He wanted to go back to grazing her skin. He could still feel, like a soft trace, the warmth from the nape of her neck. He felt like touching her and being touched, and felt something expanding, like a bubble of anticipation, in the depths of his body. "Don't take it the wrong way," he whispered. "I'm just teasing you."

He took a coriander leaf from her plate and held it in his fingers: "Coriander has always aroused me. It has such a physical scent. It seems like the scent of another person." In the warm light, the girl's face had started to fade into a nuanced, arcane shape—practically perfect. Bruce placed the leaf between her lips. He waited for her to chew and swallow. He moved his face closer and finally kissed her.

*

The sentiments he felt for Robin after his death were the same as he had felt for Robin when he was alive. A blend of tenderness, remorse, and annoyance. Robin had died with his indestructible, irritating faithfulness, before being forced to admit that it was all over: the world of the superheroes, the relationship between the two of them. He'd died just as stubbornly as he'd lived. That poor boy. That damned boy. For a while, after the murder, Bruce had feared that Robin would become a martyr, one of those figures that turn into legends, unexpectedly, just because they died young. He couldn't have taken that burden. The last thing he wanted was for the world to see him, from that day on, as nothing more than a bereft widower.

What happened, instead, was that although the news of his murder had had a certain impact, the newspapers soon tired of the case, and Robin was denied admittance to the capricious Olympus of contemporary mythology. When he was alive, he'd been too even-tempered, too predictable, too discreet. Outside his relationship with Batman, he'd never been the topic of gossip, never made a strong impression on the public, except for a small group of underground fans, obscure folk musicians and people of that sort. Who now wrote to Bruce letters of support, letters for which he felt no particular need.

He'd spent the very night of the funeral with a boy. His body had sucked in the boy's hand with the greed of a carnivorous plant. He'd sweated so much that the linen on his bed was drenched. Later, a procession of other young men followed, and after them an array of young women, and he'd never stopped sweating, begging, and drenching his sheets.

After each encounter, he woke up the following morning in his damp sheets, ravenous, in a state of dazed disturbing lucidity. Each time, he found himself breakfasting on his beloved organic cereals, or showering in his luxurious stall with hydro-massage jets, mulling over the events of the night before. Even though they were recent memories, they always struck him as profoundly alien: *Was that me? That man who was sweating, moaning, lost in pleasure? Was that really me—that grunting, drooling, begging man?*

He was aware, in a confused fashion, that a gap was opening up inside him, something that made him feel remote, more and more separate from himself. He could sense his emotions echoing in the distance as if down the corridors of a labyrinth. He watched himself live as if at the centre of a spectacle: having sex with new people, going to the gym, having his hair done, lying on tanning beds, buying the perfect creams for his skin. He was a man with a lot on his hands. He had things to do. He had an old family corporation to run, interviews to give, a body to keep fit. He had sessions with his personal trainer, appointments with his dietician, social events where he needed to be seen. He needed to stay at the centre of the world. At the centre of some world, any world.

And he needed to see his doctor, of course, and have himself checked out. With the things he did in bed, it was a good idea to have himself monitored. Doctor Szepanski asked him lots of questions. He'd always asked him questions, especially about his sexual predilections, but after Robin's death the questions increased. Bruce didn't have much to answer. What could he add to the simple fact that he loved young people? The way he loved them seemed to him eminently natural, inexorable like a destiny. He loved their intensity, their detachment, the luminosity of their skin, and the secret in their eyes.

From a certain point, it had even ceased to matter that they were males. It had been a gradual discovery. What he loved most was an incorporeal, not individual, principle, which by now he was able to recognise equally in males or females. It was a sort of spirit. That is what he loved. The elusive spirit that certain young people seemed to possess, a spirit that lived in them for a handful of years. Bruce loved that spirit, he loved that sort of soul that seemed to look out at him, always the same, ancient and fleeting, through the eyes of any boy or girl.

"So since when do you like girls?" Doctor Szepanski had asked him one day. Bruce didn't know what to tell him. He'd always known he liked girls; that he liked them even more than boys was something he'd discovered with the passage of time. He couldn't have said how much Robin's death had influenced that change, or how much of a role had been played by the fact that, as he aged, he'd started to hate the comparison between his own and other men's bodies. He'd stopped feeling enthusiasm for powerful young men. He'd even stopped going to his health club, bothered by the sight of all those youthful muscles, those carefree bodies. Young males seemed capable of staying fit with the slightest effort. To hell with them. He worked out for real. He exercised for two hours a day, he paid hundreds-of-dollars-an-hour masseurs, and stuck to rigorous diets. The bodies of young males filled him with a vague resentment. The bodies of young women never demanded a comparison.

Girls knew how to be even more ambiguous, more elusive and yet, at the same time, more compliant. A girl seemed to promise something more, access to a subtler, moister, more brilliant plane of reality. A girl seemed never to allow herself to be entirely possessed, and yet was able to enter wholly into Bruce's fantasies, into his idea of seduction. Seducing a girl was more fluid, almost choreographic. It was a scene from a perfect film. Whatever words he might say, whatever gestures he might make, they echoed better around a girl's body. They slid more easily over her fine skin.

The world, for its part, went on taking for granted that he liked men. Gay associations invited him to their events, the press listed him among the most influential gays on the planet. For a while Bruce had let things run their course. One evening he had even found himself as a guest of honour at a gala charity banquet, in London, sitting next to Elton John. The dinner had a theme: *the rainbow*. Every dish had been prepared so that it contained the six colours of the rainbow flag. Purple cabbage leaves, which Bruce detested, had been added everywhere as garnish to ensure the presence of that colour. Elton John wore a suit custom-made for the occasion, clearly inspired by a wild chromatic fantasia, and glasses adorned with multicoloured sequins. Bruce had watched him out of the corner of his eye all through the evening, as though he were observing a rare tropical parrot. *My God*, he had said to himself. *What am I doing here?* He liked dark clothes. He liked sexy young girls. He didn't have many topics of conversation with Elton John, and the smell of cabbage made him sick to his stomach.

He had tried to shed his image as a gay icon by telling a couple of interviewers the way things were. But the myth persisted. To the eyes of most people he was still the king of homoeroticism, a sexual beacon for homo males of half the planet. Men of all ages came on to him in the most unlikely situations: in an airport lounge. In the changing booths of a boutique. In a dentist's waiting room.

On another public occasion, during a speech he gave in Texas for the inauguration of a museum, a group of anti-gay activists had protested against him with whistles and catcalls, holding up signs:

SUPERGAY, SUPERSHAMEFUL

DOWN WITH GAY BATS

LEAVE OUR YOUTHS ALONE

Bruce had kept his cool, flashing a scornful smile and continuing his speech, until he spotted another sign:

YOUR BOYFRIEND TOOK IT UP THE ASS IN CENTRAL PARK

At that point he walked off the stage. Until then, he hadn't realised there were people like that, men and women who ran internet sites with Nazi overtones, who signed petitions demanding the incarceration of homosexuals in concentration camps, who chartered buses and clocked up hundreds of miles to protest against homosexual, or supposed homosexual, public figures. The gay associations responded by bringing lawsuits. To all appearances, there was a war being waged. But what did it have to do with him?

The investigation into Robin's murder, in the meanwhile, had pursued that very lead. The police were considering the theory of a homophobic murder. The theory had awakened a new fireball of media interest, then everything had gone cold again. The investigation never made any real progress. Bruce didn't think much of the homophobic lead. He didn't put a lot of credence in other leads, either. When it came to Robin's murder, any ability he might have to imagine a logic, a truth that might exist beyond the veil of the facts, came to a halt. That death appeared to him as mysterious and natural as a trail designed by the wind. He had the impression that he could do nothing but contemplate what had happened. His whole life he had always reacted to events. Now he could only observe them as they emerged, around him, like statues in an expanse of fog.

He was sixty years old. Sometimes the thought filled him with astonishment. Astonishment in his throat, on the tip of his tongue. Astonishment at the thought of the things that were happening, the things that had happened once and for all: the years, the boys, the girls, the rainbow flag, the Batman costume, the scent of the vials of amyl nitrate, his own face reflected in the eyes of a corpse, the frozen puddle of blood on the dirt of Central Park. All those things. All those events. And the nameless criminals. The ones who had murdered Robin, leaving Bruce free, and abysmally alone.

*

The girl was a bad kisser. She kissed like a girl. Bruce shoved his tongue in deeper, further back, into the soft regions of her mouth, seeking out the flavour of the coriander and of the salad she had just eaten. That was one of the disadvantages. Young people didn't know how to kiss.

Of course, that wasn't the only disadvantage. Young people, to tell the whole truth, tended to be passive. Pretty passive. Young people didn't know how to carry on a lively conversation. Young people appeared to understand everything, because they were trained to put on that air of cool knowingness, but then they'd come out with some nonsensical or banal point of view. Young people were insubstantial. They seemed always on the verge of evaporating. Young people were people you'd be well advised to get rid of as quickly as possible, because over time they took more than they could ever give back. Young people only knew how to say one word—me, me, me—and Bruce wasn't that inclined to talk about the me of other people. That's what young people were like. Still, he couldn't stop loving them. As for tonight's girl, there was no denying that she seemed better than most people her age. He grazed her petite breasts with his fingers, cupping them for a minute in his hands. "Little one," he whispered. "I think it's time to go to the last room."

Bruce had tried, in the past, going out with women closer to his own age. He'd experienced the complicity of two mature bodies. He'd enjoyed the pleasure of conversing with someone who didn't constantly demand blandishment, stimulation and teasing, someone with whom it was possible to speak as equals. He remembered taking a bath with one of those women. He remembered mirroring himself in her eyes. At the decisive moment, he'd been incapable of carrying on further. He couldn't fall in love with the hands of a mature person. Young people could be inept in a thousand ways, boring and irritating in a thousand ways, and yet there was always that precious spark in them. There was something about young people. In some of them, there was that incorporeal hint, that sort of spirit that Bruce was searching for.

They entered the bedroom. During the previous tour of the house, Bruce had skipped that room to preserve the surprise. Here too the lighting was well designed. An amber-coloured light, whose source was impossible to locate, filled the room. The girl took a few steps, naked, exquisite, into that dreamlike light. The floor was made of a russet wood, with a strip of black wood that led, like a trail, to the large bed floating in mid-air. "A magnetic bed," she observed. "So there's still a little love of technology in you."

"Oh, this isn't technology," he said, as he began to strip. He braced himself against the bed and took off his shoes. "It's just a magnetic field, nothing could be more natural."

"Interesting," she said, with an ambiguous smile. "Being on it must be a bit like flying."

"Flying," Bruce repeated, as he tugged his shirt out of his trousers. Something about the way she had uttered the word, *flying*, echoed in his head. "Strange," he said. "I've known several people in my life who knew how to fly. Superheroes, I mean. And yet I never had any desire to do it myself."

The girl said nothing.

A suspicion surfaced in Bruce's mind. "You wouldn't be one of those people who think they can do it… That is, you wouldn't be one of those people who are convinced they have superpowers, would you? Or even worse, you wouldn't be one of those who *have* superpowers, would you?"

She stopped short in the middle of the bedroom. "Of course not. Why do you ask?"

Bruce went on unbuttoning his shirt. "Sometimes… sometimes young people come here with that kind of idea. They wait for the opportunity to ask me if I can help them become superheroes. As if there were still something interesting about being a superhero." Contracting his abs, he took off his shirt; he carefully laid it on the shelf next to the bed. Undressing was almost as much of a ritual as getting dressed. He mulled it over for a few seconds, then he added: "But now that I think about it, not the girls. For as long as I've been seeing girls, not one of them has asked me to help her become a superhero."

For some reason the girl sighed. "And neither do I," she said. "I've never wanted to be a… to be one of you. I think I have other wishes."

Bruce sighed, too. He could feel the anticipation growing in his body, in his stomach, an increasingly hot impelling bubble. He cleared his throat. "Wishes?" he asked with a note of amusement, to show that he was still in control. "Oh, you kids don't have any wishes," he teased her. "You have fantasies, which is another matter."

The girl smiled nervously, clutching herself. Bruce guessed she must be feeling as impatient as he was, or perhaps afraid. Inexperienced people were often afraid. "All right," she conceded. "If I can't say *wishes*… Let's just say that I have other ideas about my future."

"You kids don't even have ideas," Bruce honed in. "At the very most, you have sensations."

"All right," she said again, in exasperation. "Let's at least say that I have a destiny."

"You have a destiny?" Bruce said, like someone uttering an exotic word. "And exactly what would your destiny be?"

She shrugged. Then she dropped her arms by her sides and stood there before him, in apparent surrender.

Bruce shivered. He decided the time had come. "Listen," he said, his voice faltering with a mixture of excitement and sudden tenderness. "This is your destiny in the immediate future." He leaned against the bed again, trembling slightly. "Now you're going to go in there, into the bathroom, and wash your hands. The lights are on, leave them that way. From here I'll be able to see your shadow while you wash your hands. Take your time washing them, and be infinitely thorough. Let the water run for a long time. I want to hear you washing your hands. I'll be here, I'll be waiting for you."

The girl hesitated, absorbing the orders she'd just received. Then she got moving.

Bruce heard the sound of running water. He finished undressing and lay down, naked, on the levitating bed.

He imagined someone watching him. He flexed and relaxed his muscles, all together, quivering to the sound of water from the other room. He could distinguish every tiny splash, the sound of every jet of water in the sink. He closed his eyes and opened them again. He leaned over, picked up a vial of amyl nitrate from the shelf, and snorted. Then he lay down again. The bedroom ceiling seemed to pulsate, above him, like the wall of an immense organ. He lost himself in that pulsation, in that half-light, as everything seemed to become more intense: the density of the bed underneath him, the soft sensation in his stomach, the flow of his blood, the noise of water from the bathroom. When the sound of the tap ceased, his penis leapt instantly erect.

*

The girl came back from the bathroom. She stopped about ten feet away from the bed, looking down at Bruce, who lay there waiting. He lifted his head. "Little one, why are you so far away?" he asked, in a gentle, almost fatherly voice. "Don't worry. It'll be easy, you'll see."

She came closer. Bruce writhed on the bed. In the liquid light he made the muscles in his chest and abdomen ripple, he took his penis and aimed it, in jest, straight at her like a weapon. She didn't seem to be especially impressed. She stayed there staring at the tattoo that Bruce had on his left pectoral. "When I saw it in the picture on the calendar," she said, "I didn't understand. I thought it was a scar."

"Oh no," he said, touching his chest. "It's my tattoo. A souvenir from the old days," he sighed, in a faraway voice. Reality around him had started to change. He heard the sounds growing remote. He could sense things slipping into the distance, he could feel the air becoming rarefied, as he hovered in that sea of arousal and anxious expectancy.

She went on staring raptly at the tattoo on Bruce's flesh. It depicted a small black bat. "Batman," she uttered. "Batman."

"Listen," he panted, very slowly, as though they had now lurched into another level of reality, a slippery, unprecedented level, where everything had to be explained with care. "Listen closely," he said. "There's some lubricant on that shelf."

She shook herself, and followed the direction of his gaze. "This?" she asked.

"Squeeze some out and lubricate your hand," he panted.

The girl seemed to hesitate. "Shouldn't I wear a glove?"

"Don't worry," Bruce replied. He writhed again on the bed. He explained: "Tonight you've washed your hands enough. I looked at your fingernails, they're nicely trimmed." And since she was still hesitating: "Don't worry, it's all okay in there. I get myself checked out often. It's all safe and soft, and it's just waiting for your hand."

She looked at her right hand, with an incredulous gaze, as though awakening from a strange dream. Then she nodded and picked up the lubricant.

Her fingers slid in first. They slipped in, joined together in a point, exploring forwards like curious probes. When the main knuckles reached the ring of the anus, the girl stopped.

"Add more lubricant," Bruce exhaled. "Turn your hand slightly."

"I can't do it," the girl whined, her voice cracking with something that, for an instant, sounded like a quake of panic.

"Turn your hand," Bruce moaned.

The taste of amyl nitrate filled his throat. He was holding his legs high, his feet resting on her shoulders. When her hand was inside, he breathed hard and relaxed completely. The hand impaled him like a tender crochet hook. He could feel it pushing deeper into the intimacy of his body. His heart seemed to fall mute as if surprised by the intrusion, then resumed beating with a new, almost aching awareness. "Now make a fist," he begged her. "Gently!" he moaned straight afterwards.

All that remained in the bedroom was their breathing. The music from the other room had stopped. In the enveloping silence he looked at the girl, obscure and dazzling in the dim light, disfigured from the tension and intensity of the moment. He swallowed and sought out her gaze. "Little one, why won't you look at me?" he invoked. "Where are you, little one? Stay here, stay here with me, I beg you…" She raised her eyes, her gaze plunging into his, and that contact felt to Bruce like a moist, immensely physical thing. "That's it," he said. He was starting to sweat in a pleasurable way. "It's beautiful to look at you now."

She was sweating too. The panic seemed to have fled, leaving her in a sort of unruffled astonishment. "Batman," she said with a strange smile. "I can't believe this is happening…"

"Here with me. Concentrate, stay with me."

"Why didn't you want me to use a glove?" she breathed, moving her fingers ever so slightly in his intestine.

"Oh," Bruce moaned. "To feel you. Because I want to feel you."

"And why didn't you get in the opposite position, on all fours? It would have been easier," she went on.

Bruce had the impression he wasn't perceiving her words through his hearing. He could sense them vibrate throughout his body. He could sense them reaching him through their locked gaze, through her hand, diffusing throughout him, vibrating through his organs. "To see you. To feel you," he went on moaning.

"Batman," the girl repeated. She tried to look away, then went back to looking at Bruce through hooded eyes. "What do you feel?" she asked.

Bruce made a grimace that almost resembled a smile: "Oh, baby. I'm yours, I'm simply yours."

"You're mine?"

"I am," he said, taking a breath and letting the air out slowly. "Peace," he declared. "I feel a clear, tender sense of peace. Fulfilment. It isn't just sex," he added, nodding towards his penis, which by now lay supine, pallid, and inert against his lower belly. "It's something more profound. Something much more intense." He stared at the girl and noticed a drop of sweat cutting down the open space of her forehead, fast, like the first drop of a summer downpour. "And you," he breathed dreamily. "What do you feel?"

The girl seemed to concentrate. "I feel moisture. Tightness. I feel the beat of your heart," she said.

"I know," he said, and at that point they stopped talking and just looked at one another, in a state of abandonment. Bruce sensed the hand pulsing inside him, or perhaps it was his entire body that was pulsating, with both violence and tenderness, around her hand. It was all there, it was all inside him, an instant of naked and perfect fulfilment. He let himself float in that peace, in that absence of desire, well aware that those sensations would not last forever, well aware that they always dissipated. He lay there in that state, in stillness, even after she started to talk again.

He didn't allow himself to be taken by surprise at the words the girl spoke. In a certain sense, he immediately knew what it was about. In a certain sense, her words didn't strike him as all that absurd, or all that upsetting, as though a part of him had known those words from the very beginning.

"There's something you should know," she said. Her face seemed to keep on fading into the shadows of the room. Once again, Bruce seemed to see other faces bob to the surface, like wreckage emerging from the ocean depths, on the skin of her face. He even thought he saw the Robin of the earliest years, or perhaps the face of some other boy, or some girl he'd met over time, or maybe someone he'd never even met, only dreamed of. Even her voice had become arcane, impersonal, a voice that announced at last, solemnly: "I'm here to kill you."

Bruce's body had a spasm. The hand inside him felt sharper. And yet he continued to feel no fear. He went on breathing at the same pace; apparently, there had been no transition, no break between the fulfilment of before and this new awareness. He waited for something more noticeable to change inside him, or else in the girl, something that would herald unequivocally the seriousness of her words. "So I'm about to die," he mused in a hesitant voice. "Who sent you?"

"Don't worry about that," she replied. "Your friend, who I persuaded to introduce me… He has nothing to do with it. He was acting in good faith."

"Then who?"

"It doesn't matter now," she said, wearily. "You don't need to know. Don't ask questions. What good would that do?"

Bruce felt his thoughts spreading out in all directions. He could feel them braiding into weird spirals. *If someone wants me dead, that means I still count for something*, he told himself with a foolish, final burst of pride. "Who talked you into doing this? Were you sent by the same people who killed Robin?"

Suddenly, the corpse with its eyes wide open appeared in his mind. He saw the morning frost on Robin's rigid, almost amazed face, and the scratch marks that Robin's fingers had left, before he died, on the hard soil of the park. He saw the frozen eyes that seemed to gleam with an undying love for Bruce. He saw all this. That was when he felt utterly lost. Robin was dead and he was about to follow him. Love squandered would remain squandered, the world's loneliness would remain unchanged, there was no more time and no redemption—no final glory. *I'm going to die naked on a magnetic bed.*

"You were recruited by the people who murdered Robin," he ventured. "Are you some kind of group or something like that?" The hand was icy inside him. Bruce felt it make a brusque, not yet definitive, movement, a movement that caused a deep and dark pain to spread, like a foam, through his body. "They'll catch you. You'll spend your life in prison."

"I've got nothing to lose."

"Wait," he implored her, sensing with a spasm that all this was real, abysmally true. "You're the last person who'll ever see me alive," he said, as if that could change anything. He received no reply. "I guess I deserve this. I was a hero. I promised to free the world, I promised to rescue other people. But I never loved them. I don't think I did. I don't think I ever loved anyone," he reflected in his panic, as in a confession, thinking he could detect something, deep down, in the girl's gaze. It was the spirit. That sort of soul that Bruce had pursued, over the years, from one person to the next.

A shiver cut through his body. A disconcerting void sank down in him. He imagined the people who would find him, the policemen who would walk into this room, maybe it would be that Detective De Villa, he imagined him staring down at his naked corpse, coldly, or with pity, or who could say what reaction. So he opened his mouth and, as though that audience were already there in the bedroom, shouted out his last lines, in a tone that verged on an absurd triumph: "You're not enough for me. No one's enough for me."

He deluded himself that the girl was about to speak again. He felt a new wave of pain growing, he felt it arrive from a distance, he felt it spring up like the breath of a dawn breeze. "Wait," he tried to add, but before he could get out the word he felt the ripping tear in his belly.

Book Three

BRUCE DE VILLA

MARCH 2006
&
1970S — EARLY 1990S

The days followed each other in an apparently orderly manner. They dropped one on top of another like tumbling dominoes, so fast and mechanical that it was almost possible to hear the sequence of their fall. Months before, the nation had taken in the news of the death of Bruce Wayne, the renowned Batman, with a certain amount of shock and obscure scandal. Even though the young murderess was arrested immediately, the trial hadn't begun until a few weeks ago.

In the press, articles on the trial featured the inevitable wire service photographs, pictures of a tanned Bruce Wayne, clearly posing with a contrived air. Sometimes the newspapers preferred to use a close-up of a famous black resin sculpture that portrayed the Dark Knight staring straight ahead, with a leering grin, the mouth twisted into a grimace that verged on the obscene. He'd been an egocentric when he was alive. He was still monopolising the stage now that he was dead.

No one suspected that another event would soon shift the nation's attention away from the notorious trial. An even more spectacular and tragic event. An event that would drive a thorn, once and for all, into the country's heart, into the whole planet's heart.

In just a few weeks' time, traffic would stop in the streets of New York. People would get out of their cars, stream from the buildings, shudder as they raised their eyes to the pillar of smoke pouring out of the building of a famous hotel. It would happen in just a few weeks. A gory explosive attack would kill Franklin Richards, America's most beloved son, the perfect blond young man, the icon of the last possible youth, as he sat helpless in a sauna. The country would shed tears as it lost one of the last crumbs of its innocence.

The event was lurking, unknown, close at hand. It was imminent. It was about to lacerate the curtain of unexpected occurrences, and bound onto the stage of collective pain.

For now, no one suspected a thing. Or, perhaps, almost no one. In fact, there was one man who had a number of presentiments. This man was another Bruce. His name was Bruce De Villa and he worked as a journalist. He was about thirty-five, of average height, with short prematurely greying hair and large dark eyes, always midway between an expression of irony and a form of melancholy, mysterious awareness. Bruce De Villa. He often appeared lost in thought. He could feel the flow of presentiments vibrate with growing frequency, he could sense it in his lungs and his stomach and in some other indefinite region of himself. He couldn't say with precision what was about to happen. He could perceive a dense, menacing event drawing closer, and wondered how it could be that everyone else around him failed to sense it. Couldn't they sense the looming disquiet, drawing ever closer, like a threatening storm front?

What this man knew in advance was that death was looming on the horizon for a couple of famous ex-superheroes. That was his knowledge. He could foresee the deaths of superheroes. He'd never asked for that knowledge and didn't really know what to do with it. To have such knowledge was a bizarre power and, for now, he preferred not to speculate too much about it.

*

The façade of the courthouse rose up, luminous, glowing an intense white in the early spring sunshine. The waves of traffic noise seemed to bounce off the façade like the echo of a rip tide, as journalists and spectators lined up at the entrance to make their way through security. Among them was Bruce De Villa. After waiting his turn, he held out his press pass and stood, with slight impatience, under the eyes of a security guard. He was wearing a brown heavy cotton suit and a pale blue shirt. He had Italian shoes on his feet and overall he gave the impression of knowing how to preserve a certain style even on the tight budget of a freelance journalist. The guard handed back his pass and asked with a trace of a smile: "De Villa. You wouldn't happen to be any relation to that detective?"

He nodded with no particular surprise. For some time now, he'd heard that question with increasing frequency. His brother was one of the detectives who had worked on the murder case and he'd appeared on television a few times to comment on this challenging investigation. His brother. Detective De Villa with his bloodshot eyes. Without another word, Bruce pocketed the pass, slipped through the entrance, and headed off across the marble-floored lobby, stepping silently.

The courtroom was pretty crowded. A buzz of voices filled the vast room. A harsh light shone down from the ceiling, illuminating the faces of the eager spectators, making them look like so many fleshy flowers under greenhouse spotlights.

Half a dozen television cameras were roaming through the crowd, hunting for well-known faces. Although the trial had been dragging on for weeks now, most of the networks were still airing daily updates. The inevitable daily updates. After all, this was one of the most sensational trials in recent history. A trial in an obscene and tragic criminal case, the trial for the murder of a giant of superheroism. The trial for the grisly killing of Batman.

Bruce De Villa made his way into the courtroom. He walked past a few rows of seats before someone waved in his direction. He recognised the familiar face of Alyson Rhodes, a colleague as well as a long-time close friend. They'd known each other for years but only recently were they seeing much of each other again, as they were covering the same trial. Bruce edged along the row, stepping on more than one person's foot, until he reached a seat next to her. "Huh," he huffed, letting himself down onto the chair. "I thought I was late."

"Late for what?" was Alyson's reply. In her voice there was a note of both sarcasm and resignation. She worked for the *New York Observer* and, like Bruce, she regularly attended the trial hearings. "I can't imagine there's about to be a dramatic turn of events here."

Bruce nodded as he settled in his chair. It wasn't hard to understand what Alyson meant. Apart from filling the news reports, the trial didn't seem to be achieving a great deal, dragging on, increasingly slow and fruitless, filled with obstacles and grey areas. The young defendant seemed unwilling to reveal the identity of the masterminds behind the crime, whether or not she even knew who they were. People were starting to talk about the existence of an obscure, deadly group. Bruce had no particular theories on the case, but thanks to his presentiments he did know that this was only the beginning, and that the old world of superheroes had begun to die with a death that was final, definitive, and beyond redemption.

"Bruce?" Alyson questioned him with a glance. "You're lost in thought, as usual. I know what you're thinking about."

"You do?" he challenged her.

"You're thinking that this trial has turned into a grim circus."

"Maybe that's what I was thinking." He smiled but offered no further explanation.

"Listen, we're reporters," she said, taking a pragmatic tone. "That's how it works. Even when the show turns grim and perverse, as it has with this trial, we need to stay and watch until it's over." Alyson was the kind of woman who knows how to frame a topic in direct terms.

Bruce took in Alyson's words. In that period he was writing for an Italian newspaper. His assignment was to write pieces about the world of America's ex-superheroes, and the idea of *watching the show until it's over* fitted very well with the sensations that by this point the whole scene inspired in him.

The hearing was starting late that day. Bruce accepted the chewing gum that Alyson offered him, and as the taste of some bizarre chemical flavouring spread over his tongue, he scrutinised the audience around him.

The television cameras continued to roam the courtroom, ravening and bored, like fat bluebottle flies. That day, the main star seemed to be Joseph Szepanski. He'd been Batman's trusted physician. He smiled contentedly under the lights of the television cameras, his skin pulled as tight as sun-baked leather. Among reporters there were rumours that the elderly doctor was about to publish a book of explosive revelations, though the exact subject remained secret. In the meantime, Szepanski never missed a chance to be in the public eye. During the previous court sessions, numerous other characters had popped up in the audience, either because they were friends of the victim or just to take advantage of the attention focused on the trial. The gallery of assorted VIPs had included the artist Nathan Quirst, the former mayor Rudolph Giuliani, an array of directors who were rumoured to be planning the definitive biopic on the Dark Knight's life, writers with meagre reputations, and even the victor of a recent season of *American Idol*. All those people. That procession of faces. Just like Alyson had said: a grim circus.

Over the course of the various hearings, moreover, some ex-superheroes had made their appearance. Personalities like the ageing Thor, the elderly Daredevil, and other has-beens from the old scene. The kind of figures that Bruce and his brother, the future detective, would once have given anything to lay eyes on. So many years ago. When they were two little kids who spent their days collecting articles and press accounts of the exploits of the superheroes. When they memorised the interviews given by their superhero idols. When they lived half an hour outside of New York and they worshipped those people, who seemed to inhabit a world of sophistication, filled with epic and unattainable intensity. So many years ago. Bygone days. So immensely remote.

Bruce took one last look around the courtroom. No sign of his brother, Detective Dennis De Villa. The police officer with the perpetually reddened eyes. Bruce had spotted him in the courtroom during some of the previous hearings. He wondered where he was now and what he was working on… He didn't know much about his brother. Over the years, he and Dennis had practically become strangers. He stopped looking for him in the courtroom audience, at last, feeling the usual mixture of detachment and distant, lingering regret.

∗

According to the findings of the investigation, each girl was given instructions before her night with Batman. Each was informed about what he liked to do. Some of the girls did it for money, others for the thrill of an encounter with the man and the legend. They were generally recruited by old friends of Batman, friends who knew his predilection for young, androgynous, fair-skinned girls. That's what had happened dozens of times before and that's what had happened with the defendant. The girl had managed to catch the attention of one of Batman's old friends, who had arranged an encounter for her with the famous hero, without suspecting her actual intention.

Her name was Mara Jones. She was nineteen years old and was the daughter of the owner of a real estate agency specialising in luxury apartments. She'd been arrested the night of the murder as she wandered through the West Village not far from Batman's residence, spattered with blood and in a confused state. She had short dirty-blond hair with a honeyed shade. Some freckles, green-grey eyes. She had a sinister beauty and there was something estranged about her gaze, midway between the naïve and the robotic. The television news reports beamed around half the planet tended to show her back, or her profile, or else to focus on details of her face: eyes, mouth, chin, the curve of an ear, as if the direct sight of that face was somehow too unsettling. Or else, more likely, it was a way of exciting the imagination of the viewers, offering single shreds, appetising samples of the young defendant's appearance.

For months now, the mass media had been buzzing furiously around the case. News reports about the defendant and the circumstances of the bloody murder were mixed with morbid gossip about the life of the victim. Batman was said to have made occasional use of crystal meth. Batman was said to have spent eleven thousand dollars a week at fashion boutiques on Madison Avenue. Batman was said to have tried to seduce the actor Leonardo DiCaprio when he was nineteen. Batman was said to have tried to seduce the actress Chloë Sevigny when she was eighteen. Batman was said to have tried to seduce… That kind of gossip.

The circumstances of the murder, moreover, had obviously fed the ravenous jackals of sarcasm. The internet was crawling with sacrilegious hymns to the art of fist-fucking and grotesque porno videos with main characters renamed Mara Jones. A hip-hop singer had a hit record with a corrosive, contemptuous ballad about the death of the former hero.

Old friends serving as pimps, young girls playing along, a stark fixation with himself and with erotic rituals with girls more than forty years younger than him… The life of the man who had once been known as the Dark Knight, one of the most glorious superheroes of the old days, had become in recent years something intensely tragic, intensely ridiculous.

Bruce De Villa agreed on that point. He recognised the pathetic arc of his former idol's life. But unlike most people, he wasn't scandalised by the details of Batman's intimate life, he felt neither a sense of scandal nor a sense of moralistic outrage, or at least not entirely. That wasn't the point. What he felt was a kind of cold, detached torment.

As a boy, he'd idolised Batman as the hero he loved best. Bruce De Villa remembered the excitement whenever he found some slender article about the appearances of the Dark Knight. He remembered how he'd adored the chronicles of that mysterious figure, who back then avoided photographers and microphones. Who could ever imagine that one day... As a boy, he was far from imagining that the heroic exploits that captured his fancy were the last sensational deeds of a world already slipping away. Far from imagining that one day he'd be a journalist covering a trial for the murder of the great hero, and that his brother Dennis would take part as a detective.

And yet, now that the death of the former hero had happened, Bruce considered it without astonishment. Truly without astonishment. He contemplated that death as if he were observing the ruins of a landscape after watching it wobble for a long time, from a distance, until the ineluctable collapse. He'd long felt a presentiment of that death. He'd known about Batman's murder months before it happened, just as he could now feel a presentiment that fatal events were about to take place in the lives of other ex-superheroes.

He supposed that this capacity for presentiment was a kind of odd superpower. He also supposed he knew where that power might come from. It was, he supposed, a sort of inheritance.

*

"You have a secret," Alyson declared as they emerged from the courtroom at the end of the day's session. They walked out onto the sidewalk and into the sunlight of late morning. They crossed the street, zigzagging through the waiting taxis while a warm breeze gusted towards them. "I've been watching you. You've been walking around for weeks now with that thoughtful, distant look on your face."

"I get it," Bruce tried to laugh it off. Next to them, the sidewalk was partly occupied by a construction site. In the air there was a scent of freshly poured cement. High above, a crane was manoeuvring with impassive gracefulness. "Are you trying to say that there was a time in my life when I didn't have a thoughtful, distant look on my face?"

Alyson gave a short laugh and didn't push further. "Bruce De Villa. The most mysterious man I've ever met." The sunlight glinted on her glasses. She was a good-looking woman and hadn't changed much since Bruce first met her, back in college. Of the two, he was the one who had taken on a lived-in look, with his white-sprinkled hair and his large unquiet eyes.

It must be more or less lunchtime. Alyson dragged him to one of her usual restaurants, a place on the second floor of a building not far from Chinatown, where they sat at a table near a window. They studied the menu, printed in a round typeface on recycled paper. It was a vegan restaurant. One of those restaurants where the name of every dish seemed to be stamped with the seal of approval guaranteeing that *this food won't make you sick*, the seal of approval that *this food is good for your soul*, one of those restaurants from which animal pain, and by extension, all the guilty pain of the world, had been rigorously excluded.

"Anyway," Alyson said, after they'd ordered. She took off her glasses, laid them on the table, and sat looking at him with her limpid gaze. "At least tell me how your articles are going. Are you a big hit in the Italian press?"

"I guess so. I hear they like my pieces in Rome." Bruce worked for both American and Italian papers and had written his most recent articles for *La Repubblica*. Before he could say anything more, the waiter arrived with their drinks. Bruce had ordered an organic beer and Alyson had opted for a freshly squeezed juice of some Amazonian fruit he'd never heard of.

"What are you putting into your articles?" Alyson sampled her juice and nodded with satisfaction.

"Well," he said, without much enthusiasm. "Just what's happening. All this. Old glories on the sunset road. American heroes dying with a forearm up their ass."

"Bruce, don't try to be a cynic. It doesn't suit you." Alyson tilted her head to one side as if to study him more closely. She wore dangly silver earrings, which swung with every movement of her head. "I meant, what are you reporting about the investigations? More important, how do you think they are going?"

Bruce didn't answer straight away. He took a swallow of beer and let his throat absorb the cool foamy flavour. "For the moment, I don't know what to think."

"I don't understand why you don't ask your brother for information," she pressed him. Her earrings were swinging like tiny church bells. "Any other journalist would try to take advantage of having a brother involved in the investigation."

"I've never taken advantage of my brother's work. It would seem odd to start now." Bruce flashed a reticent smile and slumped back in his chair. Apart from brief, chance meetings during the hearings of the trial, he and Dennis hadn't talked in months. Or maybe he should say in years. Maybe he should say: since the day their mother died, many years ago, they'd never been able to talk seriously.

A few minutes later their orders were brought to the table. The dishes emitted an appetising aroma. It was the sacred time of food. They seized their forks, both of them, every organ in their digestive system eager to do its work, jaws, organs, enzymes, glands, a biological mechanism millions of years old and ready to spring into action, for the umpteenth time, in the muffled atmosphere of a New York restaurant. They had both ordered wheat steaks and fried squash sticks. It might not have been Bruce's favourite cuisine, but he was enough of an omnivore to adapt to Alyson's tastes.

He sat there, looking at the woman in front of him. Many years ago, they'd had a relationship and had lived together in a small apartment in the East Village. Sensing his gaze, she raised her eyes. Their gazes met and remained locked in a tranquil, friendly sense of intimacy. "My God," she said. "I remember the first times I cooked vegan food for you. You were so suspicious."

"I was not suspicious at all," he did his best to defend himself.

"Oh yes you were," she maintained. "You even made me call your mother to ask for some Italian recipes." Alyson smiled, then tilted her head to one side again, squinting her eyes with the expression of someone who was sliding down a long and not always easy chain of memories. "Bruce, living with you really was odd," she ventured, without resentment, in a tone of affectionate bafflement. "So many years have gone by, and I still don't know what was happening with you at that time. Or, for that matter, exactly what happened to your mother."

Bruce drank the last gulp of beer. Even now, when he thought about his mother, his throat burned as though he'd been shouting for a long time.

He concealed his emotions and shrugged. Inside him, the taste of the meal merged with the pungent flavour of memories. The time he lived with Alyson in the East Village, his parents' old house in Clifton, the old box in which he and his brother collected newspaper articles about superheroes, his father, his mother, the untroubled Italian family they seemed to constitute. The end of his mother…

He was grateful that Alyson pushed away from the table and stood up, just then, breaking the silence and suggesting that they go and have—why not—a delicious and conclusive cup of coffee.

*

When the day was over, he returned to his tiny bachelor apartment and took a shower. He stood sighing under the hot stream of water, motionless, eyes closed, until the hot water ran out. He dried off with a bath towel and studied himself in the mirror, two Bruce De Villas that seemed to eye one another, naked, from opposing and irreconcilable worlds. He wandered through the apartment with the towel wrapped around his waist, waiting for the unease he could feel clinging to him to evaporate into the evening air. It had been a gruelling day. The day's trial hearing, his lunch with Alyson, the afternoon spent in the New York newsroom of the paper he was writing for, doing his best to speak in fluent Italian.

Even though he had mail to deal with, he gave himself a break on the sofa.

On TV he ran into the usual late updates on the trial. He preferred to turn the channel and stumbled onto an episode of *Come Take a Plunge with Namor*, that talk show whose host, with a conceited air, spoke from inside an enormous glass bowl filled with multicoloured fish. Old Namor. The Prince of Atlantis, the old glory of the seven seas. The programme on the next channel was the show featuring Mystique, the female mutant who once seemed to frighten the nation, and who now entertained it. Bruce sat and watched her host the show, sinking deeper into a reverie, until the end of the programme.

He shut his eyes. He couldn't stop thinking about superheroes. The living ones and the ones already dead. He tried to relax and finally lost himself in the rhythm of his own respiration, until everything seemed to quieten down and the sound of the TV became distant. He bobbed for a few minutes in a pleasurable void. The sofa was a yielding mass beneath him, so soft, almost liquid, and for a few gentle minutes he had the impression of floating in Namor's fish tank. How long would this phase of his life go on, this extended chapter of regret, yearning, and separation from the heroes he had once adored, and from the events of his childhood and youth? He lifted his head from the sofa. There was someone else in the room. A woman was crouching under the table, like a little girl playing hide-and-seek, and was looking in his direction with a bewildered smile. Bruce rubbed his eyes. He felt his heart shrivel. "Mama. What are you doing there?"

She was the same age as always in Bruce's memories and dreams, a vague age similar to his own age now. She was wearing one of her flowered, slightly hippyish dresses, and she remained under the table as though she really were playing hide-and-seek, either waiting to be found or convinced that she could hide, forever, from whoever was trying to find her. She seemed to gesture for him to join her. Together, they might be able to hide more successfully. Her smile was small, complicit, and melancholy.

"Mama, you can't keep hiding under there. Come on out." Bruce got up from the couch and stood there, watching her uncertainly. He could sense in his nostrils the scent of his mother's hair, which looked wet and freshly washed. "You can't stay under there."

"Bruce," she said. "Bruce."

He grabbed her arm and tried to drag her out, but she seemed impossible to move. Her body was inexplicably heavy. His mother looked at him with sadness. He let go of her arm and took a step back, without understanding what had caused that sadness: whether the fact that he had tried to pull her from under the table, or the fact that he had failed to do so. He asked her to forgive him in a subdued voice.

"Oh Bruce." She hunkered down even more under the table and looked at him with more intense sadness. "Don't feel bad for me. You have to go on, Bruce. You have to go on."

He staggered. He tried to brace himself against the wall but there were no walls around him and that's when he awakened with a start.

From the quality of the darkness and the silence out in the street, he understood that it was the middle of the night. The television was still on.

On the screen, they were rerunning a movie from the Nineties, a teen comedy full of music from that time and characters who referred to the internet like it was something exotic and new.

He shuffled into the kitchen, dizzy in his head, and drank a glass of iced water. He thought back to his dream about his mother and to the scent of her hair. While the city outside seemed to sleep and traffic barely wheezed past on the nearby highway, he stayed there drinking water, his back against the refrigerator door. A grown-up man in the dark of a New York night. A man in his mid-thirties, riven with memories and strange presentiments, two opposing streams of time meeting inside him, endlessly, like watery currents in the heart of the ocean.

———————

I WAS TWO YEARS OLD when my father managed to win the green card lottery, and we left aboard an old Alitalia jet plane, on an October day, flying across a steel-grey Atlantic. My brother hadn't been born yet. I can practically see us: a father and a mother with Italian blood, a young son with an American name. My father had named me Bruce, the same first name as Batman, even though back then that's not what he had in mind. That wasn't why he chose it. All he wanted was a name that would sound American.

My father had dreamed of America for years, and here's something I've often wondered: where exactly does a dream begin? I suppose that it springs up in some distant, mysterious place, and it takes solid form in the consciousness with geological slowness, with dazzling speed, not unlike a kidney stone inside a human body. My father had dreamt of America ever since he was a boy, even though it was late for that dream, though it no longer seemed to make much sense, and the time when his compatriots left en masse for America had ended half a century before. In him, that dream still lived on. It continued, tenaciously, out of an excess of faith, or out of simple inertia. That dream picked us up and swept us away, like a foaming wave, to set us down in the womb of a new home.

*

The place was called Clifton, New Jersey. One of the dozens of Cliftons in America. It was a half-hour's drive from New York City, a small town with no high buildings where the wind blew, in ragged gusts, through the space between one house and another. Like in any other American town, the sky seemed to hang low, spying on everyone, with no way to escape its gaze. The sky seemed like an immense sentinel. In a big city, people could hide from the eye of God, tucking themselves away in the secrecy of a thousand cement towers. But in a small town, there was no shelter. American small towns seemed designed to be flat, orderly, and exposed, so that an eye overhead could keep watch over them, at all times, the way a child might look down on a model city for dolls.

The banks of the Hudson River were a handful of miles away. New York was there, both near and far, like an ambiguous beacon, an elusive promise. On Sundays my father would take us for walks in Manhattan or down to Coney Island, where the amusement park rides spun and the wind gusted with the scent of the ocean and smoke from hot dog stands.

They said that the hot dog was invented on that beach. On the crowded beach of Coney Island. A century earlier, a German immigrant had come up with the idea of selling hot wurst sausages in a bun, an idea possessing the perfect naturalness that belonged, always, to successful ideas. That was the kind of story my father liked to tell. I was small, at the age when the mind absorbs everything. The first memory of my life would be a hot dog burning my tongue, and a T-shirt indelibly stained with mustard.

*

After about a year of American life, my brother was born, and with Dennis the family seemed to be complete: four people, four bodies. A big enough number to fill the house.

Meanwhile, my father was trying to find his path. That was proving much more challenging than expected, a slippery path that seemed to lead, each time, to some hostile territory. Keeping a job seemed beyond his abilities. His terrible temper, limited patience, and little ability to relate to his bosses, didn't qualify him for success. In Italy he'd worked for the post office. During our first few years in America, he changed jobs half a dozen times, each job less satisfying than the last, none of them lasting more than a couple of months. He was convinced that one day he'd be able to go into business on his own. The day would come when he would be the boss. My mother scanned the wanted ads, helping him to fill out job applications. "Do you promise that this time you won't get yourself fired?"

In the end, he was hired to work in a slaughterhouse ten miles or so from Clifton, where for some reason, by what seemed like a surprising miracle, he managed to keep his position.

Of course, it must not have been an enjoyable job. He never told us exactly what he did all day, but I think it had something to do with the process of administering the electric shock. The phase in which the animals are stunned. He would grab electrodes and use them to stun four-hundred-pound veal calves, one after another, before they were hung up on a hook and butchered. Although he showered every evening before leaving the slaughterhouse, he didn't always seem able to scrub that smell off himself. The smell of bled flesh. For the first two days he'd vomited at the end of his shift, then he'd got used to it. He used to say that they'd never fire him, because the work was too disgusting and they'd never find anyone to take his place. That was his theory, and I think it made him feel strong, like a martyr of some kind, a man capable of doing the dirty work.

A few years later, when Reagan emerged onto the political stage, my father started watching him on TV and telling us that this man inspired confidence. This man would open new horizons. "I can tell that something's about to happen." My father believed that sooner or later his chance would come, and he'd be able to quit his job at the slaughterhouse, and that everything in our lives was on the verge of changing.

Every Sunday morning he attended church, where he sang himself hoarse with psalms, prayers so filled with promise and mystery that he sometimes remained mute for the rest of the day. In Italy, the most Catholic country on earth, he'd never set foot in a church. In America he felt the judgement of God. I don't know if he thought he'd made mistakes in his life, but I know he would never have easily confessed them. Whether as an Italian or an American, he was still the same proud, stubborn man as ever.

*

At first, practically no one noticed my passion. After school, I'd developed the habit of taking refuge in a public library, where a girl worked whose main activity seemed to be chewing cinnamon-flavoured gum, and where I had free access to the shelves. I was about eleven, old enough to leaf through newspapers and magazines like *Newsweek*, *Time* or else *People* or *Vanity Fair*.

I always managed to find something. I would find accounts of the exploits of Reed Richards and his group. I would find reports on illegal smuggling rings that had been broken up by Daredevil or else on the controversial events involving the rebel mutant Mystique. I would find interviews with bad-tempered figures like Namor the Prince of Atlantis, interviews with Wonder Woman about her battles against both crime and male chauvinism, editorialists' commentaries ranging from the outright hostile to the completely exalted. By that point, no one had much to say about Superman, who even then was already looking elderly and decrepit, but in back issues I found articles about him too. I would extract old magazines from the cardboard containers where they were stored, with the skill of an archivist, going back months and years in search of the articles that interested me. I reconstructed the stories of all those people. Superheroes. I read each article over and over again, studying each picture, so raptly that I caressed the razor-sharp edges of the pages, sometimes, until my fingertips bled.

I was fascinated with Batman more than with anyone else. I loved the deep, enveloping black colour of his cape, which flowed behind him like a kind of shadow. I remember the infamous case of the serial dog killer, that maniac who had dognapped and decapitated thousands of dogs in the New York area before the Dark Knight caught him. I remember the reports on his spectacular incursions into the scenes of gang wars. In the pictures that appeared in the newspapers, Batman was barely visible in the distance, often blurred. In those days, he was an elusive figure; he never gave interviews, he steered clear of the spotlight, and played on his own aura of mystery.

According to what I read in the newspapers, there were quite a few eye-witnesses who had met Batman in person. Unfortunately, I wasn't lucky enough to know any of them. As a consolation for that, I knew people who had seen other superheroes: my classmate Ralph, for instance, had seen Wonder Woman at the opening of a shopping centre. I envied him that sighting for years. Too bad that Ralph was an idiot. All he could seem to say about it was how disappointed he had been. "Buddy, you won't believe this. That woman has small tits."

Eventually, the girl in the library started noticing me, and telling me that I should spend my afternoons outdoors. "That's enough reading. You're not going to meet any superheroes in the library. Why don't you go outside and run around with the other kids?" Maybe she was right. Sometimes I did go out and run around with the other kids, of course, but all things considered I preferred magazines with razor-edged pages. I preferred interviews with superheroes and photographs of the enigmatic Batman. I was a twelve-year-old who lived in Clifton, and for the moment my only opportunity to meet superheroes was in the pages of those publications.

I started to plunder the library. I tore out pages or cut out the articles that interested me, when no one was looking, when the girl was busy with another borrower or chatting on the phone or chewing her gum.

As for my father, as soon as he found out that I liked Batman, he assured me that one day I'd be disappointed. "That man," he said in a contemptu-ous tone. "A faggot with a cape."

I don't know where all that scorn came from. Back then, no one knew anything about Batman's life. I don't even know whether my father's scorn came from the hypothesis that Batman really was a faggot, or rather from a deeper, crueller hunch. The hunch that superheroes would never save a thing. Never save anyone. "Someday you'll be disappointed." Or maybe it all boiled down to something much simpler, that is, the fact that my passion hurt him. To some extent, my father wanted to take Batman's place. He would have liked to be a superhero, or maybe just a hero to his son.

As time passed, he started changing the channel whenever a news report about one of the superheroes appeared on TV. He was increasingly reluctant to talk about them. People with superpowers. People who were too free, too ambiguous, people that somehow, I believe, triggered an intimate sense of crisis in him. In contrast, my mother seemed untroubled by them. She was the one who started slipping me a few dollars, now and then, on the sly, so that I could go and buy the magazines I wanted, instead of ripping the pages out of the ones at the library. "We all need our heroes."

My brother Dennis, too, was looking for heroes. It didn't take him long to find them in my collection of news clippings. He didn't love any of them in particular: he'd take a fancy to one superhero, then another, and he'd sit there studying pictures of them with a kind of solemn intensity, sometimes greater than my own. We'd spend late afternoons in our bedroom reading my newspaper clippings, while our mother was in the kitchen making dinner, and that, for years, would be the perfect composition, the idyllic scene of our lives: two brothers reading accounts of their heroes' exploits, a mother preparing a meal alone, while a father finished his shift at work, some miles away, applying electrodes to the head of a terrified beast.

Then, one night we heard them arguing. They were speaking in a rapid Italian, as dense and intertwined as a close-knit fabric, but it wasn't hard to figure out what had happened. The girl at the library had phoned to protest about my devastation of the library's collection. There was even a risk that the library might demand reimbursement. Obviously, I'd never be able to set foot in the place again. Not only that, but my father insisted that I discard a certain object. It was the worst imaginable punishment. I would have to get rid of the box where we boys kept our news clippings.

The following morning she came into our bedroom, sat down on my brother's bed, and started fiddling idly with the hem of a blanket. "I told you not to damage the magazines in that library," she tried to scold me. Then she addressed the two of us in a soft voice, slightly scratched by a note of melancholy: "He doesn't hate your heroes. He's just worried about your well-being." She paused, gripping more firmly the edge of the blanket, and her eyes caressed us in the light of the bedroom. "Hide that box somewhere safe. And don't let your father see you reading that stuff again."

She had this small childlike smile that would vanish just as fast as it appeared. At the time, she must have been in her early thirties, and in my memory she seems to be no particular age, beautiful with an eternal and elusive beauty. "It'll be our secret," she whispered, and we both nodded our heads, ecstatically, like allies of a mysterious queen.

*

She really was beautiful. I know that lots of people think the same of their mothers, but I know for sure that she was beautiful. My male teachers would stiffen self-consciously when she turned up at a school event, and men would turn to watch her go by on the street. I have no idea how my father managed to win her heart, stealing her away from the admirers who no doubt had trailed behind her. She had a delicate nose, small ears, and dark eyes whose shape I had inherited, but which in her seemed to emanate a dense, almost solid reflection. Her teeth flashed a spontaneous whiteness. Her chestnut hair tumbled over her shoulders in waves. Dennis and I would stand and admire her when she washed her hair, in the bathroom lined with ceramic tiles, hypnotised by those dark, wet locks, until she burst out laughing and snapped at us: "What are the two of you staring at? Are you trying to make me blush?!"

She wore flowered dresses, vaguely hippyish, a little out of fashion. By then, we were into the Eighties. Our mother couldn't stand the ridiculous way people decked themselves out in that period, the padded shoulders, the shiny fabrics, and all the far too ostentatious stuff. She got no thrill from that kind of dressing up, and after all, even if she had possessed show-offy clothes, she would hardly have needed them. She didn't socialise much. Our father was less and less interested in going out and rarely took her anywhere. When she put on one of her flowered dresses, or fixed up her hair, she seemed to do it just for my brother and me. For our admiring eyes. Or perhaps just for herself. She dressed up to remain in the realm of the kitchen, the room in the house where she spent her time, alone, burning scented candles, listening to the radio, and making food.

She had brought just one book with her from Italy. It was a book of recipes. When dinner time rolled around, intense aromas spread through the house, exquisite, floating in the air like a magic spell, scents that seemed to come all the way from the Old Country, from that distant homeland, as if the wind had blown them across the ocean. She cooked crunchy square pizzas in the electric oven, brimming over with tomato sauce, oregano, and round olive slices. The spaghetti on our dining table was al dente, wholly substantial, very far from the overcooked, practically disintegrating worms that I'd sometimes happened to eat at a classmate's house. On other evenings there was a dense, almost creamy risotto, made with mushrooms or with asparagus, basil, or artichokes. On Sundays it was time for ravioli, floating in a mirror of clear broth, over which we would sprinkle a mantle of ground parmesan. There were roasts cooked in red wine. Potato gnocchi sprinkled with butter. She couldn't always find the ingredients she needed, or sometimes she'd decide to experiment, so she'd add an American touch. Maple syrup would garnish some traditional pastry from northern Italy, or peanut butter would give its aroma to a sage focaccia. She'd spread cream cheese on a pizza. Tiramisu went through a series of evolutions, changing and transmogrifying, losing one ingredient, acquiring another, until it turned into a fluffy cheesecake.

Our mother's food had an intimate flavour. It had a complete warmth, it penetrated both stomach and spirit the way any good food will do. I wonder whether that's exactly what good food is for. To make the people who eat it feel less lonely. Her food had the same effect as a hug; it never left us feeling lonely, and yet she, the woman who made it for us, spent much of her life in solitude.

She had no girlfriends. She'd left all her relatives behind in Italy. I might happen to come home unexpectedly, after school or after I'd been out somewhere, and find her sitting in silence at the small kitchen table, immersed in the dying light of afternoon. I might catch her off-guard, twirling a lock of hair around her finger, shrouded in an invisible cloak of melancholy. She seemed so distant. When she didn't know she was being watched, she tended towards a rapt expression, like someone listening for a lost signal.

Now I know that what she missed wasn't her life on the other side of the ocean. She didn't miss her relatives, or at least that wasn't what her yearning was mainly for. What she was yearning for was literally herself, in a way that at the time I could not understand.

*

The first warning that strange things were happening in our home came to me when I was about twelve, one winter evening when I was supposed to go over to a friend's house after school. It had been windy lately. The weather reports predicted snow. My classmate didn't show up at school that day, the victim of a flu epidemic that had emptied several of the desks in my classroom, and so I had returned home unexpectedly, panting from the bike ride, my cheeks glowing from the chilly snap in the air. I thought my mother would be happy at my surprise arrival. I thought she'd welcome me home the way she always did.

I walked into the kitchen. It was instantly clear that something was wrong. My mother had heard me come in and was waiting for me, gripping the edge of the table, her face ashen and appalled. I would never forget the look on her face. We stayed there looking at each other in the greyish light. Neither of us spoke. I don't know what I was thinking just then, I do know that I could feel her terror invade me, passing as if by contagion from her body to mine.

"Mama," I said. That's when I heard it. It came from upstairs, from her and my father's bedroom. It was the sound of footsteps, I think, the unmistakable sound of someone else's presence. "Mama," I said again, my mouth going dry, feeling a sudden need of reassurance. I knew that my father was at work, and that my brother Dennis had to be at school. The sound of footsteps grew louder.

"Listen to me," she said. "Listen to me, Bruce. You need to do something for me. You need to run over to the store to get some sugar. We don't have a single grain left in the house. You'd better go right away, you'd better go now." She seemed to have recovered, she was speaking with extraordinary calm. There was a shadow around her eyes. She ran a hand through her hair. "You'd better go right away, Bruce."

I raised no objections. Outside, the wind had a bitter edge. The sky was a sterile white and the streets were almost deserted. I pedalled slowly, barely breathing. The fear had ebbed with the movement of a tide, leaving an icy void inside me. It took me a long time to run that errand. It took me half an hour, much longer than necessary, and when I got home everything seemed to have returned to normal. She was listening to the radio, a cup of tea in her hand. She took the grocery bag out of my hands and gave me one of her smiles. No more noise was coming from the bedroom.

It would take me years to realise the truth, even though I think I knew it all along. I suppose everyone always knows the truth. Everyone knows it from the beginning, they just have to decide to look at it. Over the years, I would glimpse scattered fragments, symptoms of something that was right there, before my eyes, something I was still too young to recognise entirely. There was the frequency with which my mother changed the sheets in her bedroom, the kind of detail that men tend to overlook, and which I registered one day unintentionally, as I watched her fold the laundry. All that freshly washed linen. There was the number of perfumed candles burning so often throughout the house, as if to cover up the scent of some intruder passing through. There were the dirty glasses that I noticed sometimes in the kitchen sink, as if we'd had guests, or my mother's mysterious weariness, on certain evenings, even when she said that she'd had a quiet day. There was the episode when, as I was arriving from a distance, I could have sworn I'd seen a man leave our house and drive off in a grey Mercury. As far as I recalled, my father's boss drove a Mercury that same colour.

I must have been the only one who noticed these doings. No word issued from either my father or my brother. Every night we sat around our square dining-room table, eating the dinners my mother made for us. The four of us, night after night. My father dominated the tone, depending on whether he'd come home from work in a good mood, angry, or merely depressed. There were times when he just sat at the table, eating without a word, ceding the floor to the television set's monologues, and to the jingles that resounded throughout the room. At times like those, my mother might chance to stare at me. I was the elder son, the one who noticed odd things. The one who registered mysterious details. She must have known that, and that's why we sat there looking at each other for a few seconds, like a pair of secret accomplices.

Later, in bed, I would lie in the dark listening to the silence that was interrupted only by a passing car or the voice of some drunk down in the street. Dennis slept in the bed next to mine. He rarely slept peacefully. He tossed and turned all night, engaged in furious wrestling bouts with the bedclothes. The next morning, he would say he couldn't remember his dreams. He did pretty well in school, even though his teachers considered him to be something of an introvert. Sometimes he'd wake up and fire a question at me, without preamble, certain that I was listening. If what superheroes did was save ordinary people, who was in charge of saving superheroes? Would any superhero ever come to our house? And if he, Dennis, ever decided to leave one day with a superhero, would I feel lonely? "Go to sleep," is all I would say, embarrassed by those childish questions. I don't know whether he was conscious at those times, or if it was a sort of somnambulism.

One night he asked me whether I would marry our mother when I grew up. I felt like getting up and slapping him in the face. "Don't talk nonsense," I snarled. Half a minute passed, then I heard him start breathing deeply again and tossing and turning, lost in some dream that he wouldn't remember.

*

We weren't a well-to-do family. We lived just above the threshold of what at that time, in that part of the world and for that portion of mankind, was considered the basic standard for a dignified lifestyle. A roof over our heads, a car, a television set. Basic health care. We may not have scrimped on our groceries, but we sure did on clothing. We never travelled. My father's pay cheque was reliable, and covered the bare necessities, but it left us vulnerable to unexpected expenses. And over the years, there was no lack of unexpected expenses.

When Dennis needed braces, the money arrived from our Italian grandparents. When the engine of our car coughed and died once and for all in a shopping mall parking lot, my mother inherited a small sum from another relative. When the slaughterhouse hit hard times and my father's pay cheque stopped coming for two months, it was another inheritance from distant relatives of hers that kept us afloat. We seemed to be lucky. Some benevolent star was shining down on us. My father wasn't happy to scrape by on these windfalls, it made him feel less independent. Still, what other choice did he have? As for Dennis and me, we joked about feeling like heirs to some age-old dynasty. All hail those unknown relatives. All hail to the ageing uncles and aunts back in Italy, who died off one after another, at the right moment, thinking on their deathbed of their distant niece.

A similar thing happened with my studies. When I was seventeen I found myself at a critical point. I couldn't see many possibilities. I was a pretty good student, but not enough of an academic star, nor of a sports star for that matter, to hope for a scholarship that would get me through college. I'd have to try to get a loan. Everything seemed so complicated, and things were quite foggy in my own mind. One night my father came home with a piece of paper in his hand; he held onto it for a moment and then, at last, he handed it to me with an awkward gesture. "When you're done with school this year, you might think about this." It was a photocopied form for me to fill out. An application for a job at the slaughterhouse where he worked. It was an off-white sheet of paper, paper that stuck to my fingertips, making me think, for some reason, of the sticky wafers that people swallowed in church. I felt like gulping down that sheet of paper, so that I could make it vanish forever.

A few days later, it was my mother who resolved the situation. She told me she needed to take me somewhere. Where she took me was to a bank, where we sat down, side by side, in a small office that reminded me of a doctor's waiting room. When the bank officer came in, my mother told him that she wanted to open an account. "In my son's name. In the name of Bruce De Villa."

Her first deposit was one thousand dollars, which she pulled out of a crumpled paper bag. I can still see those bills. I can hear the rustling as the banker counted them, and recognise their smell, the pained odour of money, as it wafted over to my nostrils.

Outside the bank, my mother didn't have much to say. "I'll deposit more money into this account. It's for your college education. There's no need to mention this to your father."

Where that money came from was a question I didn't dare to ask. She offered no explanations, nor did she try to pawn off the usual story on me. There was too much awareness, too great a complicity between the two of us for her to drag out, yet again, that ridiculous old chestnut about her distant relatives.

This was no ordinary day. My mother was giving me the gift of a future, ironically enough, on the very day when I ought to be giving her a gift. It was her birthday. She was thirty-eight that day, and she was still a dazzling beauty. With the passing years, her features had remained delicate, clearly etched, with only a few wrinkles above her cheekbones, like scratches left by the finest of needles, revealed here in the street by the sunlight hitting her face. As we walked home together, passersby shot her the usual glances, arousing in me a blend of pride and ill-defined disquiet.

That night we celebrated her birthday with a cake she had baked herself, on which she had written her own name with a drizzle of melted chocolate:

SILVIA

My father had come home with a present, a bouquet of tiny scarlet roses that he laid in her lap, without a word, as if it were a puppy that she could care for. My mother caressed the flowers. That bunch of roses didn't strike me as much, puny and commonplace, just like all the presents my father gave her, at least that was how it looked to me. And yet she seemed genuinely touched. They embraced and for a moment something seemed to pass between them, some kind of warmth, a flow of attraction so deep it seemed almost painful. I wondered if that's what being married meant. That heartbreaking attraction, that unbridgeable distance.

I hadn't bought anything for her. After our visit to the bank, I'd been too stunned. I felt a chilling amazement at the thought. My destiny was taking shape. I'd emerged from the fog of uncertainty, I could contemplate what would become of me: I'd escaped a future as a slaughterhouse worker. I would be going to college. For me, that night should have been a double party. I should have been overjoyed. And yet all I felt was a trace of some emotion that then and there I couldn't identify, a heavy feeling that seemed to press down on the pit of my stomach. I guess it was a sense of guilt. Over the passing years, I would become quite the expert.

Before falling asleep that night, I told Dennis about college. He greeted my news with a long silence, then he asked whether that meant that I would be leaving home. "Huh," I replied nonchalantly, pretending the thought had never occurred to me. "I guess it does. Maybe I'll try to get a college room."

His silence stretched out. The sensation of something pressing down on my stomach intensified, and I realised I hadn't been very tactful in the way I'd broken the news to him. "One day, you'll go to college too," I said, trying to make up for it.

From his bed, I continued to hear a wall of silence. The darkness of the room enveloped us, only partly relieved by the faint glow that filtered in through the window. Long after I'd assumed he'd slipped into a slumber, Dennis' voice suddenly reached me: "Will you take the old box of newspaper clippings when you go?"

I wasn't sure what answer he was looking for. "No," I ventured. "I'll leave it here with you for safe keeping."

Silence again. I couldn't tell whether he was pleased with that bequest. In fact, for some time now we'd both lost interest in news about the superheroes. And by now there wasn't much news to be had, anyway. Many of them were retiring, while others were migrating from the news sections to the gossip and show business sections. Everyone knew that Batman no longer fought crime, that he was leading a leisurely existence, living on his money and with his boyfriend.

Believing in those people had been great. It had all been intense and wonderful, but now what was left of it?

So long, superheroes. The superheroes could go and live their own lives. I would live mine. And in time, Dennis would find his path too. We lay there on our sagging mattresses, two brothers in the darkened bedroom, eyes open wide, staring at the vague striations of light projected by the window on the ceiling, unsuspecting of everything that was going to happen to us, the experiences that would face us, the men that we would become, and the way that each of us would accept—each in his own way—the ambiguous gifts of the future.

*

I lived in a student residence of City College for a few months, until I met a girl on the journalism course. Alyson had a place in the East Village and it wasn't long before I moved in with her. It was a studio apartment perched upstairs from a second-hand clothes store, regularly invaded by tiny cockroaches that she swept out every day, with a broom, refusing to exterminate them with insecticides. She was unwilling to kill animals, whatever the species. So, of course, she wasn't about to eat them. Alyson belonged to a student vegan association and took part in lengthy seminars on subjects such as the concentration camp ideology of intensive animal breeding or how to control humanity's aggressive impulses through a meatless diet. "To say nothing of the fact," she would confess, "that animal toxins are terrible for the skin."

Back then, she wore a pair of black Bakelite glasses, which she'd bought who knows where. I suspected she didn't need them at all and that she wore them to give herself an intellectual appearance, but to my eyes they just gave her an extra touch of provocative appeal. She wore her hair pretty long. It was black hair, darker than my mother's, and it contrasted nicely with her milk-white complexion. In bed, her breasts barely quivered when she breathed. I can still see us, our bodies naked and light against the backdrop of the sheets, after sex or floating in the sweet laziness that comes before sleep, as she expounded her nutritional theories for me.

I didn't mind going along with her dietary regimen, even though my motivation had less to do with any real support than an effort to economise on meat. At lunch, I'd compensate with the occasional hamburger at the student cafeteria. Apart from groceries, expenses included my share of rent, college tuition, my subway pass, and miscellaneous items. Officially, as far as my father knew, I supported myself by working part-time in a bar. I actually did spend a few hours every week behind the counter of a bar on the Bowery, a noisy place that held concerts, poetry readings, and meetings of obscure squads of artists. But that work wasn't enough to support me. The lion's share of my income came from my mother, through the bank account in my name. We'd never mentioned that bank account again since that day. You could almost question whether something that never gets mentioned even actually exists, but that bank account definitely existed, I withdrew cash from it often, and every time I did, I found that a new deposit had been made.

I called home a couple of times every week. My brother would ask me how things were in New York City as though he were asking about a place on the far side of the planet. Whenever I tried to tell him anything about my life, he'd sink into a resentful silence. "I'll come back to visit you soon," I assured him. "Do whatever you want, Bruce." "How's Mama?" "Why don't you ask her yourself?"

He'd never forgiven me for leaving home. By then, my brother Dennis was fifteen, he'd grown to be as tall as me and even stronger, and he smiled just the way our mother did. A smile as fleeting as a falling star. He was no longer the kid who tagged around after his big brother. He was no longer, either, the kid who dreamt of running away who knows where with some superhero. In the end, I was the one who had left home, and after I did, his introverted personality blossomed like a strange flower, revealing unexpected sharp angles, a blend of intense emotions, reserve, and a surprising rigorous strength. He didn't seem to have many friends or, as far as I knew, girlfriends, but he seemed to get by and his grades at school were quite good. After getting over his mania for superheroes, he'd started training, becoming involved in a form of martial arts with an unpronounceable name, a sport that demanded long periods of preparation without resulting in a direct clash with the opponent, a sport that made me think of a solitary, ambiguous, solemn battle against oneself.

Sometimes I'd wake up in the middle of the night, filled with homesickness and a mysterious uneasiness. And sometimes Alyson would wake up with me. "Did you have a dream?" "I don't know. My brother. My family," was as much of an explanation as I could provide. Alyson wrapped her arms around me, and before falling back to sleep she'd whisper in the darkness: "Why don't you do the easiest thing? Go to see them."

Ever since classes started, I'd made fewer and fewer visits to Clifton. It was hard to go back there. It wasn't until I left that I understood, consciously, how grim the atmosphere was in my family's home. Back home, there was my father, with his unpredictable temperament. Back home, there was my brother with his air of a too-serious teenager. Most of all, back home there was my mother with her loneliness, her beauty, and her secrets, the mysterious provenance of the money with which she supported me. Back home, there was a truth, and whatever that truth might be, it sucked the oxygen out of the air like a relentless, invisible fire.

*

In March, regular classes were suspended for spring break. For a few days, the campus emptied out. Alyson went home to see her folks, and I finally had to admit that I couldn't come up with any more excuses. One afternoon I caught a bus from the Port Authority terminal. I remember that the feminine sexy scent of some previous passenger hovered over my seat. I remember sucking in that smell as if it were an anaesthetic, and allowing myself to be transported out of the city.

Leaving New York made me feel like a space colonist who was venturing, at his own risk, outside the protective confines of the colony. Like many provincials, I had developed an overblown pride in the metropolis to which I'd escaped. It hadn't taken long for me to acquire the sort of mistrust and hazy resentment that many New Yorkers seem to harbour towards everything that has the unforgivable defect of, quite simply, not being New York.

Sunlight shimmered on the road. Outside the bus window, other vehicles were nothing but incandescent fragments. The New Jersey landscape lay before my eyes with its blend of green and residential areas, highway interchanges, gas stations. From the roof of a McDonald's, the silhouette of their clown mascot seemed to scan the traffic on the road like a sentinel. As the bus drove into Clifton, it passed the library I went to as a kid, and I wondered what had become of the librarian, the girl who chewed cinnamon gum. I wondered whether the old archives of news magazines were still stashed away in there. Who could say. I thought about all the time I'd spent hunting through those magazines for the subject that obsessed me, hundreds of magazines with torn-out pages, pages filled with holes, snipped and clipped, like they'd been subjected to some maniacal form of censorship.

It was incredible to find everything exactly where it always had been. Even my folks' little house was right there, with its motionless appearance and the back door ajar.

As I walked in, I found a dense penumbra. I came to a halt, disorientated. A sense of alarm came towards me from within the house, making me wobble in the dark hallway. When I tried to swallow, my throat produced something like a crackle.

I stuck my head into the kitchen. My mother was staring towards the door, as if expecting me, an unmissable look of fear on her face. That look. That ashen face. I had a sense of déjà vu. The air in the room seemed to freeze, to become as solid as glass. We stayed there, staring at each other, paralysed, while from overhead came the sound of footsteps. It was all the same as that other time. All just like that afternoon, years ago, and I hoped that once again she would thrust a couple of dollars into my hand and send me to the store to get a bag of sugar.

My mother didn't move. I was eighteen, old enough not to run away, old enough to remain motionless, this time, as the footsteps descended the stairs.

A man walked through the other door of the kitchen. I wouldn't know how else to describe him. A man. Middle-aged, unremarkable face. The kind of man who might have stood in line next to me at the checkout of a supermarket. The kind of man who might have been in a car stopped at a red light while I was crossing the street, the kind of man I could have passed any day on the sidewalk. A walk-on part, an anonymous shred of humanity. I could have run into him anywhere, no question, but now he was in the house where I'd grown up, standing in front of me in my mother's kitchen. The intruder touched his tie. He gave me a look and seemed to wonder who the hell I might be. He turned to my mother and in the tone of a teacher evaluating an exercise: "Not bad at all. As usual. Could you tell her to smile every once in a while? That'd be nice." He nodded goodbye and left.

We remained there alone. My mother picked up a dish towel and dried her hands. She threw open the window to let in a breath of air. "Stay here," she said, without looking me in the eye.

I heard her climb the stairs. I heard her footsteps, lighter than the man's, as she moved towards the bedroom. There was a silence. A shiver ran up my spine. It was a deep, unnatural silence that lasted about a minute. I had no idea what was happening, nor what was the meaning of the man's words. I imagined myself walking straight out of the house, without leaving a trace, pretending I'd never witnessed that scene.

My mother's footsteps came down the stairs. She reappeared with a weary smile, pulled out a chair, and collapsed onto it. I collapsed onto a chair myself, exhausted, weakened by the thought that a man like that, nondescript and without a past, should have anything to do with my mother's life.

"I thought you said you were coming tomorrow," she sighed.

"I'm sorry," I said. And I really was sorry. About getting the day wrong, about the situation I'd witnessed. "A misunderstanding," I whispered, astonished that it should all come down to such a trivial thing. A misunderstanding. I'd said I would be there one day, she had meant a different day. It was so easy not to understand one another. Misunderstandings hide everywhere, like so many bacteria.

"Don't ask me for an explanation," she implored.

"I didn't intend to."

She ran her fingers through her thick, fine hair. She did it carefully as though afraid she might make a noise. "Your brother will be home in half an hour."

"I'll wait for him," I replied.

"We've missed you. I imagine it's nice, down there in New York," she said, continuing to caress her hair. She seemed determined to pretend that everything was normal. "One of these days," she added, "you could bring your girlfriend to visit."

I laid my arms on the table, even more exhausted, as the light of afternoon waned outside the windows. "Sure. One of these days."

*

"And why on earth should I do such a thing?" Alyson looked at me squarely, with a baffled expression. We were walking along the river not far from the Christopher Street piers. Night had just fallen and a variegated lazy crowd was milling around along the Hudson.

"Oh, come on," I said. "It's not that complicated." A few yards from the river's edge, the pilings of ancient wharfs broke the water's surface like the heads of silent alligators. I contemplated the motion of the water against the pilings and then cast my gaze, like a fishing net, out towards the night-time panorama of New Jersey on the far side of the river. I cleared my throat and tried to give Alyson some contrived explanation for the reason I was asking her to call my mother, and specifically why I was asking her to do it on a certain day, at a certain time.

Alyson continued to seem doubtful. With a typical gesture, she took off her glasses as if to eliminate all barriers between us, and waited for me to offer a more convincing explanation. When it became clear that I wasn't about to add anything more, she put her glasses back on and shook her head. "All right. I know a place not far from here. At least buy me a drink," she sighed, and continued to walk along next to me.

A few days later, I boarded a bus for Clifton. Another bus, another seat to sink into. This time, no scent of a girl. Nothing but the neutral odour of the bus itself, and perhaps the smell of the sweat that clung to me. I felt hot and uneasy. I certainly questioned the wisdom of what I was about to do, and yet I didn't see any way to avoid doing it. The need to know had been building up inside me for years. It was a Friday afternoon, one week exactly after my last visit. The same time of day. Whatever had been going on last time, I guessed the same thing was going on now.

I got to the house and stood in silence outside the back door, breathing softly, until I heard the phone ring inside. Five on the dot. I let a few more seconds go by, calculating how long it would take for my mother to reach the phone. Then I slipped inside. It all seemed simple, almost too perfect. I could hear my mother's voice: "Alyson? Bruce's girlfriend?"

From the corner of the kitchen where she kept the phone, my mother would be unable to see me as I crept towards the stairs. She wouldn't see me start up the steps, nor would she hear me, focused as she was on the conversation, as I cautiously headed upstairs.

"I told Bruce to bring you here sometime. It would be nice to meet you. What?" An incredulous pause. "He told you to call me and get a recipe?"

I set my foot on the top step. For a moment I swayed, as dizziness swept over me. Until then, it had been simple, a harmless, almost petty adventure, little more than foolish bravado. I could have turned around with a victorious smile, without venturing any further, happy just to have come this far, like in one of those kids' games where you have to capture the adversary's flag. I'd done it. I'd slipped unobserved upstairs.

My heartbeat pounding in my head. A choking sensation in my throat. I kept going, down the hall, to the end where a zone of darkness stagnated, motionless, like the water in the loop of a river. I reached my parents' bedroom door, behind which I could hear the sound of breathing. There. If I close my eyes I can see myself. I see myself at the threshold of that door. I'm about to discover something, something I don't want to discover, and I wish that someone would come and grab me, at that precise moment, and drag me away from the half-light of the hallway.

I barely pushed the door. The chilly door handle. Through the crack I saw the scene. I saw a man on the bed, a stranger, another unremarkable man, different from the man who was here the week before. I saw his naked body. The off-white flesh, a few hairs on his back. I saw the woman underneath him, also naked. I saw that it was my mother. My eyes were burning but I kept them open. It really was my mother, on that bed, her hair scattered across the pillow, with an indecipherable expression on her face, neither disgust nor pleasure, as the man grunted on top of her.

I could still hear the voice, my mother's voice, talking on the phone downstairs. My mother was in the kitchen. My mother was on that bed. As the man began speeding up his pace, she turned her head, and her eyes met mine. I took a step backwards. Something in my chest seemed to swell up, burning like an ember caressed by the breeze. I'd figured it out. Perhaps I let out a moan, but it merged with the moans of the man as he came.

When I got downstairs, my mother had finished the phone call and was waiting for me. She'd heard my footsteps. She'd guessed everything. There were two cups of tea on the table. By now, not many explanations were necessary. After all, I'd spent years reading about people with strange powers.

I sat across from her. The tea was piping hot, it tasted of sugar and infinite misery.

The man came downstairs and made his appearance in the kitchen, fully dressed, his face still sweaty. His fat neck was red and mottled. He seemed to have a more cordial personality than the guy from last week: mistaking me for the next client, he gave me a pat on the back. "Enjoy her, young man. She's hot and wet."

I shut my eyes, gripping the tea cup, resisting the temptation to smash it into his face. It wasn't hard to imagine blood all over that unremarkable face. His face lacerated by the shards of my cup.

When I opened my eyes again, the man had gone. My mother was standing in front of me, trembling. Before going upstairs, she took a deep breath. "Bruce," she whispered. She bit her lip until tears came to her eyes. "This will be our secret," she said. "You're the only one who can understand. Neither your father nor your brother can ever know about this. Our secret, Bruce."

*

To a certain extent, I think she was relieved that I had found out. She'd kept her secret for too many years now. She refused to tell me how long she'd been receiving clients in the house, but I had to guess that it was since Dennis and I were children. It must have been since then. Maybe it had been since my father first got his job. I still remembered the day when, as a child, I had seen my father's boss at the slaughterhouse leave our place. It wasn't hard to guess in retrospect who had persuaded him not to fire my father, and how he had been persuaded. Not hard at all. It all fitted together. The history of my family emerged, before my eyes, like an ancient inscription from under a layer of sand.

From the few things she told me, and from what I was able to guess, I reconstructed the story of her power. She had discovered it immediately after her arrival in America. It consisted of the ability to double her body for short periods of time. To create a double. Another body identical to her own, a perfect twin. At first, it happened rarely, on occasional afternoons when she was alone at home. She would lock herself in the bathroom, take off her clothes, and extract that second body from her own. It demanded a level of concentration and a physical effort that was impossible to define, something that made her sweat and tremble.

She and her double. My mother's second body never spoke, it just looked out on the world wide-eyed. She gave it baths in the tub. She washed its hair. She cared for that frightened second body. Once she had kissed it on the lips. She hugged it for hours at a time, to protect it, to feel protected, and sometimes, after reabsorbing it into herself, she felt an urge to weep, a remorse not unlike what a murderer must feel.

She was careful not to mention her secret to anyone. And she had no fantasies about becoming famous. She wasn't interested in fame, even supposing her power could bring her some fame. At times, I have wondered whether things might have gone differently, and whether she could have used her powers in another way. Would I have preferred to see her working in television? Would I have wanted to see her make a stab at a career as an old-school superhero, like the ones I loved so passionately as a boy: fighting evil and all those dusty illusions from the old days?

I doubt that she felt sufficiently heroic, or that she felt a sufficient hunger for attention. She wanted her children to have a normal mother. Not that she worshipped normality or anything like that, it was just that she wanted to protect them. Fame and television struck her as dank things, as toxic as black mould. She felt the urge to shelter her sons. In America you could never be sheltered enough. She had a family, and that was the only thing that mattered.

The business with the clients began during one of those money crunches she and my father fell into every few months. Gas bills and late notices on various loans piled up on the refrigerator door, stuck there with little magnets. Money crunches were like seasons. They came back cyclically, they came back always. There hadn't been much of a choice. There were a thousand ways to make use of a body, and she'd made her tortured decision. She'd decided how to use her second body. Her double had screamed with the first man. Then it stopped.

No one had ever bothered to notice the comings and goings of strange men. We didn't interact much with our neighbours. Her clients assumed she had a twin sister, a mental defective or something of the sort, a poor brainless unfortunate who was kept hidden in the house like a family secret, a sort of trained animal who had been taught, over time, to spread her legs wide.

I think that in the beginning it was once a month, just to meet some unexpected expense. Twice a month. Three times a month. The more we boys grew, the more extra expenses there were.

My brother Dennis and I had to go to the dentist. If we got sick, we were taken to see a good paediatrician. We ate good food, no frozen TV dinners or any of that garbage. We never felt poor, we grew up without luxuries, but also without privations. It was my college education, I think, that threw things into turmoil. Once I left for New York, my mother's second body had to come into existence much more often. Like a creature forced to experience a repeated rebirth, it had opened its eyes to the world at a steadily more frequent pace.

That body had stopped screaming years ago. In a certain sense, cruel as the thought might be, I suppose she really resembled a trained animal. At first, all this overwhelmed me, but not as much as it should have. It's not her, I said to myself. It's another body, another flesh.

Whether my mother still felt that urge to weep every time she reabsorbed her second body was something that I chose not to ask. That wasn't her. I wasn't me. No one was anyone, just shadows, characters in a dream, in a bizarre spectacle.

*

We went to the movies, one of those evenings, to see a screening of a restored copy of *The Mark of Zorro*. Knowing that that old movie was one of my favourites, Alyson had bought tickets. I'd seen it dozens of times. We sat there, in the darkened theatre, watching while Tyrone Power made fools of the baddies, serving justice and winning love. As always, the moment when Zorro removes his mask touched me and filled me with a vague sense of regret. Then I was surprised. I'd seen it dozens of times but for the first time I thought I understood. Here's who that character was. Zorro. I really felt I had figured out what he was. A wealthy heir who played at being a hero. Even back in the days of the black-clad swordsman, I thought to myself, being a hero was a luxury strictly for the wealthy.

There was a guest of honour in the movie theatre. It was well known that this was Bruce Wayne's favourite movie. I managed to catch a glimpse of my childhood hero, through the crowd, at the end of the screening. It was him. People were crowding around him, asking for autographs. He had a youthful appearance, and in my opinion he was a little too perfectly groomed. He looked like he was about forty although by then he must already have been about fifty. "Hey!" Alyson exclaimed. "There's Batman. Let's go get a closer look."

"I don't feel like it," I said. Batman couldn't do anything for me. Not for me, not for anybody. It had been ten days or so since I'd found out about the thing with my mother. This new awareness was still sinking down into me, deeper and deeper, into the damper layers of my consciousness. Sinking ever deeper. Perhaps there was no bottom. Perhaps that heavy secret was tearing through each layer, lacerating all resistance, and it would go on descending into me forever. I took Alyson's hand. She didn't know anything and maybe, by holding her hand, I might regain a state of blissful ignorance myself. We headed for the exit. "Why don't we just go get a hamburger," I smiled, prodding her.

"You miserable cannibal." She pointed her index finger at me like a sword and threatened me with a laugh: "Beware. I shall carve the letter S on your forehead. I shall carve an S for Soy milk."

Outside, the temperature was pleasant. The air was warm and vibrant. We headed off down the electric colours of Houston Street before cutting north. People sat idly on the front steps of buildings or on fire escapes, watching the comings and goings on the sidewalks. Bursts of laughter from somewhere. We walked along hand in hand. We detoured to make a small purchase in Washington Square Park, and that was when I recognised a couple of familiar faces among the passersby.

"Bruce De Villa! Look who's here. Guys, isn't this supposed to be a big city? It's starting to seem smaller than the crapper in my house." It was old Ralph, Danny, and Pete the Toad, so called because every time he smoked a joint his eyes would bug out. The old Clifton gang. Of all the people to run into.

It had been at least a year since I saw them last. "Jeez, guys. What are you doing here?"

"We're just looking around. We're in the right place, aren't we?" Ralph said with a wink. He had a coarse-featured face with a flattened nose and small cunning eyes. We were classmates and for a number of years, I guess, we were something much like a pair of friends. Ralph glanced at Alyson and a smile spread across his face.

I made introductions, uneasily, aware that the minute we parted company the guys would start making appraising comments about her.

"So, how's life treating you here in the city?"

"Living large," I replied with insincere emphasis. We stood there looking at each other. Even though I'd spent hundreds of nights out with them, those evenings seemed like memories from another lifetime. And to tell the truth, that's what they were. Memories from another lifetime. I crossed my arms and smiled a distant smile.

"Let us know the next time you're in Clifton."

"Sure."

"Maybe we'll run into each other." Ralph sniggered for no apparent reason. We said goodbye and it was only at the last minute, when the other guys were already a few yards away, that he hurried back and in the tone of someone confiding a secret to his old friend he whispered: "Actually, you know, I was at your house just recently."

"At my house?" I mumbled. My face stung as though it had been slapped. I felt short of breath. The scene suddenly seemed to shift colours and everything became more vivid and painful.

"Of course. I dropped by to say hello to your mom," Ralph replied in a foxy tone. He lowered his voice still further to make sure Alyson couldn't hear: "She introduced me to her little sister…" He lifted a finger and held it in front of his lips, as if to keep himself from saying anything else or perhaps to keep me from speaking. He shot me another wink and moved off to catch up with the others.

Nothing was left but the hum of the street. The void in the pit of my stomach.

"Don't tell me you used to hang out with those losers," was Alyson's comment. "The leader of the gang's breath was foul," she added in a deliberately snobbish voice. We started walking. The silence between us dragged out. Alyson looked at me with concern and asked: "Is something wrong? What was that idiot talking about?"

"I wouldn't know," I lied. "Let's go home."

*

That night, it was impossible to get to sleep. I lay on the bed, eyes wide open, careful not to move for fear I'd awaken Alyson. The light of dawn took an endless time to arrive. Infinite hours made up of infinite minutes made up of seconds that stretched out, painfully slow, like drops hanging from the ceiling. I waited for the day's first glow. It was almost morning when I got up. Moving silently, I shut myself in the bathroom. I splashed my face with cold water and brushed my teeth, for a long time, hoping to wash away the bitter taste in my throat.

I went out to get breakfast. Across the street was a 24-hour diner, where I ordered eggs, pancakes, and orange juice. Those flavours. That food. Then it was time to calculate the tip for the waitress, get up, trudge out of the place. I felt like a robot. The world was the same as ever, I was performing the same actions as ever: eat breakfast, leave a tip. Nothing much seemed to have changed. The difference was that now I knew. I knew even more than before. There is no limit to the number of things that a person can know: they accumulate one on top of another and they keep hurting, worse and worse.

I dropped by to say hello to your mom. By now I knew where my money came from. The money I lived on came out of the wallets of people like Ralph. It came from the wallets of Ralph and other guys like him, overgrown boys from New Jersey who once went to the same school as I did. Or else out of the wallets of bigger men, grown-ups, with unremarkable faces and off-white skin, men who panted, grunted, and came, with a contented sigh, on my parents' bed. My mother's bed, my father's bed.

The money I spent on breakfast wasn't all I spent that morning. I had no real plan, I was just running on a dull throbbing anger. I could feel that anger moving through my body. I could feel it shift, like a bubble of heat, from my legs to my stomach and then to my head, where it seemed to burst without warning. Vertigo. Once I reached the Port Authority station, I decided that the bus would take too long, so I struck a deal with a gypsy cab to drive me to Clifton. He wanted fifty bucks. "Fine," I said.

Fifty filthy bucks. What did that amount to? I kept having bouts of vertigo. Fifty bucks, sure. Fifty of their sighs, fifty thrusts of their hips. Fifty drops of their sperm. "It's my mother's money," I told the driver, and he shot me a furtive glance.

I had no idea what I had come all this way to tell her. When I got out of the car, I swayed like a drunk, weakened by my lack of sleep, my anger, and my disgust. I wanted it to come to an end. In whatever way, I just wanted that story to come to an end.

I approached the house. At that time, my father and my brother would have just left for the day. I found myself in the kitchen, breathless, staring at the relics of their breakfast on the table. Slices of toast. Dirty cups. A glass that bore, on the rim, the distinct traces of a pair of lips. Their relics on the table and the scent of coffee in the air. No sign of my mother. I walked upstairs, horrified at the sound of my own footsteps, at the acrid taste in my throat. I filled the hallway with the sound of my breathing. I reached the bedroom, threw open the door, and froze to the spot.

She was standing in front of me. It dawned on me straight away that this wasn't my mother. There was something strange, not quite human, in her eyes, something that made me think of the gaze of a dog. It wasn't hostile. There was a gleam of primitive wisdom, there was an absolute sorrow and passivity. This wasn't a human gaze. Otherwise, she was just like her: the hair, the face, the proportions of the body. She was naked. I could see the rhythm of her respiration, the slight movement of belly and breasts. I had never seen my mother's naked body. I wasn't seeing it now either, technically speaking; what I was seeing was its twin body.

Her skin was damp. She must have taken a bath. Her hair looked freshly washed too, and I stood staring in amazement. I knew that hair. Those damp, dark locks. I stared at her hair until she noticed my gaze, and then she startled awake from her trance. She took a lock of hair in her fingers, slowly, caressing it cautiously, as if she herself were amazed at that hair, those wet strands of silk. I'll never forget that gesture. She held the hair out to me and seemed to be asking me to touch it.

I took a step backwards. All of my anger had vanished, tumbled off me like a garment. When I recoiled, she grimaced in disappointment, almost in pain. I gulped. I stepped towards her again. There she was, her body, her rapt expression. Her docile smile. Now there was something inviting about her gaze. She opened her arms almost in surrender. Our heavy breathing. I reached out a hand and grazed her skin, feeling overwhelmed by its warmth. My fingers touched her neck, and slid down to her breasts. She moaned, her eyes still wide open. I could smell the scent of that body, a sweetish aroma, similar to some strange spice. My body adhered to hers like a magnet. It was an instant. Then I broke away, panting feverishly and with an urge to scream. I took to my heels, ran down the steps.

I found my mother in the kitchen. My chest was heaving, and I could neither calm my breathing nor conceal it. You can conceal a lot of things but not the violence of your own panting. She seemed surprised for an instant, then seemed to understand. She avoided my gaze and I avoided hers. I opened the door and left the house.

*

To forget was an impossible verb. In the following weeks, I tried my best. To forget that gaze, the sweetish aroma of that body. I did my best not to think about it in class at the university, as I struggled to grasp the nuanced poetics of some European man of letters. As I sipped from a scalding cup in a coffee shop, eavesdropping on conversations at neighbouring tables, about some unforgettable party or the tits of some classmate. I did my best not to think about it as I climbed the steps of the Public Library on 42nd Street, passing between the two huge stone lions, or sitting at a table in the reading room where, it was said, Leon Trotsky had once worked. As I sat with my eyes lost in the middle distance, lulled by the rocking movement of a subway train, or in the early morning, when those same eyes shot open after a night of dense dreams. I tried not to think about it. To think about European men of letters instead, to think of Leon Trotsky, to think of anything at all except for that gaze, and that sweetish aroma. That was the resolution I had made. Unfortunately, I was unable to stick to it. Each time, the image of that body wormed its way into my consciousness, her second body, that body as it breathed, that body with its scent, warm and defenceless.

I asked myself so many questions. I wondered what its voice would sound like if it ever tried to speak. I wondered what language it would speak, Italian or English. When it had moments of consciousness, fleeting, out of the blue, did it realise where it was? Did it have time to realise it was alive at all, before some guy walked into the room and started taking off his clothes?

Even when I was with Alyson, I couldn't bring myself to forget. I made love keeping my eyes closed, squeezed shut, pointlessly concentrating on the importance of concentrating. My attention scattered in a thousand directions. Alyson would stop and take my face in her hands. "Where are you? Look at me." Then I'd smile, tentatively. She was with me, young, intense, my girlfriend. Her eyes glowed in the semi-darkness of the bedroom. It would have been so nice to abandon myself to her. I apologised, kissed her with tenderness, and never told her about my real obsessions.

One night we climbed up to the roof of our building. It was late spring, the night was warm. We gazed over the panorama of roofs, the vast expanse of fairly low, half-lit buildings. The old East Village was all around us, silent, listening, almost surprised. A car alarm wailed somewhere. The sky was criss-crossed by whitish clouds, which reflected the light of the city and stood out, like phosphorescent jellyfish, against the dark background. Off in the distance, beyond the urban agglomeration, an aeroplane lifted slowly into the air, emitting a series of intermittent flashing lights. Its roar didn't reach us. It seemed suspended in an enchanted silence. "Look," I sighed. "There was a time when I wondered where every aeroplane I saw was going. I wished I was aboard, no matter what the destination."

"Oh," Alyson reasoned. "This is New York, kid. Where else would you want to go?"

I nodded, feeling weary. I leaned against the parapet and studied the panorama. "I was thinking," I said. "Maybe I should get a job."

"You already have a job," she replied, laying out a blanket that she'd brought up from the apartment. She sat down, pulled a small package from her pocket, and started rolling a joint.

I sat down next to her. "Not that stupid thing at the bar. I mean something a little more demanding. Something that would earn me proper money." I let a few seconds go by. "I'd like to be independent," I concluded.

Alyson went on breaking up the marijuana. "We'd all like that. Or at least, that's what we claim." She looked up and added: "I don't get it. You've always told me that your family gives you enough to get by."

"My family…" I echoed her, awkwardly. "I'd like to be independent," I limited myself to repeating.

"I can't see the point of that now. Every time you have to turn a project in to one of your professors, I see how you struggle. If you had a more demanding job, you wouldn't be able to keep up. You wouldn't be able to meet the deadlines for the coursework."

I let myself fall back, listless, looking up at the sky overhead. The whitish clouds continued to streak across it. A group of enigmatic phosphorescent jellyfish. "I could try to get a loan, like many do. I can't go on like this. Every time I withdraw money from the bank…" I broke off, sensing I was just a fraction away from confessing the whole thing to her.

"What are you talking about?" The flame of her lighter flickered between her hands, illuminating her face, and for an instant I imagined someone watching us from above, from the dappled sky, the two of us down there, alone, a boy and a girl on the roof of an apartment house, in the night, at the tail end of the twentieth century, with nothing between us but the tiny flame of a lighter. The ember of the joint glowed in the darkness and a puff of smoke wafted over to me. "You shouldn't feel guilty. If a family has the resources, it's perfectly normal to send the children to college."

"I guess that's true," I said, gloomily. Alyson came from a family that didn't have any particular problems, it was natural for her to think that way. I reached out an arm and pulled her towards me. Beneath the silent sky we embraced, the two of us joined, strangers, one body against the other, breathing together.

"Bruce," she uttered, as if my name contained within itself every imaginable sentence, as if it contained worlds. When I kissed her, I found the flavour of the joint in her mouth.

Later, when we went back downstairs to the apartment, the telephone was ringing. "Who the hell…" It was the middle of the night. I picked up the receiver. Funny how even before I heard who was calling, I clearly knew that something had happened to my mother.

"Bruce…" said the voice of my brother Dennis. "You need to come, Bruce. They had a fight. Dad put her in the hospital."

*

I slipped some coins into the coffee vending machine. The dispenser emitted a prolonged sound, gurgling, spraying the hot liquid into a plastic cup. I repeated the operation and walked back to the waiting room with the two steaming cups in my hands. I handed one to Dennis and took a seat next to him.

It was daytime by now. We'd had to wait a long time until a doctor could see our mother. There was a woman ahead of her who had been stabbed in the leg, and also a man in his mid-fifties who seemed to have taken a spill on roller skates in the middle of the night—who knows how, who knows why—smashing up his face and chipping four of his upper teeth.

Now our mother was in there, on the other side of a faded blue door, being tended to by a bespectacled physician. She had a bloody lip, a cut on her cheekbone, a black eye. Nothing too serious. At least not physically. She had walked into the emergency room with a rigid gait, dazed, like a fragile ice sculpture. I don't think she was in pain, I think she was more in a state of shock. As was I. My father had always been a temperamental man, but I'd never seen him turn violent. He'd busted her lip. He'd lacerated her cheekbone with the knuckles of his fist.

My brother had woken up in the night when he heard screams from their bedroom. Our father and our mother were having a fight. According to Dennis, a strange watchfulness had reigned in the house for the past few days. Our father, as far as Dennis could figure out, was convinced that she was having an affair with someone.

I sat there mulling over what my brother had told me. I concluded that our father hadn't figured out the whole truth but was probably getting closer. The truth about my mother's double body. That must be it. Now that I knew the truth, it was starting to loom over the others, increasingly inexorable, like an enormous mass of water. It pressed as if against the wall of a dam. Even though I was keeping the secret, by now there was a crack in the dam and it was spreading.

I blew into the cup and took a sip. "Do you think it'll take her long to get back to normal?" I asked in a worried tone.

My brother was sitting on the edge of his seat with the cup in his hand. He was wearing an old sweatshirt that he usually slept in and he had a pair of beat-up Adidas on his feet, the untied laces trailing out on the floor, inert, like lifeless arms. "Her face? A couple of weeks, I think."

I was surprised at my brother's voice. It was a grown-up voice, soft and somewhat scratchy, almost a masculine version of our mother's voice, and it stood out clearly against the background noise of the emergency room.

The voices of a couple of nurses and of other people waiting around merged with the echo of a radio that was playing, somewhere, an old blues song. I heard someone else dropping coins into the slot of the coffee machine, a metallic sound that reverberated at length, as though those coins were dropping endlessly. "That eye was so puffy and swollen," I said. "I do hope it will be as good as before."

We kept sitting side by side, two brothers, breathing slowly. There didn't seem to be any well-defined sensations inside us. He and I, alone, suspended in the void of an early morning, in the odour of disinfectant that filled the chair-lined waiting area of an emergency room.

I seized his hand. It was warm and strong. I held it for a few moments. His hand seemed to vibrate slightly, as if a secret tension were running through it. I wondered how long it would be until he too found out the truth about our mother. In my memory, his hand rests in mine. In my memory, his hand possesses a melancholy toughness, even though it is still the hand of a boy. I grip that hand. I continue to grip it. I want to tell him that I'm sorry about what happened and about what's going to happen, what neither of us know yet.

Someday, he'll become a detective and he'll see the dead bodies of super-heroes, and yet now we're sitting here, hand in hand, with coffee on our breath. Our mother's face is beaten because of a burgeoning suspicion and our father is holed up at home, like a restless animal, waiting for her to come back. "Bruce," my brother confessed. "It all seems so wrong."

*

I left Dennis and our mother at the hospital and headed to my parents'
house. The morning shone on Clifton. Irritable buses sailed down the road
towards New York City and snappy cars halted at intersections and tore
away again, leaving puffs of exhaust in the air behind them. A couple of
bored kids watched me from the rear window of a car. A young girl punk
walked towards the bus stop, solitary, proudly out of place, her face dotted
with a constellation of piercings. I stopped at a diner with the idea of getting
breakfast, but I was unable to gulp down more than another cup of coffee.

Once I got to the house, I shoved the back door open. At first, I couldn't
find my father. The kitchen was empty, steeped in a razor-sharp silence. His
jacket lay abandoned on the table. I slowly climbed the stairs and walked
down the dimly lit hallway to the threshold of my parents' bedroom. I
stopped. I had already seen this picture. Maybe that was what all my life
was about. Maybe my life was a single scene repeated ad infinitum, that
scene, the same scene, the scene of someone peering, fearfully, into his
parents' bedroom. The door swung open. There my father stood, before
me, studying me with a cloudy gaze.

Both our bodies stiffened. For an instant, it seemed we were going to
face off, and that each of us was about to swing a punch. He was bigger
than me. No question, he'd have laid me out, but I still might be able to
get in a punch of my own. At least, a fist to his face. He seemed to read my
mind. He shook his head and looked at the floor. He cleared his throat and
asked: "How is your mother?" His voice was hoarse. He shifted his weight
from one leg to the other, and repeated, without looking at me: "How
is your mother?" There was something worn-out looking about his skin,
and his shirt was rumpled, open at the chest, letting a tuft of hair emerge.

"She's at the hospital. With Dennis," I replied. "She's going to have to
get some X-rays. I think she'll be home in an hour or two." He seemed to
have a hard time taking in my words. He swayed for a moment and rested
his shoulder against the door jamb. "Is she going to file a complaint with
the police?"

"She said she fell down the stairs."

He ran a hand through his short hair. "Christ," he breathed. "Christ."
There was a pained expression on his face, the closest thing to an expression

of repentance I'd ever seen from him. He straightened his shirt and ran a hand through his hair again. "I need some air," he said.

I followed him down the stairs. We passed through the front garden and crossed the street. On the other side of the street a strip of grassy waste ground was wedged between the houses. Even though it wasn't exactly a park, the local kids went there to play, and both Dennis and I had spent our share of afternoons there when we were little. A strip of ground. My father and I walked along the grass.

I wondered what excuse he'd used to skip work that day. I wondered what we would say to each other now, the two of us, a father and a son who hadn't had a conversation of more than a couple of sentences in the last few years. We'd never been very good at this. Even when we lived in the same house, we inhabited different worlds. And most of all, I wondered what would happen if from the strip of waste ground we saw some guy, an unsuspecting client coming to see my mother, knock on the front door.

I felt my chest contract like a pump. A flow of unexpected courage seemed to surge through my body. "I don't want to know what made you do it. I just want you to assure me that you'll never do it again."

My father froze. He appeared astonished. When he tipped his head to study me, the sun glinted off the silvery stubble that lined his cheek. His gaze had hardened. "Your mother's hiding something." He stroked his chin before going on: "I think she's having an affair with someone. What else could it be? Your mother keeps denying everything. That's what made me lose it with her."

I struggled to look him in the eye. "Do you have any proof?"

"No," he replied. "Just sensations. If I ever do find out she's having an affair..." He broke away from me to put an end to the topic and walked a few yards along the grass. He spread his arms and took a deep breath. He lifted his face towards the sky, like a prophet in contact with the depths of the heavens, as the sun lit up, again, the specks of silver on his face. "Air," he said. "When we came here to live, I felt there was so much air. I felt it was easier to breathe."

I took a deep breath myself. I could still feel my chest contracting, but the sense of courage that had surged through me a short while before was gone. The air filled my lungs. I stood motionless, filled with air and uncertainty, as my father headed back towards the house. I didn't know whether to follow him. I watched him go. "Dad," I called after him.

He turned around. When he realised that I had nothing to say, he gave me a chilly glance and stuck his hands in his pockets. He seemed to hold the pose for a few moments, an Italian man in his early forties, with the street of an American suburb in the background. For a few moments he didn't move. He gave me enough time to register the harsh lines of his features, the hostile power in his eyes. "Someday you and I will have a reckoning of our own," he said.

I gave a start.

"You can't really think that I swallowed your story about working at a bar. I still don't understand what you live on, but one day I'll find out."

He walked off again. I watched him walk in that light, across that grass. I watched as he got further away. He wasn't in good shape; there was a heaviness to the line of his back and to the way his arms dangled at his sides. And yet, there was a tenacious strength in him, a sort of icy, vaguely obtuse fury, something he had brought along with him from the beginning, over the years, perhaps from Italy, across the ocean and across time. My father. However unpleasant, the conversation that had just ended was one of the most substantial we'd ever had.

*

My eyes opened wide with a start. I lay there breathing, open-mouthed, as the world around me regained consistency: the smooth fabric of the sheets, the pillow under my head, the breeze through the open window. Alyson breathing next to me. From the rhythm of her breathing I could sense she was awake. She said nothing, having decided by that time to stop asking what was tormenting me. She would just wait for me to talk to her about it. She would go on waiting. The whole world, in that period, seemed to be waiting for a turning point.

Outside, day was dawning. I could perceive the aroma of coffee from some early-rising neighbour, and the great damp peace of dawn filtering in through the window. I blinked repeatedly. I got cautiously out of bed.

"Where are you going?" Alyson sighed. "Stay here with me."

"Wait for me," I said. "I'll be back in a few minutes."

Barefoot, wearing only a pair of boxer shorts, I left the apartment and walked upstairs. I let my disquiet guide me, step by step, until I emerged on the deserted roof. From up there, I watched the sun rise. The city, motionless and majestic, received the miracle of the new light. I stood there in the glowing sunrise, practically naked, feeling full of a mysterious force, and at the same time completely helpless.

Today I know: daylight wasn't the only thing that sprang to life in that sunrise. Something new was beginning to stir in me, something that at the time appeared nebulous and that only with the passing of the years would I come to recognise. Now I know that my mother gave me more than just some of her facial features, more than just the shape of her dark eyes. A spark of the secret flame that inhabited her body had passed into mine, lived in me, under my skin, in the tiniest interstitial spaces of my flesh. I too had strange powers. But back then it was still too early to understand that.

For several weeks after the episode of my mother's beating, there were no new deposits in my account, and I scraped by on my last savings. I had almost come to believe that it was all over and that she had stopped prostituting her second body. I felt a clump of contrasting emotions in my throat. Then the deposits began again and it all went on as before, day after day, week after week.

It was summer by then, and I had summer session courses to take.

I only saw my mother one more time. It was on a quiet June afternoon. In order to avoid disagreeable scenes, I had alerted her to my arrival. She welcomed me with an angelic smile. My father's violent hands had left no marks on her, and I was afraid to ask her how things were going, almost as if any reference to what had happened might threaten to reopen, through some frightful spell, the wounds on her face. I sat down at the kitchen table while she made me a glass of iced lemonade. Even from a distance I could smell the perfume of her hair.

I suggested that perhaps the time had come to put an end to it. I hinted at a couple of possible jobs that I'd looked into. When the school year started up again, I could just attend classes part-time. I could give it a try.

I could make it work. "If what you're doing is just for me," I said, "I don't want you to keep doing it." I think my voice was shaking as I told her these things. My hands were perspiring onto the wooden tabletop.

She shook her head like someone listening to a child talking nonsense. She turned up the volume on the radio. It was playing one of the golden oldies that she loved so well. "I just adore Stevie Wonder," she said in an elusive, nostalgic tone.

"Mama. Did you hear what I said to you?"

She kept listening to the song on the radio, nodding her head to the beat, singing along with one of the verses: *I've got something that I must tell... Last night someone rang our doorbell.*

"Mama."

At last her gaze met mine. Her pupils seemed to contract and a spark of panic flickered in her eyes. She dried her hands on a dish towel. She gave me the glass of lemonade and slumped onto the chair across from me. "Oh Bruce," she said. "It's too late, don't you understand? Too late for everything. Too late to change, to turn back, it's even too late to ask for help."

Her air of resignation frightened me. She seemed to look at me from a sorrowful distance, then she went back to moving her head in time to the song. Stevie Wonder's voice on the radio. The scent of freshly squeezed lemons. Hundreds of tiny, sharp ice fragments bumped against my lips as I took a sip from the glass. I made that sip last a long time. We both kept our eyes downcast in palpable embarrassment, as the afternoon light began to catch fire, enveloping us in a sombre, gilded glow.

I couldn't stand that atmosphere. I clutched the glass tight in my fist. I set it down on the table and contemplated the traces of my fingers on the fogged glass surface. "Hey," I said, improvising a playful tone. "Let's see if you've heard this one. Do you know what goes: *riiing... riiing... riiing... aargh!*"

She peered at me in confusion, then it dawned on her what I was doing. "I can't believe this. You've never been good at telling jokes."

"Come on," I urged her. "What goes *riiing... riiing... riiing... aargh!*"

She conceded a faint smile. "No idea."

"*Riiing... riiing... riiing... aargh!...* It's Stevie Wonder answering the steam iron instead of the phone."

It took her a while to get it. "That's the stupidest joke I've ever heard in my life," she groaned, but her smile was spreading, shyly at first, then more emphatically, until the smile blossomed into laughter, strained, then deeper, a laughter that shook her body like a coughing fit, until she threw her head back. "My God," she said.

Sure, it was a stupid joke, but I felt certain that Stevie Wonder would have forgiven me.

A short while later I said goodbye. I brushed her cheek with a kiss. I walked out of the door and through the front garden, striding too fast, without turning around. Once again, I felt that bizarre and alarming sensation. The same feeling that had driven me up to the roof of my apartment building one morning a few days ago. It was the beginning of my ability of presentiment, I believe, and what I was sensing in that period, with growing clarity, was a foreshadowing of my mother's fate. I could feel it. I couldn't believe it. How could I believe in such a horrible premonition?

I had no idea what was happening to me. My superpower and my love for her were intertwined, they sprang one from the other and they each negated the other.

I shouldn't have run away like that. I should have stayed there and admired the yellow rose bushes in the front garden, the ones she watered once a day, and the pale colour of the low wall around the garden. I should have lingered to look at the windows from outside, clean, bright, and the gingham curtains that I'd seen hanging on those windows since I was a child. I should have stared at the front of the house. I should have memorised that homely scene in detail, in all its peace, before that apparent peace was overturned roughly once and for all.

I slunk away. I walked down the street. I was already a hundred feet or so away when I heard her call my name, and as I turned I saw her running towards me, her hair tossed in the air, lithe as a girl, so beautiful and desperate in the cruel light. She caught up with me and threw her arms around me, panting against my neck. "Mama…" I said in embarrassment, wondering if anyone was watching us.

She didn't let go of me. I could feel her heart beating against my chest. "Make me laugh," she begged. "Make me laugh again," she whispered, holding me tight, as I stood there, silent, mortified at the realisation that I had no more jokes, no way of making her laugh again.

*

I remember that on that day, the day after my last visit to my mother, Alyson and I spent the afternoon at the Met. We entered the museum with a donation of fifty cents each, with the brazen cheek of penniless students, and we wandered through the halls with a solemn gait, as if we were guests at a royal ball.

In a certain way it was a perfect afternoon. I remember how our voices echoed through the halls of the museum, and the sound of our footsteps on the marble floors, and the warmth of Alyson's body as she leaned lovingly against me while looking at a piece of art. It was the first time we'd gone to the museum together. We showed each other our favourite rooms. Alyson took me into the African art section, leading me by the hand as though to protect me, revealing to me the beauty of the dark wood sculptures, shaped like so many spaceships. When it was my turn, I led Alyson into the hall of medieval armour, where men who had turned to dust centuries ago seemed to have left behind their shining, metallic carapaces.

We slid effortlessly towards Greek and Roman art, and the absorbing nudity of those white sculptures, and I confessed to her that as a boy I had found myself getting aroused in those rooms. I remember how Alyson burst out laughing. "You little pervert," she kidded me. "I have to say that I lingered here myself. Beautiful bodies. Such perfect asses."

"The breasts. The white breasts of these statues."

"Too bad about the male sculptures. Have you noticed? The penis is always the first thing that breaks off."

We laughed together. We laughed a lot that day, foolishly, with perhaps just a hint of melancholy, laughing without being able to stop, on the verge of hysteria, laughing like little kids, laughing like in the throes of a giddy madness. Later, we tried to stop. We talked about things that seemed important, plans for the rest of the summer and beyond. Alyson was about to start an internship at a small news weekly. It was a great opportunity. I would continue to take summer courses and look as well for a newsroom internship. Everything seemed decided, nailed down almost to an excessive degree: the coming weeks, the coming months.

"Jeez," I confessed. "I'm starting to realise that I don't like talking about the future after all."

"What are you saying?"

"The word *future* makes me think…" I searched for the proper comparison. "I know what, it makes me think of a flavourless exotic fruit. White flesh, seedless. Possibly juicy. Partly poisonous. Impossible to say how you're supposed to peel it."

Alyson started laughing and I laughed with her.

Later, we headed home. We took a southbound subway train. I remember the trip back. I remember I could almost sense the train's effort, the train that was conveying us with a hesitant motion, pitching and yawing, lurching, as if afraid of its own destination. As we left the station, a shiver ran down my back. I was used to shivering suddenly like that. As soon as we got home the phone rang and my throat went instantly dry.

It was a summer evening, and my girlfriend and I had just returned home, coming back from our first trip together to the Met. We'd paid a dollar for the two of us, we'd laughed about the missing penises of the Greco-Roman statues. That's all it was. My girlfriend was going to cook a vegan dinner, we'd smoke a joint, then we'd lie down on our mattress, and the next day we'd go to our summer session classes. Nothing more than that. The phone went on ringing. I remember something snapping inside me, a capsule of inconceivable anticipatory grief. Frightened, I looked at Alyson. I don't remember if I said anything. I was imploring her to answer it, or maybe not to.

In the end, I was the one who reached for the phone. It wasn't hard for me to guess that it was Dennis calling, the way he had a few weeks earlier, when he called to tell me that something had happened to our mother. And in fact that's who it was. It was my brother on the phone. The news was about her.

*

My brother would tell me what had happened. From the way he told me, it was easy to guess that he knew the truth about our mother, and he'd always known—perhaps he'd known even before I did. My brother was almost sixteen when he witnessed the final scene. He saw everything, he saw it forever. From that day on, his eyes seemed to become irritated, filling up with a road map of vermilion capillaries, an effect that at first appeared temporary, then a chronic disturbance, as if the blood that had flowed to his eyes had decided not to flow away again, or had been unable to find a way back.

That day, while Alyson and I were wandering through the halls of the Met, and flocks of visitors poured into and out of the museums of New York City, and ice cream vendors were doing big business along the edges of Central Park, and the hot breath of summer panted throughout the length of the northern hemisphere... While those things were happening, back in Clifton our father did something unexpected. He came home at an unusual time. We never did find out whether the reason he returned home in the middle of the afternoon was an upset stomach, as he had said before leaving work, or was an urge to find out, once and for all, exactly what his wife did when he wasn't there. In recent times he had become suspicious.

I can see him in my mind as he enters quietly through the back door. He carries with him the scent of the slaughterhouse where he works, no doubt, and yet you can hardly blame him for that smell. When it comes to that, you can hardly blame him for the suspicions he is harbouring. He's postponed this moment for years. Then who is to blame for this evil, for the long chill that is about to descend over us?

He moves in silence down the hallway. He proceeds cautiously, noise-lessly, on his rubber-soled shoes.

Dennis wasn't home. He was at practice. When he rode up on his bicycle, and saw what was happening from a distance, he began pumping harder, riding faster, until his heart was in his mouth, and then threw the bike down in front of the house. At that point he was completely breathless. Not even enough breath to shout for help.

Our father was dragging her out of the house. He gripped her by the hair. He seemed to be possessed by an impossible burst of fury, his mouth twisted, his eyes so narrow they appeared shut. In contrast, our mother's eyes were wide open, her mouth gaping in an attempt to scream. Dennis told me that's what paralysed him. Their mouths, their eyes. Their physiognomy had been distorted, almost dissolved, and our parents had practically vanished, replaced by those two figures. They were no longer a father and a mother. They were pure fury, pure terror.

"You whore," our father was shouting. "You damned mutant bitch. After all these years, you and your bitch twin body. You thought you were so clever, didn't you? Did you think you'd be able to get away with it for much longer?"

Dennis was even more shocked. He'd never heard our father shout like that. He thought that our mother was trying to answer, but he couldn't swear that he had heard the words, or read them on her soundless lips. "I beg you. Don't take me away from the house. I can't go far. I've never gone far from the other body… This could kill me. I'm begging you."

Dennis took a few steps, hesitantly at first. He started to run. In his memory, he felt like he had no respiration, no heartbeat, like he was moving absurdly slowly, as in the classic nightmare. He reached them. He tried to say something. Probably nothing came out but a wail, and he smacked our father with the palm of his hand, square in the face, causing a flaccid, almost comical sound. If the situation were different, you'd have been tempted to laugh at that sound. Hand on face. Flesh on flesh. Our father staggered. Dennis was strong, and he knew how to land a blow, but he'd failed to wind up for this one.

Perhaps a spark of astonishment lit up in our father's eyes. Or perhaps his reaction was purely mechanical, an instinctive reflex, prompting him to take a wild, blind swing of the fist.

My brother collapsed. Perhaps our mother screamed. Dennis couldn't say. He could tell they were moving away into the distance. He saw them struggling, against the screen of daylight, like incomprehensible Chinese shadow puppets. They were moving towards the waste ground on the opposite side of the street. He saw the silhouette of our mother falling to her knees, as our father kept dragging her, and he heard her sob and implore again. "I can't go any further. I can't be this far away from her."

Dennis couldn't remember anything else. A neighbour told me that he had seen my father crying, minutes later, cradling my mother's body in his arms. I wonder where he meant to drag her. I wonder where on earth he thought he was taking her. Far away, some place far away. Maybe only over to the grassy strip, where we used to play with the neighbourhood kids, or maybe somewhere else, even further, far away from New Jersey. Maybe he wanted to take her into the city. Maybe to Coney Island. Maybe he wanted to take her back to Italy, maybe he wanted to drag her to the ocean and cross it like Moses, dragging his wife by the hair. The woman he had loved. The woman he had never fully possessed.

We never knew which of them died first. Our mother or her second body, left behind in the bedroom. When we found it, the second body was naked, sprawled across the window sill, where it must have witnessed the whole thing.

As for our mother, after dragging her for a few yards more, our father felt her become a dead weight. He turned around and saw her, ashen and senseless. The demon of fury left him instantly. A lock of hair had come away in his hand. He collapsed onto the moist grass, next to our mother, trying to shake her and staring at her in disbelief. My mother was so pale. Perfectly white. "Silvia," he called. He went on saying her name. If I'd been there, I think I'd have been doing the same. Repeating her name. Repeating it over and over again, without end.

My father held her in his arms. The neighbours said that he just lay there, holding her. They said that he blew into her face, incessantly, tenderly, as if he were trying to infuse life into her.

──────────

Book Four

MYSTIQUE

MAY 2006

Vladimir Putin was irresistible. Vladimir Putin was sexy. Vladimir Putin had steel-coloured eyes and wore a skintight T-shirt that showed off his biceps, thick and rounded like a rugby ball. The sexiest head of state on the planet. When he came in, men and women got to their feet. Every week he received a standing ovation. Vladimir Putin walked to the centre of the stage, trailing a cluster of photographers, posing with intense expressions and a steely gaze. He raised his arms in the direction of the cheering audience. He was the man of the moment. He raved some nonsense about the muscles of Great Russia, asking the audience if they wanted to see those muscles and then triumphantly hiking his T-shirt. He'd show off his abdominals at the slightest excuse. The audience laughed and new bursts of applause rang out. Vladimir Putin repeated the routine with the abdominals several times, looking around with a conceited expression, a little funnier each time, dragging louder and louder laughs out of the studio audience. *The muscles of Great Russia.* That routine never failed to get a laugh.

Commercial break.

After the pause, it was Arnold Schwarzenegger's turn, a classic of the show, and then a number by Madonna who, just like Putin, never missed a chance to show off her athletic abilities. Madonna put on a steamy dance production. Surrounded by male dancers twenty-five years her junior, she swivelled her hips until, without warning, she froze, locked in place by a treacherous shoulder cramp. The audience started laughing again. The laughter came in warm waves, like the jets of water from a health-giving shower.

The pace of the show accelerated as the finale approached. The lights of the cameras glowed at the sides of the studio. Mel Gibson appeared, a frenzied glare in his eyes, reciting random lines from his most cringe-making movies, shouting like a man possessed while the sidekick of the various numbers, Chad, tried to get him back on the track of reason. Last of all came Oprah Winfrey, striding on with a royal gait, radiant, dressed in white, showering benedictions befitting a pontiff, and beginning to recommend books that didn't exist, narrating fragments of absurd and funny plots. This was another classic of the show.

The notes of the closing theme song came up. The applause became louder and even warmer, verging on the emotional, while the last guest left the stage and finally she herself appeared, acclaimed, adored, the real star, the only actual character on the show. She stood there for a moment, in her real appearance, looking out at the studio audience and the cameras. She, who had turned herself into all those characters. She, who could become anyone, literally *become* them, taking on the semblance of the guests she chose for the show. She who made the whole country laugh. The most famous mutant in America, the unrivalled star of the *Celebrity Mystique Show*.

*

The lights of the cameras died out, in a single instant, like an interrupted dream. The theme music faded, and with it the extended applause. One last time Mystique thanked the studio audience, the technical crew, the walk-ons, and the dancers before heading to the dressing rooms with Chad. "My God," she sighed. "I am so exhausted."

"Don't even say it," Chad whined. "These shoes are killing me." He was wearing a pair of loafers that looked far too small, and was bundled into a red-sequined tuxedo that also looked too tight for his considerable girth. "Why does that costumier hate me so much?!"

"Mel Gibson was a bit overstated," Mystique thought out loud. Her perfectionism pushed her to find a shortcoming in every show the minute it was over. "I had to overdo him a little. I was having a hard time maintaining his shape, and that was the only way I could stay in character."

"I think it went fine the way you did it," Chad replied. "A crazy Mel Gibson bouncing around the studio. I thought I would have a heart attack chasing after you. To say nothing of my aching feet… Ouch!" he complained as he stumbled. "Could there be anything worse than a fatty with sore feet?"

"Oh yes, there is," Mystique answered. "A mutant who's so tired *she can't even feel* her feet any more."

They walked a little further and reached the dressing rooms. Before parting ways, they exchanged an exhausted but basically satisfied smile, the smile of two people who had finished a job, and had worked together to create, once again, the atmosphere of a hit television show. They'd done it. Another episode had gone on air.

As soon as she walked into her dressing room, Mystique collapsed on the sofa. She shut her eyes and savoured the moment. Far from the cameras, far from prying eyes, far from the spotlights of the studio. Far, far away. "Peace," she whispered gratefully in the solitude of the room.

She could feel herself breathing hard and a sense of painful excitement in her stomach. That's how it was after every show. She knew she couldn't have faced one more transformation, and yet her body seemed to demand exactly that, it seemed to want to go on transforming itself, from one shape to another, faster and faster, at a frantic pace. Her body was like an overexcited child. Like some sort of crazed animal. Now she had to find a way of calming it down, and she began breathing deeply, slowly, inhaling air, exhaling, breathing in, breathing out, closing her eyes and losing herself in that rhythm, that profoundly simple rhythm, a rhythm that was so elementary, therapeutic, and arcane. *My breathing. Nothing else.*

That was when a sound wormed its way into her ears, forcing her to open her eyes. The phone on the side table. It was an inside call. "What is it?" she sighed.

"Sorry," said a voice. It was her production assistant. "I just wanted to let you know that Gary called just before the show. It was too late to transfer the call to you, and he left a message…"

"Please," Mystique interrupted her. "I don't want messages from Gary. I don't want messages from anyone right now. I just want to relax and do my breathing exercises."

"I understand. He just asked me to tell you…"

"Hey. What do you say we talk about it later?" Mystique laughed briefly, the kind of nervous laughter she often used when she wanted to cut off a discussion.

After hanging up, she closed her eyes and went back to concentrating, doing her best to find the rhythm she had lost. She was trying to exhale all traces of agitation: out of her lungs, out of her body. Trying to expel the sense of instability that clung to her, to her limbs, in the pit of her stomach. To convince her body that there would be no more transformations, no more shapes to assume. Not any more, not now. Expel the flavour of the bodies into which she had transformed herself. Expel Vladimir Putin, expel Mel Gibson. Male bodies were the hardest. She had to expel the sensation of their weight, their scratchy chins, expel the sensation of their body hair, their chest muscles, their tight buttocks, and that small fundamental protuberance that dangled between their legs.

She started to feel a new sense of calm. A warm calm, dense as foam, gradually expanding inside her. Vladimir Putin and Mel Gibson faded away. They all eventually faded away. She was starting to feel like herself again, on that sofa, in that peaceful dressing room, whatever *herself* might mean. Herself, with her faintly bluish skin, her slender yet vigorous arms. Her mature face and her dark hair. She kept her eyes closed, floating in that peace, in the found-again flavour of her own body.

*

After relaxing for ten minutes or so she shook herself and decided it was time to get moving. She changed clothes, putting on a blouse and a trouser suit. She tidied her hair and applied lipstick. *There I am. Good as new.* At last, she swung open the door of her dressing room and at that point she gave a start, frightened by the sight of a human figure lurking in ambush. "My God, Susie," she said, bringing her hand to her chest. "I nearly tripped over you. You almost made me have a stroke."

Susie, the production assistant, gave her a worried smile. "I'm sorry," she hastened to say. She was in her early twenties and was still a girl, looking more petite than she actually was, with her fair white skin always on the verge of blushing.

"All right," said Mystique, regaining a semblance of control. "Besides taking a few years off my life, was there a reason why you were waiting for me?"

"Um… complicated situation," Susie began cautiously. "Gary… What I mean is, like I said, Gary called just before the show. He wanted to let you know… Um…" The girl stopped short, red in the face.

"All right," Mystique said again. She gave a smile, trying to reassure her that whatever it was, she wouldn't get mad. "Okay, let's hear it. To let me know about what?"

The girl opened her eyes wide, in no way reassured, before she made up her mind to talk. "To let you know that someone would be coming here to the studio."

"Okay," said Mystique in a patient voice. "Who?"

"A man. An officer. A policeman, I guess." That word, *policeman*, hung in mid-air like a puff of dust in the atmosphere of the hallway. Susie took a breath and then fired off her news: "The thing is that he's already here… Upstairs, I mean. He's waiting for you in your office."

This time it was Mystique's eyes that opened wide. "A *policeman*? Now?" She couldn't believe that Gary would play such a prank on her. "But I'm busy right now. *We're* busy, we have our production meeting."

All Susie did was to lower her eyes. Now that she had managed to deliver the news, she was breathing more freely.

There wasn't much more to say. Mystique certainly couldn't take it out on the girl. She started walking, incredulous and irritated, pounding her heels into the floor of the hallway. *Gary, thanks a lot.* In the elevator she nervously looked at herself in the mirrored wall, checking her hair and adjusting the collar of her blouse. *My God. Meeting a policeman.* She hadn't had any reason to deal with a police officer for the last six years, and she would gladly have done without it now. She was glad she'd worn that suit, because it gave her a determined, almost masculine look. *To hell with it,* she finally decided. I don't have to make an impression on anyone. *I don't see why I should. I don't see why I should feel nervous at all.*

*

The man was sitting in her office, and when Mystique came through the door behind him, the first thing that she saw was his back. The nape of his neck, close-shaven. The square line at the base of his hair. The man turned around and promptly got to his feet. He produced a smile and held out his hand. "Detective Dennis De Villa," he introduced himself.

Mystique shook his hand. She held it a second longer as if to judge its weight. She guessed that the detective must be thirty-something. Regular features. A slightly enigmatic gaze. He was in plain clothes; he wore a grey suit made of a light fabric, and at a glance he seemed to be fit. She didn't remember policemen being so fit. On the whole, he looked more like an ex-model or something of the sort than a detective. *A policeman. I'm shaking hands with a policeman.*

She sat down at her desk, across from the detective, maintaining an expression of distrust. "I'm sorry you went to the trouble of coming here," she said. "I'm afraid it really wasn't necessary."

Detective De Villa crossed his legs and nodded slightly, acknowledging the ungracious welcome. "I do hope you're right," he said. "I certainly hope there's no need for my visit. All the same, I understand that you've received some strange anonymous messages. The producer of your show…"

"Gary," she broke in. "I know Gary gave you a call. To tell the truth, I had asked him not to. I'm pretty sure there's nothing at all to worry about." She too crossed her legs and leaned back in her chair. "I don't see anything threatening about these messages."

De Villa went on nodding thoughtfully. Mystique noticed that his eyes were red as if he were, somehow, deeply moved. She wondered if the detective suffered from an allergy. That signal of vulnerability made her feel less hostile towards the man in front of her. And yet, that visit still struck her as an annoyance. It was late, she had a production meeting to get through, and she had no interest in spending time with a lawman.

"I saw a bit of the show," the detective said. "On the monitors in the control booth."

"Oh," Mystique replied with obvious sarcasm. "In the control booth? How lucky to be a policeman. I guess you manage to sneak in everywhere," she said.

"I was invited in by your assistant," he said apologetically.

"Susie? That dear girl," Mystique muttered.

"If I understand correctly…" De Villa hesitated and lowered his voice, almost as though about to ask an intimate question. "Your body can transform itself into the body of any other person you choose, right? That's your power."

"Correct."

"An interesting power." The detective tipped his head in a gesture that seemed to show respect. He thought it over for a few seconds before adding: "You're good at your work… Your show has a nice pace. Very entertaining."

"Thank you," said Mystique, wondering what the man was driving at.

"Do you think there might be some link between the popularity of your show and these messages?"

"Oh," she sighed. "So many people watch the show. I have no doubt that a few of them are crackpots. Like I said, though, I don't see anything so threatening in it."

"Or do you think," the detective pursued, "that they might have something to do with your past?" The question had come out a little harsh. De Villa seemed sorry about that, and added in a softer tone: "I mean, with your troubles with the law…"

"I see no possible link, Detective De Villa," she replied in a chilly voice. "At the police academy they must have taught you, I would imagine, not to rely on unfounded guesswork…" she suggested. "My past is truly, irrevocably *past*. I no longer have anything to do with those events, and that is as much as I care to state. In fact, I don't believe that I should discuss those matters with a policeman. Not without my lawyer."

De Villa raised both hands in a sign of surrender. "That won't be necessary," he smiled. "This isn't an interrogation." He had a small smile with a vague twist of almost childish shyness to it. The kind of smile that must cast spells over plenty of women, but which she just found annoying. "I certainly haven't come here to accuse you of anything," he resumed. "I'm here to help you. Possibly to protect you."

Mystique limited herself to a sceptical expression.

"Do you think that your power," Dennis De Villa asked at this point, "would be enough to defend you if these messages happened to… Well, if they happened to turn into something more serious?"

"What are you talking about?" She stared at the clock on her desk. "If it ever became necessary, I'd know how to defend myself from some stupid psycho."

"I understand," said De Villa. He put his hands together and sat gazing at her, enigmatic, with the rapt expression of a poker player. "I won't take much more of your time," he promised. "Tell me a little more about the notes."

Mystique considered putting an end to that conversation. She could do it. She had no obligation to waste her time talking to the guy, with his irritating questions, his ambiguous manner, and his reddened eyes. She levelled a hostile glare into the detective's eyes, and he caught her off guard when he said: "A rare form of conjunctivitis."

"Huh?" she said with a start.

"My eyes. The reason they're reddened is that I have a rare form of conjunctivitis. I've had it since I was very young."

"Oh," Mystique replied, at a loss for anything to say.

"Now that I've revealed my secret," said De Villa with another of his smiles, "maybe you would be so good as to tell me something about those notes."

Mystique was caught between the desire to respond to that smile and the urge to toss the detective out on his ear. A sense of weary exasperation seethed inside her. She picked up a pen from her desktop and drummed with it on the wooden surface. "Three notes," she finally gave in. "In the mail. Two here at the office, the third at home." She pulled open a desk drawer and extracted a sheet of paper. It was a piece of white paper, apparently blank, except for a single phrase printed in the middle. "This is the only one I kept. The other two were identical." She held it out to De Villa, who took it between his fingertips and studied it.

It was a piece of paper. A rectangle of mute, white, almost glowing matter. An anonymous note that had come in the mail, bearing nothing but that inexplicable phrase:

SO LONG, MY MYSTIQUE

Both their gazes lingered on the paper. "As I've told you more than once, it hardly strikes me as a threat," Mystique said. "Gary had no reason to call the police."

"If you don't mind, I'll hold onto it," said De Villa. He pulled a plastic envelope out of his jacket pocket and slipped the note into it. "On the contrary, I'm afraid your producer did the right thing. Did you know Reed Richards?"

"Reed?" Mystique asked. For some reason, that name triggered a slight jolt inside her. It seemed like a name from so far away. "The last time I saw him was at his son's funeral... Not much more than a month ago. It already seems like a distant memory."

"Distant," De Villa concurred. "Not much more than a month ago. I was there at that funeral myself, and in fact I remember seeing you..." He shook his head, perhaps to say that this wasn't the point, and went on: "It seems that Reed Richards received notes like this one before the attack that killed his son. Messages with a phrase of farewell."

Mystique narrowed her eyes. For a moment she felt tempted to take the whole matter seriously. A spark of discomfort shot through her, and she felt the boundaries of her body start to undulate, uncertainly, as though they were about to undergo another transformation. About to transform into something. Into someone. She took a deep breath and went back to drumming with her pen. She thought about that phrase, SO LONG, MY MYSTIQUE, and it all appeared pretty absurd. Almost comical.

"To tell the truth," De Villa said, "it wasn't only Reed Richards. Batman received the same note before he was murdered. And we can't rule out that Robin, a few years ago... Do you remember Robin? We can't rule out that he received these notes too, before dying in a corner of Central Park."

"Heavens," Mystique said. "I'm afraid I don't understand."

"Well, we don't understand much about this either," De Villa confessed. "We're still struggling to put together the pieces in this puzzle. A wave of murders in the world of the ex-superheroes... I'm sure you've heard about it. It seems that the murders are the work of a network of fanatics, an obscure group whose objective would appear to be the elimination of what survives of the world of historic superheroes. Our hypothesis is that

Robin was their first victim, that is to say something like a starting point…
The pace of the murders has accelerated now. Batman, Franklin Richards,
Reed Richards…"

"As far as I know, Reed killed himself," she objected. "He jumped off
the Montauk lighthouse."

"You're right. He wasn't murdered. We can guess that Mr. Richards killed
himself out of a sense of guilt, if we consider that he was the real target of
the attack at the George Hotel. What I meant to say is that we are currently
at a difficult juncture… a dangerous one. A truly dangerous moment. We
can no longer ignore messages like the ones you've received."

"Wait a minute," said Mystique. She was starting to understand. "So
that's what this is about. You're trying to tell me that I'm in the cross hairs
of this group. And the messages are evidence of that."

The detective twisted in his chair. "We can't rule it out."

Mystique laid the pen down on the desktop. She tried to evaluate what
the detective had told her, considering carefully, as if studying the outlines
of a shambling, bizarre geometric figure. "Ridiculous," was her conclusion.

De Villa twisted in his chair again.

"Maybe you don't understand," Mystique went on. "There wouldn't be
any damned reason for someone to bother planning to hurt me. I'm not
saying that everybody loves me." She broke off, amused at the very thought.
"Of course not. There are people who hold their nose at the sound of my
name. People who are outraged by my transformations and the way I mock
public figures, but it's nothing serious, it's all just part of the game. It's part
of the *system*." The detective tried to cut in, but she hushed him with a
wave of her hand. "One needs a motive to kill someone. *Motive*, you may
have heard of it. I spent sixteen years in prison, and I met very few people
who had wound up in there without a motive."

"This group doesn't seem to operate with a great deal of logic," De Villa
managed to interrupt her. He touched the knot of his tie as though it were
a precious amulet, and enunciating clearly, he added: "This group could
recruit anyone. Think of that girl they sent to kill Batman. They can recruit
anyone and strike whoever they please. No one is safe in the world of the
former superheroes."

"You're talking about former superheroes," Mystique replied. "That has little to do with me. I wasn't a super*hero*, I wasn't with Batman, Reed, and the rest of them. In the old days I steered clear of them and they steered clear of me. I was considered a subversive. A revolutionary. In the old days the whole country was afraid of me… Then I wound up in prison. In the old days I scared the country, now I entertain it." She raised her arms, pointing at the surrounding office, with a decisive gesture, to indicate what she had become: a woman who works in television, a woman immersed in the exhausting, ravenous, glittering, predictable realm of show business. *The queen of the show, the slave of the show.* A comedienne. A woman who had passed through the American court and prison system as if through the curves of an alchemical still and had emerged in full compliance with the prototype of a model citizen: innocuous, amusing. "A woman with no enemies," she said with a sliver of bitter sarcasm.

She leaned forward, piercing the detective with her glare, and asked him not to come around reeling off stories about weird plots, thank you very much. Plots existed in policemen's minds. Maybe there was some kind of assassin brotherhood out there, sure, why not, a group of people who had sworn death to the old superheroes, but she didn't see what it had to do with her. Not with all the things she'd already been through. As far as she was concerned, those notes were the work of some poor lunatic. She didn't need a police security detail and she didn't need policemen in her way. She'd had police and prison officers on her back for years, she'd been under their power the whole time she was in prison. No, thanks.

In fact, there was just one thing she did need, before heading off to attend a brief production meeting, and then jumping into a car that would take her home, and filling a tub with hot water and luxuriating selfishly in the pleasure of a bath. One tiny thing. An end to this conversation, please.

*

Dawn was heralded by a faint breeze, sweeping over the hill of Morningside Heights and wafting through her window screen, stirring the white cotton curtains. Mystique tossed and turned in her bed, tangled in the sheets, breathing with tiny movements of her belly.

The early morning air had a good smell. That was why she preferred to leave the air conditioning off and the window open, at least until later in the summer. The weather hadn't become intolerable yet. She stretched out on the mattress, only partly awake, while the gleam of daylight peeked into the bedroom. She was awake or maybe she just thought she was. She kept her eyes closed. She could feel something heavy weighing down on her: exhaustion, lassitude, and there was certainly a reason for all that weariness. The light grew brighter against her eyelids, forcing her to duck her head under the covers. It must be because of the show. The show always left her exhausted. The show made her electric and weary.

She stretched her legs with a grimace and tried to concentrate on memories from the night before. Her memories had uncertain outlines, like so many objects wrapped in packing material. It was difficult to tell them apart. She lay under the sheet, suspended in that uncertainty, in that languor that was both painful and pleasant. She lazily caressed her body. It was like waking up after going on a bender. Was that her, roaming the studio in Vladimir Putin's body, uttering lines with a Russian accent, stomach muscles contracted: could that really have happened? Dancing in Madonna's body, swinging her hair and shaking her hips, shooting a smouldering glance into the eye of the camera: a dream or a memory? It must have happened, she guessed it had. She couldn't swear to it. That was a typical effect of doing too many transformations at too rapid a pace, as she had to do during her weekly show. That confusion. That lassitude. Like going on a bender, that's right, or some other kind of intoxication.

She continued caressing the skin of her arms, her thighs, the line of her hips. Was that her, almost tripping over Susie at the door of her dressing room, coming close to a stroke in her fright: did that happen? And then talking to a police detective in her office, dismissing him brusquely and perhaps, she had to admit, bitchily: an actual event?! She turned over again, taking care not to open her eyes. Her nude body rubbed against the cloth of the sheets. It wasn't just her memories from the night before; thoughts of the future also had the appearance of dreams. To get out of bed and face the harsh light of day, to make a fruit smoothie while listening to the news on Ten-Ten Wins: what an odd idea. To throw on some clothes and clap a baseball cap on her head, to head out to run along the trails and steps of Morningside Park: this too was the setting of a dream.

Oh, don't do it. Don't open your eyes. Her flesh was smooth under her fingers. She breathed a little harder as the light grew stronger. It must have been about six o'clock, but that morning she was in no hurry, because the day after the broadcast she usually indulged herself and went in late to the studio. She kept running her fingers over her skin until she found, almost to her surprise, the soft mass of her breasts. A pleasurable jolt radiated throughout her body. She went on breathing through the sheet. She let her hands slide slowly downwards, then with a spasm she rolled over, her hair wrapped around her face. It was about to happen. She wanted to make it happen. She could feel the boundaries of her body waver, becoming fluid, her flesh nearly on the point of dissolving. Transforming herself in the morning was something different. It wasn't like during the show. Every fibre of her body seemed to turn upside down, and she felt herself sliding far away, until she almost vanished... Now she emitted a moan, a loud moan in a male voice. She had taken on a different body. Detective Dennis De Villa twisted and contorted under the sheet, naked, touching his muscular thighs, brushing his fingers over his groin and his hard testicles. He went on touching himself with a blend of instinct and astonishment. He ran one hand up over his chest, finding a patch of soft body hair, reaching the tiny buttons of his nipples, while with the other hand he reached down and grabbed himself between his legs. He clutched his penis. He went on thrashing, with raucous moans that sounded like sobs.

He stopped. An instant before coming a shiver ran through him, a shiver so intense that it made the bed vibrate, or maybe the whole room, and then Mystique's body reappeared, gasping, breathless, as if surfacing from a long underwater dive. She arched her back over the mattress. She didn't stop moving her fingers. The tips of her fingers stayed on the small, hard peninsula of her clitoris, continuing to brush it until it began to hurt, and until a rhythmic contraction shook her from within. She let go. She curled up panting, trying to capture that pulsation a little longer, the hot, blessed pulsation, the pulsation that started from the space between her legs and spread out, in waves, like the radio signal from some minuscule star.

It lasted a while. It died out slowly, fading away, as the lucent day triumphed. Mystique opened her eyes. The world was there, all around her, inundated with light. She sighed. In spite of her weariness, in spite of a faint, undulating sense of melancholy, she decided it really was time to get up.

*

"Listen to this," said Chad, perched on a corner of the desk and holding a copy of the book that the whole nation was talking about by now. The book's cover was in garish colours; it looked freshly printed. "It says here that Batman wasn't the faggot he seemed to be. It says he got aroused by watching girls wash their hands. It says he loved to have them stick those nice clean hands up his ass."

"Nothing new about that," Mystique replied in a sceptical tone. She crossed her arms and looked at the other people in the room, each of them poring through a copy of the same book. They were in the main production office, it was about eleven in the morning, and this was one of their daily meetings: her, Chad, little Susie, and Horace, the other writer on the show. "It's all stuff that came out during the trial," Mystique added, staring at the book in Chad's hands.

"But there's a lot more here," Chad said with a delighted smile, determined to persuade her that this was an important book. "It says that he once had a girl dressed as Zorro do it to him. It says he was considering having anal plastic surgery done on himself."

"Anal plastic surgery?" Susie echoed in amazement, looking around in search of enlightenment. She immediately dropped her eyes, blushing, disconcerted by the sound of her own words.

"Jesus," said Horace after leafing through a number of pages. "Here it talks about another poor girl. As far as I can make out, this one had sex with a certain *Cement Man...*"

"That must be Ben Grimm," said Chad. "Szepanski changed the names of the superheroes, but it's not hard to guess who he's talking about." He shifted his perch on the edge of the desk, with the casual ease of a ballerina, getting more excited by the day's revelations. That book, smelling of fresh ink. The long-awaited bombshell by Dr. Joseph Szepanski.

"*Jesus!*" Horace said again, as he went on reading. "It says that the girl had the unfortunate inspiration to give this Cement Man a blow job." Horace looked up with a mocking smile, widening his mouth almost to his ears. "Chad, can you imagine? What do you think it's like to suck a cement dick?"

"I don't know," Chad replied, pretending to think it over. "*Rough?*"

The two men burst out laughing. They laughed and laughed, satisfied with themselves, while Mystique shook her head and went over to sit on the window sill. The half-open window let a bracing breeze into the room. She brushed the glass with her fingers and glanced out at the tranquil skyline of Astoria. Low buildings alternated with old industrial structures, seedy-looking overpasses, and ongoing construction sites. "Careful not to laugh too hard," she warned Chad. "That desk is starting to creak."

"Hey," Chad protested. "That's not right. I've lost weight. I'm under 260 pounds." His short-sleeved shirt could scarcely contain his huge belly, but he didn't hesitate to spread his arms wide, with bold nonchalance, for the world to admire him. Then he waved the book in the air: "I know you don't like this kind of stuff. It's vulgar junk, no question, designed to appeal to people with their minds in the gutter. Nobody gives a damn about superheroes any more, and yet everyone wants to know what they get up to in bed. The thing is, this is a sure-fire bestseller. In the next few weeks, the country won't be talking about anything else," he declared, showing Mystique the cover emblazoned, in huge letters, with an explicit title:

THE SEX LIVES OF THE SUPERHEROES

Mystique stared at it once again. She felt an instinctive aversion for the title, the book, and its topic. The sexuality of the superheroes. She'd already got a pretty good idea of the book's contents. The umpteenth agglomeration of gossip, morbid suppositions, and bad writing. "I mean, give me a break," she complained. "I can't believe that people really want to read this junk."

"*Je-e-esus!*" Horace exclaimed, having dived back into his reading. He shot an astonished look at his colleagues. "Would you believe it?! Poor Reed Richards. Old Rubber Man... It says here that he didn't know how long his dick was."

Mystique went on shaking her head. She shifted her eyes from Horace to Chad and back again. There they were, two grown men, an Afro-American in his mid-thirties and a young Caucasian with weight problems, thumbing through *The Sex Lives of the Superheroes* with feverish enthusiasm. Ever since Chad had rushed into the office with the copies of the book, proclaiming that the publishing bombshell that had been awaited for weeks had finally come out, she had felt a subtle irritation sweep through her, a kind of irritation that almost seemed to spill over, in spite of herself, into bitter amusement. If Chad was right about this, and it certainly looked like he was, hundreds of thousands of people were going to buy that book. She thought about their foolish curiosity, about their comic excitement as they began reading. The same excitement she was seeing in her two colleagues.

"I can't understand," Susie broke in with a faint voice, even more embarrassed, "how the author found out all these private details."

"Maybe he invented some of them," Horace replied. "Who cares?"

"Szepanski was the personal physician to many superheroes," Chad explained. He sat reading through a few more lines before deciding to put the book down. He grabbed a bag of bacon-flavoured crisps from the desk, ripped it noisily open, and started crunching. "Damn, guys. Reading a book will make a guy hungry."

"I think I'd be pretty angry if my doctor wrote a book about my intimate secrets," Susie said. She seemed to think it over and then blushed, overwhelmed at the horror that anything of the sort might happen. "I'd have to agree with Mystique," she stammered at that point, without explaining exactly what it was she agreed with.

"The most famous superheroes are mentioned under pseudonyms," Chad reminded them, chomping away vigorously. The smell of his bacon-flavoured crisps filled the room. "In any case, I wouldn't be surprised if some of them were happy to be mentioned. We're all exhibitionists deep down, aren't we?"

"Speak for yourself," Mystique shot back, glancing at the clock on the wall. She wondered if they weren't wasting time talking about Szepanski. She knew the idea that Chad had in mind, but she wasn't at all sure that she liked it.

"By the way," he said. "How come there's not a word in the book about you?"

"I don't know," Mystique replied. "Maybe because Szepanski was never my doctor. Maybe because I'm a discreet woman. Maybe because I'm a woman of great personal virtue," she joked, causing both men to burst into laughter, while Susie stared at her, speechless, unable to figure out if that last line was a joke.

"I think that after this book, Szepanski will have to give up being a doctor," Chad resumed, licking the salt from the crisps off his nails. "But I doubt he cares much. This book is going to make him a millionaire."

"Okay," said Mystique, stepping away from the window. The sense of lassitude she'd woken with this morning had vanished, although a trace of tired tension was still there in certain parts of her body. She thought back to the police detective she had turned into that morning, under the sheets, and the visit from that same detective the night before. "Okay," she said again, doing her best to focus. "Enough chatter. Let's get to the point. Do you people really think that this Szepanski will be one of the personalities of the year?"

"With mathematical certainty," said Chad, who had nothing left to do by now but to wipe off his fingers on the front of his shirt. "This guy is about to experience his moment of glory. He's going to be in three-quarters of the national press and he's going to be on three-quarters of the talk shows in existence, including the programme run by our friend with the gills. The entire national gossip industry is going to live for weeks on him and his book." For no particular reason he broke off, looked over at poor little Susie, and sadistically flashed her a smile caked with masticated potato crisp goo.

The girl blushed as usual. Horace sniggered. Anyone looking at those scenes from outside would have been amazed to discover that this small team had been putting together a hit television show for years now, and that behind their surreal behaviour there actually lay concealed a formidable body of creative talent. Accustomed to the high jinks of her team, Mystique remained unruffled and picked up the book from the desk.

On the back cover was a photograph of Szepanski. The notorious Joseph Szepanski. In the picture, the doctor was beaming a perfect smile that had clearly been calibrated, to the last millimetre, to transmit a fake sense of naturalness. The skin was pulled so tight that it looked like it might rip.

Mystique kept looking at the picture. She wondered how that man could ever have been a doctor, and how a man who was so focused on the surface of his own body could grasp the depths of other people's bodies. Even though she continued to feel sceptical, she couldn't ignore the situation. *This man is about to become one of the personalities of the moment. My job is to transform myself into the personalities of the moment.*

"So he'll be a guest on the Namor show?" she asked.

"That's exactly right," Chad shot back, with the dismissive and at the same time worried tone of voice he always used when he talked about Namor, the man with the gills, the host of their chief rival show. "What do you say?" he insisted.

Mystique nodded without taking her eyes off the doctor's face. "There's something quite comical about him. I could work with this," she admitted, with the sense of sudden excitement that she usually felt when she selected a new character to turn herself into.

*

Mystique got into the car, put her bag on the seat beside her, and slumped back against the headrest. *I made it. Another day done.* The car started up, moving away from the studio and heading west, as she surrendered to the comforting rhythm of the engine. This was a moment she loved. She thought there were two best moments of each day: one was when she stopped work and let the driver convey her homewards. The other best moment, by the law of contrasts, was in the morning when she started. *I guess I love my work. I guess I love the small team of people who create the show with me. I guess I love these things, or at least I've adapted to them pretty well. I guess I've adapted pretty well.*

Outside, sunset was falling over Queens. The asphalt reflected the lowering light with the bucolic calm of a lake. Along the road, the signs for Greek restaurants promised savoury Mediterranean delights, even though the people loitering on the sidewalk seemed too hot to be thinking about dinner. It was only May but summer was upon the city. Men in shorts strolled lazily alongside girls with sleeveless T-shirts. From inside the car, shielded by the stream of air conditioning, Mystique watched the people on the sidewalk, sensing that old familiar, irrational impulse to transform herself into each of them.

She inhaled deeply and got comfortable in the seat. The driver must have noticed her restlessness, because he asked whether she'd like him to lower the air conditioning. "No, that's all right," Mystique replied. "Actually, though…" she made up her mind to ask. "There is a question I'd like to ask you. Just something I'm curious about. Today, in the production office, we talked about this book, and I was wondering if you'd ever heard of it. A book by a physician who treated superheroes…"

"Sure," the driver replied in his Hispanic accent, giving her a slightly disconcerted glance in the rear-view mirror. Mystique wondered whether that glance had been on account of the stupidity of her question. Of course he'd heard of it. "The Sex Lives of the Superheroes," Santiago recited, looking away from the mirror with some embarrassment.

Maybe the Ecuadorian driver thought that her name had come up in the book, too. Maybe that's why he seemed so embarrassed. Mystique smiled to herself and let the subject drop. The test had done one thing, anyway: it had shown that Chad had a point. Everyone knew about that book, everyone knew who Joseph Szepanski was.

He might be the perfect personality. He could be funny enough. An ageing doctor with multiple facelifts who raved on about sexual topics. The show's ratings hadn't budged in weeks, and her producers had been breathing down her neck to introduce a new character into the line-up. Starting tomorrow, she'd begin work on Szepanski. She could feel her body quiver, with a dark and almost lacerating vigour, at the thought of transforming herself into that new character.

The car came to a halt at a red light. Night was swooping down on Astoria Boulevard. A faint glow started to spread from the doors of the restaurants, while the traffic lights glittered, like gemstones, against the background of settling darkness. "There are things I don't like," Santiago confessed in the tone of someone who'd been chewing something over. "I mean, things like that book. I don't like them. I think they're wrong."

"Don't worry," she replied. "I didn't think you read that kind of book. I just wanted to know if you'd ever heard of it."

"Wrong. I think they're wrong," the driver repeated as the traffic light changed to green. The car moved off and sped towards the illuminated banks of the East River. "I was told that the book even talks about poor Reed Richards. With all he went through. I think it's wrong to talk in such a way about a person who isn't around any more," he declared in an indignant voice. "I knew Reed Richards. I was his driver more than once."

"Oh. I had no idea," Mystique reacted. She reclined her head again, without commenting further, rapt in an inevitable chain of thoughts. Reed Richards. The visit from that detective. The anonymous notes. According to what the detective said, Reed had received the same farewell notes. He had received them, and in the end his son was killed in an attack targeting Reed, and he had killed himself out of his sense of guilt, as well as over an unhappy love affair with a much younger woman, so some people said.

It had happened. All those things had happened. They had happened in that same city, not many weeks ago, and Mystique had gone to both funerals. The son's funeral, then the father's funeral.

The car hurtled across the bridge. Night had fallen over the river as well, and it looked dark and almost flat, motionless, like a slab of some mysterious metal. Mystique turned her thoughts away from the memory of those funerals. It was atrocious what had happened to both Richardses. Agreed, there was a network of lunatics out there convinced that the country needed to be rid of the remaining superheroes. Fine. But how could that have anything to do with her?

For now she decided not to think about it. There was something incomprehensible about all this, and she wasn't interested in thinking about incomprehensible situations. There were already plenty of incomprehensible situations around her. There was the stunning popularity of Szepanski's book, there were the rising ratings of the rival show hosted by the horrid man with the gills, and there was the deep mystery of how Chad would ever fit into his costume for the next show. Mystique chuckled inwardly. She didn't feel in any danger. Not any more than she had been in all her life. She shut her eyes and let the chauffeur's silky driving lull her gently.

*

The following day, after a morning spent on developing scripts for the Szepanski character, she and the rest of the team went to lunch at the studio cafeteria. The place was packed. It was a former television studio where once they had filmed the episodes of a quiz show, an enormous, high-ceilinged white box that was now filled with white wooden tables and chairs. The food counter had been installed in the former director's booth. On the far side of the room, where the backstage had once been, plate glass windows offered a view of a bare interior courtyard. Dozens of editors, technicians, writers, directors, costumiers, extras, dancers, and more-or-less well-known hosts were milling around in search of the best seating, each of them carrying a tray.

Sitting at a table in the middle of the room, Mystique and the others were talking about the next episode of the show. Horace was laying out ideas about how to recalibrate the line-up. Mystique and little Susie listened to him, while Chad seemed chiefly focused on gobbling down a huge slice of pizza. When he finally looked up, he emitted a faint belch and opened his eyes wide. "Mystique, I have some news for you."

"Don't tell me," she laughed, as she had a taste of her salad. "You're going to go get another slice of pizza."

"Oh no. Oh, I guess I should say, yes, I am going to get another slice, but that's not the news. You appear to have a visitor," he said, nodding towards the front door of the cafeteria.

Every eye at the table swivelled in the direction Chad had indicated. Over there, in his light grey suit, Detective Dennis De Villa was looking around with a calm and resolute air. There was no doubt who he was looking for.

"I can't believe it," Mystique groaned. "Now what does he want? I can't waste any more time on that guy."

"Oh come on," Chad said with a sly smile. As usual, he was in a sarcastic mood. "It could have been worse. At least they sent you a nice hunk."

"Don't move. Maybe he won't see us."

"Too late. He's coming this way."

"Oh my God."

"It's true, though," Susie broke in. "He's a good-looking man."

"Great," said Mystique, giving her a withering glare. "Thanks for that invaluable comment."

"Here comes the hunk," Chad said. "There's nothing else for me to do but go get my slice of pizza," he declared, getting to his feet and picking up his tray.

"Don't you move! Nobody move!"

"I, on the other hand, plan to finish my lunch at a table that enjoys a little more privacy," Horace stated, getting up with the same sadistic satisfaction as his colleague.

"You guys will pay for this!" Mystique exclaimed as the two traitors moved away. "Susie!" she said straight afterwards, as she realised that the girl was also preparing to fly the coop. "Don't you dare!"

"But I…"

"Hello," rang out Detective De Villa's voice. "I know it's not polite to show up unannounced at lunchtime." He gave the two women one of his small yet captivating smiles. To see him standing by the table, in the light of the cafeteria, he seemed taller than during his previous visit.

"In fact," Mystique said, ignoring the smile, "I'm afraid this isn't a convenient time. I was just talking business with my colleague," she said, pointing to Susie, who blushed, despairing, under the weight of such responsibility.

"Oh," De Villa whispered. "I assure you, I won't take a minute. I hope your colleague will excuse us," he said in a courteous voice, dishing out a new and carefully tailored smile to little Susie.

The girl swayed, looking like someone on the verge of an epileptic fit, then got up and moved off, avoiding Mystique's furious glare.

"Seriously, I'm sorry to bother you," said the detective as he sat down across from her. He furrowed his brow and added: "I have the impression that the last time we were unable to communicate very well. Please forgive me if I was a little intrusive, and let me assure you that I am only concerned about your safety."

Mystique studied him with incredulity. She picked up her fork, determined to go on with her meal and ignore the detective, then set it on the table and looked at him again. What unmitigated nerve. She knew policemen well enough. There wasn't a policeman on earth who was worried about bothering someone, much less about being intrusive.

"I don't think you're taking the matter I mentioned to you seriously enough," De Villa insisted. He seemed to wait for a reply. He glanced at her plate and caught her off guard when he commented: "Is that all you're having for lunch? No wonder you're in such great shape."

Mystique looked down at her salad. "To make the best use of my power, I need to be on a constant diet. Lots of fibre and vitamins. I also take protein supplements, if you care to know, and collagen capsules. Is that what you've come to find out?"

De Villa shook his head and looked away in a chagrin that seemed sincere. "I've done it again. I've been intrusive. I hope you can forgive me."

Mystique was perplexed. She didn't know what to think about the man across from her. The detective sat with his arms on the table, with a blend of confidence and slight awkwardness. His eyes were still red. In the light of day, the capillaries in his eyes were reminiscent of the striations in a slab of marble. Otherwise, she had to admit that he wasn't half bad. He had dark hair, fairly short and brushed back. His ears were small, the ears of a child, and they looked as delicate as a couple of flower blossoms, while his neck was powerful and carefully razored. He wore a light-blue shirt, the open collar revealing a triangle of tanned skin and a trace of chest hair. Behind the manners of a plain-clothes policeman, manners that Mystique inevitably considered slimy, it was possible to sense something interesting. Something even sexy.

She speared with her fork a piece of fresh, moist vegetable, and lifted it to her lips. The flavour invaded her mouth. She recalled that yesterday morning she'd thought about that man, or to be exact, *she had transformed herself* into that man, as she writhed beneath the sheets. She kept her eyes on her plate. She wondered whether that's what he actually did when he woke up in the morning. Whether he touched himself under the sheets, in the dawn's early light, moaning and thrusting his head into his pillow. She peeked at his hands. No wedding band. If he lived alone, who knows, maybe he did.

"Mrs. Darkholme…" the detective was saying. "That's your real name, isn't it? Raven Darkholme."

Mystique swallowed. Every lascivious thought fled from her mind, making way for a new wave of annoyance. Damn it. That man had a gift for putting his foot in it over and over. "No one calls me that," she hissed. "The last time I was called that name I was in prison."

"Oh," he said, increasingly abashed. "I guess this just isn't my day, is it?" he said, trying to laugh it off. There was something melancholy about his laugh. The reddened capillaries branched out, around his irises, in rivulets like a river delta. On the table, his ringless hands looked strong. "Any other notes in the past few days?" he asked.

"No notes," Mystique replied as she went on eating. She vaguely thought of asking the detective if he'd already eaten lunch, but she had no intention of offering him any courteous gestures. "I wouldn't be surprised if there weren't any more notes. I think we've seen the last of them. Whoever was writing them, he must have got sick of the prank."

Dennis De Villa listened thoughtfully to her words. "I hope you're right," he said. "But just in case another note does come, or in case you notice anything suspicious, or in case someone around you behaves in some odd way, or in case you have any ideas of who might be behind this *prank...*" He cleared his throat over the buzz of the cafeteria: "I'd like you to promise that you'll call me. Immediately. No matter the time of day or night."

Mystique bit her lip. For a moment she thought she would suffocate. A few yards away, behind the detective's back, Horace and Chad were putting on a little skit for her benefit. Horace had smeared his eyelids and the skin under his eyes with ketchup, making a clear reference to the detective's conjunctivitis, and was flashing winning smiles at her while Chad, pretending to be her, picked at a leaf of lettuce and fluttered his eyelashes haughtily.

It was a totally surreal scene. Mystique gulped. She covered her mouth with her napkin and just managed not to laugh. She took a drink of water to stifle the laughter that was bubbling in her stomach. It would be hard to stifle it much longer. She hoped that the detective was about to leave.

"I was wondering..." he said, oblivious to the scene being acted out behind him. He seemed to caress the tabletop for a moment, as if it were the back of a little household pet. "Well, it's just idle curiosity. But I was wondering how you can transform yourself into someone else. I mean, could you transform into anyone at all? Even someone you'd never met?"

In the meantime, Horace and Chad were going wild. Horace had smeared even more ketchup onto his eyes and Chad was throwing lettuce leaves at him as though to chase him away. Mystique let a smile escape. She regained control and forced herself not to watch her two colleagues. "Okay," she said. Even though she didn't like providing explanations on the topic, she decided that talking about it would help her to remain serious. "Sometimes, all I need is a photo. It's better if I can see part of the body... Old Vladimir, for example. The Russian president loves to be immortalised with his shirt off. I only needed a single bare-chested picture of him... I look at a person's skin, I concentrate on a piece of the body. The rest comes by itself. The other parts of the body, their way of doing things. A single piece of a body can tell you everything about a person." She took another drink of water and concluded: "In other cases, I have to see the person face to face. At least see them. In the most challenging cases, shake hands with them."

"Fascinating," said her visitor, attentive, still caressing the surface of the table. His smile really did remind her of a little boy, one of those serious boys who had for some reason grown up far too young. "I hope you don't think that's a stupid question. This kind of thing has always caught my interest. The way certain superpowers work."

The detective's serious demeanour increased her need to laugh. Laughter boiled up in her stomach, so urgent it was almost painful, not so funny any more, not even making sense, just an automatic and somewhat guilty movement. "I understand," she did her best to continue. "Now why would you be so curious about such a thing?"

He shrugged and seemed to hesitate. "When I was a boy..." He mentioned something about his childhood and a brother who collected newspaper clippings about superheroes. By this point, Mystique had stopped listening to him. She was absorbed in the bizarre vignette: those two clowns behind him trying to make her laugh, and the serious detective facing her. That detective with his captivating smile. With his moments of awkwardness, his abrupt questions, and his body, a body with which she had made much closer acquaintance, yesterday morning, than he would ever suspect. She held De Villa's gaze and thought back on what it had felt like to turn herself into him. His sturdy body. His turgid penis. She felt like laughing. She found that man sexy, there was no denying it, but she wanted to see him leave as soon as possible.

The cafeteria was emptying, and she had barely eaten half of her salad. When Dennis De Villa stood up, Horace and Chad turned away to avoid being noticed. Once he was gone, they looked over at Mystique. After a moment, the three of them burst out laughing, a hearty, liberating laugh, almost furious, contaminated by a streak of strange sadness.

*

She'd never wanted to cause any pain. Certainly not to innocent people. She'd never taken part in deadly activities, and all she was trying to do was change the system, yes: she'd just wanted to make sure that everything changed. In those days, that's what lots of people wanted, and she had wanted it more than others. She'd fooled herself into believing she could do it. She'd fooled herself that it was right to try. Mystique the mutant, the political activist, under suspicion of subversive beliefs, accused of complicity in the illegal operations of a group of armed mutants in the Seventies and early Eighties.

They'd framed her on charges of taking part in an armed robbery. There were no witnesses to her involvement in that robbery. They'd just claimed that she took part with a semblance different from her own. The perfect accusation for the perfect defendant.

She remembered the twenty-hour interrogation after her arrest, the hard chair that cut into her back, the scornful voices of the police detectives who questioned her. They had framed her for political interests, that much was clear, and during her trial a bunch of intellectuals and even a few superheroes had intervened on her behalf with public appeals. There had been that famous article by Susan Sontag. There had been petitions, but all in vain.

The time of her trial and the years leading up to it. The political discussions, the protest rallies, the hazy ideas of social liberation, the gang of mutant pseudo-revolutionaries that she and Sabrina, her old comrade in militant activism, had got involved with. She had no idea what had ever become of most of those people: in prison, or fugitives in some exotic country, or else dead or who knows what. The robberies and the arson attacks that she certainly hadn't taken part in, but which she had known about from time to time. The days when the world was split between superheroes and alleged supervillains, or supersubversives or whatever they were called. All of it belonged to the past. Obsolete ideological claptrap that by now people could barely remember.

The past was down there in the distance. The past was a muddled mass, with blurry outlines, almost dreamlike, searing and nearly invisible like a gigantic jellyfish, a shape hovering behind her back that seemed, by some sinister effect, to cast a muggy light on what she had now become. *The queen of the show, the slave of the show.*

She'd spent sixteen years in the high security section of Lexington. Some people thought it was too long, others thought it wasn't long enough. She couldn't tell whether she had paid the right price, she didn't even know what it was she was paying for: for her own illusions, for something she had done, for something she hadn't done, for what she had been or for what she had stopped being.

One thing she knew for sure was that the past had remained over there, on the other side of her life, a life cut in two by the abyss of prison. Now, the idea that anyone might go to the trouble of conspiring against her made her smile. Conspiring against a woman whose life had been cut in two. Conspiring against who? Against the woman from before or the woman she was now? Conspiring in the name of what? For the reasons of the past, for the senselessness of the present?

In the days that followed, as things began to fall apart, she would keep asking herself those questions. She would ask herself why someone was sentencing her to death. Unless it was because someone had decided to blame her for the most unforgivable mistake. The mistake of still being alive. The past was dead, she was alive. Could this possibly be her fatal mistake?

*

The event was scheduled for a Barnes & Noble book store, and by early afternoon there were hundreds of people queuing outside the front door, each holding a copy of the book. Chad had spent a couple of hours in that queue, in the heat of the afternoon, his massive body bathed in sweat. Once he got through the door, he could at least enjoy the air conditioning inside.

Doctor Szepanski was way down there. He was sitting at a table, flanked by a pair of glowering security guards, ready to hustle away any overeager readers. The doctor was signing copies of his book with a flourish of his wrist, scattering unsettling smiles in all directions. His skin had the chilly gleam of a fleshy plant. The queue was slowly inching forward, and Chad was becoming unsteady on his feet, wearied by his own weight, but he toughed it out until he was near the table. Now it was his turn. He handed his copy to the elderly doctor and looked him straight in the face. It was a hard face to read. The plastic surgery had rendered it smooth, too taut, as elusive as an abstract sculpture.

Without warning, the doctor lifted his eyes and responded with an equally penetrating stare. A frisson seemed to pass between them. Oh hell. Could the doctor have guessed? After all, that man had experience of people with superpowers, and he might have developed an instinct or something of the sort to sense when he met one. "So," Szepanski asked as he handed back the signed book. "Did you enjoy reading it?"

Mystique-Chad took the book, brushing the doctor's warm, slightly sticky fingertips. "Unquestionably," she-he lied. "I devoured every single page."

Szepanski didn't take the trouble to smile. He sat there motionless and expressionless. Maybe his face was starting to hurt, or maybe he had in fact guessed who he was talking to.

Mystique-Chad crossed the carpeted floor and emerged again into the scorching street, where she stood heaving in the afternoon heat. She really had to stop going around disguised as Chad when she went out incognito. She should find someone a little lighter. Putting on that shape and all that mass was more work than anyone needed to do in summer.

She grabbed her shirt at chest level and started flapping it to let in a little air. Two hours queuing to get close to that damned doctor, and the meeting was over in less than a minute. She felt like tossing the book in the bin. She resisted the impulse, remembering she'd promised to give it back to Chad. That is to say, to the *real* Chad.

In any case, I suppose I should be pretty happy. I managed to get a close look at the doctor.

More people kept lining up outside the book store door, with copies of the questionable bestseller in their hands, waiting patiently like a crowd of extras. Mystique-Chad huffed and walked along the sidewalk, mingling with the flow of passersby.

She spotted a snow cone stand and decided it was exactly what she wanted. She crossed the street and walked up to the stand, ordering a medium snow cone, then changed her mind and made it a large. If she was going to go around in Chad's body, she might as well order for Chad's metabolism.

The crushed ice was thirst-quenching and sugary, but its flavour did nothing to assuage the slight annoyance that lingered inside her. She couldn't stop thinking of those people standing in line. Thinking of all the book stores under siege in the entire country, of all those readers eager to learn the trove of details in the notorious bestseller. Oh, the thousands of ridiculous and morbid details. Details about Batman's perversions, about the sexual sagas of Captain America, about Wonder Woman's augmentation mammoplasty, about Wolverine's youthful erotic adventures, about the unreliable prowess of Namor, about Ben Grimm's cement penis, about the size of Reed Richards' penis, and about anecdotes concerning the innumerable minor superheroes recounted by Szepanski.

In fact, it was rumoured that the juicy chapter about Reed Richards had been popped in at the last minute, when the book was ready to go to print. And because of that chapter, Reed's private life was now the subject of discussion in magazines and on radio and TV shows. Self-proclaimed experts on sexology and male psychology chattered on about an alleged *Mister Fantastic syndrome*, which had to do with the impossibility for any sufferer, whether or not he was a superhero, to have a realistic idea of the size of his own penis. That Reed Richards had been a very private person when he was alive, sober in his personal style, and that he would never have wanted his intimate life to be discussed in public, seemed to be of no concern to anyone.

Under Mystique-Chad's arm, the book was creating a patch of sweat on her shirt. Puffs of heat were issuing from the sidewalk. A police car hurtled past down a side street, siren wailing, leaving an unpleasant stain of anxiety in the air. Mystique-Chad gulped down a slurp of icy liquid and pressed the cup against her forehead. Air surged into her nostrils, hot, heavy, in large gasps, while the bodies of passersby brushed distractedly against hers, just as hot, damp, and exhausted as she was, trailing behind them the aromas of recent showers, or else the scent of their perspiration.

Clever move. New York is suffocating, it feels like the world is on fire, and I'm walking around with a 260-pound body. She tossed the plastic cup, now empty, into a rubbish bin. She kept wanting to toss the book in as well. *There was a time when people didn't feel the need to know certain things,* she mused. *A time when people didn't need to talk about the sex life of the superheroes. They didn't seem to need to know anything about superheroes, they let them act in the shadows, almost in the realm of mythology. And they acted. Superheroes. The ones who seemed to protect the world, or the ones like me, who were accused of threatening it.*

She wished she was at home, in the cool comfort of her bedroom.

She accelerated her pace under the cutting shafts of sunlight, thinking about the book under her arm, and thinking of the people who wondered why there was nothing about her in that book. Nothing about Mystique. *The answer is simple. Simpler than anyone imagines. There wouldn't be much to say any more about my sex life. Practically speaking, there wouldn't be a thing.*

*

After her outing to Barnes & Noble, after the snow cone and a short cab ride, followed by another few blocks on foot, Mystique-Chad looked around furtively and slipped through her front door. The front door of her apartment in Morningside Heights.

She put Szepanski's book down on the hall table, next to that day's mail, which must have been left there by the cleaning lady who came in the mornings. She trudged to the bathroom and started to undress. Gratified though she was to have got near the notorious doctor, she kept feeling that mixture of sensations. A sort of ill-defined bitterness. An imprint of intensifying anxiety. She could feel those sensations fluctuating, like fish in an aquarium, in the big body whose shape she still kept.

It was time to go back to being herself. Time to abandon Chad's physical shape and regain her own petite physique, her bluish skin, her luxuriant hair. She neatly folded the voluminous clothes she had worn and put them in the closet, where a special armoire stored the clothes she used for that kind of outing: men's clothes, women's clothes, in all styles and sizes. Shoes. Belts. Baseball caps. There were plenty of XXL men's clothes. Countless oversized shirts, short-sleeved, garishly coloured, each on its own hanger. Mystique-Chad sniffed the clothes she had just taken off. They'd better go into the dirty clothes hamper.

She headed for the kitchen to get a glass of water. She would drink a glass of water and then she'd head back to the bathroom, she'd resume her own shape, and she'd gratefully indulge in the blessings of a nice shower. The sunshine penetrated through the flimsy curtains, casting on the floor a shadow of the naked, obese male body that wandered through the silent apartment. Her body. His body. Mystique-Chad.

As she went past the table in the hallway, she noticed that day's mail. She picked it up and continued towards the kitchen, leafing through the sheaf of envelopes. Bank statements. Bureaucracy. Correspondence from her agent. An invitation to an opening at a gallery in Chelsea. And last… The sun seemed to grow more intense, outside, violently pressing against the curtains.

She stopped in the middle of the light-drenched kitchen. Her respiration grew heavy, a blend of apprehension and dull rage, as she handled the envelope without a return address. She already knew what she would find inside. The sheet of paper was white and nondescript, and it bore the usual message:

SO LONG, MY MYSTIQUE

*

The arrest had been carried out at dawn, with an intimidating deployment of police forces, whole squadrons of officers in anti-riot gear and helicopters roaring overhead. They were doing things on a grand scale. They handcuffed her and hustled her into a police van. Then came a gap in her memory.

The next scene was in a windowless police interrogation room, in which a lethal chill reigned. When Mystique asked for something to cover herself, the detectives had broken out in mocking laughter. The hard cold chair that hurt her back. She had responded with an equally mocking smile, a heroic, superior smile, a martyr's smile, convinced that they might have managed to arrest her, all right, but they hadn't yet succeeded in bending her.

Those were the memories of her arrest. The scene seemed to shift forward again. Maybe she'd just passed out. Opening her eyes in the chilly light, she saw that the police officers had vanished, and there was just one man in front of her now. The man was sitting on the edge of the table. His body seemed to exude a stream of ambiguous, concealed menace. Mystique knew what awaited her. Long hours of questioning, admittance into prison, the humiliating medical examination.

When the man stood up from the table, she recognised his hands, his ringless fingers, his light grey suit, even his reddened eyes. She let out a moan. Oh no. That's not the way things had gone. What did that man have to do with any of this? Detective De Villa had never been in the room where she was questioned. Back then, he must have been just a boy. The scene was no longer a memory. *A dream, it must have turned into a dream*, she told herself, but that wasn't enough to give her any sense of relief: if anything, it increased her sense of dread.

Dennis De Villa walked towards her.

Mystique realised her wrists were free, unfettered by handcuffs. She raised one hand in his direction, instinctively, to ward him off or perhaps to touch him. She touched the man's body and felt its stunning heat. He drew closer. He said nothing, made no gestures, he just came closer. They both sighed, in unison, a sigh that filled every corner of the room.

When she opened her eyes the breeze was blowing through the window in a clean flow, piercing as a knife. She was awake. She stretched out one arm along the mattress. Her face was damp. She felt excited or perhaps upset, and she twisted under the sheets, undecided, tempted to close her eyes and plunge back into that torrid dream. Detective De Villa was even colonising her dreams at night.

She could transform herself into him, now, the same way as she had done a couple of days ago. Transform herself into him and touch herself a little and start the day with a lovely, lonely orgasm. She could certainly do it. Instead, she chose to leave the soft shell of her bed. She decided to go out for a run in the park. She felt a vague sense of guilt about the dream she'd had, guilt about herself and even guilt towards that man. Wasn't there something wrong, some kind of violation in involving another person in your own torrid dreams? Or was the violation on the part of the other person, who unconsciously, without knowing it, proved capable of breaking into such dreams?

She looked for her running clothes. She put them on with little enthusiasm, her breathing still irregular, while outside dawn grew brighter once again, muggy and impassive.

*

That day she locked herself in her dressing room and started rehearsing the character of Szepanski. The studio was immersed in silence. It was one of those days when nothing was in production and no one was rehearsing, and the whole studio floor remained motionless, uninhabited, echoing like a giant seashell.

In the secrecy of her dressing room she took off her clothes. She did a few breathing exercises and focused on the image of the doctor. Szepanski's smooth face, his cheekbones like those of a plastic doll. The flourish of his wrist as he signed copies in that book store. Mystique understood immediately, instinctively, that assuming the shape of the elderly doctor wouldn't be easy, that it would be one of the biggest challenges of her career.

Over the course of her life, she had transformed herself into hundreds of people. She had transformed herself into men, into women. In her time working in TV she had transformed herself into the most astonishing array of individuals, into Vladimir and Oprah and the other characters in the current line-up, and dozens of others like Mike Tyson, the Dalai Lama, Jimmy Carter, Yoko Ono, and Donald Trump… She had transformed herself into Sophia Loren, a radiant septuagenarian who wore dresses with plunging necklines, her tits prominently displayed. She had transformed herself into Al Gore, who strolled onto the stage with his imposing physique, striding like an overweight former basketball player, always prompting a roar from the audience. She had transformed herself into males, females, the young and the aged, withstanding the effort of that perpetual body-change, falling back on her precious breathing exercises, enduring time after time the burden of weariness it brought. She had continued to change her body. She had continued to make them laugh. She had done all this, but now it was Joseph Szepanski's turn, and for the first time she realised she had a problem on her hands.

She made a couple of unsuccessful attempts, both times transforming herself into a little old man with a swollen, imprecise, unrecognisable face, far from the unnaturally taut features of Szepanski. On the third attempt, she felt her body burn and waver, rebelling against the strain. She flopped down onto the sofa. She sat there pondering, feeling overwhelmed. *That artificial face. That rigid, expressionless, repugnant and yet at the same time perfect skin. How the hell can I take on that same consistency?*

She was gathering her strength for a new attempt when someone knocked at the door. For some reason she thought of Detective Dennis De Villa. She felt a shiver of anxiety. She considered pretending not to be there, or transforming herself into someone else, maybe little Susie or a cleaning woman, to avoid whoever might be on the other side of that door. They knocked again. She resigned herself to throwing on a bathrobe. She pulled the sash tight and opened the door.

"There you are!" Chad exclaimed. "I've been looking for you everywhere. I looked upstairs in your office and everywhere in the studio. I had to show you the latest," he said, walking into the dressing room and positioning himself in the middle of the room. He executed a pirouette and asked: "How do you like me?"

Relieved, Mystique shut the door and turned to look at him. Chad was in the midst of his weekly costume fittings and was wearing a garish green tailcoat made of some shiny material, and as always, a couple of sizes too small. The trousers clung to his thighs and looked dangerously close to bursting. Just then, he was wearing no shoes and his bare feet had a pink and puffy appearance. "Hey. I came to show you my costume, stop looking at my feet," he whined.

Mystique looked up. "Well," she said. "I'd say you look like an enormous kiwi-flavoured hard candy." She walked back to the sofa and sank into the cushion. "Didn't you ask for costumes a little less form-fitting?"

"I did," he said, eyeing himself in the mirror. "You know, that costumier hates me. But really, all things considered, I don't look half bad, do I? I think it shows how much weight I've lost," he declared, with a hint of unjustified optimism, as he went on studying himself. "How's it going with you?"

"It couldn't go much worse," Mystique replied. She brushed a lock of hair off her forehead and did her best to smile. "I just can't transform myself into Szepanski."

"Oh come on. Aren't you the one who is able to transform herself into any living human being?"

"That's just it. I can turn myself into any human being. Not into a pile of leftovers from an operating table," she said, with all the sarcasm she could muster, though she couldn't quite hide her concern. "I wonder whether we ought to consider a change of plan. Maybe we still have enough time to think of another personality."

Chad's eyes opened wide. "You must be kidding," he said. "It would be the first time you gave up on a character. Plus, the producers would never let you off the hook. Everybody's anticipating this. Gary already gave the sponsors a heads-up on the news."

"Gary," she echoed with a grimace.

Chad started stroking his chin. "By the way," he said, almost sullen, clearly thinking of something. "Apparently we got an email from a viewer. Apparently I was seen standing in line at a Barnes & Noble store yesterday, waiting to get my copy of Szepanski's book autographed. Isn't that incredible? Very odd, since I spent the whole afternoon here at the studio."

"Very odd, indeed," she agreed without losing her composure.

"Mystique," Chad sighed. "I've asked you a thousand times: please don't go around town disguised as me."

"Don't complain. It was for the good of the show," she apologised. She brushed away a lock of hair again. She noticed that a faint burning sensation lingered in her limbs, something like lactic acid in an athlete's muscles. Her body had a twinge, a blend of excitement and horror, at the thought that in a few minutes she would have to resume her effort to transform herself into Szepanski.

Chad must have sensed her state of mind. "Okay. I'm going to forgive you because I possess a magnanimous soul. Plus, I can see that we're not really looking our best today. You're not a very pretty picture, did you know that? A bluish mutant in a bathrobe, with scraggly hair, plastered across the couch in her dressing room."

"My dear," she said. "Nobody knows how to pay a lady a compliment quite like you do."

"Hey!" he said, on his way out of the door, as a goodbye and to get her to laugh. "Watch this," he said, improvising a barefoot tap routine across the floor, making a series of flaccid and ridiculous sounds.

Mystique laughed.

Chad finished his routine, took a deep bow, adjusted his green tailcoat, and finally turned and left, heading back to his costume fittings.

She sat there, alone. In the sudden silence she heard the sound of her own respiration. The dressing room surrounded her, motionless, almost alive, pervaded by that silence, by the sound of her breathing. It was time to start again. The mirror was there, brightly lit, eager to see what she could do. She got up from the sofa and pulled off her bathrobe. *Come on*, she said to herself.

*

Later on, at the end of the day, she left the studio and headed as usual for the car that would be taking her home. The sky was an impassive vault over the city, criss-crossed by grey-red clouds that seemed to be steeped, like cotton balls, in the blood-coloured light of sunset. Far in the distance, along the horizon line, blinking aircraft were rising from the strips of LaGuardia Airport, crossing their routes in the darkening sky. Mystique felt her stomach tighten. She could hardly remember the last time she'd taken a plane or the last time she'd left the city. *I'm sick of only reading the travel section of the New York Times. When we're done with this season I'll have to take a vacation. I really think I will.*

She climbed into the car and said hello to Santiago. The driver seemed to be in a bubble of distant thoughts. He shot an opaque glance into the rear-view mirror before shaking himself out of his reverie, mumbling an apology, and starting the car.

Mystique was tempted to close her eyes and rest briefly. She was not sure how she felt: sleepy, or perhaps in a state of turmoil, or just dissatisfied. Her experiments with the Szepanski character weren't going so well. The following day she'd have to work hard on it. Only when she looked out of the window and noticed how crowded the restaurants along the boulevard were, did she realise that the weekend had begun. She wouldn't be coming in to the studio tomorrow. *Friday*, she told herself. *It's Friday night*, she thought, with a chilly amazement, as she observed the people behind the restaurant windows, and the crowds strolling down the sidewalk, feeling like an anthropologist intently observing the habits of an exotic, incomprehensible populace.

She lowered her window an inch or two. The air from the street blew into her face. "The weekend always sneaks up on you," she mused aloud. "Like a rift in time. I never remember that it's about to happen." She leaned back against the seat and tried to imagine what the next two days might hold in store for her. There must be an invitation to lunch somewhere, as best she could remember, and maybe an invitation to a theatre premiere. That kind of thing. She doubted she would go.

Santiago tucked his head down, and kept steering along the boulevard. He honked at a pedestrian who was trying to jaywalk, then he speeded up, and asked Mystique, in his Hispanic accent, if she was married.

She curled up on the seat, aware of the countless implications of that question. People had expectations. People expected a woman her age to be married, to devote her weekend to her family, or at least to her husband, or at least to a lover. At the same time, people didn't know what to expect from a woman like her. A mutant with bluish skin. A television star. People would be amazed to learn that a woman like her slept alone, and to the same extent, amazed to learn that she slept with someone. "No," she replied. "I'm not married."

Silence filled the interior of the car. Nothing but the sound of the engine and the whirr of the tyres on the hot asphalt. They'd left Astoria behind them. The car was gliding towards the comforting embrace of Manhattan. Mystique let her eyelids drop, and her consciousness was beginning to blur when she realised that Santiago had started talking again.

"When we first moved to New York," the driver was saying in the tone of someone recounting an old memory, "my wife and I used to go to the zoo. On weekends, of course. There are lots of zoos in this city. You can spend whole weekends just visiting the zoos of New York. There's even one with a memorial to animals that have gone extinct, but I can't remember which one." His voice darkened, and his accent seemed to take on a dramatic cadence: "Unbelievable," he said. "You look at that memorial and you think of all those species that are gone now. All that *ending*."

"What are you talking about?" Mystique murmured, her head woolly, not particularly happy to have been torn out of her state of sluggishness. She had the impression that the driver was in the mood for some serious talk. "It's Friday night and I'd say you're about twenty years younger than me. You shouldn't be brooding about such gloomy topics."

"Ma'am, you shouldn't pretend," was his reply.

"Huh?" she asked in confusion.

The driver tucked his head down further between his shoulders and gripped the steering wheel tightly. "I know that's not the way you are," he said in a hoarse voice, almost emotional. "I mean, you don't think that everything comes down to having fun on Friday night. You don't think that certain things have to be forgotten. You don't have such a fun-loving personality. You're not so carefree, not at all, you're not the way you act on TV."

"I get it," said Mystique. She let out a nervous little laugh. "I'll take that as a compliment. I guess it is a compliment. I think I'm going to get some rest now."

But the man wasn't about to give up. He seemed in the throes of feverish ideas. "What do you say about destiny?" he went on, gripping the wheel even tighter. "That's the real cage. Destiny. We don't choose our own life stories, any more than some animal in the zoo. You think you're free? You're in a cage, same as them."

Mystique stared at him from the back seat. She stared at the nape of the man's neck, his haircut done with a clipper, she stared at his temple where she could just detect a vein throbbing. "I imagine that's so," she replied with a consciously cool tone. She lowered her window a little more, letting in exterior noise. The hum of traffic. The spirited sound of a car horn.

A few minutes later the car pulled up in front of her building. Mystique had never been so eager to slide out of the car and in through her front door. Her restful home. Her silent apartment, free of drivers raving bizarrely. She was about to exit the vehicle when the man turned around and looked straight at her. "Caged animals can do terrible things," he announced, grim-faced. "Destiny can force us to do things we don't want to. Destiny can force someone to die. It can even force someone else to kill."

Something happened. An icy jolt inside her. A lightning-fast movement in her head. It was as if the tails of several different thoughts had just been tugged, now revealing that they all formed one single thread: the notes she was receiving, the possibility that she really was in danger, the idea that the group of fanatics had actually recruited someone to harm her. Perhaps someone she knew. She stared at the driver. She stared at his face, immersed in the half-light, she stared at the gleam of those dark, deranged, heartbroken eyes.

She got out of the car. She walked stiffly to her front door.

Inside, she wandered from room to darkened room, and went to the window to make sure the car had driven away. She didn't know what to make of this. She took off her shoes and considered making a herbal tea. She checked to see if the street door was properly locked. She laughed at herself. She switched on the air conditioning and a chilly breath enveloped her skin. She had no doubt that the driver had behaved suspiciously, and that he had spoken in an almost threatening way. Mystique rummaged through her bag until she found a certain business card, and grabbed her phone to dial the number. She couldn't believe it. She was doing it. She really was calling, and stupid as she felt, she still sat listening to the ringing at the other end of the line, motionless, as if hypnotised, until she recognised Detective De Villa's voice.

*

The weather held up for the whole weekend. A warm breeze blew steadily day and night, bringing an atmosphere of summery languor. Thousands of people poured into Central Park, turning the Sheep Meadow into a dense meat market, climbing the paths of North Woods, or surrounding the banks of the little lakes. Central Park. The city's verdant heart. An oasis of artificial nature that an American landscape designer and an English architect had designed a century and a half earlier, carefully placing each tree and each boulder, providing city dwellers with a rectangular patch of bucolic, democratic peace. Crowds had poured into the city's other parks as well. They had invaded the park along the East River and the long narrow strip on Riverside. People had taken possession of every green space, driven by a ravenous hunger for light and oxygen, lolling in the meadows and sinking their fingers into the grass. People had freed themselves of clothes, pushing to the very edge of the permissible, while the onset of summer impregnated their bodies with a damp, electric, restless heat. People had filled Morningside Park as well, though in this case they were a more chaste, more modestly dressed crowd of multicoloured families with large numbers of children, enjoying sumptuous picnics on the lawn.

Mystique saw none of this. She went for her run as the sun was rising and the park was still deserted. Apart from her run, she never left the apartment. Her cleaning lady had done some shopping for her and the refrigerator was well stocked. Fresh vegetables, trays of organic food, spirulina protein bars, and other provisions from Whole Foods. No need to go out. Her apartment was a comfortable, self-sufficient, protective fortress.

The city's summery atmosphere remained outside, like a gas too dense to make its way through any fissure in the windows. Mystique cancelled the handful of social dates on her calendar and spent two days practising her Szepanski. Her sole contact with the outside world were the text messages from Chad, whose weekend seemed to be as homely as hers. Chad was spending his time watching TV, and he didn't fail to alert her when the old doctor appeared on the screen. Szepanski managed to pop up a couple of times, even in the weekend programming.

The doctor talked about his bestseller, mentioned the scabrous topics described in the book through veiled euphemisms, ignored any unfriendly comments from the other guests on the shows, and winked into the TV cameras. There was no doubt. He was a star. A number of snippets from those shows immediately went viral, and Mystique watched them over and over, rapt, hoping to pin down some new nugget that might help her to transform into that man.

As for the incident with the Ecuadorian driver, she was embarrassed that she had called Detective De Villa. She had no idea what had come over her. A woman with a past like hers, with as much experience as she possessed, rushing to call the police for something so trivial.

Now that she thought about it, she was pretty sure the poor driver had nothing to hide. She was sure he had blathered on in that weird way just because he was tired or for some other harmless reason. Sometimes people let themselves go. Sometimes they raved senselessly. She felt certain that the police would run checks on Santiago without finding anything significant, and that no group of anti-superhero fanatics was conspiring against her. She continued to feel confident that she was in no danger. Or at least that's what she kept telling herself.

On Monday, after yet another day in the office, after an interminable meeting with the writers and another equally interminable, draining meeting with her producers, as she was leaving the studio she found someone waiting for her.

In the almost deserted parking lot, the detective was leaning against the bonnet of his car. Mystique squared her shoulders and marched towards him. She couldn't believe it. She really couldn't believe that a few nights ago she had given in to the impulse to call this man.

Dennis De Villa moved away from his car and walked to meet her. "Good evening," he whispered. "I thought you'd never get here. Do you always work this late?"

"Good evening to you," she snarled. For an instant, she was flooded with a frustration so powerful it almost made her head spin. That man had already wormed his way into her dreams at night, and the last thing she wanted was to keep seeing him in front of her. "Yes, always this late. So do you, I see."

"Oh," he said, failing to pick up on Mystique's confrontational tone.

"Practically speaking, I don't work on a schedule. Let's just say I'm one of those cops who's never off duty. I never stop being a cop," he said, starting to laugh. His laughter sounded a little more mournful than usual. He turned solemn again, looked around, and said that he'd come because he had some news for her. Without warning, he headed back to his car, leaving Mystique with no alternative but to follow him.

This time, he wasn't wearing his grey suit. He wore a pair of casual trousers and a shirt that highlighted the sculpted shape of his shoulders. "That driver," said the detective. "Santiago Gomez. Apparently he had nothing to do with the notes you received or the group we're trying to track down."

"I guessed as much," Mystique sighed.

"Still, we arrested him today. We found out there was something else he was hiding."

All around them the evening smelt of burned paper, dry soil, and newly watered yards. The parking lot was silent, while from the street came the intermittent wheezing of traffic. Unsettled by the detective's words, Mystique asked him to explain.

"Like I told you, the man had nothing to do with the notes or the group… On the other hand, we did find a corpse in his house." He said the word *corpse* in a hush. He looked down discreetly and then continued: "It was his wife. Apparently he killed her months ago. It seems they hadn't been getting along since they'd moved to New York, and he killed her in the midst of an argument. He hid her body in the freezer and went on with his life. He went on working as a driver."

Mystique's throat went dry. She tried to think of something to say, but no words came. The first thing she imagined was the face of that woman, curled up in a freezer. She imagined the marble-hard skin, the sealed eyelids, the ice-encrusted hair. She imagined the body spattered with frozen blood. Crystallised tears rimming the eyes.

"That driver was no danger to you, or at least so we believe. But if you hadn't told us about his odd behaviour, we wouldn't have uncovered this murder. It was nothing but a coincidence. A *fortunate* coincidence, if we can use that term." Dennis De Villa put his hands in his pockets and stood next to the car, his eyes still downcast, the sunset at his back. His reddened eyes seemed more upset than ever. For some reason, talking about this case seemed to cost him a great effort. "A man who killed his wife," he said, as if to sum up the whole story, without another word.

"My God," Mystique pondered, struck both by the news and by the distress, unquestionably sincere, that the detective was displaying. "That's why Santiago was talking in that tone. That's why he said those things."

De Villa stood motionless. His only movement was the rhythmic heaving of his chest beneath the fabric of his shirt. Backlit, his hair was bathed in the fading glow of the sunset. Eventually, he emerged from his reverie, swung open the passenger door, and said he would take her home.

Mystique didn't reply. She was still thinking about the woman in the freezer. About the frost on her lips, her frozen organs, the chill that seeped everywhere, even into her womb. She thought of that body in a casket of ice. When the policemen lifted the lid of the freezer, did the light glitter on her skin? What did a frozen corpse smell like? Sometimes, hearing about a stranger's death caused her to suffer like this. An ephemeral yet burning pain. "I'm sorry?" she said, after a moment.

"I'll take you home. As far as I can tell, the car service hasn't yet found someone to take Santiago's place," he pointed out, looking around the half-deserted parking lot. "We arrested him less than two hours ago."

"Two hours ago. My God," Mystique repeated, thinking of the young driver. "He had such an open face. So tormented. I almost feel guilty."

"That man was a killer," De Villa said with a grimace. "Now please get in. Do you want to stand there all night?" he said in a gentler voice, swinging the car door back and forth.

Mystique took a step back. They faced each other, she and the detective, like characters in one of those TV series where members of rival gangs meet in a parking lot for an exchange of hostages, a settling of accounts, or something of the sort. She and the detective had no hostages to exchange. They didn't seem to have any accounts to settle. The breeze tousled both his hair and hers. She considered calling a taxi. Or else, if Chad or Horace happened to come by, she could ask for a ride... She noticed that the detective's car seemed very clean. De Villa was still holding the door open. There seemed to be something deeply human, almost defenceless about him that evening, in the middle of a desolate parking lot, after telling her the story of a man who had murdered the woman he loved.

They kept looking at each other. There was a moment of hesitation, a shard of time, hard, razor-sharp, like the needle of a compass hovering between two different magnetic norths. Mystique hung in the balance. Her body wavered for one final moment, and then she slid into the car.

*

The seat had a cushiony consistency. The interior of the car smelt of lavender-scented air freshener. The detective drove confidently, not too fast, heading for Manhattan. He adjusted the air conditioning and asked her more than once if she was comfortable.

Mystique struggled to answer. The news she'd just received about Santiago was stunning. She stared into the windscreen, out onto the black ribbon of asphalt illuminated by the changing lights of the traffic signals. She preferred to avoid the detective's gaze. That gaze too left her a little stunned, and at the same time curious, and mistrustful. *Mistrustful of him and of my own reactions. I feel like I am walking on a thin sheet of glass. I wonder if that's the effect that a cop is having on me, or if it's just Dennis De Villa.*

At her side, the man was driving with his cop hands, talking with his cop voice. His cop gestures. His rhythmic cop breathing. The distress he had betrayed earlier, when he announced the news about Santiago and his murdered wife, seemed to have subsided, at least in part. He seemed to be concentrating, and muttered something to the effect that the driver's arrest wouldn't solve much. He was referring to the anonymous notes. Learning that Santiago had nothing to do with the notes might be comforting, but it also meant that whoever sent those notes was still out there, unknown, with his unknown intentions.

Mystique gave a start. It was as if De Villa had touched her somewhere too sensitive, somewhere too exposed, a part of her body whose location was a mystery even to her, but that she knew must somehow exist. The notes. She didn't say a word about the new note she had received a few days ago. She hadn't discussed it with anyone and had no intention of discussing it now. She couldn't see what good it would do. She chose to bring the subject back to the chauffeur. In a calmer manner than a few nights back, when she first called the detective, she told him what Santiago had said. "He talked about destiny. That's what he told me. Something about how it was destiny that forces you to kill someone."

This time it was the detective who acted startled. He accelerated slightly, revving the engine just a bit, to make it through a traffic light. "How destiny forces you to kill someone," he said, in an awestruck voice. Streaks of light poured into the car with each street light they passed, illuminating his skin with a metallic nuance. "That must have been how he justified it to himself. Do you believe in destiny?"

"Santiago asked me something similar," Mystique mused. The scent of lavender had impregnated her nostrils, acting on her like a mild tranquilliser. "I don't know. *Destiny* sounds like a vague word to me."

De Villa waited before replying. "So then what? What else did Santiago say?"

"He talked about extinct animals." She realised that her voice had a rarefied sound to it. Due to some phenomenon, the air conditioning was leaving streaks of humidity on the car windows. "Talked about animals in cages... He asked me if I was married."

"Oh," said the detective. His voice too had taken on an odd sound. They both seemed about to add something, then decided against it and surrendered to the silence. No more noise came in from the street. The windows were fogging up as if it were winter outside.

The car appeared to be no longer moving. Impossible to see out. Mystique remained still, terrified and enchanted by those unexpected phenomena, while the lights from the street grew blurry, more and more imprecise in the fogged-up glass. It must be their breathing. There was no other explanation. Their breathing had fogged the glass. Their deep, hungry breathing. His breathing, her breathing.

Mystique's lips parted, as she felt she was suffocating, her body responding to a languid thrill of pleasure. She felt short of breath. The oxygen in the car must have been used up. They sat motionless in the airless interior, the windows closed and fogged. "I'm suffocating," she begged. Dennis De Villa caressed her face. In his smile was an infinite well of sadness. "I'm suffocating."

When she woke up she was breathing hard. Her heart was racing. It was difficult to tell whether she was recovering from the feeling of suffocation in her dream, or if instead her laboured breathing was a sign of some perverse excitement. This time it wasn't even dawn. Still dark outside. The night was silent and intact on the far side of the window.

She dragged herself into the bathroom, where she groped blindly for the switch. The light had the effect of a shot of caffeine, sweeping away the last traces of her incomprehensible dream and leaving her wide awake to stare at herself in the mirror. Her face. Her lidded eyes. In the sudden glare of light, her pupils had contracted instantaneously, recoiling like tiny frightened creatures.

Nostrils flared, lips clamped tight. She couldn't claim she looked well rested. She mustn't have slept more than five hours. To go on dreaming scenes like that was certainly no help… *This is turning into a habit. Perverse dreams involving Detective De Villa.*

Nothing she had just dreamed had actually taken place last night. She and the detective had talked about Santiago, true enough, but the car windows hadn't fogged up and the car hadn't stopped moving. Nothing remotely like it. Detective De Villa had seen her home and wished her a respectful goodnight.

What the hell is happening to you? she asked herself. She rinsed her face and dried it with a towel. The sensation of the soft cloth against her face. Once again, her body was in a state of turmoil. That night, she'd have to go on air with the show. She continued stroking her face and breathing hard through the towel, to chase that dream away, to chase away all dreams, to chase away what had happened with Santiago and the woman curled up in the freezer, to chase away the presence of Dennis De Villa so that she could think, instead, about the long day that lay ahead of her.

*

Vladimir Putin was greeted with the usual standing ovation. Vladimir showed off the *muscles of Great Russia,* making the studio audience roar with laughter. Oprah, Madonna, and the other characters were given the same giddy welcome. The show went on at a relentless pace. The sketches, the applause, the commercial breaks, the dance numbers, the walk-ons, the moments when she headed backstage to transform herself into a new character, the appearances of Chad who, in this episode, was flaunting his unequalled green tailcoat. Everything seemed to dovetail. Everything appeared well assembled, fluid, and seamless, like a perfectly smooth surface, beneath which no one would suspect the actual presence of an unexpected hole. The schedule had been reorganised at the last minute. It had become necessary to replace a missing sketch: the one that Mystique hadn't been up to performing, the sketch she just didn't feel ready to do. The notorious Doctor Szepanski sketch.

The customary meeting with the team and the director was to take place after the show. Before the meeting, while she was still in her dressing room trying to relax and to get rid of the flavour of the bodies into which she had transformed herself, Mystique heard a discreet tapping at the door. She tidied her hair and called out in a neutral voice: "Come in."

Gary Modine, the show's producer, poked his head into the room. His small green eyes beamed in the half-light of the door. "Am I interrupting something?"

"Don't worry. I was expecting you."

Gary shut the door behind him and strode towards her. He was a fairly tall man, with an understated tan and an elegant smile always stamped on his face. He was about the same age as her, early fifties, and he wore an exquisitely tailored suit. He had manicured hands. Cared-for skin, a thick white perfectly groomed head of hair. The kind of man you could picture at the weekend sipping a cocktail in some beautiful home on the ocean or else swinging a club on the most exclusive greens in the state.

"Dearest," he cooed in a well-calibrated voice. "I watched the show from the control booth. You were every bit as wonderful as ever."

"Yeah," was all that Mystique said. She let Gary get settled on the sofa and started wandering around the small space of the dressing room, feeling the usual post-show agitation cling to her.

"Of course, we have a problem though," said the producer.

"Of course," she admitted.

Gary crossed his legs. Peeping out from under the hems of his trousers was the fabric of his impeccable black socks. "Let me be frank," he said, his amiable smile still in place. "Next week, there can be no more delays. The Szepanski number is going to have to go on. The first ratings reports for tonight have us running even with Namor's show… Running even. There was a time when we dominated with an average four-point lead. Next week our friend with the gills has a good chance of scooping us."

Mystique listened as she continued to wander around the dressing room, in her robe, her body restless as in a state of insurgence. She felt the painful impulse to transform herself again, a thousand times again, transform herself without stopping until her very last breath. The post-show malaise was exacerbated by the awareness that she had failed to perform a particular transformation. The goddamned transformation everyone was waiting for. The transformation she both yearned for and dreaded. "Are we certain," she ventured, "that Szepanski is the character we really want?" She thought it over and corrected herself: "I mean, I'm pretty sure that next week I can pull it off. I'll become Szepanski. I just need a little more practice. But are we certain that he's the character we need to focus on?"

"We're more than certain," was Gary's answer. The producer shot her a gentle glance of reproof. "Next week, Szepanski is going to be a guest on Namor's show. We don't have any alternatives. Namor is going to host the doctor, and we'll have to have an even funnier version of the doctor, something more captivating than the original."

Mystique nodded distantly. She tugged her bathrobe around her and looked away, incredulous that she had to waste her time worrying about Namor. The much-ballyhooed Prince of Atlantis. The haughty sixty-year-old with pointy ears. The exhibitionist who went around, whatever the season, wearing nothing but a pair of green briefs. The amphibious man had been trying for years to beat her ratings, and it looked like he was on the verge of pulling it off. No doubt he'd be a perfect match for Joseph Szepanski. The experienced doctor might even offer some advice on how to rebuild those sagging pectorals of his. A bitter, uncertain smile flickered across Mystique's face, a smile that seemed to tremble, like a summer mirage, on the surface of her lips. "What do you think Namor'll do with the old doctor?" she asked in jest. "Get him to climb into his goldfish bowl with him?"

Gary cocked his head. In contrast with her smile, the curve on his lips looked inflexible. He barely twitched his wrist, without even looking at the watch he wore on it, as if that gesture were enough to inform him of the time. "I don't want to take any more of your time. I think I'll leave you now," he said, rising to his feet. His relaxed voice, his face with its fine-drawn features. The elegant movements of his body, his three-hundred-dollar hair-cut, the dainty knot on his silk tie, even his fine cotton socks: every detail of his person bespoke something courteous, something inexorable, as well as the eternal ambiguous softness of power. "I think you can guess what's at stake here," he hissed amiably. "The network executives are evaluating the future of the show."

Mystique nodded again. She knew what he was alluding to. *The future of the show.* Gary was alluding to the coming seasons of the programme, or to be more exact the danger that there wouldn't be any new seasons. Mystique felt a dusty taste in her mouth, and an impelling need for air. Oxygen, she needed oxygen. Her superpower prompted in her an abnormal need for oxygen. It was like a flame, consuming vast quantities of oxygen.

That was when, with the suddenness of certain dreams, the dream about the car resurfaced in her memory. The dream with the fogged-up windows. The dream in which she was suffocating, unable to open the car door, but not even trying to escape… The sensations of her dreams with Dennis De Villa. The sensations when she first learned about the woman curled up in the freezer. The sensations right now during her conversation with Gary. The variety of sensations she'd accumulated recently seemed to blend and whirl inside her for a few moments, like the snow inside a glass globe.

She was happy to see that Gary was leaving. When the man pulled the door open, a gust of air entered the room. "Oh, by the way," the producer added. "Whatever happened with that thing? Did you talk to the police? Have you received any other creepy notes?"

"No more notes," she lied. With the problems that were surfacing, with the network executives evaluating *the future of the show*, it wasn't a good idea to complicate things. Nothing on earth would make her bring up the subject of those notes again. "I think it was a false alarm. It was nice of you to worry about it, but there was no need."

"Excellent," he said approvingly. "It was best to be prudent. Always best to be prudent," he said, in a tone of refined sagacity, as he headed off down the hallway.

*

"That son of a bitch!" Chad exclaimed with surprising vehemence. "Him and his exquisite manners. Is that what he really said? *The future of the show?*"

It was the morning after the broadcast and Chad and Mystique had taken shelter in the studio cafeteria to talk in peace, without fear of being interrupted or overheard. It was an hour before lunch and the cafeteria was deserted, the tables silent, the white chairs neatly poised in readiness. Their voices echoed in the calm of the room. Outside, beyond the plate glass window overlooking the courtyard, the rain drummed down. The rain had started falling that night, driving the temperature down, quenching the fever that had held the city in its thrall, and bringing a momentary sense of ceasefire.

"That's what he said," Mystique confirmed. The sound of rain penetrated through the plate glass window. The ceiling lamps were turned off and the only light was the grey, almost metallic reflection of the daylight outside. Seeing the frustration on her colleague's face, Mystique pointed out: "Let's not put too much blame on Gary. He's not the one who decides these things."

"I know. But he can be influential."

Each of them drummed their fingers on the white wooden tabletop.

They both knew the rumours that had been circulating for a while now. Rumours that the show, even though it still had a devoted audience, was losing its lead over the rival programming. Rumours about the likelihood that this season would be the last. Rumours about the possible end of the *Celebrity Mystique Show.* Insinuating, elusive rumours, whisperings in the shadows, the kind of whispering that sooner or later was bound to spring up around every programme. In the constant struggle to hold onto a show's slot, no one was ever safe.

What Gary had said the night before was one concrete piece of evidence that those rumours might be true. It could happen. The show might be cancelled.

Mystique let her gaze wander to the courtyard outside the glass, which looked even more desolate than usual in the rain. The water dripped through the leaves of half a dozen short trees, soaking a surface of grey paving stones, dribbling towards the scattered storm drains.

They talked more about the show and the importance, now more than ever, of making the next episode spectacular and unforgettable.

They talked about it in grim, almost overanxious tones, but in time their spirits perked up. Soon they were heatedly picking over ideas for the new episode. Oh yes. Chad's eyes began to gleam again. The frustration of a short while ago seemed to dissolve in him, giving way to a series of ideas that ranged from the visionary to the absurd and camp. "How about this one? In the next episode, Arnold Schwarzenegger comes on bare-chested, striking bodybuilder poses, and then, just before walking off stage, he licks his armpits."

Mystique giggled. She wished that was enough to set things right. Some invention just a little more surreal than usual.

"Or maybe Madonna sings a version of an old hit, what, I don't know… *Like a Virgin?* Madonna sings her old hit, swinging her hips recklessly, until she's completely paralysed, and just then I come sashaying onto the stage, dressed as Madonna, squeezed into a lacy corset, demanding to stand in for her. Can't you just see it?"

This time she laughed heartily.

"*Chad versus Madonna.* It'll be a triumph. The audience will go crazy."

These ideas seemed too grotesque to make it into the line-up, but maybe Chad was right. There was no point in losing heart now. There was always hope as long as there was another episode. Madonna and Schwarzenegger would do their part. Vladimir and Oprah could help pull the load too, and then there would be the Szepanski number. In the next show, they both agreed, they'd absolutely have to include the Szepanski number.

The cafeteria staff had arrived and were prepping the counters for the lunchtime rush. Chad eyed with interest the dishes that were emerging from the kitchen. He wasn't the kind of young man who stayed down for long.

Mystique shot him a glance, and a bubble of fondness welled up in her chest. That overgrown boy. Chad had been playing her sidekick for six years now. *I've got to do this for him, too,* she thought with a surge of emotion. *I have to succeed in doing Szepanski for him, for Horace, for Susie, and for everyone who works on this show.*

"What about our friend the detective?" Chad asked point-blank. "How is that amiable hunk?"

Mystique blinked. With his infallible instinct, Chad must have sensed that this was the perfect time to needle her. "You never fail to amaze me," she replied, playing along with him. "Even knowing your twisted mental processes as well as I do, I can't for the life of me imagine why you would come up with such a question."

"Because we're in the cafeteria," he said delightedly. "Ha ha! I'll never forget the look on your face when he showed up in here."

"Ha ha," she laughed back through clenched teeth. "And to think I was just telling myself what a nice young man you are, after all."

They sat there, joking around in the empty room. Soon crowds of people would arrive, filling up the tables, shifting chairs, carrying trays loaded with food from one end of the dining hall to the other, dispersing the invaluable hint of intimacy that joined them now. The two of them. The hostess of the show and her faithful sidekick.

Outside, the rain pounded down into the courtyard with monotonous zeal. The sky had a pale silver sheen, a surface almost the colour of a mirror, a chilly impasto of clouds and light. "I think that detective has a crush on you."

"I think your brain is suffering from a sugar slump."

"Why do you take it the wrong way?" he asked. "He seemed like an interesting guy. Nice body, nice face. If only he didn't have a couple of raw T-bone steaks for eyes…"

"He suffers from chronic conjunctivitis."

"You see? You're defending him now. You care for that man."

"I'm not defending him. That man is a cop."

"You say that the police have no reason to worry about you," Chad reasoned. "But this De Villa guy keeps tagging along after you. That can mean only one thing. He's got a crush on you!"

"He's a cop," she said again.

"You could try and give him a chance. It must be a thousand years since the last time you went out with anyone."

"Too young. I don't even know how old he is. Plus, he's a cop," Mystique reiterated.

Someone turned the lights on in the dining hall.

That was when a shiver ran through her body. She started drumming her fingers on the wooden table again, thinking about the routines for the upcoming episode. She started thinking about Schwarzenegger again, about Madonna dressed in a lacy corset, about Vladimir Putin and how he'd make the audience howl with laughter.

The Doctor Szepanski routine. The decisive broadcast. Her body continued to vibrate. "Let's stop talking about the detective. Let's think about our show."

∗

People had a lot to say about a woman like her. People spread gossip, speculation, and legends about a woman like her. The ordinary, predictable effect of notoriety blended with a subtler element, verging on the morbid, bound up with the specific characteristics of her superpower and with people's inability to understand, when all was said and done, who she really was.

It wasn't just the television audience who watched her from home, the spectators who sent in complimentary emails, or those who wrote to complain about the irreverent manner in which she had pilloried some favoured public figure, or who sent in more-or-less explicit questions about her personal life. *Is Chad your boyfriend? Is it true that you're a lesbian? Is it true you once worked in a circus? When you were in prison did you find Jesus?*

It wasn't just them. First and foremost, it was the people in show business, the professionals she ran into at the studio cafeteria, or at the infrequent parties she attended, a world that ought to have been close to her, but that seemed to study her from a faraway distance.

Mystique could imagine how she looked to their eyes. A woman who had been hosting a successful TV show for six years. There was no question that her ability to transform herself into anyone she wanted was the right talent in the right place, and that no superpower had ever been used better on TV. The show had made history. People laughed at the mere sound of the show's name: *Celebrity Mystique Show*. Six years of *transformations*, six years of irreverent comedy and popularity. Of course she was the target of admiration and envy, and people had started to mutter, even before the show started losing ratings, about the possibility of it being cancelled.

People gossiped about many other things. About her habits, about her working methods, about the advertising contracts she'd decided she could afford to turn down. About the proverbial perfectionism that led her to work with a skeleton crew, a handful of trusted colleagues over whom, malicious gossips liked to hint, she exerted an iron fist. Maybe she was a control freak. Maybe her perfectionism verged on the pathological. It was also well known that she wanted no make-up artists, that she never used dressers to help in her costume changes. She wouldn't allow anyone into her dressing room. Before each show, she locked herself in to do breathing exercises. People had a vague idea of how she managed to transform herself, but apparently it required her to be naked, breathe deeply, and *concentrate*.

People seemed to agree that she had a certain dash of charisma. An unquestionable personality. *That woman can make you laugh with one glance, reduce you to ashes with the next.*

Then there were the comments on her physical appearance. She was considered a good-looking woman, though perhaps not to everyone's taste. She had a spectacular figure, given her age, but that bluish skin... The malicious ones said she looked like a corpse. Others thought that the hue of her skin gave her a touch of something exotic and sexy. To say nothing of her superpowers... Damn. What would it be like to go to bed with someone who could turn into anyone, on demand?

Too bad so little was known about her. She never gave interviews. It was said that one of the greatest regrets of Larry King's life was that he'd never managed to land her as a guest. She was such a private woman. A professional with no time for anything but her work, with an austere lifestyle, no personal secretary, no bodyguard, little if any social life. She almost always failed to show up at events where she was expected. A haughty woman, perhaps a little frigid.

What were people supposed to think about a woman with such a secret life? That she was sexually repressed? That she had unseemly vices, that she dated married men? There had to be secrets. There had to be spicy details. What did she do on Saturday nights? Did she take on the body of a seventeen-year-old girl and engage in wild orgies in a college dorm room somewhere? Did she transform herself into a man, slip on a cock ring, and indulge in gay group sex?

The more the questions descended into idle curiosity, the more time people wasted on coming up with fanciful answers. You could go overboard with questions like this. On the other hand, it was well known how much people loved to go overboard, to intertwine contorted thoughts, and waste time on a thousand pointless suppositions.

Sometimes Mystique noticed this buzz of questions, this background noise that followed in her wake from afar. It was a cold wind that blew at her back, something that involved her name without ever really touching her, without any real contact with her, with her current life or her past. Something that happened in another place. As if someone down there were organising a ridiculous party in her honour while she sat up here, proudly distant, remote, and alone.

*

Rain fell on the red brick buildings of Harlem. Rain sheeted against the windows of the shops along 125th Street, against the doors of churches that let out echoes of gospel music on Sundays, onto school playgrounds where maps of the United States were drawn on the tarmac, every state a different colour. The rain drummed on those drawings, flooding the states and making their colours fade. The rain drummed down on the street. Under the warm deluge, people walked in plastic sandals, carrying umbrellas or wearing ponchos, or else walking unsheltered.

Mystique-Chad was one of the unsheltered ones. She was walking with an unhurried gait, her clothes drenched. The water slightly burned her skin, giving her a sense of fluid purity. She leapt over a puddle with unexpected agility. Chad's massive body knew how to move gracefully. Harlem always lifted her spirits, even though the neighbourhood, she had to admit, wasn't what it used to be. She was glad it was safer now. She was glad to be able to walk down the street in the body of a white man without running any particular risk, but still, she had to admit that she missed the days when there were a few more muggers around and fewer fat people, depressed and silent, trudging along the sidewalk.

Not that she had anything against fat people. Of course not. After all, she was walking around in Chad's body, the lightest, most agile and graceful of fatties. She leapt between puddles, letting out light laughs that were drowned in the noise of the nearly tropical monsoon.

Here was the building. Mystique-Chad walked up the steps and rang the doorbell.

The woman who came to the door was a little over fifty, wearing a simple light-coloured dress and with short hair. Her eyes were fringed by heavy lashes, and they flew open in horror at the sight that greeted them: a fat man without an umbrella, soaking wet, his clothes dripping. "My boy!" Sabrina exclaimed. "Is this any way to wander around the city?"

Inside, the apartment occupied one floor of what had once been a stately home of old-time Harlem. Solid and spacious architecture, high-ceilinged rooms, hardwood floors, and fireplaces that hadn't been used in the past half-century, at least. Leaving a trail of wet footprints, Mystique-Chad followed the woman through a dimly lit room, clearly used as a sitting room-study-bedroom, into the kitchen overlooking the back. She took the towel Sabrina was offering. "You haven't been around for a while," Sabrina said, as she continued to observe the rain-soaked oversized boy sitting across from her. "Is there something I can do for you? Are you looking for something?" she asked as she put on the kettle.

"I think so," Mystique-Chad whispered. She took a look around the spotless kitchen, the row of mugs lined up on the shelf, the open window with the screen. From a building across the backyard came the bass notes of a hip-hop album. "Lately I've been having problems with a sense of… *restlessness*. I need some help to relax. Something that'll make me sleep as peacefully as a baby. Something like that excellent grass you gave me last time."

"Fine," Sabrina nodded. She got down two mugs with the Starbucks logo, added hot water and one tea bag per mug. She handed one to her visitor and commented: "I think I can help."

Mystique-Chad blew on her scalding tea, gazing with thinly disguised affection at the woman sitting across from her. Sabrina was more than just her trusted supplier. They had first met many years ago at the time of their political activism, when Sabrina was in the same political struggles as Mystique. Mutant liberation and that whole array of bizarre old-fashioned illusions. They hadn't succeeded in liberating much of anything, but they had been arrested just a few months apart.

Their stories ran parallel. They had served their sentences in different prisons but they'd been released around the same time. Since then Mystique would drop by every so often with the excuse of buying a little grass, always in disguise, and Sabrina never suspected, or gave no sign of suspecting, that the overweight young man who came to see her was her old comrade from the days of the radical struggle.

Sabrina put a sugar cube in her mug. She stirred the tea with a long spoon, blew on it, and took a cautious sip. "I like doing business with you. There are so few people left any more who ask for something to help them *relax*," she pointed out. Her thick eyelashes shaded her eyes, which brimmed with a mixture of slyness and honest concern. Since she'd been released from prison, she'd managed to eke out a living by peddling dope. Before serving time, she'd had some modest superpowers, but it had been too many years since she'd used them and she must have lost them altogether by now.

Sabrina went on with her speech. "From what I remember," she said, "there was a time when people wanted that. Back then, I wasn't in this line of work, but I did have the impression that people used to go to dealers because they wanted something to help them relax. Or at the very most, something to help them *have fun*."

Mystique-Chad kept listening to her. A trembling column of steam rose from the mug she held in her hands.

"Now all they want is something to help them tough it out, to keep them on their feet like sleepwalkers. Like cardboard cut-outs." Sabrina took a pause to sip her tea. "They want chemical crap with names I've never heard. Or cheap cocaine refined with who knows what... What do you think they use to make that crap, rejects from some paint factory?"

Mystique-Chad nodded repeatedly. She understood what the woman was talking about. Something had changed during the years they'd both spent in prison, and it wasn't limited to the capricious shifts in the narcotics market. It was something much more universal. It was something in the vibrations people put out. Something in the radio waves of reality, something to do with the world's innermost desires.

But she hadn't come to talk about that. She was here to buy some grass. Simple, pure, old-fashioned grass. Not that she was much of a dope-smoker. Sabrina's grass was just a good way to soothe the anxiety of all the pressure she'd been under lately. A way to calm the shocks of painful excitement that swept over her more and more often these days, these nights, these sleepless dawns. To keep from shuddering awake in the aftermath of some sick dream with Detective De Villa. To have some peaceful nights and get to work rested.

After their tea, and once their little transaction had been completed, they walked together to the door. "I see you on TV sometimes, on that bizarre show," Sabrina said. She stopped in the doorway, clasping her arms around herself, sniffing the scent of the rain-washed street. "You're all great. You're great. Mystique is great. Give her my best wishes, as always. I wonder if she even remembers me. Tell her that old Sabrina still thinks of her."

Mystique-Chad headed off down the street. After a few yards she turned around, and saw Sabrina standing in the doorway, in her light-coloured dress. The falling rain was cooler now. She continued down the street, a small bag of marijuana in her pocket, in the rhythmic overwhelming sound of the downpour.

Meeting Sabrina again was always a strange experience. It only took a minute for the details of the visit, the discussion of drugs, the Starbucks mugs, the taste of the hot tea, to have all vanished in a puff of flimsy, ambiguous, distant colour. The same colour that dominated her memories of Lexington. The isolation cell, the meals, the harsh light of the infirmary. The faces of the people she had met there. The visits from her lawyer. Sixteen years in prison. Sixteen years immersed in that colour, like in a sepia photograph. She wondered if Sabrina's memories of prison were the same colour.

She wondered what colour Sabrina's memories had of their long-ago political activism, of their revolutionary naivety. *Like a sepia photograph.*

*Something that must once have existed, perhaps, but in another colour, in a
different atmosphere.*

She came to the end of the street. Perhaps Sabrina was still standing in the
doorway. Who knows. She decided not to turn around, because she knew
that from where she was, she would be unable to make out any human
figure, and that there was no gesture that could be glimpsed through that
rain, which made everything blurred.

*

Transform yourself into a man. I'm begging you. I want to feel a man's body. In
the prison showers, back in Lexington, or in a distant corner of the yard
during their exercise period, the other female convicts would implore her to
transform herself into a man. Other times the female prison guards asked her
the same thing, with voices either violent or desperate, even though they knew
well that she couldn't do what they asked. She just couldn't. For all the years
she spent in confinement, her power of transformation had been inhibited
by an electronic bracelet. That had been the worst punishment of all: to be
unable to use her power, to feel it languishing in her body, in her muscles, in
the depth of her belly, down to the most intimate recess of each vein. To feel
it burn like an illness without an outlet. If she could have used her power,
would she have satisfied the yearning requests of the women in the prison?

For many long years, the torment of being unable to transform herself
was mixed with the climate of grim sexual hunger at Lexington, the claus-
trophobic solitude of the bodies around her, and the clamp of her own
solitude. The gelid odour of the bedclothes in the cell. Her bluish body,
naked, in the prison shower room.

When she got out the world was there, all around her, with its unrecognisable flavour, with its millions of moving bodies. It had taken her weeks to
get up the courage to begin transforming herself again. It finally happened
in a restaurant toilet. She'd locked herself in, undressed, and turned into
the young waiter who had just served her a lettuce-and-avocado salad a
few minutes earlier. Nothing else happened. She stood there, alone, in the
confines of a small toilet, with the appearance of some nondescript man.
She might have cried. She must have cried.

A few months later, she made her debut in show business. Mystique, mutant former extremist, a new national comedy star. Along with her fame came the rising tide of rumours, the chorus of grotesque suppositions about her private life.

But there was nothing to figure out. No secret, no shadow, no torrid secret affair.

She wasn't frigid and she wasn't apathetic. By no means. When her power was set free to manifest itself again, she had believed that soon the rest of her energies would begin circulating as well. Romantic energy, sexual energy. She'd believed that it would happen. She'd believed that she'd find someone to help her reconnect with the world, someone who would serve as an electric contact, someone she could hook up with to get back in touch, at last, with the circuit of the world's erotic current.

In that period, she'd taken a look around. Most of the men she met at work were colleagues of Gary's, or television network executives who shared Gary's style. Elegant, airbrushed men, with over-sophisticated voices, with too-perfect laughter, men who preferred five-hundred-dollar-a-bottle brandies, who were members of prestigious clubs. Men who appeared so thin to her eyes, nearly nonexistent, like adhesive decals attached, in an indelible manner, to the way of life that fed and sustained them. Mystique wasn't interested in going to bed with a way of life. She wanted to go to bed with an individual. She already found it irritating to have to interact with those men for professional reasons. Sure, she was working for them, but she hadn't reached the point where she found them attractive on any intimate level.

There were other kinds of men, creative men, writers, directors, men in show business, and friends of men in show business. Men that sent her flowers every day for weeks, men she agreed to go out with a couple of times, only to find they bored her, men full of frustrated ambitions or overabundant narcissism, men fixated with themselves who, on the first attempt at sexual intercourse, would wind up making the predictable request. Naked men begging her, moaning, sweating, chewing on the bedsheets in their frenzied impatience, asking her to take on their appearance. *Transform yourself into me. Please. I want to have sex with myself.*

And what about actors, those mysterious and sometimes alluring individuals, who could also be ridiculous to the point of tears?

There had been that television awards ceremony when she was introduced to Chuck Norris. The famous actor with the scruffy red beard. Norris had stared at her all through the evening, scratching his beard above the bow-tie of his tuxedo, shooting her a succession of nervous little smiles, asking the orchestra to play *Call Me*, and finally handing her his phone number, with a conqueror's smirk. Mystique had never felt so awkward in her life. Chuck Norris! She and Chad had laughed about it for weeks.

For a while, every interaction she had with the world of men ended the same way. A laugh with Chad.

Not that every episode was strictly comical.

She was clear-headed enough to understand that a woman who couldn't find anyone she considered attractive was, in all likelihood, a woman who didn't really want to find anyone. And she didn't understand the point of all this. What was she trying to achieve with her detachment? Was she trying to punish the world? Was she trying to punish herself?

In the meantime, sex was evaporating around her. Sex became more and more extraneous, more and more elusive. Sex was a wind that blew all around her. She could feel it but she couldn't seize it. Sex gusted in the streets of New York, ran along the entire length of Broadway, insinuated itself into the narrowest alleys, waved the flags on the roofs of the hotels. Sex swept the dust along the sidewalks, blew on the doors of the American Apparel stores and the Dean & DeLuca gourmet shops, made its way into the gardens of cocktail bars in the Meatpacking District, wafted along the riverbank, chased across the bridges, and spread out on the other side, in the relative tranquillity of Brooklyn or Queens.

She could feel it. The constant breeze of sex. She knew that she lived in one of the most seductive cities on earth, a city dominated by an excruciating lust, a sort of constant sexual exhalation. She could sense other people's sex, she could see them working away, she saw bodies attract one another, gravitate into each other's orbit to keep from plunging into the void.

It happened at work, too. It *especially* happened at work. Horace had screwed the costumier on the show, as well as the costumiers of every other programme produced in the studios, and even little Susie, timid angel that she was, had slept with a couple of the studio technicians. The dancers on the show had fucked each other, one after another, mixing and matching in every way imaginable, men with women, men with men, women with women, in such a systematic assortment that it seemed the result of some scrupulous scientific project.

The world's sexual movement was relentless, mechanical, reminiscent of a giant piece of clockwork. She observed it all without envy, with a sense of distance. She was Mystique. The woman who had survived sixteen years in prison. She was hungry for bodies, and not just the bodies she could turn herself into, but she understood that other people's bodies weren't the problem. It was her body that had grown too remote, virtually unattainable.

Her changeable body. Her proud solitary body, the body that refused to mingle with other bodies, preferring to transform itself into them, to know them without touching them.

*

On Thursday morning, Mystique dressed carefully. She put on a black cotton dress and wrapped a deep blue scarf—the blue of a sky just before dawn—around her shoulders. She wore a pair of simple sandals. She pulled back her hair and applied a discreet line of lipstick. Sabrina's grass had allowed her to get some sleep that night, and though the image looking back from the mirror might not have been that of a serene, untroubled woman, all things considered, she looked presentable enough. *I'm ready. I think I'm ready.*

At the last minute she changed her mind and arranged the scarf so that it covered her hair as well. She put on large dark glasses in the hope of going unnoticed. The simplest thing would have been to attend the funeral in the guise of Chad or someone else, but something stopped her from doing that. A funeral ceremony demanded a modicum of respectful, sincere presence. *I must attend with my own appearance.*

Forty minutes later she was in a little Catholic church in Washington Heights, where half a dozen members of the Ecuadorian community had gathered for the funeral of Rosita Gomez, Santiago's wife, murdered and hidden for months in a freezer. The woman had no relatives in New York, and none of the people present at the service seemed to have known her personally. The elderly priest celebrated the Mass in Spanish, starting a solemn plainsong at times, his voice wavering in the bare church.

The only flowers were the ones that Mystique herself had ordered, along with another wreath of unknown origin. Scrolling clouds of incense curled slowly through the air. Mystique had taken a seat in one of the last pews towards the back. At first she tried to understand the words the priest was saying, then allowed herself to be lulled by the simple sound of his voice, the scent of the incense, and the feeling of calm, sad helplessness that reigned over the ceremony. A young woman, murdered. A body shut for months in an icy casket. That body now lay in a cheap wooden coffin, over which the priest was scattering an abundance of holy water.

When the ceremony came to an end and it was time to leave the church, the few attendees recognised Mystique. A couple of them started looking around, possibly thinking that the presence of a TV star could mean the presence of TV cameras; another couple approached her for an autograph. Mystique preferred to slip away. She felt the taste of a dense melancholy in her throat. It was then that she spotted, in a corner of the church, the familiar figure of Detective De Villa.

They left the church in silence, no need to speak, walking side by side. The weather outside was a sharp contrast to the cool shadowy atmosphere inside the church. The sun once again beat down triumphant. The streets had dried off at unsettling speed, erasing all traces of the recent rains. According to the weather forecasts, a high-pressure front had settled again over the north-east coast, driving temperatures upwards. The summer was roaring back, angrier than ever. The city was about to succumb to a furious fever, and this time no quarter would be given.

Dennis De Villa took off his jacket and started to roll up his shirtsleeves. "Sorry, but this heat…" He stopped, and whispered: "I guessed I'd find you here."

Mystique unwrapped her scarf too. They stood there looking at each other, in the sunshine, on the sidewalk outside the church. "I assumed you'd come for the funeral."

"I did come for the funeral. I sent flowers. I came for the funeral and I came to see you."

Mystique ran the palm of her hand over her forehead, where a damp film was already forming. Under the heat of the sun, the sadness of the funeral seemed to dissolve into the bitterish, transparent, and liquid sensation of sweat on the flesh. "I thought that with heat like this New York's finest would relax their grip a little."

"Oh, quite the opposite." The detective had rolled his shirt sleeves up to his elbows. On his forehead, tiny drops glittered like crystals.

"I hope you haven't come to offer me protection for the umpteenth time."

"Why not?" He frowned and continued to address her with a heartfelt gaze, bordering on indiscretion, a gaze that made her glad she was wearing a pair of protective dark glasses. "Everything okay with the new driver?"

"Of course," she replied, referring to the driver who had taken Santiago's place. The car was waiting for her a few yards up the street. A new surge of perspiration was filming over her forehead, the nape of her neck, and down the line of her back. "I think it's time for me to go."

The detective shifted his weight from one foot to the other. "I could give you a ride to the studio." Even before she had a chance to answer, he added with a hint of regret: "I suppose that's out of the question."

Mystique took some time to consider her reaction. For an instant she thought of Chad, of his theory that the detective fancied her, and how amused Chad would be if he could eavesdrop on this exchange. She imagined herself at the studio, telling Chad about all this. She imagined herself giggling with him at a table in the cafeteria or in the production office, but then that image struck her as less than amusing. She could still sense in her nostrils the scent of incense from the church. "You're a persistent man. I've got to hand it to you. As you can see, right now I don't happen to need a ride anywhere."

When she started towards her car, the detective fell into step beside her. "The first time I saw you," he said in a confessional tone, "was in another church. Do you remember? The funeral of Franklin Richards. A very different ceremony from today's. I remember seeing you in the midst of the group of superheroes. I remember seeing you embrace Franklin's parents, I remember seeing you walk away, alone, through the crowd in the cathedral."

Mystique got into the car. The air inside was cool, and it seemed to penetrate her damp skin and blow into her, making her feel as if her body was empty and hollowed out. "But I didn't see you there. I'm sorry. I'm afraid I ought to be going."

Dennis De Villa leaned over the car, one hand holding the open door, his face inches away from hers. He blinked and swallowed nervously. "That day, I remember watching you as you walked away. I remember thinking that one day we'd speak, that one day we'd interact with one another. Funny, isn't it? Before I even knew anything about those notes. Before I knew that I'd have any reason to meet you."

Mystique moved towards the interior of the car, and from that short additional distance, she did her best to say with bland irony: "I think you're letting the air conditioning out of the car. I think it's time for you to shut that door. It's about time for you to let me go."

"There's just one thing I ask: give me a call if any new notes arrive," he said in a hoarse voice. "I'd like you to call me if anything else that strikes you as strange happens. And I'd like you to call me…" He lowered his voice and looked away: "I'd like you to call me even if nothing at all happens. But I guess that's also out of the question."

Mystique wasn't sure she'd entirely understood. She cautiously adjusted her dark glasses. The detective's open collar revealed a patch of his powerful chest which contrasted with his tiny childlike ears, ears that looked delicate and almost transparent, backlit as they were. On his face was a doleful expression, as though he wanted to ask forgiveness for what he'd just said. Each of his irises was a defined dark disc, surrounded by a halo of inflamed capillaries, not unlike the black disc of an eclipse. *His eyes. His lips. What is he trying to say? Is he confessing an extra-professional interest in me? Is that what this is? Is that what he's saying? And if that's what he's saying, am I possibly falling for it? Chad would laugh his head off,* she wound up repeating to herself, holding onto that thought, the familiar thought of Chad, to keep from getting lost in the unknown, contradictory feeling of embarrassment that all of this prompted inside her.

After the detective pushed the door closed, the driver started up and pulled away from the sidewalk. The car sailed over the sun-baked asphalt, past a row of buildings with decrepit façades.

A packed, weary bus was clogging traffic. Mystique was running late on that morning's appointments. She sat watching as the unfamiliar neighbourhood flowed past, still feeling lost, thinking back to the service she had just attended, the solitary voice of the Hispanic priest, the coffin sprinkled with holy water. The stiff backs of the few people present. The barren walls of the little church. She thought about those details and how they contrasted with the other funeral she'd attended a few weeks ago, the funeral of America's most beloved son.

She remembered everything about the funeral of Franklin Richards. How could she forget? She remembered the immense weeping crowd, the scent of the hundreds of floral wreaths. That funeral had been a watershed. The entire city had shuddered to a halt. She tried to summon up a picture of herself from a distance, viewed through other eyes, as the detective must have seen her on the day of that funeral: a woman dressed in black, a woman embracing the dead man's parents, a famous yet solitary woman moving off, silent, through the crowd filling the cathedral.

The sunlight was cutting into her through the window. While the driver conveyed her towards the studio, she draped the scarf over her head again, to protect herself from the sunshine. Or perhaps she was trying to protect herself from that image, the image of herself viewed through the eyes of Dennis De Villa, trying to protect herself from the idea of being glimpsed by that man, touched by his gaze, at once so intimate and so burning.

*

The music started. They lifted their arms and tried out the first steps. One two three, one two three. Gustav, the choreographer, took the pipe out of his mouth and showed them the moves. In the studio, without an audience, they were rehearsing the dance numbers for the upcoming show. The bodies of a dozen dancers were moving sinuously, scantily dressed, eyes focused on Gustav's directions. Their bare feet on the studio floor. Every move they made was in time with the others, heads moving in unison, respiration synchronised. One two three, one two three.

Mystique-Madonna was among them, in turn following the choreographer, swinging and thrusting her hips. Her lungs gulped air and her heart was racing with thrilling energy. To take on Madonna's body was always a bizarre sensation. Rehearsing dance steps was bizarre too. With her own body, she'd never known how to dance, but Madonna's body was another matter… *Like a virgin, feels so good inside.* The old song pounded away with its Eighties beat.

The young dancers were flinging themselves into the beat, all around her, male and female, with the nonchalant vigour of their youth. *Some of these kids hadn't even been born when this song first came out. Some of them still hadn't come into the world, and I'd already been thrown into prison.* There was an instant's pause. Then they all dropped, at once, she and the dancers and the choreographer, fourteen bodies grazing the floor, with the weight of their flesh, the lightness of their flesh, describing a dizzying arc and then rising again, still synchronised, in the luminous shafts of the studio spotlights.

Gustav moved in front of them. There was something miraculous about the grace of his movements. This was a gentleman half a dozen years older than Mystique, with long grey hair, a beard the same colour, and thick-lensed glasses. He wore a light-brown corduroy suit, the same suit he wore in every season, and all taken together he looked like an ageing philosophy professor, the kind of man you'd expect to run into in a library or a lecture hall in an ancient university. That image wasn't far from the truth. In fact, Gustav *was* an ageing professor of philosophy, and had retired from teaching a few years earlier to begin a new career as a successful choreographer. He hadn't changed his look since his teaching days. He showed up at dance rehearsals in his faithful corduroy suit. When the music started, all he did was take off his shoes, take the pipe out of his mouth, and start moving with unexpected agility. He had already made a name for himself with a few Broadway productions and for the past couple of seasons he'd been doing TV work.

Mystique was relieved to let herself fall under the choreographer's lead. Relieved to have someone show her the gestures to make, the steps to follow, reducing everything to the ironbound, reassuring logic of the rhythm. Relieved to let herself give in to this music, to the energy that poured over her, relieved that she was having a break from her efforts to transform herself into Szepanski.

Gustav shouted something at her. "Your pelvis! Move your pelvis!"

Oh yes. She needed to move her pelvis, move it harder, move it more sensually, move it like a pendulum, from side to side, front to back, move it like a man, move it like a woman, move it like she was black or move it like she was white, move it in the name of humanity at large.

And yet once again, a sense of anxiety stung inside her. She could feel it like a piece of shrapnel. She couldn't say whether that anxiety was due to her worries about the upcoming episode or to her meeting that morning with Dennis De Villa, at the funeral.

The bodies around her were dancing in chorus. They emitted a scent of light perspiration, like a dew, while their breathing became increasingly synchronised, merging together, one single great respiration that filled the studio, mingling with the song. *Can't you feel my heart beat for the very first time?*

Chad came onstage and joined in the dance, dressed just like her but at least twice her size. He too possessed an unexpected agility. They had worked it out that the two of them would remain onstage, dancing side-by-side, two versions of the same character: a mutant with superpowers identical to the original, same body, same skin, same muscle fibre, even the same fingerprints… And an obese transvestite who would look unbeliev-ably funny in comparison. The dance number was reaching its climax. It was all so perfect. Ridiculous, provocative, heartbreaking, perfect! They all spun around at the same time and lifted their arms, vibrating in unison, bodies hot and swaying.

The shrapnel of anxiety inside her. Mystique could feel it growing sharper. In the end, it wasn't hard to figure out the reason. It wasn't so much because of the upcoming show or the meeting with De Villa, but rather because of what she'd found, after Rosita Gomez's funeral, when she got back to her office. There had been something waiting for Mystique when she got back.

She went on dancing. She went on moving with the appearance of an athletic pop star, and following the moves of a choreographer dressed in a corduroy business suit, with a brierwood pipe in his hand. She went on moving to the beat of that song that first came out a good twenty years earlier, back in the days when she was locked up in Lexington and Gustav was teaching in some university on the West Coast and most of the people in the studio either had only recently been born or hadn't been born at all. *I am Madonna, I am Mystique. I'm in a television studio rehearsing a dance routine*, she reminded herself, as if all this suddenly looked foreign to her. The dancers' arms cut through the air. Chad's body shimmied and shook alongside hers.

When she had come into the studio a few hours ago, another note was waiting for her. It was in the usual white envelope, lying on her desk, and the envelope wasn't even stamped. This time it hadn't come through the mail. Someone must have left it on her desk while she was at the funeral with Dennis De Villa. Someone had sneaked into her office to leave her this message.

SO LONG, MY MYSTIQUE

One two three, one two three! The song was coming to an end. They all took a breath, getting ready for the finale. She and Chad and the dancers and the choreographer performed luxuriant arabesques with their arms and tossed their heads back and forth and waved their hair and spun around, moving for the last few seconds. *It's been a long while since I felt so vulnerable*, she admitted to herself. Since she had felt in such danger as she felt now, dancing in the delirium of a pop number, at the centre of a perfect and sophisticated choreography.

*

After the dance rehearsal, she took shelter in her dressing room, regained her own appearance, and indulged in a shower. The flow of water descended over her, pouring over her flesh in long rivulets following unstable courses, carving their way into the hollow between her breasts. Water on her hair.

Water on her back, on her belly, and on the dark triangle of her crotch. Water down her arms, running to her hands and hurling itself, in a cascade, as if gurgling out of her fingertips.

She raised her face to take the flow of water on her closed eyes. The sensations of Madonna's body were pouring away. The too-taut muscles, the sensation of the diminutive stature, of the slightly rounded face, the internal flavour of that vigorous body: everything was dissolving. Madonna was dissolving, leaving Mystique in a neutral, almost stunned state, waiting as always to recognise herself. *I'm coming back. My skin, my breath, the beat of my heart.*

Under the unbroken flow of the shower, she massaged her neck and her aching shoulders. She was weary. The weariness seemed to come and go in her life, in waves, at ever shorter intervals. She grabbed a washcloth, rinsed it, and started running it over her skin, her eyes closed, while the sound of splashing water filled her head, and out of her consciousness that phrase emerged, without warning, like a wreck emerging from the depths of a mighty river. *So long, my Mystique.*

She ran the washcloth over her bluish arms, scrubbed her elbows and her underarms. That morning someone had left a new note on her desk. A member of that damned group? Mystique remembered the point that Detective De Villa had made during their first meeting, about how the group responsible for the deaths of Batman and Franklin Richards was capable of recruiting anyone. *Anyone.* So the question arose naturally on its own. Was the person who had entered her office someone who worked at the studio?

For some reason, she decided to rule that out. It was something like an instinct. She had an idea of how an underground group operated. Maybe she was mistaken, but she felt pretty confident that none of the people who worked alongside her possessed the kind of opaque, grim, determined strength that was required to organise attacks, murders, or operations of that kind, to conspire on a serious basis against someone. It took that kind of strength to act consciously in the dark, to slither in the murky behind-the-scenes precincts of reality. *No one around me possesses that strength. I would have recognised it.*

Madonna was completely gone. The water temperature was starting to drop. She had spent too many minutes under the spray of water. She ought to dry off, smear her skin with aloe gel, get dressed again, continue with her day, make phone calls, confer with the show's technical staff, and all the other things she was scheduled to do. And yet she lingered under the increasingly cold water, her hair clinging flat to her head and the back of her neck.

However things stood, she wouldn't say a word about the latest notes. She could rule that out too. The idea of talking again to the police, or even to Dennis De Villa, struck her as useless and embarrassing. She wouldn't do it. She didn't want to put the show at risk. She'd always been capable of defending herself, and she felt a strong aversion for the police, plus she lacked confidence in the idea that the police were capable of protecting her. She listed all these reasons to herself. Moreover, there was one more fateful reason. Batman had been murdered and an entire floor of the George Hotel had been blown sky-high: *if whoever managed to organise all this has decided to get rid of me too, isn't it logical to assume that sooner or later they'll succeed? I doubt there's anyone who can help me.*

She stood under the now-chilly shower, breathing jerkily, paralysed but not entirely intimidated, contemplating that thought within her, that sudden, clear, definitive thought, so unquestionable that it seemed impersonal, not hers, timeless. A thought that seemed to have always been there, like an ancient inscription, carved into the walls of her consciousness. *Sooner or later they'll succeed.*

*

On Friday a group of five people, taking advantage of the unseasonably warm weather, jumped into the waters of the East River and started swimming along the Manhattan coastline. As far as could be determined, the five swimmers were staging an unauthorised preview of the marathon swim that would be held in a few weeks, as every year: twenty-eight miles through the not-always-limpid waters of the East River and the Hudson, an anticlockwise circumnavigation of the most famous island on earth. The five reckless swimmers had plunged into the river several weeks too early, without any support team or rescue boats.

The local news provided a brief report. When one of the five reckless swimmers ran into trouble and was on the verge of drowning, he was dragged to safety by Namor, who showed up *providentially* just in the nick of time. The well-known television personality, a former superhero and champion swimmer equipped with gills, told the reporters that he'd spotted the swimmers *by chance* while he was out for a walk along the riverbank. What a lucky *coincidence*. Namor had *heroically* plunged into the water, he'd rescued the thrashing swimmer and helped his exhausted fellow swimmers to shore.

Mystique and Chad giggled over the details for at least half an hour. It was obvious that old Namor had paid those five idiots, and that he'd put together the whole thing to get himself featured on the evening news in an attempt to generate some publicity for himself and the next episode of his show. It was such an obviously manufactured media stunt that even the newscasters had a hard time keeping the sarcasm out of their voices. That old exhibitionist with his pointy ears. Him and his pathetic contrivances.

The news report was so ridiculous that it restored a hint of cheerfulness to Mystique's mood. She forgot the obsessive concerns of the last few days and devoted herself to editing the scripts for the show.

But as the afternoon stretched on, the subtle dread of the oncoming weekend started to envelop her, as it did every week, only amplified by recent unsettling developments. Laughing about old Namor just wasn't enough. She felt a compelling desire to get out of there. The desire to escape from the enclosed space of the studio grew inside her until she made up her mind, gave some instructions to the production staff, invented an appointment somewhere, and had a taxi summoned. She told the driver to take her into town.

"Into town where?" the driver objected.

"Into town... I don't know. Take me to Columbus Circle."

The taxi headed off. It took some time to get to Manhattan through the thick traffic. The taxi driver turned on the radio and let the chit-chat of a radio presenter fill the interior of the cab. News about the late afternoon traffic. Weather reports about the scorcher of a weekend that was plummeting straight towards the city. And passing mentions of the news of the day, including the adventure of the five swimmers who had plunged into the river that morning, before being *luckily* rescued by Namor.

The taxi driver shook his head in annoyance. This was one hell of a day. Thermometers skyrocketing and young morons deciding it would be a good idea to swim around the island.

As soon as she got out of the taxi, Mystique scampered into a lobby of the Time Warner Center. She slipped into a restroom she had previously used for this purpose. She didn't have the right clothes with her to transform herself into Chad. Instead, she undressed and took on the appearance of young Susie, the production assistant on the show, who was just a size smaller than Mystique. She put her clothes back on and emerged into the open air. Free at last! Free to wander the city without being recognised, without running risks, free to blend into the crowd, as she tried once again to calm the nervous flames that burned her from within.

She walked down Broadway, the sun assailing her skin. Susie's complexion was so delicate. Mystique-Susie crossed the street to reach the shadier side, and continued on past the usual succession of Starbucks, health clubs, restaurants, news stands, flower shops, grocery stores, and questionable electronics outlets. She accelerated her pace to overtake a cluster of chubby women, tourists from some indeterminate European country, whose guide was holding aloft a small plastic umbrella as a sort of banner.

She made her way through the theatre district and the crowds around Times Square, pushing along the sidewalks jammed with bodies, speeding up, almost breaking into a run, while a confused knot of people swirled around her. At one street corner, a man with a guitar was singing a country song, dressed in nothing but a cowboy hat, underpants, and boots. People stopped to take pictures. The famous naked cowboy of Times Square. Mystique-Susie continued south, moving away from the chaos of the tourist zone, moving past other bodies, meeting other gazes. She felt even more agitated, and looked over her shoulder more than once, feeling silly. No one was following her.

The sweat on Susie's body had a faint, elusive scent. She kept locking eyes unintentionally with the passersby. The gazes of passersby in the streets of New York could be broken into two categories. Mystique had given this some thought. There was the category of closed, hostile glances, glances that seemed to express nothing more than the eternal, obvious question: *what the hell are you looking at?*

Then there was another category of glances. Glances that expressed something softer, something much more alluring. At certain times of day, in certain parts of the city, it seemed everyone was flirting with everyone. Men, women, everyone with everyone, without expecting consequences of any kind. No one was serious about it. Flirting in New York was a pleasurable neurosis, an almost compulsive reflex, a cheap form of gratification.

Paranoia and flirtation. Those were the two complementary modes in which people interacted on the streets of New York.

Mystique-Susie went on walking, wishing she could just close her eyes and avoid both kinds of glances. She stepped off the sidewalk and crossed yet another junction. The fumes from a hot dog stand wafted over her. She didn't stop, fleeing straight ahead, with a needlessly hasty gait, her skin red from sunlight and air, moving down the streets of that city, the paranoid city, the alluring city, and not until another jam clogged the sidewalk, forcing her to a halt, leaving her out of breath and almost staggering, did she realise that it had been a mistake to come into town. Where was she running? What was she looking for?

*

Dennis De Villa was standing in front of the full-length mirror. Daylight poured through the window, liquid, white, illuminating the outlines of his naked body, creating a fine luminous layer sheathing the protruding relief of his muscles.

He was well-built. More so than he looked with his clothes on. His shoulders were sculpted and his chest was broad. These weren't the pectoral muscles of someone who had spent time bulking up in a gym somewhere, these were real muscles, real-life muscles, squared off and welcoming. Some curly hair on his upper chest. His nipples were dark and shrunk so tight that they looked like two nodes, two clumps of hard sensitive flesh. Dennis curled up the fingers of one of his hands and ran his knuckles over his chest repeatedly, as if he were polishing them.

His skin was a pale olive hue. It was hard to tell whether that was his body's natural colour or the result of a couple of afternoons' sunbathing. If that's what it was, the absence of any tan lines meant the detective did his sunbathing naked, showing he was less inhibited than Mystique might have expected.

The legs were the part that she liked best. Dennis' legs were solid, well-shaped, slightly arched like the legs of certain athletes, and covered with a light fuzz of hair. Muscular calves. His feet looked nicely proportioned, not too long, in the sunlight that poured through the window and lit up the floor of Mystique's bedroom.

Taken as a whole, Dennis' legs seemed to contain a sort of quiet, unexpressed strength, a strength that resided there, in the lower portions of his body, where the blood was furthest from the heart, coursing through long solitary veins. As for the deep flavour of Dennis' body, the one that lay in the most hidden folds of his flesh, it was a fairly dense flavour. An almost sandy flavour. Dennis' body reminded her of the flesh of a fruit that was capable of concealing, within it, hard and inaccessible zones.

Mystique-Dennis caressed her-his thighs. She stared at his penis in the mirror, and it jerked erect in a few fast moves, as though reawakened by the simple perception of that gaze. It was straight in an almost geometric way, and just now was pointing, vibrant, nearly threatening, the tip already moist, at its own image in the mirror.

Mystique-Dennis shivered, touched her thighs again, tossed her head back, and regained her original shape. Mystique's bluish body took the place of the man's body. The tips of her nipples were just as tight as his, and now the moisture was inside her, between her legs, in the fleshy fissure that was starting to pulsate.

*

Later, in the same position, in front of the same mirror, she inhaled deeply and tried to transform herself into another man. Even though she had made up her mind not to practise on the notorious doctor that Saturday and give herself a rest, she decided to give it a try at least. In the mirror, she studied the white hairs on the chest and belly, the withered legs, and the small shrivelled penis. There was no doubt that the spectacle was quite different from that offered by Dennis De Villa.

And yet taking on an aged body didn't upset her. That wasn't the problem. To some extent, she'd always managed to find a certain beauty in all the bodies she transformed herself into, even the oldest ones, the most ridiculous ones. But Szepanski's body remained alien to her. Szepanski's body was too difficult. Mystique-Szepanski studied that body in the mirror and noted the usual problems. The lines on the face appeared blurry, the eyelids and cheekbones not taut enough. *I promised everyone that I would pull this off. I can't understand why it's so hard to do.*

She felt like telling herself that it wasn't important after all, that it was just a stupid routine on television, about a stupid doctor or former doctor who had betrayed his patients by writing a stupid bestseller. She looked at herself, incredulous, lost in the feeling that she was no longer herself, nor had she entirely become someone else, lost in the feeling that she was in the middle, in a vague and fleshy limbo.

She resumed her own shape, took a shower, and headed for the kitchen.

The refrigerator offered the habitual containers from Whole Foods. Yogurt. Prewashed fruit. Green-leaf vegetables in a transparent plastic bag, whose interior was dotted with tiny drops of condensation. *Force myself to take a day off. Now that's an exploit I find daunting.* She spent the rest of that Saturday trying to read, taking catnaps, smoking a little grass, and exchanging bored text messages with Chad.

This weekend Chad was out of town, visiting his parents somewhere in Connecticut, which meant that he had gone to Connecticut to do what he usually did at home: watch TV and consume bacon-flavoured crisps. *Can I ask you what you're doing closed up in your apartment?* Chad wrote from on high, from the vantage of his incredible dynamism. *Are you waiting for a man to fall down your chimney? Get moving! Wasn't there a gallery opening in Chelsea tonight?*

It wasn't the messages from Chad. It wasn't the sense of claustrophobia, nor was it the hot breeze that was blowing on the street door of her apartment, like the moan of some enormous mysterious beast. Instead, it was a form of ultimate pride, a sense almost of challenge, that persuaded her to do something she hadn't done in a long time. Socialise. Leave the apartment with her own appearance. She didn't care what was waiting out there: the overheated chaos of the city, the usual foolish and gossipy people, or perhaps even a gang of fanatics determined to cause her harm. She decided it didn't matter any more. Whatever the danger out there, she decided she would face the challenge and leave the apartment with her actual appearance. She got ready at her leisure and called a taxi.

The afternoon was starting to decline slowly.

The opening was being held in one of the main galleries in Chelsea, an ex-warehouse or ex-something, a huge basement a couple of steps down from street level.

At the front door there was a crowd. Plenty of photographers' flashes went off in her direction, as Mystique made her way into the place, putting on a feigned air of distraction, tossing greetings here and there. The artist whose exhibition was opening was well known. Personalities from the world of show business and the world of superheroes were wandering around, with a glass of iced wine in hand, surrounded by the typical fauna of reporters, art critics, rubberneckers, young Williamsburg hipsters, all of them with highly contrived looks.

This wasn't a situation that Mystique found particularly congenial, but as far as that went, she was here and she should at the very least take a look at the exhibition, and say hello to the artist. She got through a wall of people and emerged in the next room, illuminated by a couple of peach-coloured neon lights, where instead of finding the artist she found herself face to face with Dennis De Villa.

It was a funny thing. She didn't feel surprised. After all, the artist had some connection with the world of the superheroes, so it was natural enough that the detective should have come to take a look. Now that she saw him, Mystique had the sensation, in a way, that she'd always known she would run into him. She'd always known it, perhaps she'd even hoped it, and that sensation made her lurch, almost, as from a small internal short circuit.

*

Nathan Quirst was a successful artist. He'd had various golden periods. The first had been back in the Eighties, at the beginning of his career, when he first thought of dissolving a black dye in a tub of water, turning the water into something like ink, and lying naked on the bottom of the tub with scuba gear and two small tubes in his nostrils to run off the air he was exhaling. Unsuspecting visitors were ushered into the room and invited by a couple of assistants to immerse an arm in the mysterious black liquid. It took considerable courage to stick your arm into that tub without knowing what might be there, unseen, at the bottom. It took just as much courage to lie immersed in that blackness, motionless, without being able to see what was happening outside the tub, as hesitant, curious hands passed over his body, all of his body, until they figured out what was down there. A living man. The artist Nathan Quirst. One critic had loved the performance so much that he wrote about it in glowing terms for *The Guardian*.

His second golden period had come in the Nineties, when Quirst had embraced hyperrealism and had done a series of controversial life-size sculptures, whose details invariably wound up becoming the subject of lengthy and exhausting analyses by the high priests of British art criticism. For instance, the sculpture of Monica Lewinski kneeling in front of Bill Clinton: the luminous look that the two were exchanging, Bill's hand on the nape of Monica's neck, the fatherly smile stamped on his face.

Next came the sculptural portrait of the woman on all fours having sex with Hitler and Stalin at the same time, a work that was exhibited in London and New York, prompting vicious debates in both cases, where the realistic depiction of sex organs was more of an issue than the political message of the artwork. Such controversy had ultimately consecrated him as one of the most talked-about artists on earth, as well as putting an end to his marriage. After posing for the statue of the woman on all fours, Nathan's wife got sick of seeing herself depicted on the covers of dozens of art magazines with the penis of the worst dictator in history in her mouth.

At that point, Nathan Quirst moved to New York, where he relished his fame and began selling artworks at outrageous prices, taking advantage of the skyrocketing art market in the first years of the new millennium. He had done a few portraits of superheroes, like the one of Captain America pissing into his overturned shield, or the one of Batman flashing his pectorals, and it was this last portrait that won him yet another golden moment because of the publicity that came with the infamous murder. In fact, Batman apparently had shown the provocative artwork to the murderess just minutes before she killed him.

None of the better known artworks were on display at the exhibition in Chelsea.

On the other hand, a few of his latest creations were there, including *Meet Nathan Quirst*. This was an overpowering photographic installation that occupied an entire wall many yards high: dozens of giant prints of close-ups of girls, side by side, forming an enormous mosaic of faces. It appeared that in the New York years following his divorce, Quirst had photographed every girl he'd had sex with, taking each picture just as the girl attained orgasm. The result was a mosaic of orgasms. Intense, contracted expressions, expressions of abandonment, eyes closed or wide open, screaming mouths or lips barely parted.

But what was particularly striking about the artwork was the variety of girls. Quirst seemed to have a preference for dazzling ethnic diversity. He'd photographed girls of every imaginable or unimaginable race. Asian girls, white girls, black girls, Hispanic girls, Native American girls, girls who looked like they were European, Slavic, Russian, black girls with green eyes, girls with Asian features and freckles, girls who seemed to be the product of indeterminate mixes, girls who seemed to have the chromosomes of every possible people, and girls who were simply of indefinable origins. Possibly Martian.

Standing before the artwork, Mystique contemplated that assortment of faces as if she were in the presence of a minor revelation. She felt a little shocked. She couldn't deny feeling amused as well, that kind of guilty amusement that artists like Nathan Quirst, in all their deplorable taste, seemed to know how to inspire. Artists who were evil geniuses. Artists who were sly and spectacular. Who knew how to transform every aspect of reality into a crude, exciting, morbid object to put on display.

And last of all, she felt embarrassed. Her embarrassment had little to do with the piece of art in front of her, and much to do with the man standing at her side. Dennis De Villa. After running into each other, they had exchanged a few standard convivialities, both feigning surprise at their meeting, even though it was obvious there was nothing surprising about it. *Deep inside, I knew I'd run into him here. And I bet he knew it too.*

After the formal exchanges, they remained in silence staring at the mosaic of faces and orgasms. The awkwardness between them was a dense, sticky layer, an awkwardness that kept them divided and united at the same time, paralysed under the peach-coloured neon light.

Then the artist plummeted into their midst.

Nathan Quirst was dressed in vintage safari garb, in a beige collarless safari jacket and with a pith helmet on his head. He trailed an entourage of journalists and admirers behind him, and held a small glass of cherry vodka in his hand. "Darling," he said to Mystique in a confidential tone, although they had barely met more than once. "So happy to see you. They say that you never show up anywhere. Aren't you drinking anything? We have a first-class bar," he declared, pointing to the far end of the room.

The people in his entourage started sniggering, perhaps expecting some instant witty retort from her. The peach-coloured light was spreading over their faces, over their fashionable haircuts, their posing stances, their clothes and exquisite shoes, conferring a dainty, caramelised nuance on every detail. Rock music poured from one of the interior rooms. For an instant, Mystique perceived this scene as if it were footage for a movie, footage that one day other human beings would examine, centuries later, millennia later, in an attempt to understand the remote, paradoxical inebriation of western life.

Quirst was speaking to De Villa. He narrowed his penetrating eyes and placed one hand on his forehead as though to concentrate: "Have we met? I have the impression... You're that detective! You're investigating Batman's murder! Franklin Richards' murder! Now I remember. Now I remember," he kept saying, his hand still pressed to his forehead, shooting a lightning glance from De Villa to Mystique and back again.

She stiffened. She could read the conjecture in the eyes of Quirst and his entourage. The enigmatic television hostess and the police detective who specialised in superhero murders. They must assume that she was under his protection, or that they were dating, or perhaps both at the same time. *What a magnificent couple. Who'd have ever thought it?*

Mystique exchanged a look with De Villa, whose baffled smile seemed to express both amusement at the situation and discomfort at being under Quirst's cunning, delighted eyes.

In a way, they had become one of the attractions of the evening, the two of them, along with the artworks on display around them. They had become an artwork themselves, unwillingly, in the sticky atmosphere of Nathan Quirst's exhibition. Mystique squirmed, and flashed a smile of polite reserve: "Congratulations on your exhibition," she said to the artist. "You certainly never do things by halves."

*

At the bar, Dennis De Villa got a couple of glasses of white wine and handed one to her. Although her embarrassment at being in his company had not vanished, Mystique had agreed to head over to the bar with him. She wanted something to drink and making off now wouldn't do any good. *I've already met him. Everyone's already seen the two of us together.*

"Do you like the exhibition?" De Villa asked, as he swirled the ice in his glass so it tinkled. "I find it amusing," she replied, judiciously. She took a sip and savoured the sensation of the sparkling, ice-cold liquid. "You like it?"

"I don't know much about art," he said with a reticent smile. "Most of the artworks on display here just make me feel a little awkward." The detective gave her a look over the rim of his glass, then in turn took a sip.

Mystique watched his throat contract, and imagined the liquid making its way, like a tiny flood, through the internal canals of his body. She went on studying the detective with a blend of curiosity and ostentatious detachment. "Nathan Quirst is a cunning artist," she said, to break the silence. "An artist with a clear idea of where to strike home. I suppose that's his real work. To provoke. To entrap."

"So that's what artists do?" he honed in.

"I don't know what artists do." She paused, satisfied with the sufficiently nonchalant tone she was using: "I suppose Nathan Quirst is good at stimulating the system. He knows how to touch the right spots."

"Oh," said the detective, with an almost imperceptible start. He frowned and stared at Nathan Quirst, standing some yards away, busy with other guests. "That man's eyes… They drill into you. He looked at me like he was X-raying me."

Mystique couldn't restrain a smile: "I doubt that something so trivial would scare you." She tossed her hair, slightly, uncertain exactly what they were doing right then, in that place, near the bar of an exclusive art opening in Chelsea, as people milled around them: idle chit-chat, exchanges of opinions, provoking each other or who knows what else. "Nathan Quirst looks at everybody that way. Maybe he was considering using you as a model. Maybe Quirst wants to do a portrait of you."

De Villa seemed to take her seriously, widening his eyes in alarm. "Oh no. I really doubt that."

Mystique gave him a sidelong glance, doing her level best to conceal a curiosity that perhaps was not all that different from the curiosity with which Quirst had stared at him. His hair brushed back. The respiration of his broad chest beneath the shirt, the line of his legs revealed by the light material of his trousers. She knew that body. She knew it in detail, she knew it *from within*, even though that was not enough to understand the feelings that his body might house. She realised that she'd stared at De Villa for too long. She shook herself and went on in a mildly mocking tone: "Are you here on duty? I'd guess you're here to protect the superheroes who are attending."

"Well," he smiled. "I told you before… I'm always on duty. As for the superheroes, well, we keep an eye on them. And in any case, you know who we're most worried about…"

Mystique felt like asking him to be more specific. Were the police worried about her, or rather was it Dennis De Villa? She held back and swirled the ice in her glass, making it tinkle just as De Villa had done a short while earlier. From where they were standing, they could see at least a couple of old former superheroes. Wolverine was wandering around the room with a bored expression, followed by a pair of bodyguards who looked just as bored, and at the far end of the room was Thor, with his surly face, his long hair with that indeterminate evanescent hue of blond about to turn grey. Old Thor seemed to have downed one or two glasses too many. He was laughing louder than necessary.

Other familiar faces flashed here and there in the crowd filling the gallery, like silvery fish in the water of a lake. Raymond Minetta, the millionaire owner of the notorious George Hotel, was eating pastries at the buffet. On the subject of wealthy and grotesque individuals, who knows, perhaps even Joseph Szepanski was about to put in an appearance. He just might show up. Why shouldn't he? And yet Mystique wasn't sure she wanted to stick around to see.

She drained her glass and felt a sense of intense, gloomy out-of-placeness. A sound of applause was coming from one of the other rooms of the exhibition. The photographers' cameras flashed here and there, in silence, suddenly, reminiscent of the explosion of microscopic stars. "I'm sorry?" she said to De Villa, who had asked her a question in the meantime.

The detective too drained his glass. "That guy," he repeated. "Why does he make such a fool of himself?"

He was talking about Raymond Minetta. The man was sampling his pastries with a succession of ambiguous grimaces, apparently winces of pain, indifferent to the looks of amusement around him. That old story. The cilice or whatever other ball-crushing instrument Minetta was wearing under his elegant trousers. People had been whispering about it for years. The millionaire swallowed a pastry and emitted a throttled moan, almost a spasm, as he clamped his legs together. Someone broke into unrestrained laughter. Mystique knew of an alternate hypothesis, which she'd heard from the well-informed Chad, according to which Minetta wasn't walking around wearing an instrument of penitence under his trousers, but rather one of those pairs of rubber underpants that featured an internal dildo. A dildo up his ass. An instrument of perpetual sexual delight. According to this version, Minetta wasn't suffering at all, his recurrent moans were ecstatic sighs, and he was enjoying the last laugh on those who believed the opposite.

Whatever the truth of the matter, it wasn't the kind of truth she was interested in pursuing. She continued to feel remote. *This is why going out bores me. There are so few things in the world any more that are worth pursuing the truth about.*

The scene around her now seemed to waver, as if it were painted on wind-tossed canvas, a scene of scandalous artworks and drunken superheroes and millionaires eating pastries and people doing nothing but applauding or laughing. She and De Villa wound up looking at each other. Something seemed to spark between them, and they stood there squinting, as though this was the first time they were seeing one another, as though they were trying to recognise each other, like a pair of strangers meeting, for some bizarre reason, in somebody else's dream.

*

Outside the gallery, the afternoon had vanished. The street was immersed in the hues of a rust-red sunset. A slow procession of taxis was dropping off people coming to the opening and picking up those who had decided to leave. Mystique and De Villa moved away from that bustle, walking down the street, rediscovering the reassuring details of the outside world: the light of sunset, the outline of the buildings, the zigzagging line of the fire escapes. A couple of teenagers were playing basketball without too much energy, dribbling lazily on a court squeezed between two apartment buildings.

The breeze was blowing towards them. Mystique figured it was time to leave. Time to catch one of the taxis purring along the street, say a gracious goodnight, and go back to the comfortable solitude of home. She couldn't see any other possible moves. They went on walking slowly, hesitating. Passersby glanced at them, recognising the famous TV comedian, but no one seemed to be interested in pestering them.

De Villa cleared his throat and took on the serious and thoughtful tone that, Mystique had learned by now, heralded a question of some kind. "I was wondering how you feel in situations like this one. Situations where there are other ex-superheroes. I know that you don't think of yourself as an ex-superhero, but I mean…"

"I understand what you mean," Mystique broke in. She decided once again that it was time to leave. Their shoes produced a sharp, high-pitched sound, as if they were walking over a pile of broken glass. "Seeing ex-superheroes doesn't make me feel any special way. Tired, maybe. Annoyed, perhaps…"

She shook her head and thought it over again: "No, it really doesn't make me feel anything at all."

"Superheroes," he went on. "Superpowers. When I was a boy I wondered whether I might have them myself. But it wouldn't have made sense. I wouldn't have known what to do with them."

"That sounds a little drastic to me," Mystique pointed out. "Even if I guess you might be right. There are lots of people nowadays who have superpowers, but nobody seems to be putting them to good use." She stopped to reflect, and then added: "Why did you wonder whether you had superpowers when you were a boy?"

The detective shrugged without answering. "You guys from the old guard," he said instead. "You're the ones I'm curious about. You used your superpowers to fight and to save your lives. You thought you were using your superpowers *seriously.*"

Mystique hadn't expected the conversation to take that twist. "That's ancient history. If you're asking me what the old heroes feel when they think back to those days, I couldn't tell you. Nostalgia. Remorse. A sense of lightness. A sense of oblivion."

They'd walked a fair distance from the gallery. Just a few yards further, the sidewalk ended at Twelfth Avenue, and past that there was nothing but the banks of the Hudson.

"Remorse?" asked De Villa, with an attentive voice.

"A lot of things didn't work out the way they were supposed to. A lot of disappointment. A lot of broken promises. That's obvious." Mystique stopped short and tried to put an end to the subject: "We're really talking about a long time ago."

De Villa seemed determined to make it to the riverbank. He stopped at the side of the busy avenue and replied: "And yet the ex-superheroes still mean something. They're all that remains of an important time. They still cast shadows over the world. You have to admit that."

"Maybe so," Mystique conceded, and guessing what he was driving at, she added: "Otherwise, there wouldn't be fanatics going to all the trouble of rubbing them out, would there?"

"Then you admit you're in danger."

"I don't admit anything. I wasn't a super*hero*," she reiterated, well aware of the weakness of her argument.

"Oh, cut it out. You know perfectly well that looking back nowadays, years later, that kind of distinction doesn't matter any more." They had crossed the avenue and were contemplating the smooth-flowing waters of the river. "It was just a matter of viewpoints. You were all part of the same wave. Both you and the superheroes used your superpowers to pursue your ideas of a world of greater freedom. Too bad no one managed to achieve those ideas. Too bad that those ideas were so fragile."

Mystique shivered. It could have been the result of the detective's unexpected words, or the breeze that was blowing off the river. The taste of the iced wine she had drunk at the gallery persisted on her tongue. On the far side of the river, the sun was plunging down behind the tall buildings of New Jersey, majestic and dramatic as a defeated monarch, scattering its reflections over the scenery of the river, details glittering in the dying light: the surface of the water, the infinite interplay of the waves against the shore, the ferry boats scuttling back and forth in the distance, with their cargoes of tourists or commuters or seamen. Everything shone with such intensity. Everything in the last few minutes of the day.

Mystique hugged herself, fingers gripping her arms, and smiled, pointlessly, as she felt the wind rush through her hair. *Me and him on the riverbank. If only we weren't what we are. If only I were younger or less tired. If only those notes didn't exist. If only he weren't a cop with some obsession with superheroes. If only there had never been superheroes, if none of this had ever happened. If only it were just him and me, alone in the world, looking out over the flowing peace of the river.* "I'm going home," she said. "I'm going to get a taxi."

The detective turned gloomy. "I was kidding myself I could invite you to dinner," he confessed. "I know a place I'd like to take you. Authentic soul food. I can assure you you wouldn't regret it, it's a place worth trying."

"I don't doubt it." She tried to find words to explain how she felt, then she gave up and just said: "I don't think it would be a good idea."

"What are you afraid of? Don't worry, I won't try to talk you into accepting police protection," he smiled. "At least I won't tonight."

There was a sound of footsteps behind them. Someone was running straight at them. They both stiffened and turned around, wary and apprehensive. It was one of those suspended, extended moments, capable of containing hundreds of perceptions. The movement with which they both turned. The tension of their bodies. The noise of the traffic, the impassive silence of the river. Actually, though, the person who caught up with them had a peaceful expression on his face. When he realised that he'd alarmed them, he raised both hands reassuringly and smiled: "Sorry to scare you. I had to cross the street at a dead run."

The man was slightly older than De Villa. He had a full head of fine hair just like the detective, a little shorter and already greying. His physique was less athletic than Dennis', but he was the same height, and on the whole, there was an undeniable resemblance between the two men. "I saw you at the exhibition," the man said to the detective. "I just followed you to say hello."

"Bruce," said the detective in astonishment. "You almost gave us a heart attack."

"Sorry I scared you," the other man apologised. There was a pregnant pause. The new arrival seemed to be waiting to be introduced, then he spoke directly to Mystique: "Pleasure to meet you," he said. "My name is Bruce De Villa."

*

It was a short meeting. When Bruce De Villa smiled, his resemblance to the detective was even more marked. The same small and mournful smile. Even the same delicate ears. Only his eyes were different from the detective's. Bruce De Villa's eyes were large, with dark irises in which she realised she could see her reflection, for a few instants, a tiny image of herself in each of them. Two tiny Mystiques shone, over there, as if on the floor of distant oceans.

The improvised trio exchanged standard courtesies.

The two men, who as far as Mystique could tell must be brothers, seemed not to have seen each other in a long time, and neither of them appeared to be at his ease. "Bruce…" began the detective in a flat tone of voice, then he stopped and left his sentence incomplete. He stuck his hands in his pockets and looked off into the distance. "I didn't expect to run into you here."

"In fact," said the other man, with a tone of shared amazement. He scratched his head for a second. "I wondered what had become of you. I haven't seen you in court at the hearings of the Batman trial in a while." Since the detective didn't answer, Bruce De Villa turned to Mystique. "I'm a reporter," he informed her, perhaps to explain the reference to the trial.

Mystique nodded. Under normal circumstances, that information would have annoyed her. After the police, journalists were the category she liked least. She thought that journalists were insatiable creatures, always on the hunt like ravenous ants, always demanding interviews, statements, news, details, exclusives, confessions, and gossip. Especially gossip. But Bruce De Villa's eyes seemed too deep and knowing for all that. The man must certainly know that she was famous, and yet he looked at her quietly, without any form of excited curiosity, if anything with a trace of sadness in his gaze. A strange gaze. *The kind of gaze you would get from someone who knows something about you, maybe something that even you don't know about yourself.*

Then silence fell. The river absorbed the last rays of light. A boat chugged down the river, heading south, leaving a long soft wave behind it. The wave reached a flock of seagulls and they all rose in flight, all together in the reddening sky. Both men now stared at Mystique. Were they hoping that she'd help contribute to the conversation? It really did seem that those two had little to say to each other.

The boat's wave was splashing against the shore, weakly, almost subsiding, causing a faint lapping sound.

By studying the faces and discomfort of the two brothers, it was possible to intuit fragments of their past. A man on his own was an isolated fact, two brothers already told a story. As far as Mystique could tell, the distance between them wasn't the kind that exists between two people divided by quarrels or who knows what unpleasantness, but rather a curtain of dull, age-old pain. Perhaps they shared some grim memory from their past. A family break-up or something of the sort? She wouldn't have sworn that this was the right guess, but for that matter she wasn't too interested in probing into the details. It was none of her business.

To tell the truth, she would have settled for reaching out and running her fingers over the detective's face. She went back to focusing on Dennis De Villa. She realised she was seeing him with new eyes. That man was no little boy, he certainly had no need of consolation, and yet that's what she yearned to do: brush her fingers across his face, caress him with languid gentleness, right then, right there on the riverbank.

It was a revelation. She really wanted to reach out and do it, and that impulse forced her to come to terms with the fact that the man was becoming minute by minute more alive, more real before her eyes.

*

The restaurant was on a cross street with Lenox Avenue, in Harlem, and consisted of a tiny room with a couple of fans, small red plastic tables and a sumptuous counter behind which an elderly cook worked away, with the calm of a samurai, never lifting her eyes.

A younger woman who, to judge by appearances, must have been the cook's daughter, placed a handwritten menu before them.

"I just love this place," said Dennis De Villa. "The honey-fried chicken is the best. The fried chicken salad isn't bad either. Yes, I guess you might go for the salad. Save room for dessert."

It was a nice restaurant. The aromas coming from the galley kitchen behind the counter seemed wholesome and appetising. A small stereo played instrumental ballads. On the wall, an array of photographs depicted the two women who owned the place posing with a variety of guests, presumably customers of a certain stature, or maybe just very loyal ones. The clientele seated at the tables appeared to be locals, and the family atmosphere was without doubt more relaxed than the feeling at the gallery opening. All the same, Mystique wondered if she'd been right to come. To let herself be dragged here. On a Saturday night. Out for dinner with an attractive man with a pleasant way about him, even though he had the shortcoming of being a cop. It had been a long time since anything of the sort had happened to her.

"What were you thinking about?" he questioned her.

"Nothing." Mystique sat up straight in her chair and put on a confident attitude. "I was thinking about the menu. About what to order. About your brother..." She waited a beat and then confessed: "A little while ago, on the riverbank... It was a strange sensation to see the two of you side by side."

"It was? Were we such an odd spectacle?" he asked with aplomb.

"Of course not. That's not what I meant." Mystique decided she'd better not push it, better not ask questions, well aware that any effort she might make to get to know the man sitting across from her any better was likely to have the effect of an equal effort on his part. "What I'm trying to say..." she let slip. "Until now I'd never thought much about your life. Family, childhood, that kind of thing."

"Oh," he murmured. He gave her a sly smile and observed: "So you're saying you want to know about me."

Mystique went back to studying the menu. The stream of air from the standing fans hit her at regular intervals. The music from the stereo seemed to have been composed so that someone could get to their feet, at that very moment, and burst into song like in the middle of a musical. "Maybe so," she admitted. "You know, lots of times people accuse me of being too reserved. But I'm getting the impression that you're even more reserved than I am."

"I'm afraid I don't have a very interesting life story to tell," the detective began. Now it was his turn to keep his eyes on the menu. He looked up and started to summarise: "Born and raised in New Jersey. Italian family. My brother left home to attend university. Our mother died when I was sixteen." There was a short blackout of the light in his eyes. He waved one hand to attract the attention of the woman who was serving tables, letting her know they were ready to order, and before she arrived he finished his story: "Our father died a few years later. Joined the police when I was twenty-one. A few years in uniform before I was promoted to detective, and I'm afraid that's pretty much it. Try the fried-chicken salad. I'm glad to be here with you. Save some room for dessert."

Mystique crossed her arms on the table, vaguely stunned, staring at the menu as if it were an ancient manuscript. A man had just summarised the most important events of his life and she wasn't sure what she felt about it. Was she moved? Did she want to know more? Did she feel guilty about being nosy? "I don't think I'll be able to try the dessert," was all she said.

Dinner went on in an agreeable atmosphere.

The food that the elderly cook made for them lived up to De Villa's enthusiasm. They talked as they ate, at an even, cautious pace, avoiding overly demanding topics, sometimes with stretches of silence, like two dignitaries representing foreign countries, speaking through the filter of slow and elaborate translations.

Mystique took turns observing the man and the scene around them. The little restaurant was packed. Except for her and De Villa, the only non-African-Americans were a white family sitting at the far side of the room. Mystique stared at the family and the two blond children, peaceful-looking as they happily ate their fried chicken. Blond children in Harlem. It wasn't hard to guess what that meant. Blond children meant safe streets. Blond children meant stability, white families moving in from neighbourhoods to the south, plans for regenerating the neighbourhood, buildings renovated by famous architects, rents doubling or even tripling, old tenants evicted or unable to afford the new rents. Two peaceful, innocent blond children, busy eating their fried chicken.

"You keep excluding me from your thoughts," De Villa complained.

"I'm sorry. I was just thinking about this neighbourhood," she offered. She wondered whether the police officer would be scandalised to learn that a few days ago she had been a few blocks away, renewing her supply of marijuana. Sabrina… She thought of her old friend and her place with its high ceilings only a few streets over. She was worried that Sabrina, too, was having problems paying her rent. She thought of her and her light-coloured dresses, her kitchen with the mugs stolen from Starbucks, her piping hot tea and her placid ways.

In the meantime, De Villa had noticed the curious stares that a few other diners were directing at Mystique. "It looks like you're well known here too."

She realised what he was talking about and nodded without enthusiasm. "They're not really curious about me," she said. "All they want is to see me transform myself from one moment to the next into who-knows-who. They're curious about who I might become."

"Is that what you think?" The detective seemed unconvinced. "I think that the real target of their interest is you. I mean, you, for who you are." He set his fork down on his plate and summed up: "Excellent food. I hope you enjoyed it."

"Maybe you're hoping for the chance to see me transform myself too," Mystique went on, with a sudden urge to provoke him.

"What are you talking about?"

"Why don't you tell me," she smiled. "Who do you want me to turn into? I could go into the toilets and come back out, oh, I don't know, looking exactly like Scarlett Johansson. Would you like to be eating dinner with Scarlett Johansson?"

"Don't joke about it," he said, furrowing his brow. He seized the edge of the table with both hands and added: "I don't care about Scarlett Johansson. I just want to sit here with you."

Mystique didn't press the point. She managed to put on another smile and pretended not to notice the heartfelt tone in the man's voice. She lifted her glass and took a sip, her lips pressing against the transparent rim, while every detail around her seemed to become more vivid: the golden heads of the blond children of Harlem, the melody of the music pouring out of the stereo, the refreshing stream of air from the fans.

Dinner was over. The cook's daughter came to take away the empty plates. A little later she came back with two helpings of vanilla cheesecake and said they were on the house. *Complimentary, for our famous guest.*

"See? They recognised you," De Villa pointed out.

"It looks good," Mystique mused. The slice of cake in front of her appeared massive and emanated a fresh, creamy aroma. The very quintessence of perfect cheesecake.

"Come on!" De Villa encouraged her. "Rose's vanilla cheesecake is renowned. I told you to save room for dessert."

"I can't eat sweets. Of course, I also can't let such a lovely gift go to waste. That means you'll have to eat my slice as well."

"That won't be a hardship for me. But you don't know what you're missing," said De Villa as he gulped down a spoonful. He savoured that cool delight, shook his head, and smiled: "I remember when I came to see you in the studio cafeteria. You were eating a miserable salad and you said something about being on a diet. You got mad when I asked if that was all you were having for lunch."

"I remember," she breathed, with the impression of uncovering a long-ago memory.

"I also remember that you had a hard time speaking," De Villa went on in amusement, swallowing another spoonful. "You were doing your best not to laugh. Your colleagues were making fun of me, acting out ridiculous sketches behind my back."

Mystique's eyes widened. "You mean that you noticed? My God. You must have thought we were a gang of idiots."

He shook his head again. The creamy cheesecake had made his lips shiny. "I thought it was funny," he said, and started to laugh.

The man's gentle laughter. His lips, smeared with that moist, sugary trace of cheesecake… "True," she admitted uneasily. "It was a pretty funny scene."

In the meantime, the restaurant was starting to empty out. The white family had finished their meal, leaving behind on the table a still life of dirty plates, half-full glasses of Coke, and chicken bones. An air of languid exhaustion now reigned over the room. The exhaustion of satiated bodies, of meals consumed. Mystique sank back in her chair, weary after the long day, remembering the impulse she'd experienced a couple of hours ago, in the light of sunset at the river's edge. The impulse to brush her fingers across that man's face. That man, with his sensitive and inflamed eyes, with his manner, so gentle and yet, constantly, so tenacious and in some way distant.

Before they left, the cook and her daughter came to have their picture taken with her. The elderly Rose slid out from behind the counter and sat down beside her, while her daughter sat on the other side of Mystique. The detective took the camera and set up the shot. Mystique smiled into the camera, with her bluish skin, sitting between two black women, mother and daughter, two generations of authentic Harlemites. She went on smiling as she waited for the click of the shutter, unsure of exactly who she was smiling at, whether it was the camera or the detective, or the people who would look in the years to come at a framed photograph hanging on a restaurant wall.

*

The following morning she woke up pretty late. The alarm clock on the bedside table informed her that it was almost eight o'clock, and daylight filled the window, urgent, like the glare from some off-white bonfire. Mystique blinked. It was Sunday, no need to get up right away, though lazing around in bed was hardly her style. She rolled over with a faint dizziness. Her lips were dry. Even though she hadn't worked the day before, her limbs were numb.

She rolled over again and stared, bedazzled, at the ceiling, while her memories of the previous evening reassembled in her mind. The gallery opening. The sunset over the river. The encounter with the detective's brother, the reporter Bruce De Villa, his eyes inhabited, it seemed, by some mysterious knowledge. And then the restaurant in Harlem. The creamy smell of a vanilla cheesecake. Her picture taken with the two women in the restaurant…

The night out came to an end when the detective took her home. Once they pulled up they sat in the car, and there was an endless moment when they looked at each other in the low light of the street, each of them doubtful about the other's intentions. He had turned off the engine and then started it again, uncertain, only to turn it off again. They sat there. They sat in silence and swallowed, both of them, as if in a coded dialogue between their two throats. Mystique gave a short embarrassed laugh. She thanked him for dinner, and as she opened the car door the dome light snapped on, making the detective flinch. She got out of the car without another word and walked into her apartment, where she leaned back against the door and breathed deeply, roughly, until she heard Dennis De Villa's car start up again and move away.

She should really get out of bed. It was too late to go for a run, but she could do a little yoga indoors and make a cup of tea, and rehearse for the next episode of the show. She remained lying there, continuing to feel that weird dizziness. She guessed she hadn't been ready, last night, to invite Dennis De Villa upstairs. She wondered when she ever would be. It might not be long. In fact, she was pretty sure it would happen soon.

She twisted on the bed, feeling herself sweat and shiver, instinctively reaching up to touch her forehead. She didn't think she had a fever. The cotton sheet weighed heavily on her. She kicked it away and then pulled it back and just lay watching the curtains bellying in the warm breeze coming through the window.

She remembered that many years ago, when she was a girl first experimenting with her superpowers, every attempt to transform herself made her fall, straight afterwards, into a furious and debilitating fever. How old could she have been? Sixteen, maybe seventeen. Before going off to college, before discovering politics, before everything happened. She tried to take on the body of a girlfriend, or the body of a boy she liked or a teacher who fascinated her, and the next morning she'd wake up with her skin on fire. It had happened many times. When she was sixteen or seventeen, every attempt to use her powers inevitably ended with cool washcloths on her forehead, mercury thermometers, and Tylenol tablets.

There was almost no traffic noise coming from outside. It was Sunday and the city must have emptied out, in a mass migration towards Long Island or who knows where else. The city, too, had its fever, an intimate fever that possessed the bodies, driving them to flee or to cluster in the parks. She got up and sat on the edge of the bed. She decided that she was not a bit sick after all. No fever. She was no longer a girl, and what's more, she hadn't used her superpowers last night. All she'd done last night was go to dinner with a man. A man who was too young, *too much of a cop*, with eyes that were too red, a man with an Italian surname, with some strange family history in his past, a man who seemed to have no reason to become part of her life, and yet was doing so.

She clutched at the cotton sheet. Sitting on the side of her bed, she felt like she was teetering on the edge of a shining cliff. When she was a girl, her superpowers stirred some kind of fire inside her, an arcane and destructive and redeeming fire. It had taken time to learn to master that flame, to stop being burned by it. She'd learned to do it, though. She'd mastered it. *Now, will I be able to master what I feel in the morning air, after going out to dinner with that man?*

*

It was Monday, about noon, the hour when the sun rises to its zenith, the time of day when the skyscrapers merge with their shadows. The vertical shafts of sunlight poured down, striking the roofs and penetrating into the soil. Underground, the subway tunnels were scalding corridors, and passengers waiting for their trains dripped sweat, as they stood on the platforms, before leaping with a shiver into the chilly carriages.

The air was steaming in Astoria, too. A fluid heat was pooling in the streets, held in by the fronts of the buildings, while a police or fire department helicopter flew over the area, as if trying to cast a protective shadow over the apartment buildings. From the windows of the television studios, people looked out at the cityscape, immersed in the harsh, brutal light.

In the show's production office, Chad had been gasping at his desk all morning, despite the fact that the air conditioning was doing its best, complaining that he felt oppressed by the *sheer thought* of the heat outside. He had constructed an oversized fan with a sheet of cardboard and had been waving it in front of his face for at least two hours now. None of the others seemed very active either. Horace was typing at his computer's keyboard with the unmistakable air of someone who had been rewriting the same sentence for hours, while Susie didn't seem to have anything better to do than constantly offer everyone iced tea from a baby-blue thermos.

Mystique could sense how weary they were from the pressure they'd been under lately. She was tired herself, and the idea of transforming once again, by now, stirred nothing inside her but a sense of grim exhaustion. Still, she couldn't quit. None of them could. Tomorrow night, they'd be on air again, and they all knew how important that broadcast would be.

She was about to administer a scolding to her colleagues when, around noon, the news hit the studio.

The trial for Batman's murder was over. After months and months of hearings, the verdict had come in without warning, in the stunned heat of what was almost summer. In the aftermath of the death of Franklin Richards, the Batman case had been shoved out of the spotlight and the trial had slid halfway out of the public's memory, in contrast to the media hysteria that had churned around it at the beginning. The public liked to focus on one murder at a time. That was why the verdict came as such a surprise, shaking up the day's sleepy news reports.

Mystique and the others listened to a report on CNN. The young defendant, Mara Jones, had been found guilty of murder, with the aggravating factors of its savagery and the defendant's refusal, or inability, to tell the court who was behind the murder. During months of hearings, no information whatever had emerged about other members or possible leaders of the notorious group, the same one that later organised the attack on the George Hotel. The group that still, as the news report put it, *threatens the historic members of the community of former superheroes.*

The report went on with more details. Apparently, when the verdict was read the defendant's father had suffered a heart attack. While the courtroom was in an uproar as medical assistance was given to her father, the young Ms. Jones had maintained an otherworldly calm, impassive before the television cameras that filmed her expressionless lips, the solemn void in her grey eyes. Even though she must now expect a sentence of life imprisonment without parole, her face betrayed no feelings.

That scene gave shivers to Mystique, reminiscent of her sensations during her own trial, more than twenty years ago. She couldn't remember exactly what she'd felt when the verdict had been read. But she doubted that she'd kept the same inhuman calm as Mara Jones.

On the screen, the last image of the CNN report showed the guilty woman as she was led away by her guards: pale, androgynous, beautiful, telegenic, remorseless, unshaken, an enigmatic killer, a young sphinx. A perfect representative of the modern-day conspiracy industry. You could have studied that girl until the end of time without being able to figure out why she had allowed someone, whoever it was, to talk her into doing what she had done: was it out of gullibility, boredom, fanaticism, or just a clear-eyed belief, a conviction that an ageing superhero deserved to be murdered, whatever the price, to the point of literally ripping his bowels apart.

Meanwhile, Horace and Chad had started firing off idiotic jokes. The whole Mara Jones story was too rich a vein for them, and they were determined to get out of it every double-entendre and ironic wrinkle they could. "Such a cute young woman," Horace jested, with an allusive wink.

"So cute."

"I wonder if she'll be able *to keep her hands to herself* when she's in prison," Horace added with a snort.

"I heard they're going to make her wear a baseball glove 24-7," Chad snorted in turn. He went on fanning himself with his sheet of cardboard. "Otherwise, who can say what she'll *get her hands into.*"

"Guys. You're really not funny," Mystique admonished them.

Susie didn't get the jokes. "A baseball glove? What does that mean?" she chirped in an annoying manner. Then she turned to Mystique: "Do you want some iced tea?"

"I don't want any iced tea," she snapped, a growing wave of annoyance sweeping through her. "I want you all to get back to work. Tomorrow night we're on air."

She turned off the television as the news report moved to a series of interviews with acquaintances of Mara Jones, for the most part fellow university students and professors, asking for their comments on the verdict. The silence once the TV was turned off caused a lurching hole in Mystique's stomach. She realised that she felt sad about Mara Jones. She felt sad about the fact that she was a young woman, that she would spend her life in prison, that her former friends were giving stupid interviews to CNN. She felt sad even though Mara Jones was a murderer.

"Hey!" Chad objected. "You could have left it on, you know. We wanted to watch."

She felt sad because Mara Jones was moving off the stage, because she would be locked up forever in the twilit, gloomy interior of a prison, and that would do nothing to cast any light or bring any understanding to the outside world. What good was any of this? The trial was over and nothing had been solved. Whoever persuaded the girl to commit murder remained out of the picture, unseen, sufficiently elusive to avoid involvement, still anonymous, someone who remained on the loose, free to get rid of the next victim. Chad and the others kept wasting time. Mystique shot a grim glare at her colleagues, drunk on iced tea and trading jokes about Mara Jones' hands, jokes that Susie either failed to understand or pretended not to get. She stood watching them, disconcerted and distant, almost having difficulty recognising them and remembering what those people had to do with her life.

Her body had begun vibrating. Not really trembling, but *vibrating*. She knew she could no longer ignore the matter: did Batman's death have anything to do with her? Should she finally consider the possibility that she was the next intended victim? And what the hell could she do if she was? Take on the body of one of Mara Jones' lawyers and go to visit her in prison, in an attempt to get some information out of her?

She doubted whether she'd be capable of undertaking such a mission. Showing up in a maximum security prison disguised as a lawyer: the kind of exploit she would once have pulled off without a second thought. But now? *Now I think the most I could do is put together a TV show. That is, if my colleagues decide to lift a finger.*

When Susie walked over to ask if she wanted yet another glass of her iced tea, she felt the corrosive taste of fury gathering in her throat. It happened unexpectedly. It was impossible to control herself. She pretended to accept the glass of tea and then slowly and deliberately tipped it over, pouring the contents onto the floor. "Would you do me the favour of sparing me your damned tea?" she hissed. "Would you do me the favour of sitting down at your desk and getting back to work? Would you all please lend me a hand in putting this show together, since that's what you're paid to do?"

A chill of amazement descended over the room. The only sound was the hum of the air conditioning.

Even though it hadn't been Mystique's intention, most of the tea had splattered onto Susie's shoes. First the girl gaped at her wet shoes and at the floor, long splatters of iced jasmine tea on the ceramic tiles, then she turned red and lowered her head and walked back to her desk in tears.

Mystique's rage abandoned her like a mischievous spirit. She stared wide-eyed at what she had done. She beat a hasty retreat to her office, where she rested her head in her hands, feeling the veins throb in her temples. *I can't believe it. What's going on? What on earth was I thinking, why would I humiliate that poor girl?*

A few minutes later, Chad came in and sat down across from her. "Ahem... I have the impression that you've gravely hurt the soul of one of your colleagues. To say nothing of having ruined her shoes."

"I know. I'm sorry. I'll buy her a new pair of shoes of course."

"You don't have to tell me you're sorry. You have to tell her." Chad heaved a sigh. "If there's anything you could tell me, it might be what the hell's come over you."

Mystique brushed a lock of hair out of her face. "The broadcast, Chad. We have talked and talked about how important this broadcast is going to be, remember? Horace hasn't revised the one-liners yet, Susie was supposed to give me the details on the dress rehearsals an hour ago, and you told me you were going to head downstairs to the studio to talk with the director about the dance shots."

Chad knit his fingers together, both hands in his lap, a dubious expression on his chubby face. "Are you sure the problem is about that? You sure it's not something else?"

She took a deep breath. She held the air in for a few moments before exhaling with painful slowness. "I'm sure," she lied. "You spent the whole morning wasting time."

Chad dropped his usual cheerful expression, scowling at her. "That's not fair and you know it. You know this is the way we work. We pretend to be goofing around, we act like idiots, and we say all kinds of stupid things. There's nothing new about that, is there? It's what we do to keep from getting overtaken by panic before a challenging broadcast, and it's the way we manage to come up with the brilliant concepts that you usually like so much. We're as worried about the show as you are. And you know it. I still can't figure out what's come over you." He stood up with the gravitas of an indignant monarch, turned to leave the room, then came back and tried with a gentler tone: "Are you sure it wasn't the news reports on that trial? Mystique, level with me. Do you have some reason to be concerned?"

She denied it. Denying was simple. Denying was reassuring.

But once she was left alone in her office, she couldn't go on doing it indefinitely. All of a sudden, everything appeared clear to her, almost natural. *So long, my Mystique. Whoever arranged Batman's death has sentenced me to death too.*

She got to her feet, making the legs of her chair screech across the floor. She wandered around the room, thinking back to the first time that Dennis De Villa had waited for her in that same office, sitting across from that same desk, to warn her about the danger that threatened her. She thought back to the first time they shook hands. She thought back to the way she'd tried to bring their conversation to an abrupt end, to the irritation she'd felt at the sight of his small, enchanting smile, the enigmatic manner of a poker player in the way the detective had looked at her.

"Dennis De Villa," she uttered under her breath, brushing her fingers over the chair where he'd been sitting not two weeks ago. "Dennis De Villa," she repeated, running her fingers over the surface of the table. "Dennis De Villa," "Dennis De Villa," "Dennis De Villa," she went on saying under her breath, touching the keyboard of her computer and the desk lamp and the other objects in the office, as if she were rechristening them, overwhelmed by the intense, ambiguous resonance that the name was assuming inside her.

*

That evening, she turned herself into Chad and went to Harlem to see Sabrina. She didn't need to buy any more grass, but she found another reason to drop by. Mystique-Chad rang at the green door, waited, and when the woman came to the door she handed her a small gift wrapped in a paper bag.

"For me? What is it?" Sabrina asked. As usual she was wearing a white dress and her feet were bare on the floor of the doorway.

"For your collection."

Sabrina pulled the object out of the bag and chuckled. It was of course a Starbucks mug. "How considerate, young man. Come on in. Let's put this mug right to use."

They walked through the high-ceilinged apartment to the kitchen, where Sabrina rinsed the new mug and filled it, along with another from her collection, with a fruit juice she had pulled out of the fridge.

Mystique-Chad accepted the juice, relieved that this time she wasn't offered tea. She definitely wasn't in the mood for tea.

The atmosphere was different from the rainy one of her last visit. The smells of early summer hovered in the air. Through the window screens wafted the smells of grilling in neighbouring backyards or on the sidewalks, the smell of meat over hot coals and toasting bread, roasted corn, toasted marshmallows, and blanketing all those smells the acrid smoke of charcoal sprayed with lighter fluid. It was getting dark. Sabrina switched on a light over the kitchen counter and gazed at her guest, smiling, narrowing her long-lashed eyes. "So you've come to see me."

"That's right." Mystique-Chad took a sip. The juice was dense and orange-coloured.

"That was nice of you, young man. When I saw you at the door I wondered why you'd come back so soon. I knew you couldn't need more grass already." She waved her mug in the air, as though suggesting a toast, and said again, in a courteous yet sceptical tone: "And so you've come to see me."

"Actually," Mystique-Chad explained at that point, "let's say that I've come to say goodbye." She could smell the aroma of the fruit juice on her own breath, maybe mango or peach or apricot or perhaps a blend of the three. Her breath. Chad's breath. An unexpected thought struck her. She realised that if she died, she'd no longer be able to transform herself into Chad or anyone else, an obvious thought that still managed to prompt in her a stab of vivid astonishment.

"What do you mean you've come to say goodbye?" she asked. She narrowed her eyes further and a glint of regret flashed across her face. "You won't be coming back? You're leaving?"

"No. I don't know. I just wanted to say goodbye." She leaned the large body she had taken on against the kitchen wall, avoiding the woman's gaze and the temptation to tell her the truth. *It's me, can't you see? It's me, your old friend.* She wished she could reveal who she was. She wished she could say how she felt. She wished she could explain that this might be a real farewell, a final one, *and in fact I have a feeling that it is. I have the sensation that the circle is tightening around me.* She said nothing and stood there, in Chad's large body, next to the screened-in window.

They remained motionless, breathing, on either side of the kitchen, face to face, a woman dressed in white and what looked to be a young male, the light breathing of one, the heavy breathing of the other. Noises penetrated from outside. A dog barked in a backyard somewhere. The echo of a car engine coughing in the distance. A bug buzzed insistently against the window screen, determined to get inside the mysterious, forbidden realm of that kitchen.

From a neighbour's house, the sound of a television reached them in waves. Mystique-Chad listened. She recognised the theme music of a news programme and a rebroadcast of the report she'd seen that day on the verdict in the Batman murder trial. She set down her mug on the kitchen counter. "I think it's time for me to go."

Sabrina was even more confused. "Already? This is one of the shortest visits I've ever received. Are you sure you feel all right?"

"I feel all right." After Sabrina had walked Mystique-Chad to the front door, she headed off down the street.

The red-brick buildings stood, one alongside another, with their large windows reflecting the light of evening. The aroma of barbecues still hung around, mixed now with a scent of water-sprinkled dust, the smell of hot asphalt sprayed with water that might come, perhaps, from a fire hydrant on some nearby street.

Mystique-Chad slipped away. She felt upset and yet glad after that visit. Whatever might be about to happen, she was glad she'd said goodbye to her old friend, although in disguise. She turned the corner without looking back.

If she had, she would have seen Sabrina standing in her doorway, just like the other time. She would have seen the woman standing stiffly, hands at her sides, almost to attention, with her short hair and her bare feet.

Sabrina hadn't understood what was happening. It all struck her as rather strange. She had however understood that the person who was walking away before her eyes had for some reason said farewell to her. The breeze was tossing the hem of her dress. The air was damp and the cloak of evening was settling over the neighbourhood. Sabrina knew well who the person that had just come to see her was; she'd figured it out long ago, from the very first time. For six years, that person had shown up every so often at her place. Now, after the person turned the corner at the far end of the street, Sabrina's lips whispered a farewell in return. *Good luck, girlfriend. Good luck, Mystique.*

*

The day of the last show, she left home at dawn and started running, as usual. In the still-empty streets her footfalls and her breathing echoed like the notes of an austere musical march. When she turned onto the trail through the park the birds seemed to fall silent. A couple of squirrels on the grass raised their heads, caught off guard, tails curling in mid-air. The rustling of trees dominated everything. Mystique cut west, returning to the street, moved past the façade of the great and silent cathedral, and continued in the same direction, running past the best known independent book store in the area. She passed a boy skateboarding from the opposite direction. At that hour of the morning! Each of them started at the sight of the other as if they'd just seen an outlandish ghost.

She went on running. On her skin, thousands of microscopic glands were opening, like so many microscopic flowers, emitting transparent tears. She ran a hand over her perspiring face.

In there, inside the houses, up in the apartment buildings, protected by the breath of the air conditioning, people were clinging to their last hour of sleep, before the buzzer of an alarm clock forced them to open their eyes, yet again, to behold the strangest and densest dream of all. The world. The world! Daylight was rising and flooding the streets while a couple of bakeries were already opening their doors for business. Mystique ran along a stretch of Broadway before heading homewards again.

She threw herself under the spray of the shower, still thinking about those who were waking up in the buildings of the city. All those who were emerging from their tangled sheets, draping freshly laundered clothes over themselves, all those who were having sex to inaugurate the day, all those who were receiving the benediction of a shower over their bodies, like she was now. All those who were preparing themselves to face the hours of the coming day and who perhaps, that evening, exhausted and satisfied or else bitterly disappointed, might sit down in front of their television and watch her show. She thought of all those anonymous and faceless people and felt a stab of undefined love for them.

After her shower she ate breakfast and listened to the news on the radio and then rehearsed a few dance steps for the show, in the kitchen, as though the radio news was some wild song. She stopped and felt a sudden urge to cry and wondered whether she was losing her mind.

She wondered what the people out there wanted from their lives. She wondered what she had ever wanted over the course of her own life. There was a time when she believed that she knew what the world wanted, and the conceit of that knowledge had been the one fundamental mistake of her life.

She went into the bathroom to get ready to go out. She grabbed a brush and stroked her hair as the traffic noise outside grew louder. Whatever might be about to happen in her immediate future, she wasn't upset. She wasn't even afraid. A new, overarching, resigned calm had risen in her.

After all, she decided she hadn't lost her mind. Oh no, no question, she was sane. She smiled hopelessly into the mirror. Everything looked more and more clear to her. She had a concrete and lucid suspicion of who her potential murderer might be.

*

Roughly thirty minutes to go. Mystique was in her dressing room trying to focus. Outside the door she could hear the hustle and bustle of extras and dancers moving around, excitedly waiting for the opening bars of the theme music, as well as Susie's anxious squeaks as she tried to keep the situation under control. Mystique mentally reviewed the evening's line-up, mouthed a few of her lines, and finally sprawled on the sofa, devoid of sensation, in the typical void that came each time just before going on air.

Someone knocked at the door.

She sat up, wondering if she really had heard that knock.

At first the door didn't move. Then it swung open and the unsinkable Chad burst into the room. "Hey!" he announced in excitement. He was flaunting one of his usual flaming stage outfits and his head was covered with large rollers. "Gangway, because the way I'm getting gussied up tonight, all eyes will be on me."

Mystique blinked and went on feeling uncertain about what she was perceiving. Not because the scene seemed dreamlike, but rather because, on the contrary, it seemed almost too vivid. She observed the details of the room. Her outfits for the show hung ready, arranged in order of appearance on the clothes rack on one wall, and her shoes were aligned in the same order on the floor. "We're about to go on air again. A new episode of the show," she mused in astonishment: in a way, such a development suddenly struck her as overwhelming.

Chad didn't seem to hear her. He touched his rollers and declared, more surreal and giddy than ever: "When I get this stuff out of my hair, I'll look fantastic. The hairdresser tells me I have just the right hair to be put up in *soft ringlets*. Like a cherub in a Renaissance painting or something like that."

Mystique went on blinking. Chad's face also seemed intensely vivid. She focused on his familiar face and regained, almost inductively, the equally familiar tone that she most often used in conversations with her colleague. "My dear. You and your hairdresser talk about Renaissance paintings?"

"She's studying art history."

"Weren't you supposed to wear a wig for the Madonna sketch?"

"I will. But the rest of the time I'll have my ringlets!"

From the hallway, they heard Horace shout something, followed by a collective burst of laughter. Someone else announced that it was just twenty minutes to the opening theme.

"Listen," Chad said then. "I heard that you apologised to Susie."

Mystique nodded.

"And I heard something else…" Chad stopped touching his hair and put on a serious expression. "The director told me that you've cancelled the Szepanski routine. He says you won't be doing it this time, either."

She got up from the sofa. Once again, she looked around at the dressing room, realised she didn't know which way to turn, and decided to sit back down. "I think that routine is off the line-up for good now," she said. "I can't transform myself into that man. I don't know how to be him. It's as if that man constituted a boundary that I can't touch."

Chad mulled it over and objected: "You know what I think. I think it's a missed opportunity. But all I can do…" He seemed to mull it over again. His eyes grew gentler and a trusting smile appeared on his lips. "All I can do is accept your decision. In any case, it'll be a great episode."

"It will be a great episode," she agreed. She concealed the instinctive turmoil she felt and cracked a wan smile.

"Did you tell Gary about the change of plans?"

"Gary?…" From the way she uttered the name, it was clear she wasn't especially worried, at the moment, about their producer's reaction.

Chad looked startled. He stared at her with a new, concerned interest. But it was late and there was no more time to talk. "I need to go and arrange my *soft ringlets*. See you on stage," he breathed as he headed for the door. Before leaving he turned around, joined his chubby hands and somewhat awkwardly said: "Mystique, I have no idea what's happening to you. But I meant what I said. I accept your decision. I'm with you. I'm still with you."

Mystique was left alone. She pushed her face against the sofa cushion. She got up and fell back and realised that every breath caused her pain. She undressed and took on the first body in the show's schedule and felt the thrill of going onstage as the voice in the hallway announced five minutes to show time. A sort of blackout swept over her and a moment later someone was dragging her out of the dressing room just as the first notes of the theme music echoed throughout the studio. Arnold Schwarzenegger covered the last few yards with trembling steps. As soon as he hit the stage the applause from the audience thundered over him, making him stagger. A blast of unbearable light. Arnold lifted his arms, pumped his biceps, and spoke his first line, setting off an immediate burst of laughter. Chad and the extras spun around him like the gearing of a huge merry-go-round and the audience went on laughing and the lines poured from his lips with miraculous fluency.

There was a commercial break and a sort of blackout again. Mystique found herself in the bathroom, sobbing like a rank beginner in her first production, but she immediately regained control and took on a new body. The show started up again at the most frantic pace it had ever put on. Mystique went from one character to another in something approaching a trance state, whispering her lines to the audience as if they were words of love and dancing and singing with an ultimate and magnificent grace. The spotlights blazed above the stage like flaming meteors. Madonna whirled across the set, surrounded by the bodies of the dancers, a phantasmagoria of lithe gleaming bodies, then she danced a duet with Chad and right in the middle of the routine they looked each other in the eyes and both felt a shiver of heartbreaking perfection run through them.

The last routine came as a complete surprise. The character who appeared onstage wasn't Doctor Szepanski but someone even more shocking. The man who walked onto the stage, striking the audience dumb in amazement was… Namor! The Prince of Atlantis, the showman with the gills, the man who at that very moment was hosting the rival show on another network, the man who was trying to overtake Mystique in terms of ratings. With an audacious inspiration, she had transformed herself into her own adversary.

After its initial astonishment, the audience went wild. Dressed in his distinctive green briefs, Namor crooned an old Frank Sinatra favourite. Behind him, dancers circled in midair, dangling from invisible wires, dressed as goldfish and pretending to swim in an immense aquarium. Chad was dressed as a starfish. Namor ramped up, belting it out now. *Goodbye, said so easily, goodbye, said so quietly, goodbye goodbye goodbye*, and both the studio audience and the millions of home viewers in front of their TVs were moved to tears by the words of the song, while still laughing at the funny faces that Namor made. No one thought that this would be the last broadcast of the show. It was only later that, looking back with the benefit of hindsight, many viewers remembered this scene and saw in it, to their distress, all its sad and ultimate beauty.

Finally, she resumed her normal shape. She emerged to accept the applause at the end of the episode, and someone tossed her a bouquet. The cameras drew in closer. The audience was on its feet, clapping. She picked up the flowers, acknowledged the applause, and then, with an effort to keep her voice steady, told everyone to tune in again for the next show, though she inwardly doubted that she would be there for it.

*

Thanks to the amazing energy she had put into the episode, the *Celebrity Mystique Show* had managed to rise to the challenge of the real Namor's programme. The duel had ended in a draw. Virtually identical audience shares. Susie had brought the news while she was recovering in her dressing room.

Even though it was important news, Mystique doubted that the fact of not being beaten in the ratings race would be enough to placate Gary. Before her producer had time to show up, she got changed and left her dressing room. She had no interest in undergoing a showdown with the production executives. Absolutely not. Right then and there, she couldn't put up with anything of the sort. Out in the hallway, the laughter of Chad and all the others, clustered in one of the dressing rooms drinking toasts, echoed loudly: whatever the show's fate might be, it was worth raising a glass to what had been, without question, the most spectacular broadcast in the history of the programme. Susie had told her they'd be celebrating and urged her to hurry to join them. But instead, Mystique scampered down the hall and slipped into the elevator.

She pressed the button for the ground floor. She looked at her reflection in the elevator mirror wide-eyed, almost amazed to remember, after all those transformations, who she was after all. *This woman. This face.* She adjusted the collar of her blouse and pulled a lipstick out of her bag. Her soft lips under the lipstick. She felt guilty about having left without a word. On the other hand, she felt sure that everyone would just assume they'd see her, like always, the next morning in the production office.

Outside it was a glorious evening. A dry wind blew over the parking lot in waves, like surges of heat from some gigantic invisible fire. The sky was clear, uniform as a mirror, with just an oblong sliver of moon in the far distance, slicing through the blue expanse. Reality pulsated ever more intensely around her. Mystique kept walking through the parking lot until, as she expected, she saw Dennis standing next to his car.

Dennis moved towards her. He displayed his usual composure but he quickened his step over the last few yards separating them and his voice quavered when he spoke. "You're beautiful," were his first words.

So was he. His hair was wet, probably evidence that he'd recently showered, and the shaven skin of his chin and cheeks seemed to possess the smooth purity of marble. His fiery eyes shone brighter than ever. They walked together towards his car, wordless, without touching, as if everything had already been agreed upon. Their clothes were tossed by a violent gust of wind. "They say something's on its way," he told her. "A new change in the weather." The car started up and moved away from the studio. Dennis headed west, driving calmly, his strong hands on the steering wheel. His profile stood out against the background of the street.

On the sidewalk, a few kids were walking along, arms spread wide, leaning into the wind as though expecting to fly.

They decided to stop at a diner she knew, a quiet place never too crowded, furnished with a row of old velvet banquettes. A waitress with a gracious smile, dark-skinned and almond-eyed, came to take their orders. Mystique imagined how that young woman's eyes might see her: the famous television personality, weary after the evening's show, stopping to grab a bite on her way home, accompanied by someone who looked like a younger lover.

She was hungry now. She couldn't remember eating anything that day. She decided to order a piece of cheesecake and Dennis didn't comment, just gave an approving smile. They talked and talked. They talked in increasingly intimate terms, sinking into the old velvet seats, while the waitress on the night shift kept a benevolent eye on them from a distance.

All of a sudden, every obstacle between them had fallen away. She poured out her heart. She told him stories about her life, blending in a mixed bag of funny anecdotes, less-funny anecdotes, and personal regrets. How much she regretted having been too naive when she was young, or perhaps too proud, or maybe both. She told him about the fever, when she was a girl, every time she tried to transform herself into someone else. Her regret about not having had children. She told him about the people who wrote messages asking her to transform herself into a departed loved one, people she couldn't help because her powers only allowed her to transform herself into those who were still alive. Her regret at having spent so much of her life apart from others. She told him about the Philadelphia drag queen who staged shows in outlying bars, wearing a wig and dying his skin blue; how the drag queen had sent her a video of one of his performances with a note that said: *You may be happy to learn, since you've transformed yourself into so many other people, that someone is finally trying to transform himself into you. Too bad I don't have the kind of superpowers that would let me finish the job!*

They laughed together and turned serious again and laughed for no particular reason and almost started crying. They got up to leave. She left an excessive tip on the table. It was late when they got to her place and this time Dennis turned off the engine and there was no uncertainty about it.

*

They both got out of the car and walked into the apartment. Once they were inside, they stopped, facing each other, with the lights still off, each trying to read the other's face. She slipped into the kitchen and when she pulled open the fridge the cold pale light illuminated, barely, the silhouettes of the furniture in the room. He had followed close behind. In the lunar-like glow, they embraced for the first time and their mouths sought each other, confidently, like they'd always known one another. Dennis' tongue filled her mouth and she gulped as if trying to swallow it. She pulled away from him, trembling, covered her face with both hands, and wished that everything could remain as it was right then forever, like in a movie still, two people petrified after their first ravenous kiss.

They drank some chilled wine and moved into the bedroom, where she turned on a small lamp. Dennis set down his police handgun on the nightstand by the bed. Then he slowly undressed, as the lamp projected onto the wall the dark and oversize shadow of his movements. Mystique watched him, sitting on the edge of the bed, breathing in silence. Dennis slid off his boxer shorts and stood naked before her. He walked towards her and his cock was straining and moist and Mystique cupped her hands around it. Then she took it in her mouth and he pushed, slowly, until he hit the soft barrier of her throat.

At last, they were both naked. Lying on the bed, side by side, the man with the slightly olive skin and the woman with the bluish complexion. Mystique writhed on the sheets. On the ceiling, where the light of the lamp didn't reach, the darkness seemed to wrap itself in spirals. Dennis moved down and brushed her with his lips. He ran the tip of his tongue around the edges before sliding in, kissing her vagina as though it was a mouth. He sucked on the small knot of her clitoris, massaging it with his tongue until he felt it pulsate… The body beneath his was changing. The flesh under his tongue seemed to melt and then return, with an altered shape. Dennis lifted his face and contemplated the person into whom Mystique had transformed herself. It was a man's body. It was his own body. The two Dennis De Villas gazed, reflecting each in the other, throbbing, two naked, identical men, with the same identical cock, identical skin, identical sweat. Dennis came up, bringing his face close to the other's, his gaze in the other's eyes, closer and closer, hard lips pressed against hard lips. They clung together like long-lost twins. The sheets smelt fresh and the night awaited silently, on the edge of the window sill, populated by a thousand distant echoes.

Who was still awake out there? The night loomed over the city like a shadow cast by the wing of an immense angel. In the houses, sleepless babies were rocked by sleepless mothers. Men with elusive gazes met in the corners of parks and left used condoms in the bushes. Street-sweepers drove down the streets in their massive vehicles for the city's hygiene, sweeping away garbage and crumpled newspapers filled with now-obsolete news. Reckless squirrels froze, paralysed in the headlights of an oncoming car, convinced that the sun was already rising. Weary MTA employees drove night trains through underground tunnels, in the bowels of the city, fantasising about being different men, men who could pay their credit card bills, about flee-ing elsewhere and finding love, or losing love once and for all. The city regenerated in the darkness and in the neon lights. Night gave the gifts of both anguish and relief. "Mystique," Dennis called. "Mystique."

She came back. She resumed her own form. She was once again a woman lying underneath a man's body. She twisted vigorously while shivers ran across her skin in waves, feeling herself crushed beneath the weight of Dennis' body. She hugged him close and tried to push him away.

"Mystique," he kept calling. He immobilised her arms and pushed his face into her hair. He was sliding into her. Their bodies united. His naked flesh inside her naked flesh, that was all, just their breathing, their syn-chronised motions.

She began to vibrate and arched her hips while he thrust his hips down and for long minutes they were lost in this profound, mechanical, animal, almost choreographic movement.

Outside, the wind was blowing hard. Slow aeroplanes moved blinking across the sky and trees rustled in chorus in the backyards. Was that glow in the eastern sky a timid and early harbinger of dawn? Mystique and Dennis suddenly slowed down and each stared at the constellation of drops on the other's forehead. Both their hearts were beating in time. "Do you know who I am?" he moaned.

A shudder ran through her and she felt something give in her belly and it dawned on her that it was all just as she had suspected. "I know who you are," she moaned. "I know who you are." She'd known it since the day before, when she'd stopped to think things over in her office. Maybe she'd known it before, maybe since their dinner in Harlem, from the circumspect manner he had of talking about himself, she'd known ever since he confessed that he had seen her and desired her at Franklin Richards' funeral, she'd known it from his enigmatic glances, she'd known it since she had taken on his body and tasted his flavour, so dense and ambiguous and inaccessible. He was the man who would kill her. He was the man who had been sent by the group or perhaps, it occurred to her now, he and the group were one and the same. She opened her mouth wide but was unable to emit anything more than a whisper. "Those notes?"

"I don't know anything about them." The sweat on Dennis' face was dripping onto Mystique's face in a slow rain. He blew gently on her as if trying to dry her off. "Those notes are just as much of a mystery to me. I think someone has been trying to warn you, or maybe just bid you farewell. Of course, they gave me an excellent excuse to get in touch with you," he said, with the sound of a tormented confession. His voice broke. "Mystique. Close your eyes," he implored.

She kept looking at him. Dennis' features were dazzling in the dim light. She looked at the glare of the lamplight reflecting off his skin and the sweat beading on his forehead.

Dennis understood that she lacked the strength or the desire to fight back. He released the tension of his arms around her. He blew again on the skin of her face. He gave her a sorrowful kiss and repeated: "Close your eyes."

Mystique didn't close her eyes. She didn't know where he'd pulled the plastic bag out from. In an instant it was wrapped around her head and through the transparent plastic Dennis' face began to blur. The plastic clung to her face and began puffing and sagging with each breath she took.

Without her willing it, her body went into a series of spasms. She grabbed her breasts almost hard enough to rip them and went through a handful of final convulsive transformations. Dennis held the edge of the bag tight around her neck. The lack of oxygen forced her body to calm down, the crisis passed and the fire that had always burned ceaselessly in her chest began at last to fade.

The humidity in her breath was fogging up the bag. The light created odd reflections on the folds of the plastic. She felt the intoxicating heat of Dennis' body. She felt her own body pulsate like a single enormous heart.

It seemed to her that she was dissolving, becoming someone she had never been, someone without a name or a shape, a perfect body devoid of pain, devoid of regrets. He was holding her tight and asking her forgiveness and telling her that it was necessary, and only after a couple of minutes did she realise that she was hearing those words from a distant, unattainable place, where all this had stopped mattering.

Epilogue

SUPERMAN

JUNE 2006

According to the newspaper accounts it was the cleaning lady who found the body the next day, lying naked on the bed, with the clear plastic bag still around the head. The limbs were neatly arranged, the legs drawn out straight, the hands folded together, as if the murderer had wished to give that corpse a last semblance of peace. The body with its bluish skin on the white sheet. The white curtains quietly swelling in the breeze, a sense of tidiness reigning over the bedroom.

At first, everyone thought it was a sex game gone wrong, a theory that seemed to have been borne out by the coroner's finding that the murder had taken place immediately following or perhaps even during sexual intercourse. One more seamy death in the world of the ex-superheroes. The newspapers could barely contain their excitement. But apart from the tawdry circumstances, the identity of the famous victim suggested that the case was something more than a simple sexual incident, which drove the detectives to examine a series of other, more wide-ranging hypotheses. One after another, the investigative trails were run down and eliminated.

The murder had nothing to do with the world of show business in which the victim worked, did not involve demented fans or envious television personalities, and seemed in fact to have triggered, in a milieu that was normally so flinty-hearted and merciless, a surge of genuine grief. Show business people along the entire fame gradient talked about the news with tears in their eyes. The victim's colleagues maintained a grieving silence out of respect for her memory. A week after the murder, the victim's principal television rival, the arrogant Namor, returned on air in his show and burst into convulsive tears, floating in his giant tank as the fish swam around him, gaping in amazement.

Although more than a few questioned the sincerity of those aquatic tears, which by the way led to a rise in his ratings, many others thought his grief seemed authentic. Namor might be an overblown buffoon, no doubt about that, but he was an overblown buffoon capable of profound emotions.

Nor did the murder have to do with the victim's past history. It had nothing to do with her time in prison nor with her contacts with groups of mutant extremists in the late Seventies, events so deeply buried in the past that they had left no more traces, in the collective memory, than a sand castle in the aftermath of high tide. The victim's death had nothing to do with these aspects of her life. All that was left then was the darkest hypothesis. The nameless group. The organisation that had already carried out other murders in the world of former superheroes seemed to have struck again.

Over the course of the next few days, the highest levels of the police department were forced to make an embarrassing admission. Not only had the murderous group carried out another execution, but now it seemed possible to identify the name of its leading member. According to an array of witnesses, there was a man who had been in increasingly close contact with the victim during the last few weeks of her life. The same man appeared to have spent the night with the victim, had intimate relations with her, and murdered her, leaving the corpse on the white sheets, only to vanish into thin air, leaving no trail to his current whereabouts.

Considering the evidence piling up by the hour, it was reasonable to assume that the man in question was the most crucial member of the notorious group. The awkward point, as far as the police were concerned, was the man's identity. He was a police officer. The news sent the media straight into a feeding frenzy. A cop! Detective Dennis De Villa!

*

Because the murderer of superheroes was on the run, and hence it was impossible to obtain any current images of him or statements from him, the media had no better option than to focus on the person closest to the alleged killer, his brother. And so it was that, for a couple of weeks, the reporter Bruce De Villa was forced to defend himself from a siege by dozens of fellow reporters.

The press waited for him outside his building. They camped out there for entire days. They stalked him every time he went to buy groceries at the corner store, peppering him with questions he refused to answer. They chased after him as he ran to catch the bus. It actually reached the height of paradox when a crowd of reporters chased another reporter on his way to the news stand to buy the morning papers.

In other circumstances, Bruce De Villa might have found such an absurd situation laughable. But now, the laughter died in his throat like an ember in a wet fireplace. *My brother Dennis, leader of the notorious deadly group.* The news left him confused and practically speechless. His power of second sight had given him advance awareness of the deaths of a number of former superheroes, including that of Mystique, but it had told him nothing about how they would die, much less the identity of their killer.

He didn't have much to say to the reporters. Why were they besieging him, demanding comments and indiscretions about his brother's character? After all, what did he know about Dennis? It was very likely that by now they, the reporters, knew more about him than Bruce did. As the police gradually built up a picture of the murders that had taken place to date, casting light on the role that Detective Dennis De Villa had played in those killings, Bruce had the impression that his brother's actual life was taking shape, before his eyes, like a landscape finally freed from enveloping mists.

He found a detailed reconstruction of the murderous escalation in the *New York Post*. It began with the murder of Robin, who'd had his throat cut in a corner of Central Park several years earlier, when Dennis was a young uniformed patrolman and Robin must have looked to him, according to educated guesses, like the easiest target with which to start his career as a killer of superheroes. The reconstruction went on through the following years, which Dennis used to organise a group of sympathisers with his anti-superhero campaign, until he roped in the young Mara Jones. The scabrous death of the Dark Knight. The way Dennis began to take advantage of his position as a detective to establish contact with the potential victims. The quickening cadence of the murderous attacks. The way he apparently organised, probably with the aid of other anonymous members of the group, the terrorist-style attack on the George Hotel. The fatal error that led to the death of the younger Richards. The resulting decision of the elder Richards to take his own life. And last of all, Mystique, the television star with bluish skin, the growing intimacy between the pair, perhaps even a genuine emotional involvement, though it did nothing to prevent Dennis from carrying out his plan.

Dennis De Villa, seducer and murderer. Who could have imagined, the commentators asked, that behind those delicate eyes, in an apparent state of continuous emotional upheaval... In an attempt to find out more about the ex-detective's personality, a couple of reporters started digging into his family background. They found references to the sudden and mysterious death of his mother, sixteen years earlier, but were unable to tease out exactly what happened. For that matter, who knows whether those distant events had any significance. Dennis De Villa remained an enigmatic angel of death. If only his brother would agree to give a short interview, tell an anecdote or two, a few memories, a detail that might help to frame, once and for all, the personality of the ex-detective: a crazed fanatic, a terrorist, a cruel hanging judge working on the basis of an unknown law of morality, a reactionary determined to take the world back to a pre-superhero stage of its history?

"Aren't they sick of it yet?" asked the man who ran the corner store every time Bruce came in, trailing the team of relentless reporters behind him.

"They'll get sick of it soon, you'll see," Bruce assured him.

The intensity of the press siege did indeed begin to wane. Their voices dwindled in number, less and less insistent, as in some inevitable fade-out. Bruce had spent the last couple of weeks reducing communication to a minimum, and not only with the press but with anyone, suspending all work-related activity and choosing to spend as much time as possible in seclusion. He continued that way for a few more days. In the hope of avoiding the perils of insomnia, every night he'd drain a generous glass of warm milk spiked with an equally generous dollop of rum. He'd fall asleep with a myriad of questions echoing in his mind: those that the reporters had been asking him in vain for days, and those which in the final analysis the entire country kept asking. Would the former detective eventually be caught? Would he resurface in the wake of spectacular new murders?

Impossible questions to answer. As far as he was concerned, for now Bruce hadn't any premonitions on impending deaths. He wondered whether his premonitions would ever return and, with them, the murders. Only time could tell.

*

June was already beginning to wilt. The days were sliding down towards the scorching abyss of midsummer. News reports about Mystique's murder and the former detective now on the run evaporated slowly, day by day, giving way to the indistinct, customary buzz of stories about yet more new victims of the violence in the Middle East, yet more new sea ice melting at the poles, yet more new galloping financial crises moving like deep shivers along the skin of the whole planet.

Like every year, Broadway was assigning the Tony Awards. The film season was launching the summer blockbusters. Joseph Szepanski's book was dominating the bestseller lists. Well-to-do New Yorkers were migrating, the way they did every summer, to their beach houses on Long Island and Cape Cod... Bruce lay wide awake in his bed nearly every night, listening intently as if he were trying to capture each tiny movement of the world. Was he perhaps waiting, in the night, for one of his foreshadowings? Or was he simply trying to understand once and for all what he should do with his strange superpowers, what direction to send his life in now?

When a call came one morning from the New York office of *La Repubblica*, Bruce panicked. He was afraid that the Italian newspaper wanted to weasel an interview out of him about his brother.

But quite to the contrary, the bureau chief never mentioned the subject. Speaking in Italian, in a flat and matter-of-fact tone he just asked whether Bruce was ready to resume working again. Because, yes, there was an interview he wanted to discuss, but he didn't want to interview Bruce, rather he wanted Bruce to interview someone else. And apparently it was a pretty important interview.

At first Bruce hummed and hawed. He wasn't that sure he was interested in pursuing his journalistic career. Even though he wasn't clear what else he might do, he doubted that journalism was the path he should follow. In the last few weeks, he had sensed a number of things changing inside him. His life seemed like a building that had been blown up, and when the stones fell back to earth, they'd reassembled themselves into their exact original arrangement. Everything looked the same as before. But it wasn't.

He was thinking that over when the bureau chief decided to tell him who he was being asked to interview.

Bruce gulped. "Would you mind saying that again?"

The bureau chief laughed and repeated the name.

"Well…" Bruce paused and then went on. "In that case, I guess I cannot refuse." He had no idea how the hell the paper had managed to secure such a sought-after interview, but this was clearly a spectacular opportunity. He decided that this could be his last piece. A fitting capstone to his career. A rare interview with the most venerable of the venerable figures, the most glorious of the old glories, the father of all superheroes. He asked for the details. The interview was scheduled for tomorrow afternoon in Park Slope, at the period residence where the old man in question had founded, it appeared, a sort of school for aspiring *superheroes with serious intentions*.

Bruce didn't give the school a lot of thought. The idea that nowadays there might be aspiring *superheroes with serious intentions* struck him as bizarre to say the least. But what interested him was the chance to meet the great old man. The living legend. The inaccessible Superman.

*

The next day he took the subway to Brooklyn. He got out at Grand Army Plaza and started walking south. The day was painfully beautiful, with a sky as shiny as a sheet of glass and just one single strand of white cloud whose outline reminded Bruce of the shape of Long Island. He turned into a street lined with massive trees, where he encountered a couple of solitary pedestrians, and a female family of two mothers and a little girl in a pushchair strolling at a leisurely pace towards Prospect Park.

He looked up at the façades of the monumental houses, all of them rather austere, until he found the one he was looking for. Before ringing the doorbell he checked himself over. He was wearing the best of the two summer suits he owned and a shirt he'd picked up that morning from the dry cleaners.

He rang the doorbell. He waited. He rang again and peeked into one of the windows. Behind the curtains all he could see was a strip of hardwood floor.

At last, the door creaked and slowly swung open.

Bruce had taken it for granted that he would be welcomed by an assistant, by a housekeeper, by a bodyguard, or even by one of the students attending the school. He had taken it for granted that the elderly hero would receive him sitting in a luxurious office, or on an elegant veranda, where he would only be allowed, as if into a throne room, after the requisite several minutes in an anteroom. He was astonished, therefore, when he realised that the figure before him, framed in the rectangle of the front door, backlit by a whitish glow that seemed to reign inside the house, was none other than Superman himself.

Before then, Bruce had only seen him in person one other time, from a considerable distance, at the crowded funeral of Franklin Richards. That time, Superman had worn his superhero costume, and had hobbled forward with a hesitant yet solemn gait, making his way through the mourning superheroes. Despite his age and the afflictions of illness, he was still a charismatic figure. He had retired long ago, about twenty-five years, before the era of great superhero exploits had begun to decline, and as a result he had been one of the few to avoid being tainted by the atmosphere of gradual defeat that had later washed over the superhero scene.

They stood looking at each other. Superman was wearing a pair of navy-blue trousers. A short-sleeved shirt in a material that might be linen. He was leaning on a wooden cane and seemed to be quavering with a vague, relentless tremor. The famous face with its classical American beauty had remained recognisable over the course of the years, with his square chin and powerful jaw, even though his expression now seemed somewhat stiff and the skin drab, slightly waxen. His hair was thick, a less intense raven black than it once was, with white streaks that created the effect, here and there, of a series of veins of silver shot through a dark boulder. The eyes were still lively. Although disease had stiffened his face and slowed the movement of his eyes, those two pale blue spotlights seemed to maintain something fresh, almost amused about them. He studied Bruce and commented: "So here you are."

"I beg your pardon?" Bruce hesitated, afraid that he'd been taken for someone else. "Mr. Kent, my name is Bruce De Villa. I'm here on behalf of that Italian newspaper…"

"I know," the other man said, nodding his head longer than necessary, in a way that made it hard to tell whether he was really nodding or might be succumbing to an attack of tremors instead. "De Villa," he repeated. "De Villa."

Inside, the period home seemed to have been renovated from top to bottom. The rooms were arrayed around a large central light well that cut vertically through the building's four stories and was illuminated by a milky-white skylight on the roof. Superman and Bruce walked towards the railing that surrounded the light well. Without undue formality, the elderly man seized Bruce's arm while his other hand gripped the handle of his cane. There was still something imposing about his physical presence. *He's taller and no doubt heavier than me. The power of his arm intertwined with mine.* Through that arm, Bruce could sense the other man's tremors like a series of seismic shocks, a faint, continuous, rhythmic earthquake, almost as if Superman's body were vibrating in time to some imperceptible music, or as if that body were a sensitive wand capable of capturing the vibrations in the air, in the house, in the ground beneath them, the entire spectrum of the earth's vibrations.

"Welcome to my training centre," said the old man, a trace of mirth in his voice.

Bruce leaned over the railing. He took a look down at the floor underneath, the one at basement level. Half a dozen people were sitting in relaxed postures, legs crossed, each on a small rug, in what looked very much like a meditation session. Bruce observed the scene with slight astonishment. Were these the aspiring superheroes? Sitting on carpets and meditating? What was this? A training centre or some kind of *ashram*?

"I bet this is nothing like what you were expecting," Superman suggested. The curve that surfaced on his lips was barely a smile, but his rigid face had the expression you might see on someone who was just managing to stifle a resounding belly laugh. His arm seemed to vibrate even more. "I bet you didn't expect this."

"To tell the truth, I don't know what I was expecting."

"Of course, this isn't all the kids do with their time. Down there... down there are the lecture halls. A well-equipped gymnasium." The pale blue eyes flashed when they met Bruce's. The old man paused. "Nothing too esoteric. Quite the contrary, in fact, this is a very... practical approach. Action and meditation. A superhero can't do without either."

Down below, everyone was pretty young. They all wore jeans and T-shirts; they were barefoot, eyes closed. A short distance away from the group, a young woman who must have grown tired of meditating was sitting peacefully, tapping away at a laptop computer. Bruce wondered what had driven these people to join up with Superman. What had made them decide to pursue the project of becoming nothing less than superheroes in the proper sense of the word. *Old-school superheroes*, he thought to himself. *Superheroes who want to fight for real. Superheroes who, somehow or other, want to set the world straight. Fight evil and all that stuff? Aren't those ideas that belong to the musty past? In the space of two months, no more, I wouldn't be a bit surprised if they weren't all signed up for some dumb reality show, or taking walk-on parts in a film with Angelina Jolie.*

But he kept his scepticism to himself. He went back to listening to Superman, who was providing a brief history of some of the students. That young man sitting on a manila-coloured rug, the one with the Hispanic features, was known by the name of Spinning Top, and until recently, the old superhero told Bruce, his lips twisting with growing amusement, he'd made his living posing for stupid calendars. But in actual fact, he was a serious-minded young man. His distinguishing characteristic was that he had no fixed superpowers. Every time his body accumulated a sufficient charge of adrenaline, it developed a different superpower. Impossible to tell in advance what that power might be. The superhero with the most unpredictable powers the world had ever seen! That young woman working away on the computer, on the other hand, was a mutant and she hadn't yet chosen her own superhero name; she possessed one eccentric superpower, which consisted of negating all cause-and-effect relationships in the world around her. Guns would fire, but no one was hit. Mouths flew open, but no shout emerged.

Bruce remained sceptical. More than for great superheroic exploits, the bizarre superpowers that were being described to him seemed suitable for a performance of abstract theatre. He let his uncertain look wander around the place.

All the same, he had to admit there was a pleasant atmosphere in the house. Filtering down through the skylight was a substantial, almost solid shaft of light, not unlike what you'd see slanting through the windows of a cathedral. On the walls hung reproductions of paintings by Lucian Freud, Stanley Spencer, and other artists—or come to think of it, they might even be originals, portraits of men and women who looked out from the canvas, wordless, filled with a deeply luminous, moving, and fleshly humanity. Bruce and Superman continued the tour. They ran into a few people along the way, perhaps other students or even instructors, who limited themselves to a courteous smile. The elderly man went on explaining practical details of the school. A handful of well-to-do friends were underwriting the operation. So far no one—neither within the larger scene of the ex-superheroes nor among the national mass media or government authorities—was taking seriously the idea of training a new generation of superheroes. Old Superman was happy about that. As a matter of fact, he was actively discouraging publicity, eager to protect his protégés from outside pressure.

They reached the back door. It led to a short staircase that descended to a large garden. "This is the part of the house I like least," the old hero complained. "These steps, I mean. But I bet that with your help they'll be easier to take."

Bruce helped him down the stairs. The old man's stiff body came to a halt on the edge of each step, balancing, arms swept by more intense, almost electric bouts of shaking, that were transmitted to Bruce in a series of tiny and nearly painful impulses.

As soon as they got to the foot of the stairs, Superman broke away from him and took a few steps on his own, without even the aid of his cane, taking advantage of a momentary absence of the shakes. He squared his shoulders and stood there in the welcoming afternoon light. How old could that man be? In his eighties, at the very least. Still, in the illusion of the golden light, with rose bushes and the branches of a wisteria swaying behind him, the body of the ex-hero seemed for an instant to be as majestic as ever, and Bruce stood before him, astonished, dazzled, feeling wonderfully small. Wonderfully pure. For that passing instant, he too became what he had once been. A boy filled with trust and with the desire to stand in the presence of a great, eternal superhero.

"It's very nice here. A very nice garden, Mr. Kent."

"Until a few years ago, I did the gardening myself. The rose bushes…" Superman sighed, glancing over at the flowers close at hand, "seem to feel a little slighted." He was still standing without the support of his walking stick, though he was starting to sway. The flow of a breeze was tossing the branches. "Who'd ever think," he mused after a moment, "that I once knew how to fly? It's been twenty-two… yes, twenty-two years since the last time I lofted up into the air. In the end, just to fly a few yards… Just to fly a few yards was so exhausting that I had to throw up." There was no sadness in his voice. Every word he spoke seemed to have the tone of a calm, unforced observation. The faint smile reappeared on his tight lips. "Do you know how to fly?"

The question baffled Bruce. Instinctively, he crossed his arms. He realised he'd adopted a typical defensive stance and dropped his arms to his side, feeling naked and awkward, now, in this garden full of scents. "What do you mean? I don't have any superpowers," he chose to respond.

"Oh you don't? That's too bad," the other man said in a sly voice. His eyes were a nebula of bluish light. The rustling of leaves dominated everything else, serving as a background to their voices, thousands of leaves tossed in the breeze, louder and louder, a multitude of tiny whispering rattles. "De Villa. De Villa," the elderly hero went on reciting, in the same rapt tone he had used at the beginning, when he first repeated Bruce's surname at the front door.

The sun extended a golden patina over the gravel on the path. A little further, on a garden table surrounded by wicker chairs, a few wrinkled newspapers, probably left from that morning's reading, waved lazily in the breeze. When the old man staggered, Bruce hurried over, offering him his cane, but the man preferred to lock onto Bruce with both hands.

They both stood there trembling, clinging tight, like inexperienced skaters poised in a fragile, surprising equilibrium. "As you must know… I never receive reporters," Superman said. "Were you wondering why I agreed to meet you, Bruce De Villa?"

Bruce dropped the walking stick. The old man's weight made him tremble with effort.

The scent of the rose bushes was overpowering. A large insect with brilliantly coloured wings glided between the flowers. Superman was saying something about having gathered information, about reading the newspapers closely, and even about unleashing a small bunch of informers. By now, he felt confident he knew a lot about the De Villa brothers. "If I understood this well, my young friend… There are two brothers. Something happens to the mother. One of the two brothers… gets it into his head that he'll go and murder the old superheroes." From somewhere in the garden, or perhaps from another garden, came the sound of an automatic sprinkler. "But I ask myself," he said, "what about the other brother? What's going through the mind of the other brother? What is that uneasy spark I glimpse… in his deep dark eyes?"

Everything was becoming clear. This meeting had been a trap of sorts.

Superman had never intended to grant an interview. What he wanted was to meet the other brother, the one who wasn't a murderer, the complementary figure to the one who had killed several of his most famous former colleagues over the past few years. The smell of the wet lawn around the sprinkler wafted over to them. If anyone had been watching the two men in the garden from a distance, they might have concluded that they had fallen into a clumsy swaying bear hug. Their trembling shoulders. Their faces close together. The greying hair of the old man almost touching the greying hair of the younger. Now that he had met Bruce De Villa, the old hero was even more curious. From the moment he welcomed him in through the front door, every instinct told him that this man had certain special abilities. He had experience when it came to people with superpowers. "There's something in you, my young friend."

Bruce had no time to feel disquieted by those words. He was too busy trying to stay on his feet. His shoulders were aching. He wished he had enough strength to hold up the old hero for all time; he wished he had a steady enough body to transmit his steadiness to him, his own absence of tremors. But he was starting to sweat. He wondered how long he would be able to hold out. Why was the old hero leaning all his weight on him? Why did Superman assume that Bruce wouldn't drop him? Bruce decided that pretty soon they'd both fall to the ground. They gripped each other tighter. The leaves on the bushes went on rustling. In the end, neither of them fell.

*

Bruce had taken off his jacket, rolled up his shirtsleeves, and was now wearing a pair of gardening gloves he'd found in a tool shed. He'd started to prune the rose bushes under the old man's supervision. All the gardening experience he possessed dated back to his boyhood, in Clifton, when he'd sometimes helped his mother with the flowers in the front garden. But the work he was doing today didn't seem too complicated. Pruning some of the bushes and cutting a dozen flowers to take inside. Superman was sitting in one of the wicker chairs, and from time to time he'd toss out courteous, meticulous instructions on the best way to use the clippers. The sprinklers had turned off and turned on again, at intervals, while the breeze pushed tiny particles of water spray in their direction.

Every time his gaze met the eyes of the old hero, Bruce felt a sense of disorientation and, at the same time, of strange, immediate fullness. By now he had given up on the interview. As he continued to cut thorny stems from the bushes, encouraged by that gaze whose touch he could sense without looking over at it, Bruce did most of the talking.

He told him about a series of memories. Scenes from his boyhood. He told about his earliest memory, the first of his life, when he burned his tongue eating a hot dog, on a grey afternoon on the beach at Coney Island. He smiled at that memory. He told about how he and Dennis used to talk about superheroes, lying on their beds in the Clifton nights. He told about his mother's wet hair. About her small sad smile. Memories poured out of Bruce and seemed to hover in the air, and it almost came as a surprise not to see them glitter, along with the particles of water spray, in the late afternoon light.

The legendary hero sat listening in his wicker chair. In his lap, his hands with their liver spots barely trembled.

He told the story of his mother's double body. The off-white flaccid flesh of the man that he'd glimpsed, one day, having sex with her second body. He'd never confessed these things to another living soul. How could this stream of sincerity suddenly pour out of him? He told about his mother's death. The faces of the neighbours as they told him what they'd seen, what had been to their eyes a mysterious and fatal convulsion, a fit that had come over her during a quarrel with her husband on the strip of grass opposite their house. The coffin into which the two bodies had been secretly spirited, in a final embrace, so that they might be one again, if not in life, at least in the hour of their decomposition. The desperate perseverance that surged into him in the wake of that death, and that drove him to get his college degree in short order. How his brother was able to go to college with a scholarship, only to enlist in the police force at an early age. Overwhelmed with remorse, their father pined away in solitude and died within a few years, hammered by a state of depression and a case of stomach cancer.

"Go on," Superman encouraged him.

He told about his abilities. He had lied when he told him that he possessed no superpowers. Actually he did, however modest they might be… After learning that his mother possessed a superpower, he had discovered he possessed one of his own. A power of second sight. The first time, in fact, it was her death he had foreseen. Wasn't that ironic? In him, everything happened almost at once: he had discovered who his mother was, discovered who he himself was, and sensed that she was about to depart this life.

Over the years, he had foreseen the deaths of other superheroes. Superheroes, just the deaths of superheroes. It was something more than a sensation. It was a genuine, full-fledged *knowledge.* He knew in advance when a superhero was drawing close to the end, even a superhero he might never have met in person, as if that superhero were heading straight for the edge of a cliff and there was a sensor that alerted a guard and that guard was him, Bruce De Villa. Finding himself in the presence of a man who decades ago had been able to fly, lift a truck weighing tons, and bend a traffic light in half with his gaze, Bruce chose to stress that his own power was negligible at best.

"What about the murderer brother? Does he have superpowers?" Superman inquired.

"Oh no. Not as far as I know." He'd put down the gloves and the clippers. The branches that remained to be discarded were stacked at a corner of the lawn. Someone had come from inside the house to pick up the cut flowers; in exchange they'd left a pitcher with iced herbal tea and a couple of glasses on the garden table. Bruce and the old hero were now sitting in the wicker chairs.

"Thanks for the gardening."

"It's been a pleasure," Bruce replied, in perfect honesty.

"What other powers do you possess?" Superman questioned him. Leaning with some effort towards the table, he took a sip through the straw extending from the glass. "I can't believe this is your only power… foreseeing the death of some old superhero. That sort of ability is unquestionably… nothing but the tip of the iceberg."

Bruce stared at the pitcher on the table. The ice-cold glass he was holding in his hand. Pieces of orange peel bobbing in the herbal tea. He took a sip and recognised the flavour of lime blossom mixed with other unfamiliar plants. He closed his eyes to savour the aroma of the herbal tea and when he opened them again Superman was still waiting in front of him, with his courteous but insistent demeanour.

He felt his head spin. He sank back into the chair and gave in to the liberating, and to some extent terrifying sensation of confessing the whole truth. "I admit that there are times when I can do more. Brief, intermittent episodes… For instance, mild capacities of teleportation. If I concentrate hard enough, I can teleport small objects. Sheets of paper. Scraps of fabric. Light objects." He took another sip. The iced herbal tea gave relief to his constricted throat. "But I don't see the purpose of talking about it. Like I said, they're intermittent capacities, undeveloped and difficult to control."

Superman seemed to nod. "But you could train your powers. My young people…" he said, with an almost imperceptible tilt of the head towards the façade of the house, on which the sun, low in the western sky, was hurling its last dense rays, like a sniper shooting from concealment, "have powers that are not much different from your own. Unreliable, elusive, surprising powers…" For some reason, he raised his hands and fluttered them in the air, casting a long, movable, and somehow graceful shadow on the grass. "The superpowers of your generation are different from those of the old guard. And let me add that this… might be a good thing. An opportunity."

Bruce sighed. Whenever someone talked about generations it left him cold. The scent of the roses was still on his shirt. He drained his glass and set it down on the table.

He wondered what time it was and guessed that it was time for him to go, but first he cleared his throat and told about the last piece of the picture. He told about the farewell notes. The ones he had sent to the superheroes. The ones he had sent to Robin, Batman, Mister Fantastic, and Mystique, the ones containing a simple farewell printed in capital letters, at the centre of desolate blank sheets of paper. The ones he had written in order to slip a farewell into their hearts, a loving and woeful goodbye. Goodbye. Goodbye to those who had once filled his dreams to the brim, only to abandon those dreams and leave behind an unbearable void. He had brushed his lips over each of those notes before delivering the notes in various ways to his ex-heroes. "Even if I had warned them in a more explicit manner, I don't think that this could have saved them. I've thought it over. In a certain sense, those people seemed to have reached the end of any possible path remaining to them. They were stumbling around on the edge of a cliff…"

"And the murderer brother gave them the final push," Superman noted.

"I had no idea Dennis was involved. I didn't know exactly what would happen to any of them," Bruce said defensively, before it dawned on him that the elderly hero had spoken in a melancholy tone of jest. He noticed that Superman looked tired. "I'm sorry," he said, standing up in a burst of disappointment at himself. "I hadn't considered that you might find it tiring to be out here all this time, listening to me."

The evening grew dense around them. Scattered over the lawn, small silvery spotlights lit up in succession. A small flock of birds flew low over the grass before skyrocketing up to disappear into the now-dark sky. A woman, the same one who had brought the iced herbal tea, was coming back with a small tray. "Time for my medicine," Superman observed.

"Mr. Kent…" Bruce began. His voice cracked and he realised, to his surprise, that he was choked with emotion.

"I hope I never get… one of your farewell notes," the old hero joked. A glint appeared in his gaze. "And I also hope that you'll be willing to… consider this place. This training centre. Wouldn't that be interesting, Bruce De Villa… if you were willing to join us?"

*

He remembered seeing them after the gallery opening in Chelsea, on the banks of the Hudson River, while the sun set on the other side of the water. He remembered thinking that his brother must have been acting as a bodyguard, and noticing a certain tension between the two of them, a tension that he would have had no problem describing as erotic, but he also knew that he hadn't had a hint of suspicion about what his brother was going to do two days from then. He remembered looking into his brother's reddened eyes. He remembered wanting to give Dennis a hug, and to give Mystique one too, and he remembered not having done it. They had stood there, the three of them, each searching in the eyes of the others, two brothers incapable of talking to each other and a woman with bluish skin, continuing to exchange glances as if they were lobbing a volley of unspoken questions. He remembered Mystique staring at him as if she had suddenly understood that he was the one who had sent those notes. The one who had been saying goodbye. The sun set over the river, over the banks, over the three of them in all their awkwardness.

He replayed that scene in his head as he was walking back to Grand Army Plaza. He stopped more than once to catch his breath. He didn't feel ill. He just felt hollowed out and vulnerable in a way he hadn't experienced in years. Outside of the bounds of Superman's garden, life seemed to go on unchanged. There were streets to be crossed. Hurrying pedestrians. Some guy having an argument on his cell phone. In the big plaza, there were sculptures of soldiers aboard a chariot looking down from high atop the immense arch. The bronze warriors peered into the distance, beyond the phantasmagorical skyline of the city by night.

Bruce slipped into the subway station and waited for the train.

He clutched himself and went on wondering where his brother could be. He wondered where Alyson was. He hadn't seen her since the end of the Batman murder trial. He wondered what the young people from Superman's school were doing now that their day was over, after having meditated, after training themselves to perceive themselves, after taking lessons on how to develop their superpowers. He wondered whether Superman was still in his garden, after taking his dopamine pills, surrounded by the scent of the roses, by the glow of the silvery spotlights.

Bruce had promised the elderly hero that he'd think his offer over. Consider whether to start superhero training. At age thirty-five? In the twenty-first century? On the subway train, he slumped back in his seat and let himself be rocked by the train's motion. He reflected on the fact that the world… The world was reading Dr. Joseph Szepanski's bestseller. The world was teeming with lap dance clubs populated with girls dressed as famous superheroines of the last decades. Hordes of superheroes could find nothing better to do than read the weather report on Fox News or play themselves in pretentious docudramas. It was all so cheap and perverse.

The empire of the ridiculous was at its zenith, ruling unopposed over every corner of the planet. How could he, Bruce, subscribe to the faith held by Superman and his students?

The train doors opened and shut various times. The passengers' bodies rocked in unison. Bruce closed his eyes and sank into a tepid niche that was neither sleep nor wakefulness. Was he thinking or dreaming? Did it make any difference? He found himself back on the riverbank with his brother and Mystique, he found himself back in Superman's flowering garden, and swung back and forth between those two scenes, uncertainly, following the train's pitch and roll.

He imagined the old hero with his trembling arms and his radiant gaze, resting in his wicker chair, covered by the blanket that someone had spread over his knees. What was the legendary Superman dreaming about? An unlikely resurrection of the era of the great heroes? Or was he dreaming of going radically past that point, and throwing open the gates of a brand new age?

He could feel himself sliding down in the seat. By now, he supposed he was officially asleep. His thoughts were no longer thoughts but choreographic sparks in his consciousness.

So Superman wanted to leave his moral legacy to someone. Superman wanted to find a new Superman? Could there be a new Superman? If so, was he already enrolled in the Park Slope school? Was the new Superman around, somewhere else in the city or on the planet? Was he riding in the same subway carriage as Bruce? Was he a man or was she a woman, white or black, a mystic or an atheist? Did she dye her hair, did he have his teeth whitened by laser? Did he eat hamburgers, have political convictions, was he sterile or was he endowed with vigorous, feverish reproductive cells?

He heard the passengers get on and off the carriage. He smelt the aroma of cinnamon chewing gum and that reminded him of something… He wanted the train to go on rocking him. His mind had slipped into an indistinct territory, filled with joy and sparkling shadows. Next to him, some guys were discussing the latest news, something about a space probe about to return to earth from an important space exploration mission. He was happy to note that his brother had been shoved aside as the most talked-about story of the day. That is, provided he'd actually heard those guys talking and hadn't just dreamed them.

Oh, there was one thing he guessed he hadn't dreamed. The promise he had made to the old hero. He'd promised he'd consider his offer. The train continued on its way, pushing a whirlwind of hot air ahead of it, making the tracks screech like the strings of a viola, sending vibrations deep towards the gurgling heart of the earth and, at the same time, up towards the surface, through layers of rock and dirt, up to the sensitive stalks of the city's skyscrapers.

Tens of yards above the subway tunnel, in a tastefully furnished apartment, Alyson Rhodes put down the book she was reading and noticed that a vague tremor had just shaken the building. She decided that it was a subway train going by. The vibration was not always perceptible. On the occasions when she did notice it, she would shut her eyes and make a wish, the way you would when you see a falling star. Sometimes the wish was expressed by the depths of her inner being, other times by more surface layers. The last time, if she remembered rightly, she'd wished she could find a certain handbag on sale, and that wish had come triumphantly true.

The cat resting on a chair not far away had raised its head too, and was looking at Alyson and purring lightly. She stood up and stroked its head. For some reason she thought of Bruce. She hadn't seen him in weeks. She'd kept her distance lest he assume that she, like every other reporter in town, was fishing for news about his brother.

She went on stroking the cat and decided to go ahead and make the wish. She thought of Bruce and wished for him to have a good life. She wished that he might have the miraculous lucidity needed to avoid losing his way, and to follow his trajectory, whatever that might be, in the skies of existence.

*

It was just a few more hours until the re-entry into the atmosphere. The crew checked the instrument panel yet again while the radio transmitted the words, excited and crackling, of the technicians on the ground. The commander of the space probe joked with the technicians about the banquet he wanted waiting for him upon landing. "Guys, what do you say you set up for us… What do you say about a roast chicken fresh from the oven? After more than two months floating around in outer space, NASA rations have sort of lost their appetising appeal."

"For me," another crew member broke in, "you can prepare a piping hot apple pie!" The request was expressed with such fervour that it prompted a general burst of hilarity. Everyone laughed. The astronauts' voices seemed to break away from their bodies and hover in mid-air in the spaceship, light and echoing, as if searching for a crack through which to escape and diffuse freely into the boundless emptiness of space.

"Elaine, what do you want most?" asked the commander, addressing the one female crew member.

Elaine Ryan stopped looking at the data she'd been checking on a screen. The young astronaut seemed to focus: "For me… For me…" She shook her head and smiled. She had to admit that she had no idea, and was finding it hard to try to think once again, after living for weeks in the electrifying vacuum of space, about the variety of foods and pleasures back on earth.

Recognising Elaine's feelings, her crewmates moved towards her. They surrounded her, floating in the absence of gravity, moving as in a gentle dance, laughing, as emotional as she was. They were going home. They were returning to the embrace of their planet's atmosphere after weeks on a space mission, and this triggered in them a mixture of euphoria and subtle, heart-rending regret. They were leaving the luminous womb of space. They were leaving the realm of satellites in equilibrium, worlds suspended from other worlds, orbits intertwining with other orbits. Their voyage was over. They went on spinning in the centre of the cabin, three men and a woman with reddish hair, their limbs virtually weightless.

In the background, the beeping monitors of the electronic instrument panel were emitting an accelerating series of alerts. The earth's atmosphere really wasn't far away.

Elaine Ryan reached one of the portholes. The vehicle seemed to be accelerating, now, hurtling towards the planet as though driven by an impatient, irresistible impulse of love.

She imagined that down there the television broadcasts had already begun from the landing zone, a stretch of sea where the probe was scheduled to glide down in the early hours, and where it would be picked up straight afterwards by naval craft. She imagined that the television cameras had already focused on the sector of the sky from which the probe was expected to emerge, and that in the meantime the commentators were reporting the heartwarming detail: the crew had expressed their longing for a real earth meal. Roast chicken and apple pie.

She looked down at the globe of blue and white and emerald light. It was likely that her family was waiting up. It was likely that at the space centre in New Jersey they were following the news of the landing.

She lost herself in the illusion of the planet's perfect immobility. Waiting for her down there would be a new phase of her life. Down there she would regain the sensual weight of her own body, the arcane cycle of light and shadow. She felt changed. The space probe had taken her far away, out into a frightening and magnificent void, where solitude flipped over into a sort of unfamiliar peace, and where her body seemed to have captured a considerable quantity of wonderful, disconcerting self-awareness.

The earth shone beneath her eyes. White masses streaked the atmosphere. The colours of the surface became more and more vivid, so bright that they made the surface look as if on the verge of bursting open and giving birth, who could say, to a new and never-before-seen colour. Elaine gave a moan. The world was ever closer, with its intense shades, a giant bubble of air and matter and heat. The world was waiting for her. The world was poised, hanging beneath her eyes. The spaceship started to vibrate again, and for an instant she had the impression that it was the earth that had wobbled, almost on the point of falling, just like a ripe, wasted fruit. Elaine reached out towards the porthole. "Don't fall," she whispered, in the tone of a prayer. "Don't fall."

SEVERE

Régis Jauffret

A love story. Despite the humiliation, the whips, the latex and the bullets. Inspired by a tragic event, the murder of a banker, Régis Jauffret imagines how the story unfolded.

—

'The quality of Jauffret's language, which fluctuates between the precise and the poetic, ensures his writing never lapses into sensationalism. Severe is a dark, often brutal, but resoundingly subtle consideration of the dynamics between love, exploitation, sex and power.'   **Russell Williams**, *The Independent on Sunday*

'A universal, fascinating epic story of an unusual love affair. Again, Jauffret explores the boundaries of fiction and reality.'
Les Inrockuptibles

'A reflection on sex, power, money and emotions, *Severe* also emerges as a moving picture of a woman seeking absolution.'
L'Express

'A radioactive diamond.'   *Figaro*

'Here everybody is guilty and a victim, manipulator and manipulated at the same time.'   *Libération*

'Timeless and infernal.'   *Télérama*

THÉRÈSE
AND ISABELLE
Violette Leduc

Charged with metaphors, alternating with precise descriptions of sensations and human relationships, *Thérèse and Isabelle* was censored by its publisher in France in 1954, first published in a truncated version in 1966 and not until 2000 in its uncensored edition, as Violette Leduc intended.

For the first time in a new English translation, this is the unabridged text of *Thérèse and Isabelle*.

—

'*Thérèse and Isabelle* is written with unflinching sincerity and Leduc's progressive attitude and experimental style confirm it as one of the greatest examples of French-language erotic literature.'
Olivia Heal, *TLS*

'If the uncensored Thérèse and Isabelle reads like a fever-dream, to many it represents a long-awaited panacea.'
Thea Lenarduzzi, *Literary Review*

'Here we have extraordinary writing about sex; and, more importantly, about love, and the way it makes us feel.'
Nicholas Lezard, *Guardian*

'Thunderbolts of illicit love. A classy new translation of Leduc's masterpiece on the tyranny of love.'   ***Independent***

'Reading Leduc is like discovering a whole new nervous system.'
Deborah Levy

LACRIMOSA

Régis Jauffret

Lacrimosa unfolds through a moving exchange of letters between the narrator and his young lover, Charlotte, who has just committed suicide. Their poignant dialogue makes this epistolary novel a truly cathartic experience.

—

'*Lacrimosa* is marked by Jauffret's own direct involvement in both the real-life events and the narrative, an internal exploration deepened by his own experience.'

Russell Williams, *TLS*

'*Lacrimosa* works like a literary boxing match, a heartbreaking masterpiece where emotion is never far from the absurd.'   ***L'Express***

'Tragic and caustic.'   ***Télérama***

'Régis Jauffret has perhaps written his most accomplished novel, a work of devastating and devastated beauty: an ode to a dead lover.'   ***Le Magazine Littéraire***

'If you follow my advice, I promise: while reading *Lacrimosa*, you will both endure enjoyment and suffering. *Lacrimosa* is just made of what life is made of.'   ***Vice Versa***

'A savage epistolary dialogue made for a great novel.'

Nouvel Observateur

'A merciless tale in which honesty explodes from every page, sometimes to the point of provocation.'   ***Figaro***